What people are saying about Seven-Inch Vinyl

"The love songs that I wrote and recorded with the Flamingos will stand as a testament to the sentimentality of the golden age of rock and roll. Seven-Inch Vinyl is an emotional trip – for those of us who were there and those who wish they were."

-Terry Johnson

"From the early days of Rhythm and Blues and Rockabilly thru the DooWop era and the British Invasion, and on to the revival shows of the late sixties, Donald takes us on a remarkable journey. Enjoy the ride."

-Jon "Bowzer" Bauman

"Expertly crafted, mixing vivid, well defined characters and historic events, Donald has created a story that spans the decades. The songs sing to you from the pages of this book."

-Kenny Vance

"If you 'Remember Then,' and even if you don't...Seven-Inch Vinyl is storytelling at its best. Older readers will revel in the memories. Younger ones will learn what it was like to be a part of the generation that changed the world."

-Larry Chance

"With his novel, Donald has tapped into the essence of what it was like back in the sixties. As a performer from that era, I applaud his efforts."

-Bernadette Carroll (formerly of the Angels)

"Seven-Inch Vinyl brings to mind my days as one of Murray the K's Dancing Girls and as a backup singer on hit records with Frankie Valli and Lou Christie."

-Denise Ferri of the Delicates

Dedication

When I was eight or nine years old, I'd sit at the kitchen table in our apartment in the Throggs Neck Housing Project while my mother sat in the living room trying to watch one of her variety shows on television. Perry Como was a particular favorite. As I wrote my childish imaginings in a black and white composition notebook, I'd often interrupt her to ask, "Ma, how do you spell "sheriff" or some other silly word? She never got mad. She always spelled the word for me no matter how many times I bothered her. This book is dedicated to my mom.

Acknowledgements:

My sincere thanks go out to all those who stood by me during this long, sometimes frustrating but always satisfying journey, my wife Carol, the members of my beta group who read the complete manuscript and offered honest criticism and words of encouragement. To the talented members of the music industry who provided testimonials and a foreword, I am honored by your participation.

To my fellow authors at the Henderson Writers Group: If you ever corrected a comma, added an apostrophe or restructured a sentence at one of my readings, there's a part of you in this book. I thank you all. In particular:

Michael O' Neal, a talented graphics and cover designer whose artistic skills and talent captured perfectly the image and feeling I sought to convey with the cover of this novel. Reach him at: www.devilsplayground@live.com

Lyn Robertson, my editor, who stepped in to weed out the gremlins and glitches that inhabited my manuscript in such a timely manner. Reach her at: www.Linktolyn@gmail.com.

About the Author:

Seven-Inch Vinyl is a work of fiction. Though some characters are composites of actual individuals there was no intention on the part of the author to portray any of their actions as factual. However, with respect to historic places and events, every effort was made to be as accurate as possible.

Donald Riggio is the published author of several short works of fiction as well as magazine and newspaper articles, many of which center around his favorite topic: music from the fifties and sixties. Seven-Inch Vinyl is his first novel. He is currently working on a sequel: "Beyond Vinyl." He lives in Las Vegas, Nevada with his wife Carol.

1953
Six counties in South Carolina pass legislation outlawing Jukebox operation at anytime within hearing distance of a church.

1955
Officials cancel rock and roll concerts scheduled in New Haven and Bridgeport, Connecticut; Boston, Massachusetts; Atlanta, Georgia; Jersey City, New Jersey; and Asbury Park, New Jersey; Burbank, California; and Portsmouth, New Hampshire.

1957
"My only deep sorrow is the unrelenting insistence of recording and motion picture companies upon purveying the most brutal, ugly, degenerate, vicious form of expression it has been my displeasure to hear and naturally I'm referring to the bulk of rock 'n' roll. It fosters almost totally negative and destructive reactions in young people. It smells phony and false. It is sung, played and performed for the most part by cretinous goons and by means of its almost imbecilic reiterations and sly, lewd --- in plain fact --- dirty lyrics, it manages to be the martial music of every side burned delinquent on the face of the earth."

Frank Sinatra - writing in the November issue of "The Western World" magazine.

1958
The Esso Research Center reports: "...tuning into rock and roll music on a car radio can cost a motorist money, because the rhythm can cause a driver to unconsciously jiggle the gas pedal, thus wasting fuel."

"Rhythm & Blues had a baby and they called it rock and roll."
Muddy Waters

Foreword

In the sixties, rock and roll music became the new paradigm for success, with singing groups popping up everywhere.

Many of us started singing just for the sheer joy of it. As a young black girl living in the Brewster project in Detroit, I was not thinking of pursuing a career or even making money. There were many kids standing on street corners Doo-Wopping and that would be as far as they would ever go. However, for others, their natural talent would take them to the top. Those of us who became a part of the Motown family soon realized that we were on to something very special and magical.

Men like Mr. Berry Gordy, the founder of Motown Records had a plan and over the course of the next fifty years, their vision changed the music industry forever. The Motown sound, with its artists, songwriters and producers have all become legendary, setting the standard for popular music all over the world.

In those days it was not always easy and success didn't happen overnight. There were many ups and downs, but it was still really fun until the big business machinery set in. Amid the beautiful gowns, gold records, the world tours and fairy tale adventures, there were times when business decisions divided friendships and sometimes led many down a road of despair, addiction and for some, even death.

Today, I still love what I do, traveling the world doing concerts, celebrating fifty years in the entertainment business and enjoying my family. I have eight grandchildren and one great-grandchild. Life has been filled with many ups and downs but I have weathered the storms and come out a much happier and wiser human being. I am living proof that "Dreams really do come true."

It isn't often that a novel comes along that depicts the early history of rock and roll in such a realistic way. Seven-Inch Vinyl deals not only with the music, but also with the tumultuous times of the sixties, like the civil rights movement, and the Vietnam War. Donald was inspired by those in the music industry to create his fictional characters and artists. They are composites of those who actually made the music and in an eerie way the similarities ring true. I thoroughly enjoyed this novel about life in the fifties and sixties and an inside look at the music industry,

Touch –

Mary Wilson

Prologue:

In the 1950's, the whole world expected an explosion.

The atom bomb, the devastating, destructive device used to bring World War II to an end less than a decade earlier was a weapon in the arsenal of both the United States of America and the Communist regime of the Soviet Union.

After the armistice was signed in 1945, the five victorious allied nations along with forty-five other countries formed the United Nations, an organization whose hope it was to prevent any further hostilities by using the combined armed forces of member nations as peacekeepers. At the time, most of Europe remained occupied and divided forming an "iron curtain" between the democratic countries and Soviet Russia. The German capital city of Berlin became divided. The east governed by the Russians, and the west under the control of allied nations. In 1948, Russia pushed for reparations from West German industrial plants located solely in allied sectors. The American President, Harry Truman denied this claim and the Russians retaliated by closing off their section of Berlin declaring it a Communist State.

The following year, things became more complicated. Nearly all of Mainland China fell under the Communist rule of Chairman Mao Tse Tung. Early in 1950, Russia and Red China entered into a thirty-year mutual defense treaty creating a huge monolithic Communist bloc that many believed threatened the free world. The power of the UN was soon tested.

On June 25, 1950, 135,000 Communist troops crossed the 38th parallel and invaded South Korea. In Washington, Truman believed this to be the beginning of World War III. He immediately ordered General Douglas MacArthur to prepare a counter-assault. In September, UN forces conducted an amphibious landing at the Korean City of Inchon placing 40,000 troops, artillery and tanks, onto the Korean peninsula. The Red Chinese responded by hurling thirty-three divisions into the fray. MacArthur requested enough men and material to push the Communists back and invade China. Truman refused knowing full well that to do so was risking war with the Soviets. The "police-action" in Korea would drag on.

As the Presidential election of 1952 approached, Truman's popularity waned. He was forced to fire MacArthur when the General began to publicly criticize his Commander-In-Chief. The fighting soon reached a stalemate and it became obvious that the hostilities would not reach a clear military conclusion. The Republican candidate for President was former General and war hero, Dwight D. Eisenhower. A poll named him the "most admired living American." In his campaign he promised to clean up the mess in Washington and end the war in Korea. As a result, Truman decided not to run for re-election and in November, Eisenhower won in a landslide. He became President in a time of ideological conflict known as 'The Cold War.' Communism became the new enemy.

At home, Americans were seeing "commies" under their beds at night. A mass hysteria brought on by the threat of Communism and the fear of Atomic War swept the nation. Homeowners built fallout shelters in their basements. School children conducted duck and cover drills in their classrooms, hiding under their wooden desks to protect themselves from radiation poisoning.

With the stage set, people all over the country listened to feel good songs with innocent and inoffensive titles like, "(How Much is) That Doggie in the Window?" and "High- Lilly, High – Low" they held their collective breath waiting for the inevitable explosion to come.

But it wouldn't be the kind of explosion anyone expected.

Chapter One:

"Kentucky"

April 1953

Joseph Rabinowitz and Danny Cavelli rode in the front seat of Danny's 1940 Ford Deluxe convertible. The car, many would call a hot rod, maneuvered over the slight dips and around the easy curves through the rural landscape of North Central Kentucky. Mild spring temperatures made it comfortable to ride with the top down.

The boys were soldiers dressed in their khaki uniforms, recruits from nearby Fort Knox. Their thoughts wandered in opposite directions.

Joseph, eighteen years old, a wiry good looking Jewish kid from New York City, relaxed in the passenger seat taking in the scenery. Sheep, cattle, and horses grazed in meadows and pastures of green grass flanking both sides of the road. Savannahs of evergreens lay beyond stone or wooden fences. Long stretches of bottomland ran alongside the Ohio River to the base of Muldraugh Ridge off in the distance. He believed if he hadn't enlisted in the Army, he would never have the chance to see this beautiful countryside.

At nineteen, Danny was also a city boy, calling the predominantly Italian-American section of University Heights in Cleveland, Ohio his home. Rugged and muscular, he was handsome, street-wise, and arrogant. He possessed a rebellious attitude for authority that made him hate the Army. Months earlier he was thrust into the military after being arrested for joyriding in a stolen car. The judge gave him the choice of going to jail or serving in the military. Danny chose the latter. But, there wasn't a day since that he didn't regret it.

He yearned to be home cruising the streets of his old neighborhood. He couldn't care less about the scenery. There were more important things on his mind.

They'd driven to an auto paint and body shop in the nearby town of Radcliff. The Motor Pool Sergeant at the base had told him that the shop offered discounts to soldiers in uniform. The tip paid off. Danny was quoted a fair price for the work. All he needed to do now was decide on just the right color.

Joseph and Danny became friends early in their basic training in North Carolina, on the day they got their first G.I. haircuts. Danny was mad as hell to have his civilian locks sheared off. The Jewish kid looked even worse when clumps of his own brown hair lay beneath the barber chair. His ears stood out from the sides of his head making him look like the movie star Clark Gable. Danny made the mistake of teasing him, saying he resembled a holocaust survivor. The comment infuriated Joseph and a fistfight ensued. Danny had the better of him hands down, but he admired his spunk. They vowed to watch each other's back from that day on.

They volunteered for the Tank Corps and were assigned to the same M41 Bulldog Tank in Armored Training School at Fort Knox. Joseph qualified as gunner on the Main 76MM Cannon. Danny trained as driver and lead mechanic.

It was the third member of their tank crew, a lanky, fair-haired country boy named Darryl Hoffman that Danny had to thank for the convertible. The Ford originally belonged to Hoffman who drove it out from his home in Galveston, Texas, after he was drafted. At the time, it was a beat up jalopy, but from the moment Danny laid eyes on the vehicle, he wanted it. The game of poker provided the solution.

He maneuvered the Texan into the nightly stud poker games in the barracks and soon collected enough markers to force Hoffman to hand over the ownership papers in order to reduce his debt. Danny had big plans for the vehicle and, with the help of his Army buddies he started to customize the car.

They sanded the car's body, priming it to a dull, gun gray finish. Then they fine tuned the V-8 engine, and installed a new Mallory ignition before they rolled and pleated the black Naugahyde interior. Only one question remained, would it be finished in time?

Half a world away the Korean conflict raged on through its third year. Even though peace talks were taking place in the Korean city of Pamunjom, young soldiers on both sides were still fighting and dying. The harsh reality was Joseph and Danny could soon receive orders sending them off to war.

For now, they were on their way back to the army base. Jo Stafford's recording of "You Belong To Me" played on the radio. Suddenly, a loud popping sound came from the engine. A long billow of steam rose between the seams of the louvered hood. Both driver and passenger bolted straight upright.

"Holy shit!" Danny yelled as the Ford swerved toward the right shoulder of the road. "What the fuck is going on?"

"Danny, what are you doing, man?" Joseph said.

"Okay, okay I got it!" Danny put both hands on the steering wheel, to regain control of the car and his composure. "It's just the radiator, Joey, it's okay."

Joseph lifted his backside off the seat trying to see through the column of steam. He noticed a tall white sign a short distance ahead. The sign depicted a five-pointed red star with the word TEXACO printed across it.

"There's a filling station up there on the right," he told Danny.

"Yeah, man I see it. We can make that easy."

Danny eased up on the gas pedal and guided the car onto the shoulder. The Ford rumbled over the rough gravel separating the roadway from the dirt surface beneath the sign.

The filling station was little more than a single gas pump atop a concrete slab connected to a buried gasoline reservoir tank. A white wood framed building stood a bit further back from the road. A big, lazy hound dog lay motionless on the ground at the base of the sign and made no attempt to move as the Ford pulled up. The station attendant, a short, grizzled old-timer dressed in greasy overalls and a baseball cap came out of the building and approached them. Joseph got out and stood by while Danny waited to speak to the attendant.

"Nice set of wheels you got here, son," the older man said as he wiped his hands on an oily rag he took from the pocket of his overalls.

"Yeah, thanks. I need some water for the radiator."

"I can see that."

"Well, that's just great, pops. But instead of just standing there, why don't you do something about it, okay?"

"Relax, soldier boy, water is something we got plenty of around here. We'll just wait a spell till that motor cools down a might. Then we'll open her up and have a look-see, make sure you didn't bust a hose or something worse."

Danny got out and joined the mechanic at the front of the car. The older man used the rag to protect himself from the heat as he popped the hood. More steam rose into the air. Both men fanned it away from their faces.

"You know, this here vehicle will last a lot longer if you was to take better care of it."

"Geez," Danny hissed with a grimace before he called out to Joseph. "Do you believe this guy, telling me how to take care of a car?"

Joseph shrugged his shoulders in reply. He had a question of his own for the mechanic. "You got anything cold to drink around here?"

"There's a freezer box with soda pop out back in the office there."

Joseph asked Danny, "You want a soda?"

"No, man I'm good."

Joseph took his folded garrison cap from his belt and placed it on his head. As he walked toward the white building he heard the sound of a guitar playing. It was a simple chord progression in three quarter time sounding jazzy in parts, quite unlike the hillbilly music played on local radio stations or the popular styles of Jazz he remembered from home. The music came from inside a mechanic's bay adjoining the office. In his curiosity to hear more, Joseph got sidetracked and changed direction. When he got to the open bay door, he peered inside.

There, the hulking figure of an old colored man sat in a wooden rocking chair. He played a six-string acoustic instrument with a fervor and intensity that was, oddly enough, familiar to Joseph. Still undetected, he moved to get a better look at the musician.

The guitar player had a full head of white hair. His face unshaven for some time, the bristles of his white beard stood out in contrast against his dark complexion. Based on the man's weather worn and wrinkled features, Joseph guessed he was in his late sixties.

He worked the fret board with his left hand to form harmonious bar chords. At times he bent the strings against the frets to produce a moaning sound. He plucked the strings with the fingers of his right hand without the use of a pick to create a bass and rhythm pattern at the same time.

The results were rich in tone owing to the high quality of the guitar, the deftness of the musician, and the echo effect created by the high ceiling of the hollow garage bay. When the old man saw Joseph, he stopped playing and smiled.

"Howdy," he said from behind a wall of white teeth.

"I'm sorry," Joseph apologized, "I didn't mean to interrupt you."

"No, no…not interrupting at all. Come a little bit closer son, I don't bite."

"My buddy's car overheated on the highway," Joseph said.

They both looked out at the Ford. The steam had dissipated and the mechanic had unscrewed the radiator cap. Danny stood close by overseeing the entire operation.

"Fine looking automobile. What's he got under the hood?" The old man asked.

"I don't know much about cars," Joseph confessed.

"But you *do* have an ear for music?"

"Yes, I always have. That was the blues you were playing, right?"

"Thas' right. You a fan of the blues are you?"

"Some. But what you were playing, that's different from anything I've heard."

The old man grinned. "I guess round here we throw in a little western swing…country… maybe even a bit of gospel just for good measure. Do you pick?"

Joseph didn't understand the question.

"Guitar, do you play?"

"Oh, no I don't."

"So you're just a hip cat then?" Once again Joseph was unfamiliar with his meaning. The older man explained. "A hip cat is what we call a white boy who digs rhythm and blues music."

"Rhythm and blues? I've never heard it called that before. I don't know how *hip* I am. But I've listened to a lot of it since I've been down here so- yeah I guess you could say I dig it."

"Good for you. You boys stationed at the Gold Reserve?"

"No, we're in Armored School. Off to Korea soon, probably."

The old man shook his head. "War is a terrible thing."

"That's a beautiful guitar you have there," Joseph changed the subject.

"Yeah, she's a dandy, my very own Senorita." He cradled the instrument then laid it across his lap.

"Senorita?"

"Uh-huh, made by Bacon and Day. They call this model the Senorita. I've had mine since thirty-eight." He reached down, picked up a soft cloth from the guitar case at his feet and rubbed the scalloped top deck of the instrument. Joseph watched as the man moved the cloth along the mahogany finish like a father bathing his infant son. After placing the guitar back in the case, he stood up and offered his hand.

"My name's Chanticleer, but folks round here, they just shorten it to Chanty."

As they shook hands, Joseph felt the hardened calluses at the top of his palm that extended up to the tips of his fingers, caused by long years of hard farm labor. Joseph felt safe in assuming that they were also the result of working the frets and strings of his guitar.

"Joseph Rabinowitz, I'm from New York."

Chanticleer gave him a broad smile. "I kinda figured as much son, judging from the way you talk."

"You get many New Yorkers stopping by here do you?" Joseph asked with a hint of sarcasm, Chanticleer took no offense.

"Son, I ain't exactly spent all my days sitting in this here rocking chair. I been up North, worked the jazz circuit all around Chicago, St. Louis and thereabouts. Been to New York too, played the Cotton Club in Harlem with Cab Calloway and Duke Ellington back in thirty-four."

"What made you come back here?"

"Got homesick is all, I reckon," the old man said with a laugh.

The mechanic appeared outside the garage bay door.

"That fancy Ford out here just went dry of water. The hoses is all fine –ain't no damage. Them bein soldiers I don't figure you wanna charge them anything?"

"That'd be fine Lester."

"Gotcha boss," the mechanic replied and moved off.

"He called you boss, you own this place?" Joseph asked.

"Well, let's just say I'm what they call a silent partner. I made enough money playing music around the country. Came back down here and bought this place, built me a small house out a ways further. But Lester there, he does most of the work. Folks round here seem to feel better if that's how things go."

"Yo, Joey!" Danny's voice interrupted them. "Where are you man? Come on let's go!"

Joseph glanced outside. The hood of the convertible was closed and Danny was behind the wheel.

"I gotta go. It was real nice meeting you Chanty."

"Same here, young Joseph, you drop by anytime and we'll talk more about music."

"I might just do that, thanks."

Joseph waved to the smiling colored man and hurried to the car. He took his cap off and hopped into the front seat just as Danny gunned the engine. The convertible threw up a cloud of dust and gravel as it sped back onto the main highway.

"Did you hear the music that old man was playing?" Joseph asked.

"Goddam nigger music. You like that crap?"

"I think it's different…interesting."

"They started playing some of that shit on a few radio stations back in Cleveland before I left," Danny complained, "It was starting to catch on too. Can you believe it?"

Joseph said nothing, but yes, he certainly could believe it.

Music had always been a big part of Joseph's life. His father, Solomon Rabinowitz had been a piano virtuoso with the Berlin Symphony Orchestra, a well-respected man of class and distinction. This was during a time when being Jewish wasn't yet considered a crime in Germany. But Adolf Hitler's rise to power and the rampant anti-Semitism that followed frightened many German Jews. He and his wife Myra immigrated to America in 1933.

Solomon achieved some success in his adopted country and may have reached greater renown had fatherhood not intervened with Joseph's birth in 1935. Instead, he acquired a position as Professor of Piano Instruction at the prestigious Julliard School of Music in New York City.

♫♫♫♫♫

Danny pushed past the speed limit to make up for lost time. The convertible had gone some five miles further down the road, when he caught sight of a vehicle traveling in the opposite direction. It too moved at a high rate of speed. As the gap between them closed, Joseph also became aware of the vehicle, a black Chevrolet pick-up truck. It drove dangerously close to the yellow line dividing the road.

Danny inched the convertible to the right but the pick-up showed no intention of slowing down. It seemed the driver was deliberately engaging them in a game of chicken.

"What's with these guys?" Joseph said.

"Fuck if I know!"

Danny bore down behind the steering wheel confident his driving skills and reflexes would be quick enough to avert disaster. The vehicles closed to within a hundred yards of one another, close enough for them to see two teenage boys in the cab of the truck, proud of the havoc their horseplay was causing. A third teenager stood in the truck bed peering at them over the cab of the Chevy.

"Get ready, Joey. This is gonna be close man!"

Joseph braced his hand against the frame of the door's fly window. The pick-up sped toward them. Danny noticed the Chevrolet bowtie logo on the hood of the truck coming squarely at his face. At the last minute the pick-up veered to the right and whizzed past them. The teenager in the truck bed hurled a half empty beer bottle at them as they went by.

"Here y'are General, he cackled. " Have a beer on us!"

The two soldiers felt the bottle zoom between their heads and crash into the rear passenger door panel. Both of them were showered by the beer and shattered glass.

"You crazy bastards!" Danny cursed as the truck disappeared down the road. "I'll rip your fucking guts out for this!"

♫♫♫♫♫

The roughnecks in the pick-up truck didn't hear Danny's threat. They roared with laughter at the outcome of their prank, and looked to find yet another victim. One soon appeared in the distance, a lone figure on a motorcycle. They increased their speed to overtake the biker. But as they maneuvered into position to attack the Harley Davidson, they recognized the rider. They knew him from high school as someone not to be fooled with. They flew passed the Harley without incident.

The cyclist stared at the truck through dark sunglasses. His hands riding high on the chopper type handlebars. He opened his motorcycle to third gear and the 23 horsepower engine propelled him forward.

Chapter Two:

"Teddy"

Teddy Boyette exhibited his teenage rebelliousness in a different way than his reckless schoolmates in the Chevy truck. He did it with his attitude and his look. White, short-sleeved tee shirts and tight blue jeans flapped at the cuffs over black motorcycle boots, served as his standard attire. He wore his dark black hair combed back in a ducktail, made slick by thick Dixie Peach pomade. Easily five foot ten, he stood tall and slender with striking good looks and smooth features. He was a junior at Radcliff High School, about to turn seventeen, the only child of a local chicken farmer and his wife.

Teddy guided his Harley across the yellow centerline, and braked to a stop at the Texaco station on the south side of the road. He needed advice and he'd come to the one person he knew who could help him. Working the kickstand down in a fluid motion while dismounting, he took off his sunglasses. He continued with a swagger to the office where he'd find Chanticleer. But the black man was already standing outside.

"That the McVie boys went screeching by like that?" Chanty asked.

"Yup. Them and Tiny Cassidy with 'em. Up to raising some hell on the highway."

"No doubt. Those boys gonna get themselves killed doin that one of these days. I wonder why they ain't in school? Come to think of it, boy, why ain't *you* in school?"

"Ahhh...I cut my classes." Teddy knew his answer would

disappoint his friend.

"Now Teddy, I told you more'n once I wasn't gonna let you come by here to jam if it meant you was cutting school to do it."

"I didn't come by to jam."

"Then, what's with you boy?"

"Ain't nothing going right for me, Chanty."

Chanticleer shook his head and let out a chuckle. "What's got your dander up this time?"

"It's about that talent show I told you they was having at my school. I had to submit the song I planned to play to the committee. Dang it, Chanty they ain't gonna let me sing the song I picked. They say it's improper!"

"What song was you planning to do?"

"I put together this revved up version of that Hank Williams tune "Move It on Over." Teddy was proud of what he'd done with the song. "The committee turned it down."

"So, sing something else?" Chanty made the solution sound so easy. Teddy shifted his weight from one foot to the other. He waved a negative motion in Chanty's direction.

"I been lookin' forward to this show for a long time, singing in front of a real audience, making my mama proud. Nobody's got the right to tell me what I can't sing."

"This don't sound like it's got too much to do with making your mama proud."

Chanticleer was right. Teddy's attitude had more to do with the fact that, once again, someone in authority was telling him what to do. It was bad enough when it came from his parents at home or his teachers at school. He wasn't going to let it carry over as far as his music was concerned.

"Listen here Teddy," Chanticleer reasoned with him, "you got a real talent boy. The day is gonna come when people will sit up and take notice of that. But you can't force it on folks. It has to happen natural like. And you can't do it all alone. You're gonna need people to help move you along. You won't *get* no help if you keep defying folks all the time. And it won't do you no good to get all riled about it either."

Teddy managed a smile at his friend's solid advice. "All right Chanty. I'll sing a different song."

"Good boy. Do you know 'The Old Wooden Cross'?"

"Aw, Chanty that's a church song! What are my friends gonna think if I sing a church song?"

"I thought you was doin this for your mama?"

Teddy crumbled. "I know the words but I don't know how to play it."

"Well then c'mon inside and we'll get to teachin it to you."

Unlike the soldier who stopped by earlier, there was no question as to whether Teddy Boyette was a hip cat or not. He'd grown up listening to the music of the poor coloreds working the farms and fields of the surrounding area. The sorrowful laments they called the blues impressed the boy at an early age. He listened to country music nightly on the radio in his family's parlor, he embraced the gospel sounds of the hymns he heard and sang in the Church where they worshipped.

Teddy had begged his parents for a guitar from the time he was ten. For two years they'd put aside enough cash to order one from the Sears Roebuck catalog and gave it to him the following Christmas. But the boy had no idea what to do with it. The only person he knew that played guitar was the colored man who worked at the service station where his daddy got gas.

"Don't you go bothering Chanticleer with any of that guitar nonsense now Teddy," his father warned him the first time he heard his son ask Chanty to string the guitar for him.

"That's all right Mr. Boyette. I'd be happy to help the youngster, maybe even give him a lesson or two."

"Can he Daddy?"

"Can't be paying you for no guitar lessons Chanty," his dad told the old man.

"Be my pleasure to do it, in my spare time of course, no charge."

"Well," Mr. Boyette reasoned, "That'd be okay I reckon."

"Oh boy!" Teddy shouted.

"You come around any time you like," Chanty told the youngster.

Teddy rode out that very next day on his bicycle. His guitar slung around his back on a makeshift strap he made from a rope.

He watched Chanty string the guitar. The old man showed him how to tune it by turning the pegs that stretched the strings to a precise point to get just the right sound. He learned simple chords, playing until his fingers ached from the coarseness of the steel wound strings. It would be that way until hard calluses formed on his fingertips.

Chanty taught him progressions, where to play on the neck to remain in key, how to transpose chords into different keys until it was as automatic as the multiplication tables he learned in school.

♫♫♫♫♫

Joseph Rabinowitz became a frequent visitor to the Texaco station, riding out by bus in civilian clothes. He sat with Chanty on the porch of his house snacking on raw green onions and sipping cold bottled beer. Joseph enjoyed listening to the old man play and the stories he told.

One day, Joseph asked, "Where does it all come from Chanty, the blues I mean?"

The lines in the old man's forehead deepened as he thought long and hard for an answer.

"The blues I know comes from the sharecropper plantations I growed up on in the Mississippi Delta country. Before that it goes way back to the slave times. My Grammy recollected to me 'bout the times when the boss field hand would come around bout daybreak callin' the workers out to the cotton fields. They sang out whilst bending low to pick the good cotton from the bottom bolls. They sang out for the water boy when they got thirsty but they sang loudest of all when the field boss shout out, 'quittin time!' Ha ha ha! Even at night, bone tired from work, they took to singing and dancing. Weren't no drums allowed to the slaves back then so they clapped they hands and stomped they feet, playin' fiddles and banjos. They griped about the big boss man, hard times and some man or woman what done 'em wrong."

"And you Chanty, how did you get started?" Joseph asked.

Thinking again Chanticleer began to relate, perhaps for the first time ever, the events of his early life.

"I was partial to the Jews harp and harmonica when I was a pup. First time I heard blues guitar was in a railroad station round - ought six maybe. I seen a man strum the strings with a pocketknife. Some years later I had a guitar of my own. In time, a man name of John Lomax come around sayin' he was from the Library of Congress in Washington, lookin to make recordins of sharecropper songs. I knowed where Washington was, didn't know what a recordin was. Not rightly sure I knew what a Library of Congress was neither. But I said I'd give it a try. This one night, some folks gathered to where this Lomax fella set up his machine what had a big ole' horn stickin' out of it. When it come to be my turn I told him he sure better catch the songs first time 'round. I had me a fear of that there horn."

Chanty's tale took on the feel of a ghost story told around a campfire at summer camp. "They cranked up that machine and I sang me a bunch of songs. Then, they fiddled with it some, and dang me if, before long I wasn't listenin to the sound of my own voice comin back at me out of that there machine. It was scratchy and tinny. But, yes sir, it was me all right."

Lomax told him many Negro players were traveling north to cities like New York and Chicago to make good money playing the blues in clubs. Chanticleer had never dreamed of a life beyond the plantation but the prospect of escaping the hardships and poverty of the south tempted him. He packed a bag, hopped a night train, and went north.

"Did you have a family?" Joseph asked.

"I had a wife, two children," he paused, suddenly uncomfortable with this part of his narrative. "I convinced myself I was doin it for them, to make a better life and all. Prolly meant it then, can't say for sure now. I played in small clubs for my room and board, once did a gig for two pieces of fried chicken. I hooked up with Cab Calloway like I told you before. Got me enough money to buy my Senorita and some fancy duds. I toured around the East Coast and the Midwest for a number of years."

"Sounds like a great way to live," Joseph said.

"It was a hard life, Joseph. I drank too much whiskey, smoked too much reefer, and catted around with too many women. I was a church goin man when I left here. Turned out I'd spend most Sunday mornings getting over Saturday night. About that time I decided to come back. My wife had run off, took the kids. So I just settled here."

Chanticleer fell silent, lost in thought. Joseph was sure these details had been locked away in the deepest recesses of the old man's mind for many years.

♫♫♫♫♫

Whatever free time Joseph didn't spend with Chanticleer was devoted to helping Danny with his car. The Master Sergeant in charge of the Motor Pool had great respect for Danny's ability as a mechanic. He allowed him to keep his car in an area normally reserved for non-commissioned officer's vehicles.

On one particular afternoon, Joseph, Danny and one of the motor pool mechanics, a Negro named Jackson, worked on replacing the brake pads on the Ford. They took a short break, resting in the shadow of a two-ton truck. Danny was jealous of the time Joseph spent with Chanticleer. He rarely missed an opportunity to tease him about it.

"So tell me, Joey, how's Uncle Remus?"

"C'mon, Danny, knock it off," Joseph fired back.

"I figured by now he'd fixed you up with some darkie chick." Danny didn't seem bothered that his comments might offend Jackson.

"I like the music Chanticleer plays that's all."

"Yeah, Chanticleer that's right. Hey, Jackson, tell Joey what you told me about that name."

"Up yours, Cavelli," Jackson replied. Clearly, he wanted no part of Danny's foolishness. Danny wouldn't let up.

"Jackson says the name Chanticleer means cock. You hear that Joey, cock, like a rooster...king of the hen house and all that shit? So if I was you I'd watch myself around that guy...don't bend down in front of him if you get my drift?"

"Fuck you Danny!" Joseph blushed making Danny howl all the more.

When the work was done they barely spoke to one another as they headed back to their barracks. After they'd showered and changed clothes, Danny figured it was safe to speak to Joseph again.

"Did I tell you I got another letter from my sister?" Danny asked.

"Oh yeah?" Joseph responded, not wanting to sound as interested as he really was. "How is she doing?"

"She's hanging in there...says my old man is off the wagon again. That's got me worried, especially with us going overseas soon."

Danny didn't share details about his personal life with just anyone. It was good for both of them to have somebody to talk to. He first told Joseph about his family in basic training. His mother had passed away from an illness when Danny was seventeen. His father started drinking heavily, which made Danny highly protective of his younger sister, Janet. The two siblings became very close. In the first letter she sent to her brother she enclosed a picture of herself. Danny showed it to Joseph.

At sixteen, Janet Cavelli attended high school in Cleveland. Joseph saw from her picture that she was pretty with long, blonde hair that fell down her back. She looked slim with the beginning of a good figure. But it was her warm, innocent smile that attracted Joseph most, a fact he'd kept secret from her brother.

Though he never actually read any of the letters, Joseph imagined Janet was a sensitive soul with more on her mind that the usual teenage issues.

Janet always included a short poem she'd written with each of her letters. Danny didn't mind sharing those with Joseph. They were usually short, well-crafted pieces on many different topics. She demonstrated the emotions of someone mature. Joseph enjoyed every one she sent.

"Did she send another poem?" he asked Danny.

"Those stupid things? Yeah, sure, remind me to show it to you after chow."

"Why do you make fun of what she writes? Some of them are really good."

"She's a kid growing up in a tough town. She needs to wise up and face reality, not waste her time writing poetry, wishin and hopin she was someone she ain't, like Queen Gwendolyn in King Arthur's court."

"Guinevere," Joseph corrected him.

"Huh?"

"Guinevere was King Arthur's queen – not Gwendolyn."

"Who gives a shit?"

"Did she ask about me?" Joseph dared to inquire. Danny had told his sister about his new friend. He even sent her a picture of them both, taken in the last days of basic training after their hair had grown back some.

"You got the hots for my little sister, Joey?"

"What a thing to say man. I told you, I like her poems, that's all."

"Yeah, well, it's a good thing you're a nice Jewish boy from New York City, or I wouldn't have invited you to come home with me when we get leave."

They planned to drive the convertible up north so Danny could store it in his family's garage before they shipped out. It would be their last chance to prowl and Joseph wanted very much to meet Janet in person.

"How about you… you hear anything from your folks?" Danny asked.

"Yeah, I got a letter too." Joseph wanted to let it pass, but Danny prodded.

"And?"

"They're doing okay. My mom is feeling a lot better. She got a good report from her doctor last week."

"That's great man. Listen, we can still make a side trip to see your folks before we go to Cleveland," Danny suggested.

"No, we'll stick to our plan. I don't want to see them too soon before we go to Korea. It might set her back, ya' know?"

It sounded like a logical explanation. But it wasn't entirely true. The real reason for Joseph's reluctance to go to New York was because he was still at odds with his father about enlisting. It went much further back than that and it had to do with music.

♫♫♫♫♫

Joseph's earliest recollection of his father at the piano was when he was around three years old. The vibrant melodies of the masters like Chopin and Grieg filled the rooms of their apartment on Central Park West. Solomon played with the same focus Chanticleer displayed with his guitar. Joseph studied his father's movements and before long, found himself on the bench next to his father, then on his lap. His tiny hands stretched apart, resting on Solomon's forearms until they grew long enough to reach the keys on their own. He learned the scales and the rudimentary elements of the instrument. The idea that he might one day be able to re-create the music his father played excited the gifted youngster. But then, tragic events and deep sadness overwhelmed the household.

In 1939, the forces of Nazi Germany invaded Poland. All of Europe was at war. Rumors about the horrible things being done to Jews filtered across the Atlantic. In less than a year all correspondence from both Solomon and Myra's family ceased completely.

Not long after Joseph started school, the Japanese bombed Pearl Harbor drawing the United States into the Second World War. As the conflict raged and the years passed, confirmed news of death and destruction reached the family with alarming regularity. In 1944 both sets of Joseph's grandparents were murdered in the gas chambers of a concentration camp named Auschwitz.

The horror of it all was too much for Joseph's mother. She'd always been a frail woman, small framed and thin. But the years of constant worry about events in her native country took their toll on her once beautiful features. Her smooth skin became wrinkled, almost ashen in color. She suffered an emotional breakdown, and retreated into a deep depression that robbed her vitality and love of life. She exhibited severe mood swings and fits of crying.

Solomon soon became a harsh taskmaster. He permitted the anger he felt at his family's situation to drive a wedge between him and his son. Learning to play the piano was now an arduous chore for Joseph and he rebelled against it.

After the war, some Nazi war criminals stood trial in Nuremberg, Germany. Evidence revealed that over six million Jews, along with millions of members of other ethnic groups were killed in the camps. Many Nazis found guilty of crimes were executed. The world settled in to a period of healing.

As Joseph went through high school, he couldn't reconcile that so many people of his heritage were led so sheepishly to slaughter. Being Jewish now meant something different to him. He decided that he'd be one Jew who wasn't going to put up with any insults or slurs to his heritage and religion. But, even that wasn't enough.

When America began sending troops to Korea, Joseph saw this as a way to release his anger. He vowed to be part of it. The day after he graduated high school he went against his parent's wishes and enlisted in the Army.

♫♫♫♫♫

Soldiers stationed at Fort Knox played a waiting game. Orders sending them into combat had been delayed twice. Ongoing peace talks were at a stalemate call ups for more troops were temporarily halted. That was fine for most of the GI's but Joseph wasn't happy. An armistice now would cheat him out of his opportunity to fight in the war.

Saturday night found Joseph, Danny, Hoffman and Jackson throwing back beers at their favorite watering hole, a roadside tavern called City Lights. The bar, owned by two veteran Army buddies from New Jersey, catered to the drinking habits of Northern soldiers. It was one of those dimly lit smoky places offering a haven for GI's from cities like New York, Chicago, and Detroit. Large black and white pictures of these places decorated the walls, along with those of famous ballplayers and prizefighters. The tunes in the corner jukebox featured Frank Sinatra, Tony Bennett and Rosemary Clooney and was quite devoid of any country and western talent.

The bar was also popular because the owners flagrantly ignored the Jim Crow laws designed by the southern states to ensure segregation between the races. Those laws called for separate areas for whites and coloreds with regard to dining, restroom facilities, and drinking fountains. That wasn't the case at City Lights. Many local women frequented the bar believing the prospect of meeting up with a northern soldier could be their ticket out of a dull, rural life.

Danny and Hoffman were trying their best to impress two local young girls while Joseph and Jackson sat at a table across the room. When the two skirt chasers faced the reality that they weren't going to get anywhere, they returned to the table to join their buddies.

"Looks like you two Romeos struck out big time, huh?" Jackson said with a howl.

"You figure you can do any better Jackson, you go on ahead, boy," Hoffman challenged in his deep Texan drawl.

"No thank you. Folks round here likely to lynch a poor black boy like me for doin shit like that. I'll just wait till we get over to Korea and we get hold of some of them cute little Asian beauties. Then you boys will see me wail."

"I hear that," Hoffman shot back. "That's all the poon tang any of us will be getting for a long time." The soldier drained his bottle of beer with one gulp.

"Speak for yourself," Danny threw in before taking a swig from his brew.

"What are you planning to do Cavelli, sneak one of these here bar hogs into your duffle bag and smuggle her off to Korea?" Hoffman asked.

"Maybe I ain't going to Korea," Danny answered.

"Don't kid yourself," Jackson offered. "This delay is only temporary. They don't get a peace treaty worked out soon, good 'ole Ike will have us on a transport for sure."

"Might not be so easy getting me on a transport," Danny persisted.

The others now realized what their friend meant.

"You better stop that crazy talk man," Joseph warned. "Desertion is serious shit."

Danny leaned in to the middle of the table, "Look guys, you all know I ain't no coward. But I don't feature getting my guinea ass shot off in some fucking Korean rice paddy."

"You go over the hill during wartime and they can hang your ass when they catch you," Jackson injected.

Danny grinned at his companions, "Yeah, well, they gotta catch me first."

"You think that's gonna be hard to do with you toolin around in that hot rod Ford of yours?" Hoffman countered.

They were all pretty drunk by the time they called it a night. Hoffman needed help just to leave the bar. Joseph and Jackson helped him up and supported his weight on the way out leaving Danny to pay their tab. They managed to get the Texan into the backseat of the Ford with Jackson climbing in behind him. Joseph rode in front with Danny.

"I swear to Christ, if you puke in my car I'll drop you off on the side of the road and leave you there, man."

"Don't you worry Cavelli, I'll be fine," Hoffman slurred back at him.

"You better be! Jackson you sing out if that cowboy even *looks* like he's gonna hurl."

"Let's just get out of here man," Jackson replied, who suddenly did not feel so well himself in the night air.

Danny peeled out and the convertible took off, knifing its way through the night. They breezed past the turnoff at Primrose Lane, unaware that the house about a half-mile east of the turnoff was still well lit despite the late hour.

♫♫♫♫♫

The house belonged to George and Jean Boyette and there was something of a celebration taking place. Their son Teddy had just won first prize at his high school talent show. His stirring, reverent performance of "The Old Wooden Cross" was the highlight of the show, so impressing the judges that they brought him back to sing it again as an encore. They awarded him a gold trophy cup. The family invited several of Teddy's classmates to the farm for an impromptu party. A few of them, mostly girls, lingered on.

Teddy enjoyed his newfound popularity, normally reserved for football players and track stars, but he wished the celebration would end soon. He couldn't wait until morning to drive to Chanticleer's place and tell his mentor all about the show.

But, Chanty already knew of Teddy's success. He and Lester had been at the high school, parked in their tow truck a short distance from the auditorium. They drank corn liquor from fruit jars, listening to the performance, the applause, and Teddy's encore that followed.

Chapter Three:

"...Then There Was Music"

"Candy apple red," Danny announced out of the blue.

"What?" Joseph asked.

"That's the color I decided to paint this heap, candy apple red."

They headed back to the paint shop in Radcliff so Danny could arrange for the finishing touches on his convertible. A week had passed since their drinking binge at City Lights. Nothing more was said about desertion and Joseph hoped the events were forgotten.

Danny was in good spirits. He steered the car with his left hand, his right arm extended out along the back of the bench seats.

"Think of it Joey." He conjured up a flight of fancy. "You and me up in Cleveland, cruising the boardwalk by the lake. All them fine looking chicks in bathing suits gawking at us. What'll ya' have man blonde, brunette, or redhead?"

"One of each."

"Yeah, yeah, one of each. I like that. Wait till you see the beaches up in Ohio, Joey."

"Hey, we got beaches in New York too ya' know. Ever hear of Coney Island?"

Danny's next words had purpose. "Maybe I'll see them someday. When we get back from Korea you can show me around up there." He looked at Joseph, awaiting his reaction.

"What did you say?"

"I said I'd like to see New York someday."

"No, no, not that part, the part about coming back from Korea."

"Yeah, I've been giving that a lot of thought. I hung around with a bunch of guys probably ten times tougher than any of them Chicoms we're gonna go up against over there. And besides, we ain't gonna be no pushover, riding around in a tank with three inch armor plating. So what am I so worried about?"

The two friends shared a hearty laugh until the loud blast of a horn startled them. Joseph peered over his shoulder. Danny stared into the rearview mirror. That familiar, threatening, black pick-up was bearing down on them.

"Not these fuckers again!" Danny took hold of the steering wheel with both hands.

"Take it easy, Danny!" Joseph warned.

"I'm not taking any of their shit this time, Joey!" Danny let out the stick shift and floored the accelerator pedal until the countryside flew by in a blur. The two occupants of the pick-up were equally intent on having their way. They sped up until the front bumper of the Chevy made contact with the back of the Ford.

"Bastards!" Danny wailed in anger. He jammed his foot to the floorboard, searching for every ounce of speed the convertible could give him.

"It's no use Danny! You can't out run them!"

"I can take these guys Joey! I know I can!"

The road opened up onto a long straightaway. The two vehicles were neck and neck when both drivers made the same tragic mistake. Danny yanked his steering wheel to the left, while the driver of the pick-up turned his hard to the right.

The vehicles collided with a loud crash, both of them careened out of control. The convertible spun around once. In a flash, a last glance of terror passed between Joseph and Danny. The Ford went off the road, lurched into a culvert and began to roll.

Joseph was thrown clear of the car hurtling through the air like a rag doll. He came to earth with a bone-crunching thud, and tumbled over rocks and grass. Dirt got into his eyes, his nose, and his mouth until he finally stopped rolling. Unbearable crashing sounds followed from very close by. An explosion, perhaps the gas tank rupturing, then, silence.

Joseph was dazed and in great pain, his movements severely hampered. He lay flat on his back, fought to raise his head but could not. He managed to look to his right and through badly blurred vision, caught site of the smashed, overturned Ford. Its wheels, pointed skyward were still turning, but It wasn't on fire. The explosion must have come from the pick-up truck.

"Danny?" he called out weakly. There was no answer. Blood now flowed into his eyes from somewhere on his head. The pain worsened. Silence folded in around him. Then, there was music, a piano at first, distant and soft. Chanticleer's guitar followed, slow and bluesy. Was it real or imagined? He looked to find the source but couldn't. As his consciousness slipped away, he listened and closed his eyes.

♫♫♫♫♫

When Joseph awoke, he was lying flat on something with wheels being hurried along a corridor. He could make out the large figure of a man walking alongside him. Not a doctor, but a sheriff or deputy of some kind, peering down at him with a look of great concern. Joseph felt the need to make some sort of report.

"The pick-up…" he struggled with his words.

"Take it easy, boy. You're banged up pretty bad," the lawman said.

"Black pick-up truck…ran us off the road."

"We know that, son. Family owns a spread out that way saw the whole thing. After the collision the pick-up slammed into a tree and blew sky high. Both occupants were killed instantly."

"Danny?" Joseph asked.

"Your friend? I'm afraid he didn't make it either. You lay quiet now, the doctors are gonna do all they can for you."

Joseph was scared. Danny and those other boys were dead. What possible chance did he have? The parts of his body that didn't hurt, he couldn't feel. Maybe he'd be paralyzed, lose limbs! Before any real panic could set in, the music returned, soothing and calming like a lullaby ushering him off to sleep.

♫♫♫♫♫

Lester finished talking with the owner of a blue Buick, a regular customer who stopped in for gas. After the Buick drove off, he walked to the office and stood in the doorway. Chanticleer sat behind a desk going over his invoices. He looked up. Lester had news.

"That wreck we heard about yesterday over near the Collins place," Lester said.

"Uh-huh?"

"It was the McVie brothers."

"Dead?"

Lester nodded, "Both of 'em…they was up to their usual shenanigans on the highway." Lester paused before relaying more bad news. "That Ford convertible from the Army base was involved."

The old man winced before he asked, "They killed too?"

"One of 'em can't say which."

Chanticleer decided he'd find out.

♫♫♫♫♫

When Chanticleer got to the hospital, he spoke to a surgeon named Wutherich, an Army doctor brought in from the base to treat Joseph's injuries. He gave Chanty a grim report.

"Your friend's in pretty bad shape. He suffered a severe head injury. We had to operate to relieve pressure on his brain. We gave him a transfusion and he's also got a broken leg and two herniated discs in his lower back."

"Is he gonna pull thru, Doc?" Chanticleer asked.

"He's young and he's strong. If he comes out of this coma soon, I'd give him better than a fifty-fifty chance."

"Can I see him?"

"Yes. I suppose so."

A stern looking white nurse in a starched uniform took him to

Joseph's room. He found the boy heavily bandaged, hooked to tubes and strapped to a traction device.

"Remember, the doctor says you can only stay a few minutes," the nurse reminded Chanticleer before leaving them alone.

"Can he hear me?" he asked her timidly.

"No one can say for sure. I like to think he can. It might even do him some good to hear a familiar voice."

Chanty pulled up a metal chair and sat at Joseph's bedside.

"Figured I come by and visit fer a spell," he began after the nurse had gone. "You're a sight boy. You had this old man worried I can tell you."

He leaned close in and touched Joseph's hand as it lay motionless at his side. If the nurse was right and Joseph could in fact hear him, perhaps it was time for another story.

"You was always asking me about blues men I'd known and I remembered this one fella in particular you might like to hear about. His name was Levy, Levy Morgan and he were a rascal he was…" Chanty chuckled, covering his face for fear that someone might hear him, assured no one had, he continued, "…he come down from Arkansas way … a real ladies man. He had the most perfect manicured fingernails you ever seen on a man. Well, on the middle finger of his right hand, he growed that nail especially long and he hardened it with clear polish and a coat of varnish. He shaped it with a nail file 'til he could use it as a guitar pick. He come to call it his 'itty' finger. He bragged that he'd use it on a titty and a clitty and his six string gitty. It made women folk flail and his guitar wail! Ha, ha, ha!"

Moving closer toward Joseph, his tone changed dramatically. "Joseph Rabinowitz, if you can hear me at all son, you come back to us. This world needs young men like you."

Chanticleer would return for a short time every day. He'd sit and talk to his friend, and say a prayer for his recovery. He'd been there and gone on the fifth day, the day Joseph came out of his coma.

It was difficult for Joseph at first. The slightest movements proved unbearably painful. In time he learned the extent of his injuries and the details of the crash.

A plain-Jane female Lieutenant from the Army Medical Corps informed him that his parents had been notified and were being kept up to date on his progress. Of course, they were anxious to speak to him personally. Joseph thanked the Lieutenant and assured her that he would call home in the next day or so.

"You had some tests today?" Chanty asked one afternoon.

"Yeah, more x-rays. I'm gonna glow in the dark pretty soon." There was something on Joseph's mind, something maybe only Chanty might understand. "You know, they tell me I was lucky to survive the crash."

"Lucky that the good Lord was watchin over you. That's the way I figure it."

"Why over me and not Danny or those other boys?"

"It's only natural to question such things, long as you don't mind getting no answers. Everything happens for a reason Joseph. Just you remember that."

"I've never been a real religious type Chanty, but through all that happened…out there on the highway…when I went into surgery…all those days I was in a coma, I could hear something. It sounded like music playing over and over in my head. I swear it saved my life."

"Likely as not, it did." Chanticleer didn't presume to have any special insight into the workings of a heavenly entity. He simply offered his own interpretation. "It's like because you clung onto life, stayed connected through that music you was hearing, you were able to come back to us."

"You really believe that, Chanty, don't you?"

"I do. I truly, truly do."

Later that afternoon one of the night nurses, a local married woman in her thirties, stopped by Joseph's bed.

"You have a letter young man," she announced, showing him an envelope.

"Is it from New York, my parents?"

She looked at the envelope. "No. The return address is Cleveland, Ohio. J. Cavelli?"

Janet? Joseph couldn't handle the letter with his arm in a cast.

"Would you like me to open it for you?" the nurse asked.

"Would you please?"

She sat close to the bed, opened the envelope and removed the folded pages. As she did, something fell to the floor.

"Oh, what's this?" She bent down to retrieve the item. It turned out to be a small photograph. She leaned forward and held it for him to see. It was a picture of Janet in a bathing suit, posing like a model in a magazine. He'd seen it before.

"She's very pretty," the nurse commented.

"Yes she is, isn't she?" Joseph managed a smile probably for the first time since the accident.

"Is she your girlfriend?"

"No she's not. Would you mind reading the letter to me?"

The nurse unfolded the pages and began to read:

Dear Joseph:

My dad and I wanted to write to tell you how glad we are to hear that you woke up from your coma and you're going to get better. The army people told us you were in the car with Danny. I hope you're not in too much pain. The picture I'm sending was with the personal effects they shipped home with Danny's body. He told me he showed it to you and you liked it, so I want you to have it. I hope you don't think that's too silly. We were so glad Danny found such a good friend in the army. He sometimes wrote me about the things you guys did and they always made me laugh.

It's really sad here without Danny. There's a priest from our church who comes to visit. I find it helpful, but my dad won't even listen to him. He's been drinking a lot and I worry about him. The priest says time will heal the wounds. I hope he's right.

Thanks again for being Danny's friend. I'm sorry we

never got the chance to meet in person. I hope you get better soon.

Love,
Janet

The nurse re-folded the pages and placed them back in the envelope.

"Well, despite what you told me, I'd say that young lady has feelings for you." Joseph blushed. "Would you care to send a reply?"

"I think I'll wait until I can write it myself."

"I understand. But, maybe just a short note just to let her know you read it?"

That sounded like a good idea. "Would you mind?"

"It would be my pleasure. I'll get a pen and some paper." She stood, but before walking away, she turned. "I might be able to scare up a frame for that picture if you'd like?"

"That would be great, thanks."

He dictated a short note expressing his sympathy for Danny's death. Joseph assured her that her brother always spoke with great affection for his family. He rambled on a bit about his recovery. When he decided there was nothing more he wanted the nurse to hear him say, he signed off with the words: "Sincerely, Joseph Rabinowitz."

The nurse smiled and rolled her eyes at the formality of his closing. She told Joseph that the letter would go out in the mail the next day.

It would be the best night's rest he'd had since the accident. When he woke the next morning, the night nurse had put Janet's picture into a metal frame and placed it on the meal tray for him.

Joseph worked hard to recover. The traction device was removed after some time, as was the cast on his arm. When he was able to handle a telephone, he called his parents.

"Oh, thank God. It's so good to finally hear your voice, Joseph." His mother's voice trembled with emotion.

"I know Mama. But I'm fine, really. I'm making good progress every day." He downplayed the severity of his condition.

"The Army tells us so little," she complained, "Wait, your father wants to say something."

He could hear her pass the receiver to Solomon. The line went quiet as though his father didn't know how to begin.

"Papa?"

"Yes, I'm here. I want to make arrangements to go down there to see you."

"No, Papa, please don't do that. It's such a long trip and there's really nothing you can do here. Everyone is taking good care of me. Mama needs you to be there with her."

"But she worries…we both do."

Before he could respond, his father put his mother back on the line.

"Joseph I love you very much, son." Joseph could tell she was crying.

"I love you too Mama. Try not to be too upset, it's not good for you. I'll call you every day now. I promise."

"Yes, yes. You need to do that. Call us every day."

"I promise," he repeated. "I have to go now, Mama."

"All right, son. I love you so much. You're Papa and I both love you."

"I love you too." He hung up the telephone.

Hospital aides and nurses soon had him out of bed and in a wheelchair. Every day they'd bring him to the therapy ward where he endured exhausting, painful exercises designed to bring his broken body back to normal. There were long, grueling hours, stretching the muscles in his back to strengthen them. Eventually, the wheelchair gave way to crutches and later, a cane.

On July 27, 1953, almost three months after the accident that claimed three lives on a highway in Kentucky, a treaty ending the Korean conflict was signed. Joseph Rabinowitz no longer had anyone to fight with his tank.

Not that it mattered anymore. Two days before that, a Captain from the U.S. Army Administration Office visited him in the hospital. Joseph's injuries had rendered him unfit for further military duty. The officer informed him that when he left the hospital, he would recieve an honorable discharge. The news hit him hard.

♫♫♫♫♫

After his prize-winning appearance at the high school talent show the past spring, Teddy Boyette sang at Radcliff's Fourth of July celebration. No church songs this time. He wooed the teenagers in the audience with his rowdy rendition of "Move it on Over" and several other songs. He made up his mind that he wanted to sing and make records for a living. But Hardin County wasn't the place to do it.

"That old Desoto we got out back ain't worth half of what your motorcycle would bring Teddy." Chanticleer said when Teddy offered to trade his Harley for the 38' Coupe they were working to restore. "What are you in such an all fired hurry to do, son?"

"I'm fixin' to drive down to Memphis. I'm gonna get me a record contract. I figure I'm better off in a car since I can't afford to stay in no kinda hotel or nothing, I might need to spend a night or two sleeping in the back seat."

"A night or two? You reckon two days is all it's gonna take to get a record contract?"

"Why are you talking against me on this? Ain't you the one always telling me I need to find someone to help me get started? Well, they ain't gonna come knockin' on my door, I gotta go out and make it happen."

"What your folks say about all this?"

"Aw, they don't want me to go neither. They think it's all some crazy dream. But why can't I try it, Chanty? While school is out, why can't I try?"

"Then you go on ahead and take the Desoto, as a loan. We'll hold on to the Harley for safe keeping, till you get back."

"Chanty, when I come back, I'm gonna be driving a Cadillac."

Chapter Four:

"Memphis"

Memphis, Tennessee was a bustling city south of the Kentucky border on the banks of the Mississippi River. Born out of the 1930's depression era hardships that befell whites and coloreds alike, the races came together in an integrated, urban environment quite unique to its time. Those who settled in town brought their culture and their music with them.

W.C. Handy, a self taught Negro musician, songwriter, and bandleader, sometimes referred to as the "father of the blues," helped transform the city into one brimming with promoters, publishing houses, and record companies as early as 1910. In the downtown area, blues clubs lined both sides of Beale Street, in a predominantly colored section of town.

Teddy Boyette drove passed the Memphis city limits around midnight. He pulled the Desoto onto a railroad siding and parked between two freight trains. There, he stretched out in the backseat for a few hours of much needed sleep. He had a big day ahead of him. Despite what his parents and Chanticleer thought, he *did* have a plan.

Teddy knew that the three top record executives in Memphis were Lester Bihari, Sam Phillips and Artie Franklin. Bihari ran Meteor Records out of a small store on Chelsea Avenue. Sam Phillips owned and operated Sun Records out of a similar storefront operation on Union Avenue. Teddy had decided to make his first stop Artie Franklin's hugely successful Myriad Music Corporation on the third floor of an office building on North Main Street.

He freshened up in a service station restroom, putting on the only pressed white shirt he'd brought with him. By ten in the morning he stood in front of the receptionist's desk at Myriad Music.

♫♫♫♫♫

"May I help you?" The receptionist greeted Teddy with a polite smile as he stood on the other side of her desk, his tattered guitar case dangling from one hand.

"I'd like to see Mr. Artie Franklin, please."

"Do you have an appointment?"

"No ma'am I don't."

Her smile faded, "I'm sorry, Mr. Franklin doesn't see anyone without an appointment."

"Well, you see ma'am I'm a singer and I… "

"I can see that young man. But, if you don't have an appointment, I'm afraid I can't let you in." She looked down.

"Okay then, how do I make one?"

"Excuse me?"

"An appointment, how do I go about making one?"

"Do you have a manager, someone who represents you?"

"No ma'am I don't got no one like that. I just want Mr. Franklin to listen to me sing."

"If you'd like to leave your name and phone number I'd be happy to have someone from our staff set up an audition for you."

"Audition! Yeah, that's what I want. But I'd like to audition for Mr. Franklin himself, if you don't mind?"

"Mr. Franklin doesn't conduct personal auditions. Now, why don't you just go away before I have to call the police?" She punctuated her threat with a less than friendly grin.

Chastised like a troublesome child, Teddy turned and walked away. He stormed out of the building and paced the sidewalk. Stewing in his anger and disappointment, he resisted the urge to go back inside.

Teddy wandered up the street. On the corner across the intersection he came to a luncheonette. He went inside.

The late morning breakfast crowd was breaking up. Teddy walked to the counter to the right of the entrance and sat on a vacant stool. He peered out the front window that offered a good view of the office building down the street. A waitress arrived across the counter to take his order. She was an attractive woman in her mid-thirties. Her dark auburn hair was done up in a tight, fashionable style that flipped up at the back. Make-up accented her deep green eyes. The extra button she kept opened on her brown waitress uniform called attention to her ample bosom.

"What can I get for you, honey?" she asked.

"I'll just have a cup of coffee and some toast."

"White or rye, the toast?"

"White."

"Comin' right up."

"Thank you, ma'am."

"You can skip the 'ma'am' talk there darlin, my name is Dee." She cast a flirtatious smile his way. Embrassed, Teddy felt himself blush.

The waitress made her way through swinging doors to the kitchen. She put two pieces of white bread into a toaster. A second waitress, pudgy with peroxide blonde hair joined her.

"Hey, Paula. Did you see the smile on that cat at the counter?" Dee asked.

They peeked through a diamond shaped cutout window in one of the doors.

"Yeah. He's got the whole package don't he?" the blonde said.

"You got that right."

"You looking to housebreak a new love puppy, Dee?"

"He might be good for a few kicks," Dee observed. The two women giggled naughtily bumping shoulders. The toaster popped two pieces of browned bread. Dee prepared the toast and returned to the dining room.

The young man was gone. She caught sight of him through the luncheonette window as he walked up the street. Dee didn't know what to admire more, his strong Gary Cooper-like gait or the way his tight ass wiggled as he walked.

"You must be losing your touch, sweetie you let that one slip right off the hook," the blonde next to her kidded.

"He'll be back," Dee replied.

"How can you be so sure?"

"He forgot something." She motioned to the guitar case leaning on the opposite side of the counter. The girls shared a knowing smile.

♫♫♫♫

Teddy's stomach turned flip-flops. While he'd been sitting in the luncheonette, he decided he'd given up far too easily in his quest to see Artie Franklin, allowing himself to be shooed away by his secretary. He'd come a long way seeking his big chance. If he gave up now he might as well head back home and work on his family's farm or find a job somewhere else. Before doing that he'd give Artie Franklin one more try.

As Teddy approached Franklin's office, the secretary caught sight of him and picked up the telephone. Teddy guessed she was calling the authorities.

Just then, an office door behind her opened and three men walked out. The man out front was older and did all the talking. Teddy assumed he was Artie Franklin. The other two followed hanging on his every word, eager to carry out orders.

"I'm going out for a while Tammy," Franklin told the secretary.

She tried to warn him about the young troublemaker but Teddy was already within earshot of the men.

"Excuse me, Mr. Franklin, can I have a word with you please, sir?" Teddy asked.

The three men stopped walking. The yes men shrunk backward leaving Franklin face to face with the youngster.

"Okay, kid, what's this all about?" Franklin demanded.

"My name is Teddy Boyette. I'd like to sing for you."

"You plan on auditioning for me right here in the hallway?"

Only then did Teddy realize that he'd walked off without his guitar. This flustered him.

"I know you're a busy man, Mr. Franklin, I just need to run back and get my guitar. I know if you was to just give me a chance, you..."

"Don't bother..." Franklin cut him off in mid-sentence. "I don't have the time to listen to every one of you greasers who manages to bully his way into my office."

People gathered in the hallway to watch the confrontation.

"Look kid, we promote clean talent here not juvenile delinquents. That slicked back hair and tough guy look may work on the other side of the tracks, but not here. Go get yourself a haircut and clean up some, then maybe you'd stand a chance."

People stared at him, some giggled at Franklin's chiding words. Teddy's embarrassment turned to anger. "And if you'd take your fat head out of your ass you might see that things are changing in music and its people like me gonna make them changes!"

This outburst by such an upstart against one of the most influential record executives in Memphis shocked everyone within earshot.

"What did you say your name was?" Franklin asked.

"Teddy Boyette."

"Well, I'll be *sure* to remember that."

Two uniformed Memphis police officers arrived on the scene. They took hold of Teddy, one on either side of him.

"No need for the strong arm fellas, I'll go quietly," Teddy said.

Despite his surrender the policemen pulled him toward the stairway. Once outside they were content to send him packing with a swift kick in his backside and a strong warning that he not return. They stood sentry to make sure he heeded them. Teddy walked back to the luncheonette.

♫♫♫♫♫

The lunch crowd filled the place. Teddy sat at one of the last remaining seats at the counter. Dee approached him.

"I'm afraid your toast got cold, sweetie," she said.

"I'm real sorry about that ma'am."

"And I told you about that ma'am business too, didn't I?"

The sullen young man didn't respond. Just one look told her he was stewing over some crisis. Dee slipped back into the kitchen and when she returned she was carrying his guitar case. She gave it to him over the counter.

"I put this in the back for safekeeping."

"I appreciate that...Dee."

The waitress smiled, "You look a might on the used side. Would a burger help maybe?"

"I'm afraid I'm a little off my feed."

"Well, sugar you can't be sittin' here during the lunch rush without ordering something. How about a coke at least?"

"That'd be fine."

"And don't you go runnin' off on me again, it's bad manners. You nurse that pop for as long as you like. When things thin out in here later, you and me are gonna have a little talk and you can tell me all your problems, okay?"

"Alright."

He managed a smile that made the waitress quite happy.

As she walked toward the soda fountain, a tall, balding, badly overweight gentleman came into the luncheonette. He wore an outrageously colored sports jacket and matching trousers. He took the last counter seat, next to Teddy. He looked to be in his forties and smoked a cheap, fat cigar that sent lines of smoke right passed Teddy's nose. The boy fanned the air around his head, but the heavyset man took no notice.

"What's your pleasure, Cap?" Dee asked the man when she returned and placed Teddy's Coke in front of him.

"How's the meatloaf today, little darlin?"

"Same as usual," she replied with a shrug.

"Well, I'll have it anyway with mashed potatoes, peas and iced tea...extra gravy for the mashed potatoes."

"Coming right up."

At about the same time two other men entered the luncheonette and sat in a booth not far from the counter. They were the two yes men from Artie Franklin's office. When they recognized Teddy they let out a hearty laugh. The sound caused both Cap and Teddy to look around. Seeing the men made Teddy squirm. Cap offered no reaction, probably because Dee had placed a heaping plateful of food in front of him. He looked around for some ketchup, and noticed a bottle just beyond his reach on the other side of Teddy.

"Excuse me, son, would you pass me that there ketchup?"

Teddy picked up the bottle and handed it to him.

"Better watch out how you talk to that boy, Cap," One of the record company men called out from his booth.

"How's that Billy?" Cap seemed more intent with tapping the bottom of the ketchup bottle until the contents flowed out over his meatloaf.

"He's the cat that told Artie Franklin that if he took his head out of his ass he'd learn something about the music business." He and his lunch mate enjoyed another laugh.

"That right, son?" Cap asked so that only Teddy could hear him.

"Afraid so."

"No need to put yourself on a cross over it. Fact is there's plenty of people in this town wish they had the stones to tell Artie Franklin off. That includes them two hyenas over yonder."

"Well, all the same, I wish it hadn't been me that done it."

"Can you play that thing?" Cap asked pointing his fork at the guitar case on the floor.

"I can if I ever get the chance. Are you in the record business?"

"Records? No, I'm not a record man. My name's Cap Stewart. I put on roadshows, 'The Cap Stewart Cavalcade,' you ever hear of it?"

"No, I can't say as I have. I'm Teddy Boyette from Kentucky."

"Pleasure to meet you Teddy." Cap put his fork down long enough to shake the boy's hand. "We do a lot of local shows hereabouts, sock hops, stock car rallies, and such. I got one getting ready to go out next week. You looking for work?"

"Me?" The question stunned Teddy.

"I got a feelin' I could use a looker like you to draw in all the teeny boppers on the road."

"Well, if this don't beat all? Less than an hour ago I got thrown out of Artie Franklin's office and now you offer me a singing job and ain't neither one of you heard me sing or play a single note."

"Oh, I'll hear you sing soon enough. You interested?"

"Heck yeah I'm interested. I'd be crazy to turn down a paying job!"

"Well, son, let me explain a few things about that."

Cap went on to detail how his shows worked. The Cavalcade would be out touring for several weeks. They'd play small towns in Tennessee doing one show per night, perhaps two on weekends. Several acts were on the bill, each performing for about twenty minutes. The artists all began the tour on equal footing with the more experienced at the top of the lineup. However, that could easily change once the show was out on the road. Audience reaction would determine future billing on the next stop on the tour. This way Cap ensured the performers wouldn't become complacent. They'd work harder and do their best in the hope of moving up in the pecking order.

It was all geared for the big final show at the Regency Theatre in downtown Memphis when the Cavalcade got back to town. The performers were paid for that show depending on where they appeared on that final bill.

"I know it ain't the big time you been dreaming about," Cap wrapped up his sales pitch as he finished his lunch. He took one last gulp of his iced tea. "But a lot of young performers starting out look at it as a good way to get some experience, polish up an act. It might stand you in good stead for the next time you went to see one of them record company fellas."

It made good sense, but Teddy had reservations.

"I understand that, Mr. Stewart. It's just… I was counting on making some money."

"We'll pay for your food and lodging and such while we're out. If you do real good there'll be some cash in it for you when we get back here to Memphis. You might even make enough to buy yourself a car."

"I already got me a car," Teddy informed him.

"You do? Why didn't you say so in the first place, son? If you'd be willing to haul some of the gear, I'll pay you three dollars a day and gas money."

"So, I don't get paid for singing but you'll pay me for the use of my car?"

"That's right," Cap said.

"This music business is sure nothing like I expected. Mr. Stewart, you got yourself a singer and a driver."

They shook hands to seal their deal. Cap tossed some bills on the counter to pay for his lunch and leave Dee a generous tip.

"We're holding rehearsals at the Charles Street Hall. We start at ten sharp. Being new you've got a lot of time to make up. You come on by tomorrow. I'll listen to you sing and we'll see where we can work you in. You got some decent clothes, I take it?"

The question made Teddy's heart sink. "Huh?"

"Dress clothes, button down shirt, jacket, and go to meeting outfit? You can't go onstage in blue jeans."

"Oh, I realize that. Yeah, sure I got all that stuff back at my place."

"Good. We'll see you in the morning then."

Cap gave the boy a hearty slap on the back and left the luncheonette leaving Teddy to ponder his deceit.

"Hey, baby, did I hear him offer you a spot on his show?" Dee asked as she picked up Cap's empty plate and scooped up his money.

"Yeah, he sure did."

"Well, see there, turns out you got some good news today after all."

"Not really. I lied to him," Teddy confessed. "I told him I had some dress clothes back at my place."

"And you don't?"

"Nope. Not unless you'd call two tee shirts and another pair of jeans dress clothes. Heck I don't even have me a place. I slept in my car last night. Dee, I don't know what I'm gonna do."

Dee thought for a moment before offering a possible solution. "Well, I clock out of here in another hour. If you want I can take you down to Lasky's and help you pick out a few things?"

"I can't pay for nothin like that."

"Short on cash too?"

"Damn near broke."

Dee saw this as a perfect way to further the real motives she had for helping this good-looking boy.

"Well, I guess I could take you shopping, get you the things you need and you can pay me back when you can."

"I couldn't ask you to do something like that, Dee."

"You didn't ask. I offered."

Under any other circumstances he'd never consider such a proposition. But Cap Stewart's offer was too good to pass up. Dee's plan seemed the only way out of this dilemma.

"Alright, but you gotta promise to let me pay you back with interest."

"If you insist," Dee replied with a smile. The little fish had taken the bait. Now all she had to do was reel him in.

Teddy left the luncheonette to pick up his car. When he got back to meet Dee at the end of her shift, he found her waiting outside. She'd applied fresh make-up. The alluring scent of her perfume filled the interior of the DeSoto.

She directed him to Lasky's, a clothing store that catered to the hip cat crowd located in the lobby of the Peabody Hotel on Beale Street. Dee picked out three silk shirts, one black, one yellow and one lime green, all with outrageous wide winged collars. They also purchased two pairs of black pegged trousers and a pink double-breasted sports jacket with wide lapels and padded shoulders. A thin, white silk tie, some socks and a pair of white Flagg Brothers loafers completed the wardrobe.

After Lasky's, Dee treated them both to dinner and several bottles of beer at a local fish fry restaurant. She listened as he spoke about being excited to audition for Cap Stewart, but his inability to maintain eye contact told her that Teddy was also excited in a different way.

"And you can't be sleeping in the back of your car anymore, either. I got plenty of room at my place. You can stay with me." Dee continued to spin her web.

"Well, my car ain't exactly what you'd call much on comfort. So if you got a spot where I can get comfy, I think I'd like to take you up on that."

"Oh, yeah, I got a cozy spot for you, honey, real cozy."

♫♫♫♫♫

Back at her apartment on South Street, Dee, well schooled in the art of seduction, took charge. She kissed him hungrily from almost the first moment they walked in. She led him by the hand to the bedroom and sat him on the edge of her bed. She unbuttoned her one-piece waitress uniform and let it fall to the floor. Teddy sat transfixed at the sight of this woman dressed only in her underwear. He'd kissed and fondled some of his female high school classmates before. This was something completely different. After a short step forward, she straddled one of his legs. She reached around to unhook her bra with one hand.

One quick shrug of her shoulders made the garment fall away from her body exposing her breasts and erect nipples. She moved his head close and he began to suckle her, nipping at her flesh with his teeth.

Dee fought the urge to gasp in response. This was *her* show and she wasn't ready to relinquish control. She pushed him flat onto the bed, coming down on her side next to him. Her hands roamed all over his body until she could feel his erection through his jeans.

"Sugar, you need to be out of these clothes," she whispered.

Teddy leapt from the bed fumbling with his clothing.

Dee took off her panties. She was naked and leaning on her elbows when the fully aroused young man came at her like a wild animal. As he lay on his side, she took his hand and guided it to the intimate spot inside her body, where she would achieve optimum response.

His fingers were awkward and anxious, but he proved willing and eager to learn. Urging him on with words and movements she reached a fully satisfying climax. She took some time to relax before rising up on all fours to straddle his body. Dee reached down and placed his rigid penis into a warm, wet place she knew he'd never experienced before. She rocked back and forth, slowly at first, and then she quickened her pace as her passion rose once more.

Teddy exploded violently inside her. They lay entwined like a mass of shuddering, quivering flesh. Dee melted on top of him. They kissed until their breathing returned to normal.

♫♫♫♫♫

Their cavorting made him twenty minutes late getting to the rehearsal hall the next morning. The large, auditorium had a high ceiling and sparsely furnished, except for a large wooden table set back some fifty feet from an elevated stage located at one end of the room. A sound engineer sat at the table working the dials of his equipment. Long lines of wiring snaked along the floor to the stage where they hooked into microphones and amplifiers. Cap Stewart sat in a chair beside him.

The promoter paid little attention to Teddy when he approached the table. A group of four pretty white girls, dressed in chiffon dresses, finished a song onstage. Cap stood up and clapped.

"That's a fine job, gals. That number sounded much better this time. All right, the Hollins Twins will be up next. Get your music charts ready."

Cap sounded like a confederate general commanding his troops on the battlefield. It may have been that Teddy's entrance escaped his attention but the same couldn't be said about the members of the girl group leaving the stage. Each of them took a hard look at the boy as they filed by.

Cap faced Teddy, who was dressed in a pair of the black pegged pants and his new yellow shirt, demonstrating that he indeed own nicer clothes.

"I'd just about given up on you boy."

Obviously the clothes didn't impress him. Teddy formed the words of a lame excuse, but they never made it to his lips.

"Since you're a late addition, you'll open the show when we start out. You got ten minutes to show us what you got. What kind of accompaniment do you use?"

"Sir?"

"Accompaniment, back up musicians…a band?" He motioned toward the stage where several young men with musical instruments moved around setting up for the next act. A few of them had provided musical background for the girl group as well.

"Oh, Mr. Stewart, I ain't never played with no band before. I just get up there with my guitar and sing."

Cap took a deep drag on his ever-present cigar. "Alright son, after this next act I'll have a listen to whatever it is you do."

The Hollins twins, a brother and sister team dressed in matching cowboy outfits took the stage. They performed several popular country and western tunes. Teddy was impressed with their tight harmony and professionalism.

Keeping in mind what Cap told him about accompaniment, Teddy paid close attention to the musicians playing behind the twins. There were five of them, all young, all white. One played a big hollow-body electric guitar connected to an amplifier by a long cord. Another strummed a tall, bulky stand-up bass fiddle. Two others sat behind music stands. One played saxophone, the other a trumpet. A drummer, set back furthest of all, provided the combo a strong backbeat.

When the Hollins Twins completed their set, Cap applauded

giving the performers some parting words of encouragement. He walked onstage and motioned for Teddy to join him there.

"All right, everyone," Cap's voice squeaked as he spoke into a microphone to get everybody's full attention. "If you'd all just gather around for a minute."

Everyone in the hall moved toward the stage area. Teddy grew nervous at the prospect of singing for these polished professionals. He took his guitar from its case and strapped it around his body.

"I want you all to have a listen to Teddy Boyette from up Kentucky way. He's gonna be coming with us on this trip and he claims to have a heap of talent. So why don't we all give him a chance to show us what he's got?" Cap turned to the band members who were still at their places behind him. "Slim, you hang back there on drums and Brad you stay on bass. See if you can play along with the boy. He don't have no music charts or nothing."

The two musicians gave Cap the high sign. The rest of the band filtered off the stage.

"Okay, Teddy, the stage is yours."

"Do you know what key you play in?" the bass player Cap called Brad asked.

"I start off on the C chord," Teddy told the musician.

"Key of C it is then."

Teddy began with his rendition of "Move it on Over." The drummer and bass player knew the song but not in this rocking new tempo. It took several bars for them to catch up. By the end of the song Teddy had his captive audience in his corner, and everyone applauded. For his next tune he did a blues number Chanty taught him, one with a shuffle beat the drummer improved upon by using brushes instead of sticks. Teddy liked it. Cap faded offstage and moved next to the sound engineer.

Teddy moved on to his third up-tempo tune, his confidence level rose to the point that he now moved in time with the beat. He made deliberate half turns with his upper body as he sang.

"That tom cat can sure rip it up!" the soundman observed.

"I'll put an amen to that."

"Not much bottom to his voice though," the engineer added.

"He's young. You can do something to fix that right?"

"Yeah. I'll outfit him with an A-77 ribbon mike. I can pump up the bass level from the console."

"Good."

Both men became more and more impressed as Teddy sang on. He possessed a raw energy combined with his sweet down home charm assuring Cap that his initial hunch about the boy might indeed pay off.

Teddy had daytime lessons in performing music from Cap, and nighttime lessons in lovemaking from Dee. She schooled him in the ways of pleasing a woman. Cap's lessons were similar though far less intimate.

"Eye contact, Teddy, that's the key, it's all in the eyes. There's gonna be a lot of young girls in the audience every night and you gotta be sure each of them feels extra special, like you was singing to them individual like. I know you have fun when you're up there, but you also got to think about it like it was your job, your responsibility to see that each one of them gals is glad they came to see you."

"That could be a tall order, Cap."

"Well, son, if anybody can do it, you sure can."

While the format of the Cavalcade encouraged competition, the other performers were supportive of the talented newcomer. By the time they were ready to go out on the road, Teddy had a solid twenty-minute set of songs.

♫♫♫♫♫

A caravan of seven vehicles left Memphis on a clear Saturday morning. The departure aimed to get them to their first destination, the small town of Bartlett, Tennessee, before noon. Teddy's Desoto led the way. Cap sat next to him. The back seat and trunk was packed with suitcases and other gear. The others followed close behind in a variety of vehicles including Cap's 1934 station wagon.

The show in Bartlett was to take place at an outdoor pavilion on the fairgrounds outside town, after a stock car race at the adjoining speedway. The pavilion stood at the opposite end of the grounds between the midway of rides, games, and food tents that lined the walkway to the parking lot. A soft summer breeze cooled the crowds filing out after the race. Few realized they were intentionally being herded past the stage. Those spectators who'd come to see the show stood in front as the band tuned up and played some instrumental numbers. By the time Cap appeared onstage, the pedestrian walkway had filled.

"Don't walk on by friends. Don't pass us up!" His brash, carney voice bellowed out over the crowd as he spoke into the microphone at center stage. "Welcome to Cap Stewart's Cavalcade of Music. We got us a real fine lineup of young talent ready to entertain you this evening, so gather round and have a good time! Let's start things off with a handsome young newcomer to the circuit with the face of an angel and a smile to match. Let's have a real big hand for Teddy Boyette!"

Cap stepped aside as Teddy bounded onto the stage. Many of those out front had no idea what to make of him as he strummed his guitar. He wore a black shirt and pants, his pink, unbuttoned sports jacket billowed in the breeze like a vampire's cape. Aided by the bass effect of the new microphone, his voice boomed from speakers on either side of the stage.

More people took notice. Young girls caught up in the driving rhythms of the music and Teddy's exaggerated body movements. They drifted into the open space in front of the stage. Some dragged their unwilling male companions along with them. The size of the crowd swelled to well over one hundred. Teddy did his job well. When he finished his set the audience roared with delight. Teddy left the stage to loud applause mixed with cheers and whistles.

His heart pounded the whole time, though he hadn't noticed it until now. Cap stood onstage and introduced the girl group, the

Sparrows. He then hurried around back to seek out Teddy, who still wore a huge, beaming smile.

"You're a Goddamn natural boy, you know that?" Cap said, taking hold of his new a discovery. He shook him left and right.

"That's the most exciting thing I ever done in my life, that's for sure."

"Were you nervous?"

"Fact is I think I was too scared to be nervous. But I loved it Cap. I'll be doggone, I loved every minute of it!"

"See there, what'd I tell you, a natural! Let's get you some water before you hyperventilate."

The Sparrows, and the Hollins Twins were also well received by the crowd. But by the time Tommy Payton, a torch singer in the vein of Johnny Ray finished his act, the audience numbered less than forty.

More of the same followed in the towns they played that first week. The tour turned north along US Highway 45. After they performed in Milan, Tennessee for a two-night stint at the town's Opera House, Cap gave Teddy some important news.

"Starting at our next stop in Humboldt, I want you to close the show."

"Honest, Cap?"

"You got ears ain't you son? The kids love you."

Cap planned to nurture his hot new property. He also realized that he'd have to guard against those who'd try to steal Teddy away from him. He promised himself to do just that.

Chapter Five:

"Cleveland"

The Cavelli house on West 226 Street in Cleveland, Ohio looked just the way Danny described it, a working man's home not unlike the house next door or the one across the street.

It was hot and muggy when Joseph Rabinowitz walked from the bus stop on the corner. Reaching the front of the two-story, wood framed dwelling, he paused to gather himself before continuing through the gate of the picket fence. He walked up the steps to the porch that ran the entire length of the house.

Days earlier, he'd telephoned Danny's father, Vince Cavelli, to ask if he could stop by on his way home to New York. A sense of unfinished business haunted him. He wanted to visit Danny's grave and say a final farewell. After Vince granted his request, Joseph telephoned his parents and told them of his plans.

He signed the papers severing him from the U.S. Army and collected a hefty sum of back pay. Chanticleer drove him to the bus station in Louisville where their parting was an emotional one. They shared a friendly embrace, which raised some eyebrows in the segregated atmosphere of the public bus terminal.

The long bus ride up from Louisville, Kentucky had jostled and jolted him. The heavy duffle bag he carried made his injured back ache.

There were knots in Joseph's stomach as he rang the doorbell. The knots became lumps in his throat as the door opened and Janet Cavelli stood before him, smiling.

"Janet?" he managed to choke out passed the lumps. "I'm Joseph Rabinowitz."

Her pictures did not do her justice. She wore a short sleeve, red and white plaid blouse draped over a pair of loose fitting blue shorts. Her ponytail accented her slender face.

"Hi, Joseph, come on in." Janet shifted backward. He entered the small foyer and she closed the door behind them. "Why don't you put your things in the corner there? We can go into the parlor and sit down."

She pointed to a spot beneath a mirrored coat rack hanging on the wall. He put his duffle bag down and followed her through an archway into a large living room, neatly kept and nicely furnished. Joseph sat on a sofa in the middle of the room.

"I made lemonade. Would you like some?"

"That would be great, thanks."

Janet bounced from the room through a doorway that Joseph guessed led to the kitchen. He studied his surroundings. He noticed a lot of family photographs on tables and shelves around the room. He stood up to have a closer look. Many were photos of Janet's parents. Others depicted Danny, Janet, or both at various times in their childhood. The wedding picture of Mr. and Mrs. Cavelli caught his attention the most. He picked up the metal-framed picture to study it more carefully. The photographer captured the image of two people so in love that it transcended the boundaries of time more than any spoken word could ever hope to do.

Joseph noticed the strong physical resemblance between mother and daughter. He believed Janet was well on her way to equal or perhaps even surpass her mom's beauty.

"My Mom was really pretty wasn't she?" Janet asked. She carried a metal tray containing two tall glasses of lemonade. She put it down on a coffee table in front of the couch.

"Yes she was," Joseph replied, keeping his speculations to himself. He put the photograph back in place and returned to the couch. He picked up a glass of lemonade. "Danny told me she got sick?"

"Tuberculosis. She's gone two years now. I still miss her."

"Yeah, I'm sure you do."

Janet crossed the room and picked up another framed photograph.

"This is one of my favorites." She handed the picture to Joseph and plopped down cross-leg on the opposite end of the couch.

The photograph, smaller and more recent, was of Danny and Joseph in their dress uniforms. Joseph couldn't remember where or when it was taken.

"I'm sorry I never got to see Danny in person in his uniform. He looks so handsome. You do too."

Her compliment embarrassed him somewhat. Drops of perspiration inched down his face. He reached into his pants pocket, took out a handkerchief and wiped his brow. Janet sat bolt upright when she noticed his discomfort.

"Look at you, you're sweating bullets!" She took two quick butt hops across the cushions getting close enough to take the handkerchief away from his grip and help him.

"I can go get a fan," she said.

"No, I'm okay, honest. I don't know why I'm so nervous. I mean, I know we just met and all but I feel like we've known each other for a long time, it's almost like -"

"Like being on a blind date?" Janet interrupted. They both laughed and Joseph nodded. She'd hit upon it exactly. "I know. I took two showers before you got here. I was afraid my skin was gonna get all pruney."

The nervous tension between them now broken, they relaxed and spent the rest of the afternoon talking. Janet spoke of the letters she'd received from Danny with all sorts of silly basic training stories. Most were about something stupid they'd done, some of which still embarrassed Joseph. She giggled and smiled a lot, which proved infectious, allowing Joseph to enjoy himself more than he had in a long time.

The conversation took on a more serious tone when Janet asked him about the accident and aftermath. She spoke of the sadness that prevailed around their lives in the days after Danny's body came home in a closed casket. His wake was attended by many family members and friends. Tears came to her blue eyes. She turned away so as not to let Joseph see them flow down her cheeks.

"I'm sorry." She managed to say when she faced him again. "Would you want to go to the cemetery…visit Danny's grave?" she asked after composing herself.

"Well, that's one of the reasons why I came to Cleveland. But we don't have to go right now if you're not up to it."

"Actually I go every day at about this time."

"Alright then."

"It's not very far. We can walk. Just let me go run a brush through this mop." She hurried off again and up a flight of stairs.

♫♫♫♫♫

They walked to the Roman Catholic Cemetery where Danny was laid to rest. They paused long enough for Janet to buy a bunch of fresh flowers from one of the vendors.

The Cavelli family plot was located mid-way down a row of marble headstones in the St. Peter's section. It was easy to determine the exact location since no new grass had grown over the recently disturbed earth. Joseph stood by as Janet knelt down and lovingly placed the new flowers at the base of the stone. The engraving read:

Margaret Cavelli
1916-1951
"Loving wife and Mother"

As she stood she fought back tears. "My dad says I can write a couple of lines for Danny and if it isn't too expensive we can put it on the stone. I haven't been able to come up with anything yet though."

"I'm sure you will. You've got a real talent for that kind of thing."

She recalled Danny telling her how much Joseph enjoyed her poems.

As they turned to walk away, Janet reached up and took hold of Joseph's arm with both hands. She wrapped herself around him for support. She rested the side of her head as close to his shoulder as she could. Joseph felt the curve of her breast press against his arm. He felt a sense of guilt, perhaps he should move away but he made no effort to re-position himself.

"Back at the house you said visiting Danny's grave was one of the reasons you came to Cleveland. Was there another reason?" Janet asked.

Her question surprised him. Maybe because he'd never admitted, even to himself, that he'd also come to Cleveland to meet her. Janet held on to him until they were almost back to the house and she noticed her father's sedan parked in the driveway.

"Daddy's home," she whispered, and let go of Joseph's arm.

♫♫♫♫♫

Vincent Cavelli was a hulking man in his forties. He'd worked for many years in Cleveland's thriving construction industry, where he became rugged and weathered in his demeanor. His hairline receded, the color prematurely gray at the sides. He shook hands with the younger man after Janet introduced them. His vice-like grip impressed Joseph, but his spoken greeting betrayed a whiff of liquor on his breath.

Vince, as he preferred to be called, was typical of many veterans who went off to war in Europe. There, images of death and destruction burned themselves into his brain. He returned from the bombed out cities with its starving inhabitants to find the American landscape intact and unscathed, the only country to come out of the conflict more prosperous than it was before. His children were five years older since last he'd seen them. Time created a gap that would never be regained. He sought simplicity and stability in his family life. Then his beloved wife Maggie became sick, likely from the dust and grime she breathed at the defense plant, where she worked to help support her children while Vince fought in France.

Now, he stood face to face with the last person to see his son alive, and he had no idea what to say to him.

While Janet prepared dinner, Joseph and Vince relaxed in the living room. They shared Army stories a bit too raw to share with Janet. They laughed between sips on a bottle of some local brew.

Joseph left out any reference to Danny's thoughts about going over the hill.

Janet proved to be a very good cook, and Joseph enjoyed dinner immensely. Vince had a few more beers and by the time Janet cleared the table, her father was beyond tipsy.

"That was a great dinner, Janet. My first home cooked meal in a long time."

"Yeah, my little fair haired Italian is quite a cook," Vince said proudly. "She takes after her mother's people from the north of Italy. Me, I'm Calabrese, dark, stubborn, and loud, right baby doll? Wait till you taste her marinara sauce. She makes spaghetti every Sunday," Vince added.

Sunday was still five days away and his comment caught Joseph off guard. Janet noticed his reaction.

"Daddy, maybe Joseph didn't plan to stay until Sunday?" It was a statement to her father but a question for their guest.

"I really had no idea how long I'd stay. I don't have a place…"

"We have plenty of room right here," Janet chimed in, "You can stay in Danny's room. Can't he Daddy?"

"Sure, plenty of room."

"Unless, of course, you're in a hurry to get back to New York, to your folks?" Janet worried she was being selfish.

"New York will still be there in a few days. Besides I wouldn't want to miss out on a spaghetti dinner." The idea of spending more time with Janet appealed to him. His answer pleased Janet, but Vince seemed far away.

"My son was a great kid. Sure he got himself into some trouble messing with them Pollacks over in Collinwood. Even that business about stealing a car last spring…I'd bet my whole paycheck he took the rap for somebody else on that too. Fucking judge thought he was doing Danny a favor sending him off to the Army - said it would make a man out of him. Got my boy killed is all it did, fucking judge." Then, back in the moment, he looked Joseph squarely in the eyes. "I'm glad you decided to stay around, but do me a favor kid. First thing tomorrow you call your folks and tell them what your plans are. That way they won't worry. You shouldn't do anything to make your folks worry."

"I'll do that, Mr. Cavelli, I promise."

Vince nodded, "I feel like a freight train hit me all of a sudden. I guess I'll turn in."

When he stood, it took a few seconds for him too steady himself. He backed away from the table and weaved his way to the doorway. He kissed Janet on the top of her head. "Goodnight, Sweetheart."

"Nite Daddy," she answered without moving.

"Goodnight, Mr. Cavelli."

"Goodnight, Joey."

No one had called him Joey since Danny died. For a moment Joseph and Janet sat silently listening to his footsteps on the stairs and the sound of the door to his room closing.

"Is he like this every night?" Joseph asked.

"Pretty much. It all started after my mom died. He just couldn't deal with losing her. Danny tried to stop him. He even tried hiding the liquor. Daddy beat him pretty bad a couple of times for that. When Danny realized he was fighting a losing battle, he just stopped trying. That's when Danny started getting into trouble of his own. Then daddy got real concerned and cut down on the drinking for a while. When Danny got arrested and sent into the Army, it got real bad again, even worse after they sent Danny's body home."

"Does he beat you too?"

"No, no he's never hit me." Her eyes brightened as she changed the subject. "Hey, let's go sit out on the porch."

"Sounds great."

A warm, sultry evening greeted them when they left the house.

The moon shone like a bright globe. Janet kicked off her white sneakers and stripped away her bobby sox. Then, like some elfin creature in a forest glade, she pranced along the wooden planks on her tiptoes. Janet stretched her arms high above her head as though trying to count every star or grab a cloud in an embrace. Joseph settled down on the end of a rattan porch swing outside the front window. He hoped Janet would join him, instead she hopped onto the porch railing and sat with her back propped against one of the support beams.

"That little star right there," she announced gazing skyward, "That's gonna be my wishing star tonight."

"What are you going to wish for?"

"Can't tell *you.*"

The sound of a customized car turning onto their street caught their attention. Its loud muffler roared. A Buick pulled up in front of the house directly across the street.

"Hey, girl!" a squeaky female voice called out from the passenger side of the car.

"Hello Mary Lou!" Janet yelled as she jumped to her feet to stand on the narrow porch rail. The Buick's radio blared over the din of the rattling muffler. The passenger door opened and a young brunette stepped out into the street. The girl was Janet's age though not nearly as pretty.

"The weatherman says it's gonna be another scorcher tomorrow. You wanna go swimming?" Mary Lou asked.

Janet shrugged her shoulders and turned to Joseph.

"Want to?" she asked.

"I don't have a bathing suit."

"You can probably fit into one of Danny's."

"Okay, then, sure."

Janet looked back into the street and called out. "Okay, call for us about ten."

"Oh? And who pray tell is *us*?"

"You'll find out tomorrow, nosey!"

"Okay, mystery girl, see you tomorrow." Mary Lou skipped

around the front of the Buick and into the house just as another song began playing on the radio. It had a great beat with lots of guitars and a hard-edged vocal. When the car pulled away, the neighborhood fell silent.

"That's a pretty hopping number. You know the name of it?" Joseph asked.

"Oh, that's called "Crazy, Man, Crazy" by a guy named Bill Haley, I think. You like it?"

"Yeah, I do. They play a lot of music like that down south where we were stationed. They call it Rhythm and Blues."

"Danny didn't like it."

"I know what Danny thought of it."

"All the kids here in Cleveland really dig it though. There's one deejay in town, Alan Freed, he plays it all the time. He calls it rock and roll."

Joseph thought for a moment and decided rock and roll was a pretty good name for it.

Janet had an idea. "We have a radio in the kitchen. I can hook up an extension cord and we can listen to music out here. That is, if you're not too tired?"

"No, I'm not tired at all."

"I'll be right back." She shot off like a dynamo. Joseph could finally breathe. It had been quite a day. A day that had started out with such anxiety had led to these wonderful moments. Chanticleer was right, you never know where the road of life will take you.

"Here," Janet called from behind him. He turned to find her half in and half out of the window holding a small table top radio. Joseph took it from her and placed it on the outside windowsill.

Janet joined him on the porch and this time sat next to him on the swing. They listened as local stations played songs like Kaye Starr's "Wheel of Fortune" and "Cry" by Johnny Ray. At times, Janet reached back over her head to turn the dial looking for a station that played rock and roll. Joseph soon took over that task. After one such maneuver he managed to leave his arm around Janet's shoulder. She inched closer.

A few good tunes filtered through the static from time to time. During a slow sexy ballad, Joseph leaned over and took Janet's chin gently in his hand. He tilted her head upward and moved forward to kiss her, softly at first, and then his lips lingered on hers. The night and the music was theirs.

After the radio stations signed off for the evening, they brought the radio inside and closed up the house. Joseph carried his duffle bag upstairs following Janet to Danny's old room. She opened the door but didn't go inside.

"I put clean sheets on the bed. There's a fresh bath towel in there too. That's my dad's room right next door, mine is across the way. The bathroom is down at the end of the hall. I get up early to fix my dad breakfast before he goes to work. You can sleep a little later if you like but you should get up by nine if we're going to go swimming. I'll dig some swim trunks out of the attic for you."

"I'm pretty sure I'll be up early."

She reached up around his neck and kissed him one last time. "Goodnight."

"Goodnight, Janet."

He waited until she'd gone into her room and closed her door before he left the hallway.

Moment's later, Janet lay in her own bed wearing just a tee shirt and cotton panties. She glanced up at the travel posters hanging on the opposite wall. One was of Winchester Cathedral in England, the other was a stone castle somewhere in Europe. An eerie light she called night lace, streamed through on the beam of a street lamp outside her window. The posters seemed to come to life.

There'd been other nights, while she laid waiting for sleep that she stared at the posters. She would transport herself into a mythical, medieval fantasy world where she imagined a champion, a knight in shining armor there to protect her.

Sometimes, if her father came home drunk, she could sense his presence out in the hall. Janet knew there was no way the door would offer any real protection if he decided to come inside. But he never did. She hated herself for thinking such thoughts but his behavior with Danny put fear in her mind.

Now, her dream lover was real with a face and a name. She thought about what it was like to be held in his arms, kissed by his lips. She turned onto her side, and brought her legs up and toward her body. Janet reached over her head and grabbed her extra pillow. She pulled it around in front of her, folded it into a bundle pretending Joseph lay there next to her.

One hand traveled downward, resting in the warm softness between her legs. She squeezed her legs together tightly around her fingers and uttered hushed sighs as the stirrings in the pit of her stomach began. The stirrings grew stronger as always, but this time the shuddering explosion that made her go limp was more intense than she'd ever experienced.

She let the pillow fall away as she was lost in sleep with the thoughts of castles and champions and a boy named Joseph Rabinowitz.

♫♫♫♫♫

The night passed quickly for Joseph. Dawn brought sunlight into the room but he made no effort to get out of bed. The realization that he hadn't dreamed the events of the previous day made him glad all over. He lay for a long time thinking and listening.

He soon heard heavy footsteps in the hall. The footsteps moved down the hallway followed by the sound of a door closing. Bathroom noises came next, a toilet flushing, a shower running long and hard, and then sink water through squeaky pipes that Joseph guessed was Vince shaving. After a brief silence more footsteps re-traced the path passed his door and downstairs.

Joseph waited several minutes before rising and repeating the same bathroom ritual, only without the shaving. He dressed and went downstairs.

He found Janet and her father in the kitchen. Vince ate his

breakfast. Janet, wearing shorts and a blouse stood at the stove.

"Good morning," Joseph said.

"Hiya' kid. Have a cup of hot java," Vince replied. Sober now, his tone was more agreeable. Janet flashed a half guilty smile Joseph's way.

"Did you sleep okay?" she asked, pouring him a cup of coffee.

"I sure did."

"How do you like your eggs?"

"Scrambled is fine."

"I made bacon…Do you eat bacon?"

It was the first time the issue of his being Jewish came up. Even Vince looked up from his plate anticipating his reply.

"I eat bacon. I'm not orthodox."

Janet seemed relieved, "Take some toast."

Joseph took a slice from a dish on the table and buttered it. Janet placed a plateful of eggs and bacon in front of him but she didn't join them at the table.

After breakfast Vince stood, took one last gulp of coffee, and made his way around the table. "I've got bowling tonight," he announced. Janet handed him his metal lunch pail as he leaned over and kissed her on the cheek.

"I remember."

"You two kids have a fun day."

"Thanks Mr. Cavelli," Joseph said.

"We will, Daddy."

Once they were alone her mood lightened.

"Since he's going bowling he won't be home for dinner. That means we can hang out with the gang and go for pizza or something."

"Sounds like fun."

"I'm gonna do these dishes and go take my shower. That'll give you a chance to phone your parents like you promised my dad. I'll lay out some swim trunks for you to try on and we'll get ready to go, okay?"

Joseph nodded. She had everything all planned out.

His call to New York put him in touch with his mother. She was happy to hear from him but somewhat disappointed about his change in plans. She made no real issue of the news but made him promise to stay in touch. They exchanged words of love before hanging up.

Outside, Janet introduced Joseph to her friend Mary Lou and her boyfriend, Tommy. They squeezed into the back seat of his Buick for the ride to the Lake Erie shoreline that offered swimming and other activities. Janet monopolized the conversation, telling her friends all about Joseph. Mary Lou giggled a lot while Tommy cast suspicious glances in his rear view mirror.

They met up with three other boys and two girls at the boardwalk. There were too many names for Joseph to remember.

The group separated by gender into the bathhouses where they changed into their swimming gear. Joseph stood off to one side by himself. The other boys took this as some kind of act of modesty. They exchanged whispered remarks about him. Joseph put his tee shirt back on. He was the only one with his upper torso covered when they joined the girls outside.

Janet looked wonderful in her one-piece bathing suit, the same one she wore in the picture he had. She seemed curious as to why Joseph still had his shirt on.

"Do you get sunburned easily?" she asked.

"No, not really, I just..."

Janet reached out and grabbed the bottom of his shirt as if to lift it over his head.

"Well then let's get rid of this..." The shirt rose to the middle of his back and Janet noticed the awful bright pink scar. The imprints of his stitches were quite discernable. Janet, mortified by what she'd done, let go of the shirt hoping none of the others had seen. "Oh, Joseph, I'm so sorry. I had no idea!"

"That's okay. It's enough to frighten anybody. The doctors say it'll fade away."

"Does it hurt?"

"No, not really," he assured her.

The group spread out two large beach blankets across a patch of Lakefront sand they staked out for themselves.

After a while, the silent treatment and cold shoulder became quite evident. This Jew boy from New York had come to their turf and was messing with one of the girls from their crowd. Finally, one of them, a runty scrub of a boy, grew brazen enough to challenge him.

"Tell me something, don't it bother you to wear a dead guy's bathing suit?"

Everyone became quiet. Before Joseph could respond, Janet flew into a rage.

"Toby Haskell…you turd! I oughtta cream you!"

Joseph had no desire to fight with any of these boys but he was prepared to do so if necessary. The two young men stood and squared off opposite one another.

"Cool it, Janet." Mary Lou's boyfriend Tommy took charge. He placed himself between the two would-be combatants. "And Toby, you shut your butt hole."

Toby suddenly didn't seem so confident. Tommy's next comments were directed to Joseph. "Sorry for all this, man. It's just that we miss Danny a lot. You was his buddy in the Army so any friend of his is welcome here."

"Thanks," Joseph said.

All three boys returned to their places on the blanket. Janet remained angry, upset by what happened. Joseph consoled her with a smile touching his hand to her cheek. Things soon got better from that point on. Later, they left the lakeshore and headed for a local pizza parlor where they hung out listening to music on the jukebox.

The extra few days he planned to stay in Cleveland carried beyond Sunday's spaghetti dinner and well into the following week. Joseph and Janet weaned themselves away from her crowd until they spent almost all their time doing things on their own.

Chapter Six:

"Laughing Sal"

The Euclid Beach Amusement Park became the center of their world. Almost every day, Joseph and Janet walked to the corner and took the city bus to the end of the line, which left them at the parking lot outside the main entrance.

Before venturing through the stone archway, the aroma of freshly made popcorn balls and cotton candy wafted through the air to greet them. They strolled passed the kiddie park. Young children rode the carousel and tamer rides under the watchful eye of their parents. Joseph and Janet headed to the thrill rides. They screamed with delight after riding the Flying Scooters or the twin wooden roller coasters named Gemini.

Some days they'd pack a lunch and eat on the sprawling picnic grounds, or munch down hot dogs and root beer served from wooden kegs. They'd mischievously toss jellybeans at the huge, grotesquely painted plaster statue of a hag-like woman dubbed "Laughing Sal," above the funhouse entrance. Loud music and shrill recorded laughter blared from hidden speakers, annoying adults and frightening little children.

Twilight found them walking out onto the fishing pier. They leaned over the wooden railing to drop crumbs into the water, to feed large fish schooled against the pilings below. They'd stay long past sundown when the amusement park became a wonderland by night.

Janet loved listening to Joseph. He painted wonderful word pictures of New York City, his family, and his plans for the future. He told her of his dreams about making a career in the music business.

"You mean you want to be a dreamy singer like Eddie Fisher?" she asked.

"Me? I couldn't carry a tune in a suitcase."

"But, you told me your dad was a concert pianist. Talent runs in the family, right?"

He dismissed her compliment. "No, I could never hope to play music the way my father does. But there is something I think I *can* do. I hear all this stuff going on in my head. I'd like to put all that together, arrange it in some way, the instruments, the voices."

"That sounds so cool."

Janet spoke of castles and far off places she yearned to visit one day. She described a fanciful world with deep forests, pools flanked by weeping willows, inhabited by pixies, trolls and sprites.

"Just like in your poems?" Joseph asked.

This embarrassed Janet, "You know, I got mad when Danny told me he showed you my poems. Then, when I found out what good friends you were and how much you enjoyed reading them, I made sure I put one in every letter I sent. I probably meant them more for you than Danny after that."

Her revelation touched him. He blushed.

"I liked all of them," he confessed.

"You're not fibbin, are you?"

"Cross my heart. Do you have others?

"I have lots of them. But you'd probably laugh at them."

"I never laughed at them before. But if they're real private, personal, forget I asked."

There were private things in some of what she wrote, as private as any girl might put in her diary. But there were also things she'd like only for him to read.

"No, it's okay. I'll let you read them sometime - maybe."

Sometime turned out to be her father's next bowling night.

♫♫♫♫♫

It had been raining all day. A band of severe thunderstorms swept in eastward off the lake. The air grew heavy, a warm breeze preceded each down pour. Inside, they listened to the radio, a favorite new pastime. Raindrops clattered against the windowpanes at their heaviest. Flashes of lightning accompanied rumblings of thunder, distant at first, then closer and, in time, distant again as each cell moved off.

"Do you still want to read more of my poems?" Janet asked.

Joseph nodded and smiled.

"C'mon, I keep them up in my room."

She skipped up the stairs ahead of him. Joseph arrived on the upper landing pausing at the doorway to her room. He inched forward, taking note of the scent of her favorite perfume, the stuffed animals and dolls neatly positioned atop her dresser. He also looked at the two posters on the wall across from her bed.

He found Janet on her hands and knees, partway under the bed like a burrowing gopher. When she came out she held several tattered composition notebooks she'd squirreled away under there. When she stood she clutched the books close.

She motioned for Joseph to sit with her on the edge of the bed. She seemed unsure as to whether she wanted to carry through with her offer. Joseph sat down, finding her mattress girlishly soft. Janet held the books out and he took them.

"If you laugh at me, I'll never speak to you again, I swear." An idle threat, she knew she'd never be able to carry out.

"Can't I laugh if I think they're funny?"

"See!" Her reaction was girlish. She hopped to her feet, placed her hands on her hips and stamped one foot on the floor. Punching him hard in his arm, she tried to yank the notebooks away but his grip wouldn't allow it. When Joseph realized she was serious he offered the books back to her.

"Indian giver," he teased.

"No, go ahead. You can read them."

As he opened the first book, Janet shimmied away to the head of the bed. She picked up one of her pillows and held it in front of her body like a shield. She bit on the edge of the pillowcase.

Time passed with the pitter-patter of the rain on the roof as Joseph read the book cover to cover. The compositions were a wonderful mixture of lighthearted, teenage observances told in short, melodic verse about things like dragonflies, sleeping cats, and sad eyed puppies. Other, longer pieces were more mature, encompassing deep, emotional feelings like the dream of falling in love or the heartache of losing someone very near and dear. The poems seemed to sing to him from the thin blue lines on which they were written.

"Just a lot of silly girl stuff, huh?" she asked.

He looked at her over his shoulder. "Some of it is, yes. But all of them are really wonderful, even the silly ones. I'll bet you could have these published in a book someday."

He put the notebook on the bed, inched closer to Janet taking her into his arms. He kissed her deeply. Joseph gently moved her down flat on the bed, positioning himself almost on top of her.

They took a big risk. If Vince came home early and discovered them like this, there was no telling what he might do. But they were beyond caring.

Joseph slid a hand down the small of her back passed her waist until he cupped the cheek of her backside, pulling her closer. Janet reached under his shirt seeking out his scar. She traced it gently with her fingertips like any other part of his body she explored.

Joseph fumbled with the button of Janet's shorts. He managed to get it open but had difficulty making further progress until Janet lifted herself off the bed. She reached down and slid her shorts and panties to her ankles and shook them off with her feet. She trembled when Joseph touched her bare abdomen. His slow, tentative manner made it clear that he hadn't much experience with other girls. That made this magic moment even more magical.

She tensed. Joseph was about to find out that she wasn't a virgin. How would he react? What would he think about her?

In the next heartbeat, he was there, touching that private part of her body she willingly shared with him. Emboldened by her reactions, Joseph moved a finger inside her. Flames of passion heated their blood. Janet welcomed his explorations.

They paused long enough to get fully undressed and Joseph once again took control in a delicate, loving manner. He raised himself over her naked body. Janet bent her knees and parted her legs to receive him. She closed her eyes as he moved downward to penetrate her. Joseph moved with slow easy thrusts and Janet reacted in kind until they were moving in a fluid motion, in sync with the rhythm of the rain still falling outside.

Janet gave in to her passion and allowed herself to moan as her body reached a long, shuddering orgasm. Joseph moved toward climax. It took every ounce of effort he could muster to pull away from Janet's body at the last possible second.

The young lovers lay spent and breathless for what seemed like a long time. When they gained some sense of composure, Janet got up and went to the bathroom. She returned with a washcloth wet with warm water and a little bit of soap. She washed him without saying a word. The rain had stopped by the time they got dressed to go downstairs. They were sitting together on the porch when Vince got home.

Later, Janet felt the need to tell Joseph about her past experience with a boy. It had in fact been Toby, the smart aleck from the Lakeside who'd taken Janet's virginity.

"It was stupid and I shouldn't have done it but we got to kissing and touching. It felt nice for a while, but he prodded at me and it hurt and all of a sudden there was blood. We both got scared and didn't go any further. After that, I never let him touch me again. But I've experimented some, by myself."

"You don't need to tell me any of this," Joseph said.

"I wanted you to know."

"Tonight was my first time."

"Not even in the Army?" she asked.

"Not even in the Army."

"I'm glad."

The couple sought out other opportunities for stolen moments together though they paid greater attention to being careful. They immersed themselves into a magical realm inhabited by just the two of them. As with most things magical, the spell could be broken by some unwanted act of reality.

On an afternoon jaunt at the amusement park, they ducked into a large indoor arcade to get out of the late summer sun. Joseph won her a cuddly stuffed teddy bear playing Skee Ball. They giggled as they squeezed into a photo booth that took a strip of six photographs in less than a minute. They made funny faces for the first five poses but Joseph put his arm around Janet before the sixth flash of the camera.

"C'mon, Janet, make this a good one so I have a nice picture to remember you by."

Janet stiffened as the camera clicked for the final time. The strip of snapshots processed inside the cabinet and dropped into a metal slot on the side of the machine. Janet picked it up to look at them and Joseph pressed close behind to peek over her shoulder. They laughed at the first five shots but the sixth made them quiet. In that photo Joseph smiled but Janet wore a serious look on her face.

They didn't speak much on the ride home and it wasn't until the bus deposited them at their stop that Joseph felt the need to explain.

"I don't know what made me say that back at the arcade, about wanting a picture to remember you by? It was an awful thing to say."

"That's okay, Joseph, really. It's just that until then I hadn't given much thought to the fact that you'd be going home soon. It made me kinda sad, that's all."

"Janet, I love you, and I never want to be away from you, but I've been here almost two weeks. Eventually I have to go back to New York and you have school here."

"Don't back up Joseph. You just told me something wonderful, that you loved me. And I love you too. But if you back up now, apologize for it…"

"I'm not apologizing for anything Janet."

Her eyes widened like a Cheshire cat. "I want ice cream."

Joseph knew this was her way of saying that there had been enough serious talk. He took her by the arm and led her off in the direction of the nearest ice cream parlor.

♫♫♫♫♫

In bed that night, Joseph struggled for a solution to their situation. Before giving in to sleep he had a plan.

The two of them discussed it the next day. Janet agreed to go along but with one stipulation, that she be the one to tell her father. Joseph argued that it was his job to do so, but Janet knew better. She was sure Vince's temper would lead to a disastrous confrontation. Janet had to tell him herself.

Vince was busy at the workbench in his garage, when he noticed Janet standing outside.

"What is it, honey?" He stopped what he was doing.

"Daddy, there's something very important we need to talk about."

"What's wrong, Janet?"

"I love you very, very much and I know what I have to say is going to make you angry. I'm leaving home. I'm going to New York with Joseph."

"Now, you just hold on one second, you're not doing anything of the sort!" He reached out to grab her but she'd managed to position herself far enough away. Vince came up empty.

"I'm in love with him daddy and he loves me!"

"You're just a couple of kids for Crissake!"

"Daddy, I'm sorry," she was crying now, "But if I stay here alone with you something real bad might happen, we both know that."

A wave of guilt washed over him. The torment his demons visited upon him by his drinking placed vile, sickening thoughts in his mind about his own daughter. But this was the first indication he had that Janet suspected them. He sobbed, burying his face in his hands. Janet's fear gave way to sorrow. She moved forward to cradle her father's head in her arms.

"Can you ever forgive me, sweetie? You're all I have left. I'm surprised you haven't run off before now."

"I just can't stay here anymore," Janet said.

They sat together and cried for a long time.

Vince got drunk that night. Janet remained in her room. They decided it would be better if Joseph didn't stay in the house for his last days in Cleveland. The Casey's, Mary Lou's family from across the street, let him sleep on their couch. Instead of sleeping, Joseph sat vigil at the front window to keep an eye on the activities at the Cavelli house.

When he next saw Janet's father, Vince was sober, somewhat calm but stern.

"Do you really love my daughter, Joey?"

"Yes, I do, Mr. Cavelli. I love her very much."

"Then I suggest you take good care of her, kid." If it was a warning or a threat, Joseph believed it was quite unnecessary.

They'd cleared the first hurdle. A still higher one remained.

Chapter Seven:

"New York City"

For Solomon and Myra Rabinowitz, the news that their son Joseph was bringing Danny Cavelli's sister home with him, was alarming and confusing. It alarmed Solomon. To him it demonstrated yet another example of his son's impulsive and rebellious behavior. It confused Myra because the telephone call they'd received from Joseph days before to ask their permission to carry through with his plans, showed a sensitivity she never knew he possessed.

Joseph's mother had grown old before her time. The recovery from her breakdown had been slow but she'd made progress. Solomon didn't appreciate the fact that his son's actions might deal his wife some sort of setback.

Solomon exuded all the attributes of a college professor. His hair, a dignified grayish color matched a neatly trimmed beard and moustache. He remained impeccably dressed even in his relaxing hours at home. His deep voice always seemed to raise an octave when he spoke to his wife about their son.

"He claims to be in love with her. What does he know of love?"

"I'm sure she's a wonderful girl."

"Wonderful girl or not, he's only known her for a month! And she's so young, only sixteen, correct?" He spoke to her like a professor.

"I was only thirteen when I went to the conservatory to listen to you play."

"That was different," he mocked the comparison, "You came with your classmates as part of your studies."

"So you thought, so perhaps my parents thought as well."

"What are you saying?"

"Every girl in my class had eyes for the great Solomon Rabinowitz. We all knew you were destined to do great things with your music. All of us wanted to be noticed by you."

Solomon raised his eyebrows at her admission, "I noticed."

"I made certain you did. And did you care that I was so young when you took me boating on the lake…or when you had lunch with me nearly every day, or when we…"

"Enough of this!" He cleared his throat determined to bring the topic back to where it belonged. "He's bringing this girl here, to our home, to stay with us."

"He says it's only temporary."

"Yes, and just what do you suppose he means by that?"

"We'll know what he means when he tells us," Myra defended her son. "Solomon, what in the world's come over you? Our son is lucky to be alive. It's only because of some miracle that he's coming home at all. The least we can do is listen to what he has to say and advise him if we can."

Solomon uttered a sarcastic chuckle. "When was the last time we could advise that boy of anything?"

"We mustn't judge them just because they're young," Myra scolded him.

After all these years she still made him take notice.

♫♫♫♫♫

Janet's first look at the Manhattan skyline left her in awe of the place she would soon call home. They approached the city on a Greyhound bus traveling through the neighboring state of New Jersey. For the first time, she saw the towering skyscrapers that formed the tip of Manhattan. To her, it looked like the bow of a mighty ocean liner cutting a path between the two rivers that flanked the island, the East River on one side, the Hudson on the other.

The closer they got to the city, the taller the buildings seemed.

They appeared so tightly packed together that surely there wasn't room between them for people to walk or traffic to flow. The bus turned off the New Jersey Turnpike to the portal of the Lincoln tunnel. The next mile took them ninety-seven feet beneath the surface of the Hudson River, emerging on Manhattan's west side where the perspective changed dramatically. The tops of the buildings were now obscured from view as the bus moved along amid the mass and humanity of a workday lunch hour.

Janet thought that the crowds of pedestrians crossing toward each other at every intersection resembled opposing medieval armies charging their enemies in battle on some European plain. It made her happy to think that New York was a place with towering stone castles and battling armies of knights.

The bus left them at the Port Authority Bus Terminal on 42nd Street, where they freshened up in public rest rooms. Janet changed into the nicest thing she owned, a loose fitting dark dress purchased for Danny's funeral. She combed her hair, and decided against wearing make-up. Joseph donned his dress uniform for what he vowed would be the last time. They walked to the nearest subway station for the ride uptown.

Janet carried Joseph's duffel bag and one suitcase of her own. Joseph struggled with two other pieces of luggage containing her belongings. Crowds of New Yorkers racing around them made their journey through the underground corridors more difficult.

"Why is everybody rushing?" Janet asked, bothered by the near frantic pace.

"This is New York, Sweetheart. This is how things are."

The subway platform was stifling hot and foul smelling. It became worse when they boarded the crowded subway car and found no empty seats. Janet gripped her knees together to balance the suitcase between her feet. She reached up to take hold of a strap designed to keep passengers from falling over on one another as the train sped noisily through the darkened tunnel.

They got off at West 86th Street and climbed the stairs that would take them back to street level and the light of day. Janet felt like a washed out dishrag, certain that her efforts to look nice and make a good impression had all gone for naught.

They walked to West 87th Street and the apartment building Joseph called home. Their footsteps echoed on the polished floor inside the lobby. An elevator took them sixteen stories upward. Secretly, this idea of vertical living frightened Janet.

The entire, exasperating experience proved worthwhile when the door to the Rabinowitz apartment opened and Joseph's mother, Myra, laid eyes on her son. She clapped her hands together and smothered him in hugs and kisses that embarrassed him.

"Oh, it's so good to have you home again." She ushered him into the apartment with Janet following behind. As the heavy door closed behind them, Janet made note of the hardwood floor covered with plush rugs red and blue in color.

Solomon remained in the background, not showing much emotion. Now, with Joseph there, in the uniform of his country, he couldn't conceal his pride. Once Myra allowed Joseph to breathe again, father and son shook hands and embraced.

"Welcome home, son," Solomon said.

"Thanks, Papa."

Joseph motioned Janet forward.

"Mama, Papa, this is Janet Cavelli."

Janet smiled. Myra put her hand on Janet's shoulder emitting a smile of her own. "So very nice to meet you, my dear."

"How do you do young lady?" Solomon stepped forward to take her hand in greeting the way any elegant European gentleman would have done.

"I'm so happy to meet you both," Janet gushed. "Joseph's told me so much about you."

"And there's so much we want to hear about you, too." Myra spoke in the soft voice of a perfect hostess. "But you both must be exhausted after your long trip. Solomon, why don't you and Joseph show Janet to her room?" She leaned in closer to Janet. "You can start getting settled in while my husband and I fuss over our son some more."

"I'd like that," she said. "I want to thank you both for letting me stay here."

"It's our pleasure, dear," Myra told her.

The men picked up her luggage and led the way. As she followed along, Janet continued to survey the old world styling and furnishings of the Rabinowitz home. The sofa, chairs, tables and lamps were of superb craftsmanship. The place had a warm, homey atmosphere.

The room where Janet would be staying was small. It contained a single bed, a bureau for clothing and a dressing table with a mirror and chair. After she unpacked, she thought about her house in Cleveland with a porch and a big spacious backyard. She walked to the window and glanced outside. The view overlooked the splendor of Central Park, a sprawling, pastoral landscape spreading out for as far as the eye could see. Janet decided she now had the biggest backyard anyone could ever imagine.

♫♫♫♫♫

Janet did her best to fit in to her new surroundings. She wanted to make sure Joseph's parents didn't think of her as some silly teenager, whisked away from home by the first boy to come along. Solomon exhibited a standoffish attitude, though he remained cordial and congenial.

She and Myra hit it off dispelling her concerns. The older woman was warm and friendly in an old world way that Janet had never experienced. As she took on more and more of the household duties, Janet displayed a sincere interest in learning about Jewish culture and traditions. Myra taught her to cook traditional dishes like brisket of beef and potato pancakes she called latkes. It was easy to see that the couple was deeply in love and planned to make a life together.

Meanwhile, Joseph tutored Janet on the fine points of becoming a New Yorker. She soon got around on the subway like a native, able to differentiate between the east side and west side, uptown and down. Janet developed a taste for the street cuisine of dirty water hot dogs smothered in mustard, sauerkraut and pushcart onions. She came to love hot pastrami sandwiches from the Kosher Deli on Amsterdam Avenue and flying flimsy paper kites on the great lawn of Central Park.

As summer ended, Joseph set out to find himself a job. He pursued his dream to work in the music business, but the industry didn't welcome him with open arms. He camped out in the lobbies of record company offices, where he was repeatedly told he lacked experience. No one seemed willing to give him a chance.

Before Halloween he took a menial job as a shoe salesman in a busy store not far from where they lived. As part of his quest to learn all he could about the record industry, he started reading Billboard Magazine on a regular basis.

Billboard was a weekly publication that, since 1940, kept charts documenting the popularity of the different styles of music. In 1948 their reporter, Jerry Wexler suggested that the magazine change the name of the chart previously known as "race music" to rhythm and blues, or R&B.

From the magazine, Joseph learned that rock and roll was growing in popularity. A Negro vocal group called the Orioles had their record "Crying in the Chapel" cross over from the R&B chart and rise to number 11 on the pop music chart, the first non-white act ever to do so.

There were other innovations in the business besides content. All the major companies now used the new 45-RPM record on most releases. The existing format, the 78-RPM disc, was ten inches in diameter and made out of thick, heavy shellac, which broke easily. The grooves on the 78's held only three minutes of music per side. Forty-fives were made of a more flexible vinyl material and seven inches in diameter. The larger center hole allowed for smaller grooves providing better sound quality. These discs held up to five minutes of content on each side.

Joseph decided to be patient and to learn all he could about the music business while he waited for a break.

♫♫♫♫♫

Phil Gambetta walked out of Nick's Sandwich Shop on Mulberry Street, clutching a paper bag containing six veal cutlet parmigiana hero sandwiches. He savored the aroma of homemade tomato sauce as it wafted from the bag.

One month shy of his nineteenth birthday, lean and tanned, Phil was like most young Italian males brought up in the lower east side Manhattan neighborhood known as Little Italy. What knowledge he neglected to learn in high school he supplemented with education he gained on the streets in the year since the Board of Education grudgingly issued him a diploma. He ran with a street gang called the Hester Street Cavaliers, where he earned the reputation of being a truly dangerous individual. He didn't take any lip from anyone and often resorted to violence to settle disputes.

When his talents brought him to the attention of one of the lieutenants of the local crime boss recruiting neighborhood muscle, Phil eagerly took the job. He was relegated to being a go-fer or a flunky, but he remained confident he'd someday move up in the organization. For now he accepted his role, kept quiet, and followed orders.

Phil turned onto Broome Street, a cobblestone thoroughfare made narrow by cars parked on both sides. The neighborhood was alive with activity. Somewhere, a car horn blared.

"Hey you kids," the driver shouted, "Get outta the way!"

"Up yours, mister!" a grimy urchin hollered back.

A woman leaning out a fourth floor tenement window called in an Italian Neapolitan dialect, "Pasquale, go find your sister, she needs to come upstairs now."

Further along, in front of a poultry market, an old woman and shopkeeper argued.

"This chicken is all feathers…too tough to eat." She shook the freshly killed bird in the man's face.

"Senora," the shopkeeper pleaded, "What you want from me, eh? I already give you my best price."

As his made his way through this landscape, Phil noticed some activity taking place up the block in front of his destination, the Carozza Social Club. He quickened his step, arriving in time to see one of the club members, a numbers runner named Fat Rudy Pasqua, shove a young man Phil's age out the front door and down to the pavement. When Phil recognized the younger man he called out to Rudy, who was moving forward to inflict further harm.

"Yo! Hey Rudy, ease up man! He's cool."

Fat Rudy, a short, barrel-bellied hood looked at Phil and ceased his charge.

"You know this asshole?" Rudy barked, breathless from the unwanted exercise.

"Yeah, that's Richie Conforti, man. Me and him went to high school together."

"Yeah? Well he came strolling into the club like he owned the place. Good way to get his friggin' head broke. I thought you was supposed to be watchin' the door?"

"Mister G sent me over to Nick's to pick up lunch. I was only gone for five minutes."

Rudy reached out and snatched the paper bag from Phil with one quick swipe. "High school, huh? Well you better educate the creep a little more." Rudy turned and walked back inside the Social Club.

Phil shifted his focus to Richie, now back on his feet, brushing sidewalk dust off his plaid jacket. Black chino pants, white shirt and socks, and a pencil thin necktie completed his Ivy League look. He was shorter than Phil, slight of build, with a flattop style haircut.

"Damn, Richie, you okay?"

"Yeah, yeah…thanks Phil, I'm alright. Jesus, I thought that guy was gonna kill me."

"He sure as shit might have if I didn't come along. What the hell were you thinking to walk right in there like that?" He guided Richie over to the curb. They leaned against the front fender of a parked Oldsmobile sedan. From that vantage point, Phil could talk to his friend and keep an eye on the door of the social club at the same time.

"I'm selling magazine subscriptions door to door. I came

by, looked in and seen a bunch of guys playing cards, so I went inside."

"Magazine subscriptions? I thought you was going to City College?"

"Nah. I decided college was for chumps."

Richie neglected to tell Phil that he'd indeed gone on to college for one semester before becoming too lazy to study and continue.

"So, how did you get into this magazine stuff?"

"I filled out a coupon on the back of a matchbook cover. You know, one of them 'be your own boss' kinda things? Say, Phil, you work here?"

"Yeah. I'm in with the Viola mob," he boasted.

"Shit! You work for Gugie Viola? This is his place?"

Don Gugliemo Viola ruled the lower east side. Even now, frail and in his seventies, the mobster was still feared and respected by everyone. Richie's use of his boss' derisive nickname annoyed Phil. He looked around to see if anyone else heard it.

"Cool it Richie. The guys inside don't like civilians calling him that."

"Civilians? Who do they think he is, Mussolini? And you, does he let you do anything more than be a doorman and pick up his lunch?"

Phil resented his tone. He remembered Richie as being one of those kiss ass, know it all kids in school. He always had his homework done and never got detention. He was also a finagler, always looking for an angle and ways to put things over on somebody. However, he came from the neighborhood and that made him okay.

"I do other things." Phil said defensively. "I got high hopes…a lot of good ideas of my own. Someday I'll approach Don Viola with them. Anyway, it beats selling magazine subscriptions door to door."

"Don't knock it. I got some ideas too. Lately I been thinking about that book we read in high school, Tom Sawyer. You remember it?"

"No, man, not really," Phil gave an honest answer.

"Well, in this book, this kid Tom Sawyer is supposed to paint a picket fence around this house. But he's lazy see and he wants to goof off. So instead of painting the fence himself, he talks all these younger kids into doing it for him."

"Oh, I get it, he worked a con on 'em?"

"I figure maybe I can do the same thing. If I find a bunch of kids to go around and sell subscriptions for me, all I'd need to do is pay the brats a couple of bucks and keep the rest of the commission for myself."

"Sounds like a pretty good scam to me," Phil agreed.

"The more I sell, the bigger the territory I get. They even give out prizes to the salesman who sells the most subscriptions every month."

The wheels in Phil's brain turned just fast enough to recognize opportunity. "Ya' know Richie, maybe I could help you out with this thing. I got a lot of connections in this neighborhood. I could scare up a whole bunch of kids to work for you, river to river."

Richie, the finagler, was being finagled himself and he knew it.

"I… a… wasn't thinking of taking on a partner, man."

"But you really could use a guy like me. Most of these kids around here are just wiseass punks. I know how to keep them in line, make sure they don't give you no shit…protect your interests…see what I'm saying?"

"I tell you what Phil, give me your telephone number and I'll call you in a day or so."

"Yeah?" Phil became suspicious. He took Richie's fake leather order book and used a pencil lodged in the binding to jot down his family's telephone number on a blank form.

"You won't give me the shaft on this, right, Richie?"

"No, man, I'll definitely be in touch."

Richie held out his hand and they shook on it. Richie then headed off toward the subway. Phil lit a cigarette and took a deep drag. He glanced inside the social club to see that the men were still busy with their lunch. Phil felt smug in the thought that he'd weaseled such a clever deal with Richie. All he had to do was be a bully. That was something he was very good at.

Richie Conforti stood on the subway platform waiting for the uptown local. He too gloated about the arrangement he'd made with his former classmate. Though dim-witted and dangerous, an enforcer like Phil Gambetta might be a handy man to work with.

Chapter Eight:

"Christmas"

The second week of December, Joseph took Janet to see the Christmas tree at Rockefeller Center. Throngs of tourists and native New Yorkers alike flocked to the midtown area to take in one of the most famous seasonal attractions the city had to offer.

Big, wet flakes of snow flurried down between massive skyscrapers, taking forever to reach the pavement, where they melted on contact. Janet was bundled in a heavy, navy blue pea coat. Joseph had on a black leather jacket with the collar turned up around his face, his bare hands buried deep in both side pockets.

They entered Rockefeller Center through the public space between the two buildings that made up the commercial complex. The approach to a sunken plaza was lined with life-sized figures of angels blowing trumpets, wooden soldiers, and gingerbread people. Onlookers crowded along the perimeter railing of the plaza to peer down on the ice skating rink, where dozens of skaters of all ages moved in a slow, wide circles.

The couple squeezed their way into a space at the railing. Joseph stood behind Janet, his arms wrapped around her waist.

Directly across the way, the spruce evergreen towered some sixty feet high in front of the seventy-story RCA Building. The tree was adorned with assorted colored lights, garland, and other decorations. White clumps of freshly fallen snow gathered on the ends of the branches. Though Janet craned her neck back as far as possible, she couldn't see to the top of the building where the uppermost floors disappeared into low-lying clouds.

"Oh, Joseph isn't it all so wonderful?" She wiggled free of his embrace and turned to him, her arms reached around his neck. "What kind of a tree can we have at the apartment?"

"We don't put up a tree, honey," Joseph said reluctantly, "Jews don't celebrate Christmas." It was a detail she'd somehow forgotten. "I'm sorry sweetheart. You know if it were up to me, we'd have all that stuff. But it's my parents' home and, well, we have to respect that, right?"

Janet twisted her mouth into a comical frown that made Joseph laugh. Then, her face brightened in that pixie-like way he'd come to love. She scooped up a mitten full of loose snow from the railing and tossed it into the air over their heads. Most of it came right back in her face, but she didn't mind a bit.

"Know what? It doesn't matter." She spun around and raised both hands out in the direction of the giant spruce. "This can be our Christmas tree! We can come back on Christmas morning and exchange our gifts right here. We *can* exchange gifts with each other, right?"

"Yes, silly, of course we can. But I already have the best gift any man could get. I got you, babe."

Sometimes her man said such wonderful things. She stood on tiptoes to kiss him hard on the lips.

♫♫♫♫♫

Christmas Day services at the First Baptist Church of Harlem located on West 125th Street and St. Nicholas Avenue was always a joyous occasion. The all-Negro congregation filled every pew. Everyone dressed in holiday finery proclaiming their adoration for Jesus Christ in a reverent celebration of his birth, complete with hand clapping and singing that shook the walls.

A superb choir made up of men and women ranging in ages from teens to senior citizens led the singing. They wore long, flowing, red satin robes and sat in an area set aside for them to the left of the preacher's pulpit.

After a stirring sermon by their white-haired pastor, three young female members of the choir rose and stepped forward. They were teenagers from the neighborhood, two sisters and a cousin. They looked awkward and shapeless in the robes that dragged along the floor when they walked. Their hands were covered almost to their fingertips. But they were confident and sure in the way they handled themselves vocally. They sang the traditional hymn, "Just A Closer Walk with Thee," with their voices blending in close harmony and perfect pitch, keeping a moderate beat to the accompaniment of the church organ.

The congregation sat quietly at first, with only an occasional utterance by someone calling out, "Sing it, children."

By the time the youngsters reached the third verse, the rest of the choir began a hushed, harmonic background. Soon, the entire congregation stood and swayed to and fro with the singers. Inspired by the reaction to their performance, Evelyn Rhodes, whose strong contralto voice anchored the soloists, extended and bent her notes. Her voice soared in strength and volume leading to a rousing, crescendo finish. Her heart pumped proudly. Though she was certain it was a sin of pride, Evelyn loved the attention.

♫♫♫♫♫

At the Boyette farmhouse in Kentucky, Teddy's mother baked breakfast biscuits in the oven. It would be the first of three sumptuous meals for a full day's menu of food and baked goods. There was added reason for celebration. After being away performing for Cap Stewart in and around Memphis, her son had come home for the holidays.

In the front room of the house, Teddy and his father, George, entertained their guests. Cap had been invited home to meet Teddy's parents. Having no real family of his own, he happily accepted. Also present was the Reverend Watts and his wife.

Reverend Watts was the pastor of the Evangelical Church where the Boyettes worshipped, and where Teddy sang at services earlier that morning. The clergyman and his wife accepted the Boyettes' invitation to breakfast. The family had recently made some significant donations to the church with some of the money Teddy sent them. But this was the first time the pastor had ever been in the Boyette home.

"That's a fine looking Christmas tree you got there, George," the neatly dressed preacher commented. He gestured to the decorated pine tree standing in one corner of the room. "Is it from your place here?"

"No, Teddy brought it in last night," George answered as he filled his pipe bowl with fresh tobacco, leaving it for Teddy to explain.

"I took it down out of Chet Wyman's meadow just like I always do."

"Usually by this time in the season old Chet is standing out by his front gate with a shotgun trying to discourage that sort of thing," the clergyman quipped.

"Aw, he didn't mind, Reverend. This year I paid him for it." The others laughed. Cap remained quiet, avoiding the hometown banter.

"You did a wonderful job on the hymns you sang at the service this morning, Teddy." The austere Mrs. Watts spoke up. "You have a lovely voice."

"Thank you ma'am. It was an honor to be asked to do it."

Not everyone in the congregation approved of Teddy's singing. Several elders expressed displeasure with some of the stories that circulated about Teddy's shows in Tennessee. Word reached Radcliff that their town's new favorite son engaged in lewd behavior on stage and sang songs with lustful lyrics. One or two reports went so far as to brand it *the devil's music.* But Reverend Watts wouldn't be so quick to condemn the source of new donations.

Jean Boyette appeared in the doorway.

"I hope all this conversation has given everyone a hearty appetite. Come to the table. Breakfast is ready."

Teddy stepped aside to let everyone pass as they headed toward the kitchen. His innocent smile brought a blush of color to Mrs.

Watts' face.

After the hearty and delicious meal, Reverend Watts stood from his place at the table. "Mrs. Boyette, I've long held that breakfast is the most important meal of the day and I hope you'll forgive my wife and I for having to 'eat and run' as it were. Christmas Day finds us with many more stops to make around the area."

"We understand perfectly, Reverend," George said. "I'd like to thank you and Mrs. Watts for honoring us with your presence this morning."

After a round of fond farewells, the Reverend and his wife took their leave. The Boyettes and their remaining guest settled in to enjoy the rest of their day, culminating in a delicious supper that included a roast and more baked desserts than any three men could handle.

After clearing the table Teddy helped his mother in the kitchen.

"You looked real nice today, Mama," he said.

"Why, thank you, Teddy. I didn't wear anything special though."

"The pastor thanked me for the big contribution you and pa made. The money I sent home was a gift. It was for you and Pa to buy yourselves some nice things...some new clothes..."

"Your daddy bought whatever we needed for the farm. The rest we gave to the church. Heck, I got more dresses than I need. No sense spending money on clothes for me to just sit around this ole house."

"There's gonna be a lot more money coming in and soon, too. Mr. Stewart's got real big plans for me."

His mother listened, but his explanation was ill placed on her.

"Teddy, you know I've always wanted you have everything you ever dreamed for in your life. But this talk about your future is something for you and your Pa to decide on."

His parents had been disappointed when he ran off to Memphis in the summer and didn't return to finish school. Despite the fact that he'd sent most of his money home, Teddy knew there would be no guarantee his folks would approve of him pursuing a career as a singer, especially now the way some people talked about his kind of music.

Teddy made his way into the front room where he found his father and Cap chatting. Cap excused himself. "If you gents will allow me I'm gonna walk off the effects of Mrs. Boyette's fine home cooking, go outside and sample one of these here imported stogies Teddy gave me for Christmas."

He produced a long, dark-textured cigar from his shirt pocket and ran it along under his nose, taking in its rich aroma. He stood and headed for the front door.

"Better put on a coat there, Cap, or you'll catch your death," Teddy advised. Cap grabbed both his overcoat and hat before leaving. Teddy sat in the chair he'd vacated.

"It was a nice holiday, wasn't it, Pa?"

"Yes, son. It sure was. Your Ma and me appreciate all the nice gifts you gave us."

"Oh, it was nothing Pa, honest. And it's just the beginning. Why, Mr. Stewart says…"

His father cut him short. "I know what all this is leading up to, boy," Teddy expected a stern lecture about how his plans for a singing career was foolish and how they needed him to stay at home to work on the farm.

"Son, farming is the only life I ever known. Hard work, sacrifice, keeping my family fed and a roof over our heads, that's all that was ever important to me. But, you ain't no farmer son. I guess I've known that for a long time. I been listenin' to all the things Mr. Stewart's been saying and I don't claim to understand it much, but if he thinks that by you doing them shows, you can make a passable living at it, well I guess that's what you oughtta be doing."

"I can't tell you what this means to me, Pa. Thank you."

He glanced back over his shoulder and noticed his mother standing there, smiling. Teddy guessed she'd heard the whole conversation.

"Excuse me, Pa. I gotta go tell Cap the good news."

Teddy sprung to his feet and rushed out the front door, ignoring his own advice about putting on a coat to brace against the cold.

A thick cloud of cigar smoke emanating from inside the shed next to the house betrayed Cap's presence. Teddy dashed across the open distance and into the shed. He retold the conversation he had with his father with excitement, pleasing the promoter.

"That's great news, Teddy. I knew your folks wouldn't stand in the way of your success. And I'm glad they trust me to look after you."

" Course they trust you, Cap, we all do."

"I know that son. But we've come to a point now where we gotta make things official between us so we can move ahead with our plans. Come this spring we're gonna go out on the road again, with you as the headliner. We'll rent us a bus and ride in style. I'll book dates in all the big cities, Baton Rouge, maybe even New Orleans."

Cap knew R&B music caused quite a stir all along the Gulf Coast, a perfect opportunity for Teddy to cash in on this new style.

"It's gonna require a big investment on my part. I think we need to have something legally binding between us."

"You mean a contract?"

"That's exactly what I mean." Cap reached into the inside pocket of his overcoat, and produced several folded papers. "I took the liberty of drawing up this document appointing me as your manager. It gives me the authority to make all your professional and business decisions for the next ten years. It also entitles me to forty percent of your earnings over that same time. For my part, I agree to pay all the expenses and costs associated with your career. That means you'll never pay for anything out of your own pocket."

"And what about a record deal, Cap?"

"All in good time, son, all in good time. You stick with me, and all those fat cat record people are gonna come crawling out of the woodwork looking to sign you."

"That sounds fine, Cap. Just show me where to sign," Teddy took the papers.

"Hold on there hoss, you might want to have someone look that thing over for you, show it your pa, or your family lawyer maybe?"

Cap took a big risk in offering this advice. He knew full well Teddy wasn't old enough to sign a binding contract. He relied on Teddy's trusting nature and desire to become a singing star to blind the boy to any legality.

"Mr. Stewart," Teddy answered in earnest, "We ain't got no family lawyer I know of, and I doubt my Pa ever had anything to do with no contract passed a handshake and his good word. So if that's a good enough way for him to do business, I suppose its good enough for me too. So why don't you just hand me a pen and we'll get this thing done right here and now?"

Cap smiled, reaching into his coat a second time, producing a fountain pen and handed it to Teddy. "Just sign on the line where your name is typed on the last page."

Teddy held the papers against a wood planked wall and signed them turning control of his singing career over to the man he trusted most in the world.

"You won't regret this, son," Cap said as Teddy handed the contract and pen back over to him. Using the same plank for support Cap affixed his own name to the document.

♫♫♫♫♫

Joseph and Janet followed through on their plans for Christmas Day. They were up and out after a quick breakfast, taking the subway to Rockefeller Center. They found the usually bustling city to be quiet, the streets were almost deserted, and many of the stores were closed. When they arrived at the plaza they sat on an empty bench to exchange gifts.

She presented him with a gift box containing a pair of black imitation leather gloves. Joseph appreciated the gift of something that he needed. In turn, he gave Janet a small square box, neatly wrapped. She felt certain he hadn't done it himself. It excited her to know her gift was something special. Janet removed the wrapping paper and opened the box. She let out a gasp when she saw it contained a white gold engagement ring with a small diamond in a simple setting. Tears ran down her cheeks.

"This diamond ring is the most beautiful thing I've ever seen."

Joseph slipped the ring on her finger and kissed her for a long time.

They were home by nightfall. Janet had removed her ring. She and Joseph agreed it would be best for her not to wear it until he told Solomon and Myra about their engagement.

After supper they settled in with Joseph's parents in the living room listening to the radio. Solomon sat in his favorite easy chair reading. Myra's knitting needles clicked, but she paused frequently to rest her hands. Joseph dozed, stretched out along the length of the sofa, his head resting on Janet's leg as she sat on the opposite end.

Perry Como's rendition of "Ave Maria" played on the radio. Joseph let out a loud snore. His father looked up from his book. Janet leaned forward nudging Joseph's head.

"C'mon you, go to bed. You have work tomorrow."

Joseph stirred and managed to sit up. He yawned and, though still not fully awake, stood and stretched. Without another word he left the living room. Janet felt sad that he had to go off without her on such a special night. She listened to a few more songs before rising. "I think it's time I turned in too. Goodnight to you both."

Myra looked at Solomon and gestured to remind him of something. He reached behind his chair to retrieve a gift-wrapped box.

"Oh, Janet?" he called to her.

"Yes, Mr. Rabinowitz?"

He crossed the room and offered her the box. "Myra and I..." then, words escaped him. "Merry Christmas, Janet."

Surprised and embarrassed, she looked beyond Solomon to where Myra sat beaming. She took the box, opened it and peeled away a thin layer of tissue paper revealing a green and white wool pullover sweater. Janet removed the garment allowing the box to slide to the floor. She unfolded the sweater and held it up in front of her body.

"It's perfect. But, I feel bad. I didn't get either of you a present. Joseph said…"

"Come here, my child," Myra motioned to her. Janet scurried across the room and plopped at the foot of Myra's Queen Anne chair. The older woman put her arms around her.

"Perhaps you don't realize all you've already given us? You brought our son back home. He was a sad, angry young man when he left to go into the service. We worried we might never see him again. Then, that terrible accident that killed his best friend…your brother…and left him in that awful coma. Then he met you and any fool can see he loves you so much. You brought happiness into our home. We're eternally grateful to you for that."

Janet got to her feet and helped Myra to stand. Solomon moved closer and the three of them embraced.

"Thank you both. Thank you both so very much," Janet spoke through tears of joy.

They were truly a family from that moment on.

Chapter Nine:

"Down the Aisle"

By 1954, there were over two thousand AM radio stations in America. They ranged from small 250-watt local operators to the major 50,000-watt stations. When the weather was right, those signals could bounce along the ozone layer in much the same way a flat rock scaled across the surface of a quiet pond.

But the golden age of radio was over and the medium was in big trouble. Revenue had fallen from $215 million in 1950 to $40 million in 1953. Almost overnight, television had stolen radio's crown. The number of TV stations more than doubled from between 125 to 349 in 1953 alone. It became apparent that for radio to survive, it needed to re-invent itself. Popular music provided the answer.

In Kansas City, Missouri, Robert Todd Storz, a radio maverick sought to increase the ratings for a group of radio stations that his family owned throughout the Midwest. He conducted a survey of local restaurants, taverns and other locations to determine how often the most popular records were played on jukeboxes.

The results surprised him. In almost every instance, patrons chose the same titles over and over. Storz believed the same thing could work in radio. He applied the concept at his station, WTIX in New Orleans, and saw ratings improve. When rival stations initiated a top twenty play list, Storz doubled his station's list to forty songs. He also fine-tuned the shows, insisting his on-air personalities speak in a quick, rapid-fire style. They broadcast short, sensationalized headline news reports and jingles. Listeners were encouraged to call the station and request specific songs they wanted to hear. Storz debuted the first forty-song reverse order countdown survey of the hit songs of the week. Soon, stations all across the country were doing the same thing with shamefully little or no difference.

Ratings soared and Top 40 radio was born. Teenagers everywhere listened to the sound of the big beat.

♫♫♫♫♫

Joseph Rabinowitz and Janet Cavelli were married on April 10, 1954 in a traditional Jewish service at the Beth Shalom Synagogue on West 100th Street. The guest list was small. Solomon and Myra were all that remained to represent Joseph's side. Though invited, Vince Cavelli did not attend his daughter's nuptials, but he did send a generous gift. A handful of friends from the neighborhood, along with Joseph's boss from the shoe store and his wife, were also in attendance. Solomon treated the gathering to dinner in the private room of a nearby restaurant.

The bride and groom spent their wedding night at an inexpensive midtown hotel, where they were free to be playful and noisy in their lovemaking.

Their financial situation dictated a move. Since they couldn't afford to live in Manhattan, they rented a one-bedroom apartment on McLemore Avenue, in the Bronx. They furnished their new home with Joseph's back pay from the Army and money they'd received as wedding gifts.

Though it was something of a sparse beginning, they were determined to get by.

"I mean it Joseph," Janet told him, "I can do my part. If I get all dolled up, fix my hair and make-up, I can look older and get a job waiting tables."

"Hey… I don't know if I like the idea of my wife getting dolled up to go to work. I know how guys flirt with sexy waitresses."

"Quit that, you! You're not gonna be stuck selling shoes all your life. With me working, if something comes along in the music business, you won't have to worry about changing jobs."

"I'm not having any luck finding anything, sweetheart. Maybe it's not in the cards for me to even be in the music business."

His sudden self-doubt bothered her. "Careers don't just happen overnight." Then, she caught him grinning at her. "Joseph Rabinowitz, are you laughing at me?"

"No, not laughing…just trying to figure out how I could be so lucky to marry the most beautiful, sexy, and intelligent woman in the world."

♫♫♫♫♫

A flat bed truck owned by the Zerega Monument Company moved across the expanse of the Bronx-Whitestone Bridge that connected Queens and the Bronx. The driver and his co-worker, Dominick Seracino, were tired from a long day of delivering headstones to a cemetery in Forest Hills. As they approached the tollgate on the Bronx side, Dominick noticed a large cluster of red brick buildings under construction on an area of open land below.

"You know what they build there?" he asked the driver. Despite being in America for over twenty years, Dominick still spoke with a thick Italian accent.

"Apartment buildings…city housing project, you looking to move, Dominick?"

"Somebody told us the city's gonna tear down all the buildings where we live to make room for the new highway."

Dominic was right. Many tenement buildings in the Bronx were leveled as part of a multi-million dollar urban renewal program to make way for the Cross-Bronx Expressway, connecting the George Washington Bridge from New Jersey to the New York bridges leading to Queens and Long Island.

"You might want to look into it then," the driver continued. "Those apartments are supposed to be for low income families."

"I tell my wife," Dominick said.

Dominick and Rose Seracino were both in their early forties.

As an immigrant laborer, Dominick was barely literate so it fell to Rose, a second-generation Italian, plain, pretty and well schooled to handle many of their business matters, like paying bills and doing the banking. They had a fourteen year old son named Johnny Boy, and two daughters, Jacqueline, eleven, and Tina Marie, nine.

The day after Dominick told Rose about what he'd seen on the bridge, she took the subway to the offices of the New York City Housing Authority to pick up an application for rooms. She and Dominick filled out the paperwork providing information about their financial status and housing needs.

Weeks later they received a letter from the Housing Authority. The family was approved for a three-bedroom apartment.

The Throggs Neck section of the Bronx was a quiet, residential, suburban area three blocks from the water of Long Island Sound. Many residents had protested the building of the project. To them, the term "low-income families" meant an influx of a minority population certain to increase crime and bring down the value of their homes and property.

To the Seracino's, and many families like them, it was a godsend. Dominic was closer to work. The three children were sure to get a better education, perhaps even attend parochial school, if they managed their money right.

They moved into an apartment on the first floor of a three-story building on Sampson Avenue, a street on the perimeter of the project. The building faced a similar structure across an open area, to form what tenants came to call "the court."

Newly planted saplings and green lawns flanked asphalt walkways. Wooden benches were spaced evenly apart on slightly raised cobblestone aprons. Friendships formed between the mothers who sat on those benches during the day, watching their children at play or tending to infants or toddlers in baby carriages and strollers. The project offered a new start for these thirty-six families living in close proximity, a diverse mix of ethnic, cultural, and religious backgrounds.

Friendships also formed between the many children living in the court. The two Seracino sisters played jump rope, tag and potsy with other girls and there were enough boys Johnny's age to form teams for sports. They painted bases in the asphalt of Sampson Avenue and played stickball every day in the summer and touch football in the fall until it got too dark and too cold to be outside for any reason.

Johnny boy had dark curly hair and a cherub's face. His wide, sad brown eyes marked him as shy and sensitive. He enjoyed western movies, watching television and he possessed a vivid imagination that set him daydreaming at almost any time.

Most of all, he loved listening to his mother's collection of phonograph records.

Chapter Ten:

"The Southern Tour"

Cap Stewart officially dubbed it, "The Teddy Boyette Show." True to the name, he built the tour around his talented young singer. Aside from the technicians, stage hands, and the three-piece band to back up Teddy on stage. The only other performers would be the Hollins Twins, the brother and sister act from Teddy's first tour. They warmed up the crowds of the deep south with their hillbilly harmonies.

Beyond that, Cap encouraged local promoters in the towns and cities where he booked the show to hire one or more local acts to appear on the bill. People were apt to buy tickets for an act they recognized.

A full slate of shows would take them southward along US Highway 51, through Mississippi and into Louisiana, traveling over three hundred and sixty miles before finishing in the big market cities of Baton Rouge and New Orleans. Cap purchased and refitted a used Streamliner bus, which he had repainted with Teddy's name emblazoned on both sides beneath the obligatory, "Cap Stewart Presents" logo.

There was one other detail Cap needed to address before they headed out.

Since arriving back in Memphis, Teddy had once again taken up with the waitress, Dee. He stayed at her place where they resumed their fling. Cap didn't like the situation, especially after Teddy told him the gist of a conversation he'd had with Dee about their contract.

"I don't pretend to know much about these things sweetie," Dee had told him. "But forty percent of what you earn seems like an awful lot to me."

"The way I look at it, forty percent of nothing don't amount to very much at all."

"But suppose he makes good on all these plans he's got for you?"

"Well then, I guess he would have earned his share, right?"

Dee didn't say anything more, knowing that to criticize Cap would be seen as meddling.

That's exactly the way Cap perceived it.

"You can't let yourself get tied up with a woman like Dee," Cap later warned.

"I'm sure she didn't mean no harm by it. She's just looking out for me is all."

"That's my job now, boy. Some women got a real talent for manipulating men with their bedroom ways. Next thing you know she'll be trying to hook you into getting married, complain you're never home...always out on the road. If you wanna ball and crawl and climb the wall with this here gal, that's fine. But hear me good. You put an end to it before we leave."

Cap painted an ugly picture of things, his words more of an edict than friendly advice.

Teddy planned on breaking the news to Dee during dinner at a ribs place they liked on Beale Street. But as time grew short, a pang of guilt washed over him and he decided he couldn't wait. He put a wad of rolled up cash on the dressing table next to her.

"What's all this?" Dee asked without picking up the money.

"That's just to pay you back for all the clothes and stuff you staked me to last year."

"There's more there than I ever gave you."

"Well, you let me stay here and all, and I figure I owe you for that too."

"But then we started something personal, I never expected to be paid back after that."

"I know, Dee. I'd just feel better about things if you took the money."

His words stayed with her all through dinner. She drank more than usual and Teddy didn't want to say anything to her that might cause a scene. Dee was tipsy by the time they got back to her place.

"I'm gonna be missing you so much when you're out there on the road." She moved in close to hold him and sensed his uneasiness. "You promise to call me every night?"

"I don't see how I'll be able to do that, Dee, what with us traveling so much…"

She cut him off with a drunken cackle. "I'm just kidding, Sweetheart, just kidding. Fact is I don't figure we'll see much of each other after tonight, do you?"

Her comment rocked Teddy. Was she setting a trap or making it easy for him?

"We'll always be friends, right?" Teddy asked.

"I don't spread my legs for just a friend, Teddy." Her smile and any semblance of pleasantry was gone. Teddy couldn't find words to respond. "Relax, honey, I've been given the brush off a time or two in my life. Ain't no big deal."

"I wish you wouldn't feel that way. I owe you an awful lot, Dee."

"You don't owe me a damn thing. Fact is, I'm the one probably owes you. If that fat assed, God Almighty Cap Stewart turns you into a big star, I can always say I fucked Teddy Boyette when he was a nobody!"

Dee walked into the bathroom before surrendering to tears.

Teddy spent the night sleeping on the sofa. Dee was gone when he woke. He thought of leaving her a note, but he didn't.

♫♫♫♫♫

The southern tour kicked off in the town of Senatobia, Mississippi two nights later. The sellout crowd cheered all through Teddy's act.

He sang raucous, upbeat tunes like "Lawdy Miss Clawdy" and "Hard Luck Blues." Female hearts fluttered as he whispered lyrics to sexy ballads like "Harbor Lights." Even the male members of the audience tapped their feet to "Blue Moon of Kentucky" or the song that had become his signature tune, "Move it on Over."

More of the same followed in Sardis and Batesville. In the larger city of Tupelo, Teddy appeared at a local drive-in theater. He sang from the roof of the refreshment stand between showings of a double feature. A large crowd surrounded the building. Others watched and listened from inside their cars. They showed their appreciation by blowing their horns and flashing their headlights in a combination of sight and sound that delayed the start of the feature attraction for almost an hour.

The entire tour proved to be one success after another. Then, some miles south of Meridian they came to the town of Castlehurst.

Often, the local promoter would be on hand to meet them when they arrived. This time, the person waiting didn't appear happy when Cap got off the bus.

"Mr. Stewart?" The slim, middle-aged man in a rumpled suit stepped forward to introduce himself. "My name is Earl Wellington. We've spoken over the phone."

Cap recognized the name and shook his hand. "Why, sure Mr. Wellington, right nice of you to come out to meet us."

"Mr. Stewart, I'm real sorry to have to tell you this but there seems to be a problem with the show tonight."

Before he could say more, their attention was drawn to a siren from a dark sedan with sheriff's markings. It came to a stop not far from where they stood. A scrawny gent in an ill fitting tan uniform got out of the car and approached them.

"Sheriff Tyler," Wellington addressed the officer with both respect and fear.

"Earl." The sheriff nodded a greeting. He looked passed the two adults. Teddy and his band were off the bus, standing in the street. The sheriff's gaze was far from friendly.

"Sheriff, this here's Cap Stewart."

"Afternoon, Sheriff." Cap smiled through his growing sense of anxiety. He extended his hand to the official who shook it with little enthusiasm. "Mr. Wellington was just telling me there might be some problem with the show we're doing here tonight?"

The sheriff's response was terse, almost venom-like. "Ain't no *might be* about it. The show's cancelled."

"Why?"

"News travels fast in these parts. We've been hearing that your boy there is fond of singing that jungle music the coons like so much. That may be okay in some places, but here in Castlehurst, we're decent church-going folks. We don't want our young people exposed to that kind of vile trash even if it is a white boy singing it."

"But Sheriff, young people everywhere love Teddy's music."

"We don't give a rat's ass about everywhere. We won't stand for it here."

"But I have a contract…"

"Mr. Wellington here realizes he made an honest mistake… didn't know what he was getting into when he booked your show. You're both reasonable businessmen so I expect you can resolve this thing to your mutual benefit."

"Would you have any objection to us at least spending the night here before we continue on?" Cap asked.

"You're more than welcome to enjoy our hospitality. But I wouldn't give much thought to continuing on. You see, I've been in touch with some of the other places you plan on playing, they feel the same way about things as we do. They don't want you either."

Cap's heart pounded and the blood rose to his cheeks. If he lost control and lashed out at this arrogant bigot he'd only be buying trouble for his entire troupe.

"Sheriff, I have solid commitments all the way down to New Orleans."

"Suit yourself, but it's a long way to the Louisiana state line. Some of these country roads can be real treacherous, lots of wrecks, rollovers and such. Best advice I can give you is come mornin' you turn this here safari of yours around and head on back the way you came."

His threat clearly understood, the sheriff returned to his car and drove off.

Earl Wellington finally spoke. "Mr. Stewart, I'm real sorry about all this. If you'll come by my office in the morning, we can settle things up."

When Cap failed to respond, Wellington hung his head and walked away.

Teddy moved forward. "That hick sheriff can't do this, can he Cap?"

"It appears he just did."

"So, what's gonna happen now?"

"I don't rightly know. But it won't do no good to stand here in the middle of the street bellyaching about it. Let's get checked in at the hotel."

♫♫♫♫♫

The members of the tour occupied several connecting rooms at the Castlehurst Hotel. The tour bus driver, named Corrigan, picked up a meal of burgers, fries, beer and soda. As they all gathered in one room, they ate and discussed their options.

Teddy offered, "I say after we pull out of this shit hole in the morning we circle around and find us a back road to the next town."

"And suppose that son-of-a-bitch sheriff is right and they don't feel no better about us there neither?" Slim Reed, Teddy's drummer asked.

Corrigan, an experienced open road trucker added. "The law in the next town might not be as accommodating as they was here and do more than just try to scare us off."

Bernadette Hollins, the female member of the Hollins Twins asked. "You mean they might do something to hurt us?" Her voice quaked with fear.

"This here is Klan country girlie, things like that been known to happen all the time." Corrigan warned. He spoke of the Ku Klux Klan, the racist organization whose violent acts against coloreds ran rampant throughout the south.

"That's it then, we gotta' turn back," Bernadette's brother Andy said. He was right. Having a young girl along with them made the option of challenging the sheriff's threat impossible.

"I can't believe this crap!" Teddy exploded. He stood and paced the floor like a caged cat. "Everywhere we been so far, folks love the show! It's only music! How can music hurt anyone?"

It was a question no one in the room could answer.

Later, Teddy and Cap sat alone in the room they shared, sipping sour mash whiskey from a metal flask Cap carried.

"How much do you stand to lose from all this?" Teddy asked.

"Can't rightly say. It all depends on what the promoters in the other cities do. Hopefully, they won't sue for breach of contract."

"I'm real sorry about this Cap."

Cap let out an intoxicated chuckle, "Boy, what are you sorry for? None of this is your fault. Just a lot of ignorant people in this world is all it comes down to. I'm an old carnival man son. In the morning when I'm thinking clearly I'll come up with something. There are lots of towns we bypassed along the way and some we already played would love to have you back for a return engagement. I made you a ton of promises, son, and I intend to keep every one of them."

In time, Teddy either fell asleep or passed out. Cap mulled over their situation. He was well aware that none of it would have happened if Teddy was an established artist, with a string of hit records played on the radio.

There had already been several small record labels interested in signing Teddy. But they wanted exclusive rights to the singer. That meant they didn't want Cap in the picture. He wasn't about to let his bread and butter slip away from his control so he kept it all a secret from Teddy. Cap also knew that any good lawyer could get the boy out of the contract they'd signed. Keeping Teddy out on the road performing bought him time. But, time would soon run out. He had to find a record company that would agree to the terms he dictated.

Chapter Eleven:

"A Rickety Old Piano"

Janet couldn't tell exactly what had caused the nightmare, the science fiction feature she and Joseph went to see at the Loew's Paradise, or the banana split they shared at Jahn's Ice Cream Parlor afterward. It was probably a bit of both.

"So what was it about?" Joseph asked when told about the bad dreams in the morning.

"I'm not really sure. The end of the world I guess, Communists."

"Communists?"

"Joseph, I'm smart enough to know that when these movies talk about invading aliens coming out of the sky, they don't mean little green men from Mars. They're talking about the Communists, the Russians and the terrible things atomic weapons can do."

She sounded frightened, and she wasn't alone. Many feared the world was on the eve of destruction and they could become the last generation on earth if nuclear war broke out.

"It was only a movie, Sweetheart."

"The Senate hearings on television are very real, Joseph. This Senator McCarthy says there are Communists in our own government."

Senator Joseph McCarthy from Wisconsin directed investigating committees to root out Communists wherever they could find them. His ranting and verbal attacks on witnesses were televised nightly making him one of the most feared men in America.

"McCarthy is an idiot. He's always accusing people of this, that or the other thing but he never has any real proof to back it up."

"I'm sorry. I don't mean to be such a scaredy cat. But, someday, we're going to have a family. Bringing a child into a world that's about to blow itself to bits is… kinda frightening."

Joseph got up and stood behind his wife. He bent over and wrapped her into a protective cocoon. "Your he-man will protect you and our babies from the bombs, the Communists and even those little green men from Mars."

"Know what? I believe you really could."

♫♫♫♫♫

Janet made good on her offer to go to work. A new hairstyle and more make-up did indeed make her look older and she dressed to highlight her good figure. She got a job as counter girl at a small Greek coffee shop near the entrance to the IND subway line. Her morning work hours had her serving commuters their first cup of coffee on their way to work. Tips were good.

One morning, after the breakfast rush, a man dressed in a wrinkled suit sauntered up to the counter.

"Hi, what can I get you?" She asked with a smile.

"Is the owner around anywhere, sweetheart?"

Janet half opened the swinging door behind her. "Mr. Yanitz, there's a man here to see you," she called out.

Tom Yanitz came through the door. With his curly hair, thick black moustache and stubble chin, the Greek-American looked more like a cook than a restaurant owner. Janet busied herself by refilling sugar shakers close enough to hear the conversation between the two men.

"Good morning sir." The salesman began his pitch. "I represent the Rock-Ola Jukebox Company and we have an exciting offer for you today. I can put our top selling model in here in less than a week. It plays those 45's the kids go crazy for. Over one hundred selections at the push of a button."

"Ahhh, if I put a record machine in here, I'll have a gang of no good kids hanging around not spending any money," Yanitz complained.

"They'll be spending money all right. They'll be feeding it coins like they feed peanuts to elephants at the Bronx Zoo."

"Some of the kids they got in this neighborhood belong in the zoo. Where would I put the damn thing anyway?"

The salesman looked around the main dining room.

"How about up against that far wall back there where you got that rickety old piano? Is there an outlet on that wall?"

Yanitz and Janet both looked at the upright piano standing beneath a painted mural of Greek ruins.

"Yeah, there's a plug back there," Yanitz said.

"Perfect spot for it," Janet interjected.

The two men laughed.

"Well, if the help likes the idea…I guess it's settled." Her boss's remark sent Janet off with a blush in her cheeks.

Yanitz had Janet serve the salesman a free cup of coffee while they sat filling out the order form for the new jukebox. Before he left the diner, the salesman put a three-dollar tip on the counter. Obviously, he thought her comment to her boss helped make the sale.

Later, Yanitz surveyed the area where the jukebox would go.

"Pepe!" he called out.

A short, well-muscled Puerto Rican man in his twenties appeared in the doorway of the kitchen. "Yeah, boss?" the dishwasher asked.

"When you see the sanitation men, ask them when we can put this piano out for pick up?"

"Sure thing, boss." Pepe went back into the kitchen.

Janet approached her employer. "Are you just going to throw it away?"

"Yeah, I got no use for it. I'm not even sure the stupid thing works."

"Well, then, can *I* have it?"

"Do you play the piano?"

"No, I don't. You see my husband and I don't have a lot of furniture in our apartment. I think a piano would look great in our living room."

"Yeah, sure, go ahead. If you can get it out of here before the garbage men take it.

As Yanitz walked off, Janet realized the enormity of the task she'd given herself. She wanted the piano to be a surprise for Joseph, so she needed some way to get the instrument home. She hurried into the kitchen to find Pepe again.

"Pepe, I need your help."

"What you need, sweet pea?"

"Mr. Yanitz says I can have that piano but I don't have any way of getting it home."

Pepe looked up from a metal sink filling with steaming hot water, "Where do you live?"

"Not far… McLemore Avenue."

"That don't sound too bad. We got the dolly we use to take the garbage cans out at night. We could put the piano on that. But if the boss found out, he'd be pissed."

"Tomorrow is banking day. Mr. Yanitz leaves early on banking day."

"Yeah, yeah, that would work. But we'll have to be quick like Speedy Gonzales. I'll get my cousin to give me a hand and we'll wheel the damn thing right through the streets. What floor do you live on?"

"Third," she said, hoping her answer didn't kill the whole deal.

"Dios mio!"

"Please, Pepe, I really need your help. I can give you a couple of dollars… please?"

"You're a nice girl Janet. Okay, I can get another guy to help us drag it up the stairs. Just give us a few bucks for some cold beer, okay?"

"Oh, thank you Pepe. You're a doll!"

♫♫♫♫♫

Joseph arrived home the next night to find an upright piano against one of the bare walls in their living room. Janet beamed as she waited for his reaction. When he smiled, she had great fun telling him the story of how it all came about.

Joseph tried a couple of the keys. The sound it produced was quite sour.

Janet scrunched her nose. "I think it might be a little out of tune?"

"I'll say."

"Your father can fix it though, the next time they come over, right?"

"If he can't, nobody can."

"You're not mad at me for doing this without telling you, are you?"

Joseph took her in his arms. "No, honey, I'm not mad. I think having a piano in the house is a pretty cool idea."

Chapter Twelve:

"Leo Klein"

Joseph discovered the Harmony Time Music Shop at the bottom of a hill, on Fordham Road, a shopping district and transportation hub for bus routes and subway lines in the Bronx.

As he surveyed the glass display windows that flanked the recessed entrance, he saw some musical instruments, record players and accessories. But there was also an overabundance of non-musical items as well. Costume jewelry, toasters, blenders and other kitchen appliances grabbed the focus of any potential customer.

Inside, Joseph found the store to be narrow and cramped. A counter ran ten feet down the length of one wall. The other wall consisted of shelves of varying height, displaying all types of merchandise. Two aisles, formed by waist-high wooden bins ran down the center to the back. The bins contained older, 78-RPM records and a modest number of 33 1/3 long playing vinyl albums. There wasn't much in the way of rock and roll or R&B titles in evidence, but Joseph managed to pick out a few that interested him and might have some value to other collectors. He imagined what he would do if he owned a store like this.

He approached the counter and found himself behind two young teenage girls being waited on by a thin, balding, bespectacled man in his forties.

"Do you have the record, 'Gee' by the Crows?" one girl asked.

The man needed little time to respond, "No, we don't dear."

"Okay, thanks anyway."

The girls left the store.

Emboldened by this exchange, Joseph put his albums on the counter. "Does that happen often?"

"I'd have to say it's not unusual for customers to leave without buying anything." The older man barely looked up from ringing up Joseph's purchase.

"They didn't buy anything because you didn't have what they wanted. Do a lot of teenagers come in asking for new records?"

"Sometimes." The shopkeeper peeked over the top of his wire-rimmed glasses to look at the young man who asked so many questions. "These kids, they have no patience. I try to tell them I can order any record they want, but they just…"

"They go someplace else?"

"I suppose so. Do I know you, young man?"

"My name is Joseph Rabinowitz."

"I'm Leo Klein. I own this place, fifteen years now."

"You've been a businessman a long time, Mr. Klein. I don't need to tell you that it's bad for business when customers leave your store and go elsewhere to find what they need."

The boy was right about one thing Leo Klein knew his business. He came from a long line of "sellers." His father, uncles and grandfather before him made their living going door-to-door when Jewish families dominated the Grand Concourse. They sold clothes, jewelry and other amenities from briefcases they carried. They offered furniture and household items from catalogs, all on the installment plan with low interest. Housewives all along the Boulevard could count on weekly visits by one of the Klein brothers to hawk new wares or collect a payment.

"I've been a businessman long enough to know when someone is trying to schmooze me. Just what it is *you're* selling young Mr. Rabinowitz?"

"Kids today don't mind spending their allowance money on the things that they want, like hit records."

"That crazy stuff?" Leo made a disapproving face. "It's just a fad."

"That's where you're wrong, Mr. Klein. If you know what records to stock and how to market them, you could make a lot of money. Even if you're right and it is just a fad, why let all the other record stores in the neighborhood make all the profits in the meantime."

"And I suppose you're just the man who knows all that?"

After a long conversation, Leo Klein hired Joseph that very afternoon and gave the young man free rein in dealing with the record inventory.

First, Joseph put all the old 78's in a bin labeled "Discount." Priced to sell at three for a dollar, local bargain-hunters cleared it out within a week. Armed with the proceeds from the sale and an insider's knowledge of the current record charts, Joseph went to a local record distributor in Times Square, and acquired a wide selection of 45's and LP's, sure to suit the tastes of teenaged record buyers. Janet helped him make up a colorful paper banner for the display window which read, "We Now Stock All The Latest Top Forty Hit Recods."

He then built a wooden rack consisting of two rows with five slots in each row. He filled the slots with records from the Billboard Top Ten Survey. Joseph hung the rack on the wall behind the counter where every customer could see it. Before long, business boomed just as he'd promised.

His ideas didn't stop there.

"Leo, there are boxes full of appliances downstairs, stuff that's probably been there for months. It isn't selling." Joseph told his boss. The basement of the store, a large damp room with thick, bare walls and a concrete and clay floor was cluttered with merchandise that must have been there for months before his arrival.

"Just what would you suggest we do?" Leo asked.

"Let's turn this place into a real music store. We can re-stock and sell record players, clock radios, table radios, hi-fi consoles all sorts of things like that." Joseph had one concern. "But, what do we do with all that stuff in the basement?"

This time Leo had the answer. "Two words…clearance sale."

They chuckled at the brilliance of the idea.

The sale was a huge success. Soon the display windows were

full of the new inventory. Adults were also drawn to the shop in search of the latest hi-fi equipment and radios, all of which became big sellers.

♫♫♫♫♫

On September 7th, 1954, popular radio disc jockey, Alan Freed moved from Cleveland to New York City. Radio station WINS made him a lucrative cash offer that included nation-wide syndication of his show and a free hand in producing live concerts.

At first he filled the role of late-night disc jockey, on the air from eight to eleven in the evening. He quickly became so popular that his broadcast expanded to four hours a night, four nights a week. Joseph and Janet became avid listeners.

There was another new personality on the air they enjoyed. He called himself "Big City" J. Munrow. His show aired on WNBA radio late every Saturday night. It was called "The Midnight Special." During his program, Munrow played two continuous hours of older records. He was obviously a student of the music and Joseph learned a lot from the stories he told. On one particular Saturday night, he played a record but made a mistake in identifying the group performing it. Joseph and Janet were cuddled on their couch listening. Joseph sat straight up when he caught the error.

"He got that wrong. That's the Crew Cuts singing that, not the Chords."

"So call up and tell him. I know the request line number."

"Nah, I couldn't do that, I'd be embarrassed."

"Silly head, *he's* the one who should be embarrassed. He's supposed to be the expert."

"You really think I should?"

Janet rolled her eyes and sat up. She reached around to the end table and picked up the phone. "You can be thick as a brick sometimes."

She dialed the number and after a short wait she was put through to the deejay. Janet handed the receiver to Joseph who was quite tentative in correcting the radio personality. He was glad when Munrow reacted so positively.

"Yeah, that's easy to do. It's not often two groups have a hit with the same tune." The song was "Sh-boom" and two groups, a Negro group called the Chords and a white group called the Crew Cuts, had separate versions climbing the charts at the same time. "Thanks for the call. You sound like a guy who knows his stuff."

Joseph now felt comfortable enough to continue the conversation. "I have quite a record collection. Been at it for a while now."

"Is that so? Maybe you can grab a few gems and bring some them by the station sometime, let me have a look at what you got?"

The invitation stunned Joseph who could only manage the childish reply, "For real?"

"Not while I'm on the air of course, but yeah, sure, bring 'em by my office."

Joseph made an appointment to meet with Munrow. Three days later, carrying a shopping bag full of records, he stood face to face with the disc jockey. He felt awkward to discover that Munrow's physical appearance didn't quite match his commanding on-air persona.

The man across from him was in his late-thirties. Short and somewhat portly, he wore black, thick-rimmed glasses. After introducing himself and shaking hands, Joseph received yet another surprise.

"Hello, Joseph. You can call me Jacob."

As it turned out, "Big City" J. Munrow was actually Jacob Miliewski, a Polish Jew from Sheepshead Bay in Brooklyn.

The two men spent the bulk of the day talking about records and music. Joseph told Jacob about his job at the music store and how his ideas had improved business. The deejay was indeed impressed with some of the rare R&B records Joseph had with him.

"I don't suppose you'd to let me borrow some of these to play on my show over the next few weeks?" Miliewski asked.

Joseph was flattered though taken aback by this request. Recognizing his hesitancy, the deejay sought to sweeten the offer.

"I tell you what, just let me borrow the records and when I play them on the air I'll tell my listeners they're on loan from your shop. I'll even mention the address a couple of times."

Joseph knew this bit of free advertising would be great for business, and probably make Leo Klein turn cartwheels.

"It's a deal." Joseph had made his first contact in the radio industry, a contact he hoped would pay big dividends in the future.

♫♫♫♫♫

It was Thanksgiving Day before Solomon Rabinowitz got the chance to tune his son's piano. While Janet and Myra roasted a turkey in the kitchen, Solomon sat with his shirtsleeves rolled up working with a tuning fork, levers and wedges, setting the pins of the instrument to just the right pitch. He'd been at it for nearly three hours. Joseph admired his father's skill.

"Pretty tricky, eh Papa?" Joseph asked.

"Several of the strings are stretched rather badly. They should hold as long as you don't plan on doing a concert at Carnegie Hall."

Joseph sat on the kitchen chair that served as a piano bench, he reached forward to play a few random notes, then some chords. The sound was now rich, full and perfectly in tune.

"Well that's a heck of a lot better," Joseph remarked. Then, with a look of deep concentration, he began to play the opening strains of Debussy's "Claire de Lune."

Solomon was impressed. "You remember it?"

Joseph stopped, but did not look at his father. "Some, not all."

He continued with the piece until he became aware that Janet and his mother had come out of the kitchen to listen to him. He grinned, changed tempo, and broke into a boogie-woogie style of playing. His fingers glided across the keys. Janet exploded in a howl of laughter, clapped her hands and shook her backside in time with the rhythm.

"Woo-hoo! Go daddy-o!" She shouted.

Solomon made a sour face and waved his hand at Joseph in mock disgust. “Ahhh. You call that music?”

Joseph stopped playing, and the four of them had a good laugh. Joseph stood and gave his father an appreciative pat on the back. “Thank you, Papa, the piano sounds just fine.”

“It sure does,” Janet agreed. “Do you think you could give me lessons sometime?”

Her request got a rise from both her husband and her father-in-law, who looked at one another in surprise.

“Are you serious?” Joseph asked his wife.

“Yes, I am. I think I need a hobby.”

“What about grandchildren for a hobby?” Myra caught everyone off guard with her comment. The frankness of her question amused them.

“That too, Mama. Your son and I are working on that, believe me.”

“What kind of talk is this?” The topic embarrassed Solomon. The two women laughed. Solomon changed the subject. “I’ll gladly give you piano lessons but only if you promise not to play any of that wild, be-bop baby nonsense…at least not when I am around.”

Janet hugged her father-in-law tightly around his neck, “Okay, Papa, I promise. Now, we better check on that turkey.” She and Myra headed off to the kitchen to tend to dinner.

♫♫♫♫♫

Working under licenses granted by Bell Laboratories, an electronics company named Texas Instruments came up with a practical, inexpensive mass-market use for a solid-state amplifying device called the transistor. The low frequency device was only suitable for audio applications. It seemed logical for someone to develop a small, hand held radio.

Soon after, the Regency TR1 transistorized radio went on the market. It was five inches high and used four germanium transistors powered by a battery. The company believed that with cold war paranoia sweeping the nation, the transistor radio would become an essential survival tool every family's fallout shelter needed. They missed their market by a wide margin.

The radio *would* become essential, not for survival against a nuclear attack, but for the survival of the American teenager. Now they could listen to their own brand of music whenever and wherever they pleased. It created a form of aural integration. Songs had no race. They had no color.

Chapter Thirteen:

"King of the Wild Frontier"

Leo Klein, his wife Gloria, and their sixteen-year-old daughter, Marlene, finished dinner in their apartment on Pelham Parkway. Marlene cleared the table as the adults spent a few minutes together before Gloria left for her weekly Mahjong game at the Adleson's apartment two doors down the hall.

"This is going to be the biggest Christmas season we've had since the war ended," Leo bragged.

Dark haired with sharp features, Gloria Klein was a vain woman, who always tried to look glamorous and younger than her actual age. She pampered herself with trinkets and jewelry. Gloria had no real interest in the business beyond the profit margin, of which she kept close track. As long as she could indulge in her vices, shopping at Macy's and Bloomingdale's, a two-week vacation every summer in the Catskill Mountains and weekly visits to the beauty parlor, Gloria remained a happy woman. She was even happier lately since the Rabinowitz boy starting working for her husband.

"I'm telling you, that kid has got some great ideas," Leo went on.

"You should give him a raise."

"I already did, twice. He deserves more but he never asks for anything."

"Well, I hope he doesn't come in one day and tell you he's opening up his own shop."

His wife's comment made him think, until he dismissed the whole idea. "Nah, he wouldn't do something like that."

"So, what's it all mean, Leo?"

"It means, my dear, that if business keeps up like this maybe we can start looking for that house in Scarsdale you want so much."

Gloria's eyes widened. She dreamed of owning a house in that plush area of Westchester County north of the city. Her younger sister already lived there with her husband, a lawyer. To think that she too might be able to afford a house in Scarsdale made her very happy.

"Give the kid a raise, Leo, a big one." She stood and walked around the table, lingering behind him long enough to plant a kiss on his head. The peck left a spot of red lipstick between the thinning stands of his hair.

"Does Marlene have homework?" Leo asked.

"She's all finished. She wants to watch that Disney program on television tonight."

"Television," Leo scoffed, "another fad. Joseph will want to put those in the store next."

"That might not be such a bad idea. Nearly everyone we know has one. The Feldman's own two."

"Two television sets? That's ridiculous!"

Gloria was halfway out the front door. "I'm sure you're right, dear. I love you."

The heavy door slammed shut before he could respond.

An hour later, Leo sat in his easy chair reading the Daily Mirror, a newspaper he bought every morning but seldom got the chance to read anymore. Marlene sat cross-legged on a throw rug in front of their Dumont console television set. She was a smart, studious child who'd yet to fall prey to the worldly pleasures her mother embraced so vigorously.

At seven-thirty, the ABC television network broadcast another weekly installment of Walt Disney's "Disneyland," a popular show that premiered in October.

The current king of animation and creator of Mickey Mouse had moved into television production as a way of financing his pet project, Disneyland, a huge amusement park he planned to open in

Southern California.

On this night, viewers watched the image of Disney behind his desk. In the background, a bouncy tune began to play. Disney's image faded into a series of hand drawn sketches that resembled the panels of a comic book. The lyrics of the song described the illustrations. They told the tale of Davy Crockett, King of the Wild Frontier. Crockett was a simple backwoodsman from Tennessee. He fought Indians, served in Congress and would go to his death in a desperate battle at a place called the Alamo. Disney told his viewers that this would be the first of three installments, entitled "Davy Crockett: Indian Fighter."

Leo hardly took notice but Marlene was transfixed. So were thousands of other viewers.

By the time the second and third episodes of the Davy Crockett saga aired in February of 1955, the entire country was caught in a "Davy Crockett" marketing frenzy. Consumers spent millions of dollars on toys, books, clothing, or anything linked to the television hero.

♫♫♫♫♫

"We're selling fur coats now?" Leo asked Joseph when he arrived at the store to find him unpacking one of five large cardboard boxes, which contained dozens of furry looking items. He picked one up and examined it. "Or rats, maybe? They have tails. They could be rats."

Joseph took the item and placed it on his boss's head.

"They're coonskin caps, Davy Crockett caps. All the kids want one."

Boys and girls everywhere played frontiersman games in backyards, vacant lots and city streets. They all wanted to look like their favorite hero. The demand for raccoon fur had jumped from 25 cents a pound to $8.00 a pound.

"So we sell hats instead of records?" Leo asked, unaware of how silly he looked.

"No. We sell records, too." Joseph reached down and handed Leo a 45 record in a paper sleeve. "This one is headed up the charts like a rocket."

Leo read the sleeve. The record was called, "The Ballad of Davy Crockett," by Bill Hays.

Walt Disney realized that since Crockett's story unfolded over three separate segments airing nearly a month apart, he needed some way to tie them together to flow easily from one episode to the next. What better way than to have a catchy little tune, with several verses, to remind viewers of what transpired before?

"Coonskin caps?" Leo complained. "Joseph, really?"

Leo didn't notice the attention he was getting from a small child, browsing through the store with his mother. When the boy of about seven saw the hat on Leo's head, he wandered away from his mother's side. He stood next to Leo, staring up at him.

"Mister," the wild-eyed youngster asked, "is that a Davy Crockett hat?"

Leo looked at him. "Why, yes it is, sonny."

"Mommy! Mommy!" The boy hurried off yelling to his mother. "Look, they sell Davy Crockett hats here! Can I get one, Mommy, please?"

Leo took the hat off his head. "We can get more of these, right?"

Joseph had a big smile on his face. "Yes, Leo we can get all we could possibly need."

Chapter Fourteen:

"The Recital"

Alan Freed's rock and roll shows at the Brooklyn Paramount Theater introduced fans to a fertile crop of talented newcomers such as Ray Charles, Chuck Berry, Little Richard and Jerry Lee Lewis. Joseph and Janet rarely missed a show.

They settled into the comforts of a routine married life. Two days a week after work, Janet went for piano lessons at her in-laws. She didn't consider herself a serious student, she had fun, she *was* learning, and she enjoyed her visits with Myra.

Joseph monitored the music world from behind the counter at the record shop. He saw dozens of independent record labels springing up all over the country. Major companies like Columbia, Decca and RCA formed subsidiary branches to release rock and roll records. He had a gnawing, disturbing feeling in the pit of his stomach that it was all passing him by.

A new plan materialized in his daydreams. He was lost in thought when a customer appeared at the counter and snapped him back to the present.

Joseph recognized the young, skinny, light-skinned Negro boy dressed in jeans and a tee shirt, as one of their regular customers, usually interested in Jazz instrumental LP's.

Joseph asked, "What can I do for you today?"

"I was wondering if you could... maybe put this up someplace?" He handed a folded page of loose-leaf paper across the counter. Joseph struggled to read the teenage scribbling:

Wanted:
Bass Guitar Player
To join local band
Call Curtis: TY2-9080 (after 5 pm)

"Are you Curtis?" Joseph asked.

"Yeah, Curtis Tinnsley."

"Pleased to meet you. My name is Joseph Rabinowitz. What instrument do you play?"

"Saxophone. I play trombone too, but these days mostly just sax."

"You must do a lot of rock and roll, huh?"

Curtis nodded. "Yeah, we're getting into it a lot more. Seems like that's all anybody wants to hear these days."

Joseph chuckled. "You guys any good?"

"I think we got a pretty good sound, just me and a couple of kids from school. We got an accordion player and a drummer, but we need a bass player real bad."

"I'd be happy to put it up. Would you mind if I wrote it over – maybe even type it out?"

"No, go ahead. Gotta be better than my chicken scratching. Thanks, Mister."

"My pleasure, and a…call me Joseph, okay?"

"Ok, Joseph."

Joseph typed the ad and tacked it to a bulletin board next to the rack of 45's.

A week later, Curtis returned. "Hiya Joseph," he said with a smile.

"Hey, did you see your ad up there on the board?"

"Yeah, man, that's what I came in to tell you. You can take it down."

"Huh?"

"A kid came in here the other day and saw it. He called my house and came to our last rehearsal. The guy is really good, man. He plays both bass and electric guitar. We asked him to join the band."

"That's good news. Congratulations."

"I really appreciate what you did for us." Curtis reached into his pocket and took out two admission tickets. "I don't know if you'd be interested. My school is having a recital in two weeks. My band will be in it. I got these two extra tickets. Maybe you'd like to come? If not, you could give them to somebody else."

"That's really nice of you Curtis," Joseph said as he took the tickets from the youngster. "I'll talk to my wife. If we aren't busy, I think we might like to go."

"Cool, man. Maybe we'll see you there. Thanks again, Joseph." The young boy added as he turned and walked away.

"Thank *you*, Curtis."

Joseph was glad he'd been able to help the young musician. When he got home he told Janet the story. She was happy to have tickets to a show, even if it was just a high school recital.

♫♫♫♫♫

The Jonas Bronck High School on Jerome Avenue resembled a fortress more than an institute of learning. The hallways were immense and the staircases built of tile and metal. Even the slightest whisper or footstep echoed throughout.

The auditorium on the main floor was built theater style. Three aisles sloped down passed rows of wooden seats bolted to the floor. A thick burgundy curtain with billows of material draped over a top rail on heavy metal hooks. Since there was no reserved seating, they settled into a row midway down one aisle.

"Can you see okay?" Joseph asked, once seated.

"Um-hum, I'm fine." Janet hooked her arm around his and leaned in close to him. They were both excited to see someone from their neighborhood perform.

The auditorium filled to near capacity and the school's matronly principal appeared onstage. She gave a brief welcoming speech and introduced several school officials and other community dignitaries.

Then she brought out the glee club and asked everyone to stand. The audience rose in silent respect.

The group of some twenty boys and girls of varied ethnic backgrounds stood center stage. They sang a passable rendition of "The Star Spangled Banner," accompanied by the school's music teacher seated at a baby grand piano at stage right. They received modest, respectful applause for their effort.

Once the crowd sat down again, the glee club continued with their segment of the program, highlighted by the Broadway show tune, "Ole Man River." The reaction was more enthusiastic by the time they left the stage.

The recital continued with a line of six young ballet dancers, pirouetting their way through several dance movements. A boy followed them with a clumsy magic act. Next, a rather snooty piano prodigy of about fifteen marched stiffly across to the piano and played his segment. The ovation he received seemed loud and overlong. Apparently the crowd was well seeded with his family and friends.

This prompted Joseph to lean closer to Janet and say in a hushed voice that came out louder than he'd intended, "He's no Van Claiborne."

"Shhh, be quiet, you," Janet scolded, "his family might be sitting right behind us."

A short intermission followed. As Joseph stood to stretch his legs, he recognized Curtis among a group of students setting up musical instruments. He also noticed another person working further in the background. The man, closer to Joseph in age, was on his haunches connecting wires and cables to electronic equipment. Before Joseph could get a better look, the houselights dimmed. The show was about to resume.

Curtis and the rest of his combo took the stage. They wore white shirts, red ties and black chino slacks. They appeared confident and cool.

"These are the kids I told you about," he whispered to Janet.

"Neat." She paid close attention to the events onstage.

The principal introduced the boys as the Curtis Tinnsley Combo. They began with a stirring version of "Lady of Spain." The accordion player, a short, chunky kid looked lost behind the huge mother-of-pearl instrument strapped across his chest, yet he handled the keys and chord buttons with well-practiced skill. A lanky colored youngster on drums set the tempo with a solid backbeat. The young man Joseph knew to be the newest member of the band, a Spanish kid, tall, lean like a matador thumbed a four string electric bass guitar while reading sheet music from a stand. Curtis, on his sax, held it all together with hand signals to the others, a true and talented leader.

For their second selection they did a haunting ballad called, "The Unchained Melody," followed by a cha-cha, "Cherry Pink and Apple Blossom White."

"They're real good," Janet commented during the enthusiastic applause that followed.

Joseph nodded, clapping loudly.

The principal stepped onstage again.

"It is now my great pleasure to introduce to you the stars of tonight's program, Evelyn and Althea Rhodes, along with their cousin Roberta Johnson."

She stepped aside as the three colored teenage girls moved forward. This was a lot different from singing at their Baptist church in Harlem. Their red, dangly choir robes were gone, replaced tonight by pink dresses with flowing skirts.

The band played a short intro for a catchy tune called "Mr. Sandman" followed by their rendition of "It's a Sin to Tell a Lie." The girls slowed the pace for the song they'd saved for last, a ballad "Sincerely." Their lead singer, Evie Rhodes exhibited great stage presence. She used well-timed head movements and sweeping arm gestures, backed by the others singing pinpoint harmony. After the final note, there came an explosion of applause filled with warmth and appreciation. The girls curtsied politely and seemed to glide off the stage, waving to the crowd as they went.

Inspired by the ovation, Curtis and his combo hurled into "Shake,

Rattle and Roll," by Bill Haley and his Comets, a rocking number from start to finish that provided a fitting end to the evening's festivities. The crowd reacted wildly.

When the lights came up, people scurried about, leaving the auditorium. Joseph watched Curtis and his band break down their equipment.

"What say we go down and say hello?" he suggested.

"Do you think we're allowed?"

"I don't see why anyone would stop us."

"Okay. Let's go."

Holding Janet by the arm, they weaved their way along to the front of the auditorium. As he predicted, there was no problem gaining access to the stage. He headed straight toward Curtis who smiled when he saw Joseph approach.

"Hey, man, I'm glad you could make it," Curtis said.

"Yeah, I am too. You guys were terrific."

"Thanks." The rest of the band looked their way. "Hey, Freddie, c'mere, man," Curtis called out. The accordion player joined them. "This here is Mr. Rabinwitz," he mispronounced Joseph's name, "he owns the record store on Fordham Road."

"Just call me Joe," Joseph said. "I don't own the record store, I just work there."

"I'm Freddie Christie. That's our drummer, Gary Tracy, over there. The bass player is Raymond. You probably know him from your store."

Joseph exchanged greetings with the others and introduced his wife. She waved to them and smiled. Joseph wanted to know more about the man working the electronics. "Was someone from the school recording the show?"

"No, he's with us," Freddie said. "That's my brother Mickey. He's into electronics so we asked him to come and tape us and the girls."

"You mean that trio that closed the show?"

"Yeah, Evie is in our homeroom class. They were good right?"

"Yeah, they were great."

"Do you wanna meet my brother?"

"Sure," Joseph answered. He followed Freddie back to where the man packed his equipment.

"Hey, Mick, I want you to meet Mr. Rabits." This botch of his name was even worse than the first. "This is the guy that found Raymond."

"The name is Joe," he said, as they shook hands. "I really didn't find anybody. All I did was put up the sign Curtis gave me."

"Well, we're glad you did. Raymond fits in perfect with the other guys."

Mickey was a muscular young man with wavy black hair slicked back in a ducktail.

"I think you're right." Joseph motioned to the recording equipment. "That's quite a setup you have there."

"Yeah I suppose so. It's something I got into when I was over in Korea."

"I was in the service myself," Joseph blurted out without thinking.

"Really, did you see any action?"

"No. It was over before I could ship out." This had become his standard answer.

"I was in the signal corps, communications. I worked with the radiomen. We taped a lot of stuff for the front line guys, USO shows and shit like that. When I got home I kept messing around with it."

"This what you do for a living?"

"Not this exactly. I take a training course on television repair under the GI Bill. That's gonna be the next big thing."

Just then, the trio of girl singers approached from the wings area. They'd changed from their stage outfits into street clothes. They were giddy and excited, evidence that the adrenalin rush from their performance had not yet worn off.

"Hey, Curtis," the girl Evie, called out, "when can we hear the tape?"

"I don't know. Ask the expert."

Evie looked at Joseph.

"Not me," Joseph pointed to Mickey, "he's the guy you want."

"I'll run off a copy and Freddie can bring it to school on Monday," Mickey told her.

An older Negro woman followed the girls through the curtains. She struggled with the weight of the dresses she had draped over her arm. Evie and the other girls snapped to attention.

"Evie, what in the world are you girls doing, dawdling about back here? If you don't get a move on, we'll miss our bus. Hurry along children."

"Coming, Aunt Eleanor." She and the other girls shouted their goodbyes as they scurried off with the older woman.

"I think we should be going, too," Janet said as she joined the group.

"Yeah, yeah we better go." Joseph suddenly suspected they might be intruding on a special moment for those onstage. "Congratulations again. You were great."

There was another round of waves and nods as Joseph and Janet walked away.

"Thanks for coming, Mr. Rabbibs." Curtis called out.

"Call me Joe," Joseph said a final time.

♫♫♫♫♫

On their way home they stopped at the candy store on the corner for a pint of hand packed butter pecan ice cream. Soon, they were propped up in bed in their underwear. Janet leaned on his chest. She fed tablespoons of ice cream alternately between both of them. Joseph seemed distracted.

"What's the matter, don't like butter pecan anymore?"

"I'm frustrated, sweetie. Selling records has become just like selling shoes. People walk into the store, tell me what they want, and I sell it to them."

Janet knew he wanted his place in the music business to be more of a creative nature. She loved his ideas on how to structure the way records sounded and how the songs should be put together.

Joseph continued, "I've stood in that empty basement in the store looking at those dirty brick walls and concrete floor. I've talked out loud just to hear my voice echo back to me. I can just *picture* it, a recording studio, with a piano, microphones and instruments all over the place. Tonight we saw Curtis and his band, met those girl singers…even that guy Mickey who knows all about electronics and stuff. It's like somehow, something is coming together all at once like…like…"

She finished his sentence. "Fate?"

"Yes, just like fate. It reminds me of the things Chanty used to say, about how everything happens for a reason."

After he'd outlined more of his plan, Janet asked, "Do you think Mr. Klein would go along with all of this?" She rested on his chest, feeling him take in deep breaths.

"I can't be sure. It's a big step. I know Leo trusts me. But he's got a lot of expenses what with the new house he's buying in Scarsdale."

"But, suppose he doesn't…go along I mean?" She sought to find out just how far Joseph's planning had progressed.

"I guess then I'd have to put things on hold for awhile, at least until I can make a move on my own. Whether or not Leo comes aboard, I plan to do this, Janet. It might put a real dent in our savings though."

"That's what savings are for, right?"

"We had plans for that money. It's supposed to be for when we start a family."

There wasn't exactly a king's ransom in their savings account at the Dollar Savings Bank, only what they'd managed to squirrel away from her tips and his bonuses.

She made a twisting half-turn to look him in the eyes. "I know. But we don't need it for that…yet. I think your idea is really great. Mr. Klein is smart. You've made a lot for money him. There's no reason to think he wants to stop now. When are you going to talk to him about it?"

"Soon," Joseph recognized the sour puss on his wife's face. "You think I'm backing up on this, don't you?"

"I think we're out of ice cream." She tilted the empty carton up for him to see.

"Do you wanna go get some more?"

"Can we?"

"Not dressed like this we can't."

"Last one dressed is a rotten egg." She tossed her end of their blanket over him to get a head start. Joseph laughed.

He made up his mind. He'd talk to Leo the next day.

♫♫♫♫♫

It was a financial commitment Leo couldn't make without consulting with Gloria. The three of them met the next evening at Leo's home. They sipped hot tea and munched on rugallah Joseph brought from a local Jewish bakery.

He spoke with great confidence about his idea. His facts made sense. The numbers and predictions on projected profits were most impressive. Neither Gloria nor Leo interrupted. When he finished, the Kleins looked at one another in some secret method of communication developed over years of marriage.

"My brother, Norman, can handle all the legal matters," Gloria said to Leo.

Leo nodded and looked at Joseph, "He's a lawyer."

This talk of legal matters prompted Joseph to explain. "I'm afraid I don't have a lot of money to put up for my end. But I'm more than willing to sign a note agreeing not to take more than just a salary from the profits until my part of the start up money is paid back."

Joseph was relieved neither of them asked what would happen if there were no profits.

"That's a very fair condition, wouldn't you say, Gloria?" Leo said.

"Yes, it is," Gloria agreed.

It would be a full and equal partnership, a generous arrangement on Leo's part. He would control the purse strings, dispense the funds, approve expenses and sign the checks. Joseph would be in charge of all creative and artistic matters. The two men shook hands on the deal. Leo had just one more question for his new business partner.

"Joseph, I know how to run a business. But do you know how to make hit records?"

"Yes, Leo, I think I do."

Chapter Fifteen:

"The Studio"

Through Curtis, Joseph got in touch with Mickey Christie and told him his ideas to transform the basement of the record store into a recording studio. Mickey offered his help and a day later, he stood in the basement with Joseph and Leo.

"We wanted your opinion on some things before getting a contractor," Joseph told him.

"Contractor? That's gonna cost you an arm and a leg," Mickey said.

"Not worth it?" Joseph asked with concern. He suddenly envisioned his dream project never getting off the ground.

Mickey made a point to be more positive. "I just meant you have your work cut out for you." His eyes scanned the room. "That area back there where the old coal bin used to be, that's hardwood. It probably makes for a great natural echo chamber. I wouldn't touch that at all."

Coal burning furnaces once heated homes and businesses in New York City. Weekly deliveries of smelly, black chunks of the mineral were made by truck and dispensed through metal doors in the sidewalks, clattering down chutes into wooden bins. The chutes were gone, but in many cellars, the bins remained.

Mickey continued, "You'll have to lay down a new floor and drop the ceiling, put up some insulation and dry wall…new wiring. You're also going to need a shitload of electric outlets."

"An electrician we have." Leo knew of another of his wife's relatives.

"What about a control room?" Joseph asked.

"Back in that corner by the stairs I think." They headed in that direction. "It should be big enough for a sound console, recording equipment, and four people."

"Sounds expensive," Leo said.

"Look, Mr. Klein, I know a lot of guys who are always on the lookout to make some side money. I'll ask around, see if I can put a crew together for you," Mickey told him.

"That would be wonderful young man. Joseph tells me you are getting into television repair?"

"Yeah, I get my certificate in a couple of weeks. Then I'll need to find a job someplace."

Leo made an offer. "I've been thinking of selling TV's here in the shop. It might be a good idea to also offer the services of someone who repairs them. Television is going to be the next big thing you know?"

"I think so too," Mickey agreed.

"Oh, yes. We can put a placard in the window, something like: *For expert TV repair: inquire within.*"

"I don't know what to say, Mr. Klein."

"You don't have to answer now. Give it some thought. It was a pleasure meeting you, Mickey." The two men shook hands.

Leo went upstairs, leaving them alone together.

"Did you have a hand in that?" Mickey asked.

"I *might* have made a suggestion." They both laughed. "Listen, Mickey, we can always use an extra pair of hands here at the store. With a sign like that in the window it'll be like having your own shop, no rent, no overhead."

"Well, I'm not taking no charity. If any repair work comes my way I'm kicking back a percentage to Mr. Klein."

"I'm pretty sure Leo had something like that in mind as well. And besides, once we get up and running around here we're going to need a recording engineer. Interested?"

"Man, I don't think I know enough to call myself any kind of engineer. I learned it all by trial and error, real seat of the pants stuff."

"That's what we're all doing around here."

Mickey thought for a moment, "I'm getting married in a couple of months. Mr. Klein's offer might be the head start I need. You got yourself an engineer."

"Great. Let's go tell Leo the good news." They started for the stairs. "Getting married, eh? Hey, what do you say we get together and double date sometime?"

"Yeah, sure man, we'd dig that."

The two couples went out that following weekend and several times more until they became good friends. Mickey's fiancée, Linda McBride was a busty, gum-smacking brunette who worked as an operator for the telephone company. She was fun to be around even though she came off as being a bit ditzy at times. Janet liked her and they spent a lot of time together while Joseph and Mickey worked on the studio.

Gloria Klein's nephew was an electrician. His company installed all the wiring and outlets needed in the studio. Mickey found three young workmen from the neighborhood. He set them to work installing the dry wall, flooring and drop ceiling. They also constructed the sound booth to Joseph and Mickey's specifications.

One of the workers suggested they bring in some old rugs and mats to change the acoustics in different parts of the cellar. Curtis and the members of his combo gathered whatever they could find, and cut them into pieces of varied lengths and widths. Leo questioned them as to where they came up with the material.

"We found them in a backyard over on Sedgwick Ave," Curtis told him. "We figured someone was throwing them away."

"That's what we used to call foraging in the Army, Mr. Klein," Mickey kidded.

"Well, I think they call it larceny here in New York." Leo dismissed it all with a wave of his hand.

Several days later, Mickey got a tip on where to find some used recording equipment.

"A guy I know says there's an Army Navy Surplus store out in

Long Island City that might have something we'd be interested in looking at."

Joseph, Mickey and Leo, armed with his checkbook, drove to Queens. The tip paid off. In the surplus store, they found a Presto five-input mixer board and a PT 900 quarter-inch tape recorder. Though not the most up-to-date equipment, it was portable, dependable, and it suited their needs and budget. The owner of the store sweetened the deal by throwing in several cases of used Ampex recording tape.

Joseph and Mickey worked on their hands and knees running wires and cables through holes bored in the walls to provide connections to the microphones, amplifiers and speakers within the studio.

Curtis and his combo came in to "road test" the room. They performed several songs for Mickey to put down on tape, working until everyone was pleased with the result.

The recording studio in the basement of a record store in the Bronx was ready.

Chapter Sixteen:

"A Rising Star"

There had never been any question in Joseph's mind about whom he wanted to record in his studio.

When he last spoke to Chanticleer it was to tell him about getting married to Janet. There was a lot to catch up on after he telephoned the Mobil station in Radcliff. He eventually got around to telling Chanty about the recording studio and his desire to have him make records. A long silence followed. Joseph thought there might be something wrong with the connection.

"Chanty, are you there?" He asked, raising his voice.

"Yes, Joseph, I heard you, son. That's right good news about the studio and all. I'm flattered by your invitation, I truly am. But there ain't nobody wants to buy records made by a crusty old coot like me."

Joseph pleaded his case. He told Chanticleer he believed there was indeed a market for good blues music in New York. The renewed silence on the other end meant the man in Kentucky wasn't going to change his mind. But, Chanty did have a suggestion for his young friend.

He told Joseph about Teddy Boyette and his yearning to get a recording contract. If Joseph was prepared to take a chance on an aging, black guitar player, might he be willing to give Teddy a try?

"Well, if he's as talented as you say he is, I think we *might* be interested."

They spoke again over the phone two days later. This time Chanty was at the Boyette's farm along with Cap Stewart, who monopolized most of the conversation. He introduced himself as Teddy's manager and outlined a long list of conditions to be met if Teddy was to audition for him. Joseph listened with interest, but was non-committal. That was, after all, Leo's department.

Joseph talked with Teddy for a few minutes. The singer sounded excited and grateful. Then Joseph spoke to Chanticleer.

"Are you coming north with them, Chanty?" he asked.

"Teddy's folks would like me to if that's all right with you?"

"Absolutely. It would be great to see you again."

"And I want to get a chance to meet this little girl you married," he chuckled.

"She's dying to meet you too. I'll be in touch with Mr. Stewart as soon as we've made all the travel arrangements."

As Joseph expected, Leo complained mildly about spending money for three round trip bus fares and two hotel rooms for a week, even if they were in the most modest Times Square hotel. But he soon conceded.

♫♫♫♫♫

A week later, the reunion between Joseph and Chanticleer took place in the lobby of the hotel. The two men embraced warmly while Janet, Teddy Boyette and Cap Stewart stood nearby. With the introductions out of the way, Chanticleer had kind words for Janet.

"Janet, you're prettier than he ever could have described to me. I hope he appreciates you?"

"He treats me pretty good …so far," she responded, making everyone laugh.

Joseph turned his focus to Teddy. "How do you like New York?"

"Oh, I'm real excited to be here. I ain't ever seen anything like this before."

"Have you been out exploring?" Janet asked.

"Oh, no, ma'am. I ain't made it passed the doors yet. I'm afraid I'd fall down and get swept away by all that's going on out there.

"Well, we need to change that and, I'm just Janet, okay?

Janet's comments reminded Teddy of Dee the waitress. "Okay, Janet."

She turned to Joseph. "We can take him to see some of the sights before you put him to work can't we?"

"Absolutely. We're not due in the studio till tomorrow." Joseph answered, certain his wife had something in mind.

"Great. Chanty, would you and Mr. Stewart care to join us?" she asked.

"No thank you, darling," Chanticleer declined gracefully. "I don't think I could keep up with you young folk."

"That bus ride played heck with my arthritis." Cap added. "I'm gonna spend the rest of the day stretched out in my room. Just make sure you keep a close eye on our boy there. We wouldn't want him getting lost on us."

Everyone smiled at Cap's remark.

Joseph and Janet ushered Teddy out of the hotel and into the crowded street. They strolled toward Broadway and Forty-Second Street. The sights and sounds they experienced overwhelmed Teddy. They took him to the top of the Empire State Building. It was windy on the observation deck of the skyscraper, one hundred and two stories above the ground.

"This here is the tallest building in the world, ain't it?" Teddy asked with fascination.

"Yes, it is," Janet, answered. Being this close to him, she could sense his electricity. He had a sparkle in his eyes as he gazed out at the panoramic view.

"I never dreamed I'd ever see anything this wonderful in my whole entire life. Why, I bet I could almost see all the way back home from here," Teddy said.

Joseph grinned. "Not quite that far but, I agree, from here the whole world opens up to you."

It occurred to Joseph that his remark might prove prophetic. A new world *was* about to open up for this fresh-faced young man from such a humble background.

♫♫♫♫♫

The studio bustled with activity. Curtis and his combo were set up and introduced to Teddy. Leo and Cap Stewart sized one other up for the business negotiations to follow. Chanticleer stood off to one side charming Janet and Linda with stories of the New York City he remembered from the old days. Mickey sat in the control room preparing for the session.

When Joseph entered the studio he motioned for everyone to gather around him. In his hand he held something special for Chanticleer.

"As most of you know, Chanty here is the man who inspired me to do all this. He's the modest type and refuses to take any credit for what's happened. But, this is one thing I'm not going to let him refuse."

He handed the older man the large, manila envelope. Chanty opened the envelope to reveal its contents, a single sheet of white construction paper, circular in shape, the exact size of a forty-five record. An art student at Curtis' school had skillfully sketched the image of a strutting rooster in thick ink. The combs and wattles of the rooster were pronounced and detailed. The body lay precisely around the diameter of the hole in the center of the record. The hackle, tail and saddle feathers were drawn with a flourish at the back part of the label while the bird's thin legs and feet extended toward the bottom. Fancy lettering spelled out the words CHANTICLEER RECORDS across the top.

Chanty had difficulty looking at the others.

"At least you had the good sense not to put *my* picture on it." His comment amused everyone. "Just let me say that I'm deeply touched by all this. But, Joseph is right. I don't take no kinda credit for any of it. If it's true that I played some small part in putting you talented people together, then I'd just as soon we thank the good Lord and not me."

The group applauded.

It was time to get down to the business of making music.

"Chanty, would you like to come into the control room?" Joseph asked.

"If it's all the same to you, I'd like to sit off in the corner there with the young ladies. I promise to be as quiet as a church mouse."

"That's fine."

Joseph, Leo and Cap Stewart headed toward the control room, leaving Teddy and the musicians to make their final preparations.

Teddy handed Curtis a sheet of loose-leaf paper. "This is a list of the songs I do when I'm out on the road... simple stuff...easy to follow. I mostly sing in the key of C." Teddy said, proud that now he could provide that information.

Curtis reviewed the list. "Yeah, we know some of these. The ones we don't you can show us, okay?"

"That'd do just fine."

Inside the control room, Mickey and Joseph sat behind the soundboard with Cap on a folding chair behind them. Leo stood braced against the closed control room door, his arms folded in front of him.

When Mickey saw through the panel of glass that Teddy had strapped on his guitar, he flicked the switch that opened his microphone to the studio speaker.

"Teddy, I need to get a sound level on your vocal mike," his voice boomed out.

Teddy moved forward. "Testing, one, two, three, testing."

"Sounds good." Mickey replied before pressing the record button on the tape machine. "Teddy Boyette audition tape, take one."

On Mickey's cue, Curtis counted off and Teddy launched into the rocking tune. Right away, Gary was mixed up on drums. They stopped and started twice more before getting it right. The mishaps rattled Teddy to the point of his becoming giddy. The faint hint of a chuckle came across on the take that captured the entire song.

The band needed some help on how to play the country and

western arrangement on the next number, a Hank William's tune Teddy re-worked called, "Mind Your Own Business." He fell into a groove and even began his gyrating stage moves putting two more tunes on tape before they were allowed to take a break.

While those in the control room studied the playback, the boys in the studio joked together like old friends.

"You shake your ass around like that when you're on stage?" Raymond asked.

"Course I do." Teddy answered with a sly smile and a feigned air of conceit. "The chicks go crazy for it, man." The musicians laughed. Teddy glanced into the corner where Janet sat, he suspected she and Linda had heard his wisecrack. He lowered his head.

What the girls heard, was nothing compared to what they'd seen. Linda leaned in close to Janet to make sure Chanticleer didn't hear her.

"That guy has the cutest ass I've ever seen," she whispered with glee.

"Linda, your mind is always in the gutter." Janet chastised her girlfriend, and then added in her own well-guarded whisper, "he's got dreamy eyes, that's for sure."

"I couldn't get *my* eyes to go above *his* waist," Linda said boldly.

Mickey's voice came over the speakers, "You boys ready in there?"

"Hey man, you guys know any Dean Martin songs?" Teddy asked the band.

"Are you kidding?" Freddie answered. "Dean Martin is like God in my house. Which one you want to do?"

"How about, 'You Belong to Me'?"

"You got it, man."

Teddy took off his guitar and laid it on the floor next to him. When Freddie got the high sign from Mickey, he played a short accordion lead-in to the familiar pop tune. Teddy sauntered up to his microphone and sang the ballad in a sweet, gentle manner. The four men in the control room were surprised by this selection. Teddy nailed the take.

"I thought he was going to start making out with the damn microphone on that one," Linda commented, aloud this time. Janet simply nodded in agreement.

The session continued for another thirty minutes. Then, Teddy called out toward the control room.

"Mr. Rabinowitz, can you hear me in there?"

Joseph cued the P.A. speaker. "Yes, I hear you, Teddy."

"I promised my Mama I'd do a special gospel song for her. Would you mind?"

"No, not at all. You go right ahead."

"The tape is running whenever you're ready," Mickey told him.

As he eased his way into, "The Old Wooden Cross," Teddy couldn't help but feel that he was somehow, conveying what Chanticleer spoke of earlier, a way to thank God for the opportunity to follow his dream. When he finished, he looked in Chanty's direction. His mentor beamed with pride.

Those in the control room had business to conduct. By way of silent agreement Joseph stood and the three men prepared to leave. "Joseph," Leo began, "I think perhaps you and Mr. Stewart and I should have a talk upstairs?"

"Want to have the boys pack up?" Mickey asked.

"No, they're having a ball in there. Let them play for as long as they want," Joseph replied. He motioned for Cap to follow Leo out of the room as he brought up the rear. Mickey settled back to enjoy the jam session about to take place in the studio. He also took the time to put a fresh reel of Ampex tape onto the recorder and switch it on.

♫♫♫♫♫

The Jewish businessman from New York and the carnival hawker from the south sat across from one another at Leo's desk. Joseph remained standing off to the side.

Both negotiators were confident in their abilities to outdo the other. Cap believed he held an advantage. This Rabinowitz kid was eager to sign Teddy, a fact that would hinder his partner's attempts to make any outlandish demands.

Joseph opened the talks. "I have to tell you, Cap, we're very impressed with Teddy."

"Course, you realize he'd sound a lot better with his own combo backing him up?"

"That's understandable," Joseph offered.

Leo said,"You know, I can't help but wonder why there hasn't been any interest in Teddy from any other record labels?"

The question caught Cap off guard. He tried to worm his way around it. "Well, it's a long story, Leo, but let's just say Teddy pretty much burned his bridges with the record people down our way."

Leo wasn't fooled by Cap's explanation. "Still, if you were willing to travel all this way to work for our little enterprise, you can't really expect too much."

It became obvious to Cap that he was being double-teamed. These two had already developed a strategy to get what they wanted.

Joseph moved to reinforce their position. "We'd like to sign Teddy to a recording contract. But, as Leo says, we're a small outfit just starting out. We can't offer much."

That was the other side of the coin and Cap knew it. To walk away from any kind of a record deal would crush Teddy. Cap was in a tight spot. His only way out was to make sure his personal interests remained protected.

"You're aware that I have an exclusive contract with Teddy as his manager and I handle all his business matters?"

Leo nodded. "We're not looking to interfere with any arrangements the two of you may have. But, if he does sign with us, we expect to play a major part in how he's marketed from here on. He records here in New York. We arrange his performance schedules, television and radio appearances, concerts."

Cap could live with that. His percentage deal with Teddy would add to his take.

"I have a full slate of tour dates scheduled back home that takes us through Labor Day."

Joseph took charge. "Then I suggest we get Teddy and his band back up here as soon as possible to record a single for immediate release. We'll give you a supply of the records to sell at the shows or distribute to local disc jockeys. That way we'll get full exposure."

"That's a fine idea," Cap agreed.

The terms of their contract were fair to all parties with regard to length and royalty payments. Joseph and Leo also agreed to pay some up front money. Handshakes sealed the deal with Leo assuring Cap he'd have the necessary papers drawn up before they left town.

Their business completed, the men went back down to the studio. The jam session was over and everyone was milling around. They grew quiet as Joseph and the others approached, Cap grabbed the spotlight.

"Well Teddy," he announced, "it appears you have a record contract with Chanticleer Records."

He slapped the young man squarely on the back. Teddy blushed accepting hearty congratulations from everyone. Janet and Linda kissed him on the cheek. Chanticleer embraced him. Joseph and Leo stepped through to shake his hand.

"Happy to have you with us, Teddy," Joseph said.

"Thank you, Mr. Rabinowitz. I'm sure grateful for this. I won't let you or Mr. Klein down."

Cap spoke again. "Thanks to these nice folks I think I can afford to buy us all dinner. What'll it be?"

"Pizza…pizza!" A youthful chorus chanted.

"How about it Teddy, you up for some real New York Pizza?" Janet asked with a smile.

"I don't recollect I know much about pizza. Is it good?"

"What?" Linda exclaimed. "Man, are you in for a treat? C'mon, sweetie, there's a lot we need to teach you." She took him by the arm and led him away.

♫♫♫♫♫

Later, at home, Joseph and Janet undressed for bed.

"Did you see Linda all over Teddy tonight?" Joseph asked.

"Do you think Mickey was jealous?"

"I doubt it. He knows she likes playing the little town flirt."

Janet slipped naked into bed and under the covers. Joseph got in next to her. She snuggled and spooned close to him.

"Well, well," he teased, "looks like Teddy got you all hot and bothered, too."

"It's my he-man has *me* all hot and bothered." She gave him her best Marilyn Monroe pouty smile. "I checked the calendar. I'm ovulating. Let's make a baby."

Sparked with electricity by the events of the day and their determination to conceive, every touch tingled and excited them.

The intensity of their fulfillment left them spent and breathless. In the quiet that followed, Janet dozed off only to be awakened later by a strange dream. Joseph was no longer beside her and she was about to get up when she heard the faint tinkling of piano keys coming from the living room. It made her smile.

Details of what had awakened her filtered through her consciousness. In her dream she was making love - not with Joseph but with Teddy. Maybe it was the power of Joseph's suggestion or perhaps it was the pizza, but it bothered her nonetheless. As she listened to Joseph play, she lay back upon her pillow hoping the dream image would not return.

But it did.

Chapter Seventeen:

"The Pixies"

The weekend after Teddy went back to Kentucky, the Chanticleer Records family celebrated again. Mickey Christie and Linda McBride got married in the church of St. Therese of the Roses. Mickey's brother Freddie played hymns on the church organ. Seventy guests gathered for the reception at the Chateau Pelham Catering Hall. Curtis' band provided the entertainment. After the ritual cutting of the wedding cake, the festivities wound down.

"You guys sounded great tonight," Joseph told Curtis.

"Thanks Joe. It's a special day."

"Yeah, it sure is. Listen, I hope you and the guys aren't too disappointed about Teddy bringing his own band back with him?"

"Nah, stands to reason he's comfortable with his own guys."

"You know, we're going to sign other singers to the label. I hope I can count on you guys to play behind them too - maybe give *you* a title like musical director or something like that?"

"Musical director, me?"

"That's right. I even thought about approaching those girls from your school recital."

"You mean Evie Rhodes?"

"Yeah, that's her."

Curtis had concerns. "I don't know about that, Joe. Evie's mom is awful strict. It was like pulling teeth just to get her to let Evie sing at school. Usually the girls are only allowed to sing in church."

"Well, I'd still like to try."

"I'll have my Mom call hers and see if she'll meet with you."

"Thanks Curtis," Joseph said before heading back to his table to share a piece of wedding cake with Janet.

♫♫♫♫♫

Since forming their partnership, Richie Conforti and Phil Gambetta achieved much success selling magazine subscriptions for the Planet Publishing Company. Employing the strong-arm tactics of Phil and his gang of bullies, they had no problem convincing naïve youngsters, elderly residents or immigrant families to order magazines, even though some of their customers could barely speak English, let alone read it.

The two men ate lunch in a crowded pizzeria on Mott Street.

Lucy Giarardi, a crass neighborhood girl with a bad reputation, interrupted them. "Phillie, can I have a quarter for the jukebox?"

Phil, with a mouthful of food, hardly missed a bite as he fished in his pocket for some coins. "Here, here's two quarters. Now go away and don't bother me while I'm eating."

She took the coins and smacked on her bubble gum as she walked away.

"I don't know why you bother with that broad?" Richie asked with disdain.

"She likes me," Phil answered.

"She puts out," Richie challenged.

"Ahhh, you're just jealous."

As Phil devoured his sausage and pepper sandwich, Richie kept a keen eye on Lucy and a group of teenagers gathered around the jukebox on the far wall.

"Don Viola gets a piece of whatever comes out of that thing right?" he asked.

"The Don gets a piece of everything in this neighborhood. You know that."

"I was looking at the national sales numbers this morning. Six of the top ten magazine titles the company publishes have something to do with music."

"So what?"

"That means there's big money in that rock and roll shit. That's what."

♫♫♫♫♫

Convincing Gladys Rhodes and Elenore Johnson to sign a recording contract for their daughters would be no easy task. Joseph sat across from them in a diner in Spanish Harlem. Both women eyed him suspiciously. He recognized Mrs. Johnson as the woman who picked up the girls after they sang at the school recital. The stout, stern faced ladies drank iced tea even though Joseph offered to buy them lunch. Fearing it might be a short meeting he ordered coffee.

They'd agreed to meet with him only after speaking to Curtis' mother. She'd told them what she knew about how Joseph helped the young boy from down south and his plans to make records with other local kids. Now, he was telling them how talented their girls were and that he wanted to offer them a contract. When he finished, Gladys Rhodes acted as spokesperson.

"Listen, mister, my sister and me been raising these kids on our own for a long time. Elenore is a widow and my man…he just up and left us. We all live together, two grown women and three kids in one apartment. I work two jobs, day and night shift. That's why I couldn't be at the school to hear my girls sing. Evie and my niece graduate next June, but Althea got one more year to go. They need the best education they can so they can get a high school diploma so they can go out in the world to a get a job. How can I be sure all this foolishness about singing on records is good for them?"

"I understand Mrs. Rhodes. There are a lot of talented young people making good money by making records. The girls can make more money working for me than by working in a bank or in an office. And I assure you both that singing for us will never interfere with their school work in any way."

"And you'll pay them for singing now?" Mrs. Johnson wanted

to know.

"Yes. But, because they're minors, you'll be in charge of their money. They won't be able to go on tour or anything until after Althea graduates. But they can make records right now and probably earn enough money so that you can get a bigger and nicer place to live.

Gladys looked at her sister whose gaze begged to accept the offer. She decided it was worth the risk.

"Alright, Mr. Rabinowitz, you got a deal," she said. Her sister smiled.

With Mickey on his honeymoon, it fell to Joseph and Curtis to put Evie's trio through their paces. On their first visit to the studio, the girls listened to the raw material from Teddy's audition tapes. Joseph worked up some vocal harmonies and Curtis helped arrange the songs they planned to record when Teddy got back.

During a break in the session, Evie drifted into the control room. She hovered over Joseph's shoulder and didn't wait for him to acknowledge her.

"So, the plan is for us to sing back-up for this Teddy guy?" she asked.

"For now, yes."

"And then what?"

"Maybe back-up some of the other acts we sign. I don't know yet."

"My Mama said you had a lot of nice things to say about us. Did you mean it or was it just a way to get what you wanted?"

"I meant what I said," Joseph looked up at her.

"Why can't we make our own records right now?"

"You will, in time. Like I told your mother, you're too young for that. If you had hit records, you'd have to go out on the road, and you can't do that until you finish school. Till then you'll have to be content being…"

"Pixies?" Evie interrupted, "Flittering in the background on our little pixie wings?"

Joseph liked the image. "Pixies? Exactly! In fact, I think that's what I'll name your group. The Pixies."

"You're not having any of my nonsense are you?" she asked.

"Is that what this is, nonsense?"

"You go ahead, have your fun. I can be patient. But, don't make me wait too long. I got big plans for my future." She smiled and walked off. Joseph believed she meant every word.

♫♫♫♫♫

"Got a minute?" Joseph surprised Janet while she prepared dinner in the kitchen.

"I have chicken in the oven," she replied. She could tell he had something on his mind, "I can give you five minutes tops."

"That's plenty. Come with me."

She followed him into the living room. Joseph led her over to the piano, where they both sat on the bench. He played a piece of music Janet was sure she'd never heard before. It had a slow melody augmented by wonderful chord changes.

"That's beautiful, Joseph. What is it?"

"Something I wrote myself. You see, all the songs Teddy's done for us so far were recorded by someone else. He needs some *original* material, songs no one has ever heard before. You know what I mean?"

"Sure I do. But you need to have words for these songs, lyrics?"

"I do have words for them, Janet." He reached for a folder on the music rest, took out some sheet music and handed it to her. He replayed the song he'd written, while she read the words printed below the lines and spaces of the music staff. It didn't take her long to recognize the words.

"Joseph, this is one of my poems."

He stopped playing and looked at her. "That's right sweetheart, and if you're mad at me I wouldn't blame you one bit. If you don't want me to use them, I promise I won't. When I decided to write these songs it was your poems that inspired me. They make great lyrics, they really do. I worked hard on them Janet and well…they just - they just fit."

"How many songs did you write?" she asked.

"Four, so far, and I want to do more, a lot more."

"Are they all like this one?"

"One is. One is more up-tempo, a real rock and roller. The other is like a cha-cha, great to dance to."

"Has anyone else heard them?"

"No one but you. Do you want to hear the others?"

"After dinner. The chicken will burn."

Janet walked to the kitchen. Her poems *were* personal. Joseph never should have taken it upon himself to turn them into songs for everyone to hear. Then again, in a way, she felt good that they inspired him. She trusted him to be true to his word and not use the poems if she wished.

After dinner they went back into the living room. Janet sat on the couch while he played all four songs. This time he tried to sing the lyrics he'd written. She grinned.

"I know…I'm no Teddy Boyette," he confessed.

Joseph was right. The lyrics did fit. But, to know that it would be Teddy's voice singing on the records was the deciding factor. Janet told him it was okay to use her poems.

Chapter Eighteen:

"Alchemy"

The first order of business for Teddy when he returned to New York was for him and the members of his band to learn the new songs Joseph had written. To accomplish that, they all got together at the studio and sat around the piano. When Teddy took his guitar out of its case and laid it across his lap, Joseph was surprised.

"That sure looks familiar," he said.

It was Chanticleer's Senorita.

"Yeah," Teddy explained, "Chanty give it to me just before I left...for luck. I tried to talk him out of it. But, you know Chanty."

"He has a world of confidence in you, Teddy. You mean a lot to him."

"I know that. I'll do right by him, Mr. Rabinowitz. I'll do right by all of you."

The young singer proved to be an eager and willing student. He learned the four new songs and made them his own with solid performances. He also worked well with the Pixies, who sang background on a few of the numbers. All three girls warmed to Teddy. Evie soon agreed that it wasn't such a bad thing to sing with this good-looking white singer. Tracks of three other songs from Teddy's stage show were laid down before the day's work was done.

On the final day of the session, five more songs were recorded, including two gospel numbers, "The Old Wooden Cross" and "How Great Thou Art." Freddie Christie played piano on both songs and the girl's choir training paid great dividends.

They had twelve songs in all, enough for six two sided records.

Joseph would decide which two songs would go to make up Teddy's first single release. Leo and Cap came up with a marketing strategy that would be two pronged. Cap would push the records at shows and distribute them to local disc jockeys to encourage airplay. Joseph would stay in New York, trying to accomplish the same thing, to make Teddy Boyette a star.

♫♫♫♫♫

The process of putting sound onto vinyl can compare to a medieval type of alchemy that caused individuals to be burned at the stake for witchcraft. Wizards were required to perform such magic.

Leo delivered Teddy's master tapes along with the necessary information and logos required for the label to the wizards he'd hired at the Berliner Record Processing Plant in Newark, New Jersey, a small company with a good reputation and affordable prices.

The first step in manufacturing a record was to create a lacquer-coated disc called an acetate. A disc recorder with a stylus made of sapphire to ensure superior recording quality, captured the audio signal fed from the tape. The stylus moved across the disc at the exact speed of forty-five revolutions per minute, cutting precise spiral grooves as it went around. After painstaking inspection through a microscope, the acetate was then test played. If approved, it became the master disc, and never played again.

An electroplating process then bathed the acetate in silver, nickel and then copper to create a second metal disc called a mother. This disc was plated a second time, resulting in a stamper copy.

Bags of powdered vinyl heated into soft, soggy clumps called biscuits were placed on a hot tray next to the operator of an automatic hydraulic press. The press contained two molds mounted face to face with a hinge at the rear. The stamper disc for the "A" and "B" side of the record was placed one above and one below the molds. After the labels were positioned, the powerful machinery was put into operation. Steam heat forced the vinyl material into every tiny groove. The result was an audio equivalent of a photograph negative identical in every way to the first. The same machinery trimmed the ragged edges of the record, affixed the labels and punched a hole in the center. The record was bathed with water, which instantly hardened it. The process was repeated, pressing records at the rate of one every fifteen seconds.

And so it was that a thirty-nine year old factory worker held the record with the label featuring the logo of a strutting cockerel. It was her job to randomly listen to a number of newly pressed records looking for defects or imperfections before passing them on for shipping. She was the first person to ever hear Teddy Boyette's voice on a seven-inch vinyl record.

Chapter Nineteen:

"Johnny and Bobby"

Johnny Seracino adapted well to his surroundings in the Throggs Neck Housing project. He'd lost much of the baby fat from his face and body. Nobody called him "Johnny Boy" anymore.

He leaned on a lamppost in front of a seven-story building further down the block looking to meet up with someone he knew only by sight. When he spotted the boy coming out of the building, Johnny headed his way.

The other teen walked with a confident swagger in his gait. One hand buried deep in the pocket of his black chino slacks. In the other he held a lit unfiltered cigarette deftly between his middle and index fingers. He was taller than Johnny, slender with a full head of brown hair tussled on the top of his head in no particular style. When he caught sight of Johnny, his eyes darted back and forth, suspiciously.

"You're Robert Vitale, right?" Johnny asked with a half nod. All New York street kids used this greeting instead of a handshake.

"Bobby's my name. I don't like to be called Robert."

"I'm Johnny Seracino I live down the block."

"I've seen you around."

"You know Laurie Lombardo?" Johnny asked.

"She goes out with a guy in my building."

"Yeah, I know. She's in my class at school. She told me you know a lot about singing?"

"I know some. You a singer?"

"I mess around with it."

"Yeah? Well I'm more serious about it."

"That's what Laurie told me. I was wondering if maybe you could teach me some stuff? I wanna' try out for the choir."

Bobby took a deep drag on his cigarette, "You some kind of church boy?

"I go to church. Something wrong with that?

"No offense. Don't get so uptight. You a tenor, baritone or what?"

"I got no idea, man."

"Well, that's the first thing we need to find out. You busy right now?"

"Nope."

"Walk me up the hill. I gotta get some smokes. When we get back we can play some records and see what we got to work with."

Sampson hill was five steep blocks of private homes that led to the local business district on East Tremont Avenue. The two boys got acquainted as they walked. Bobby was something of a loner who didn't hang out with other guys his age.

Johnny was surprised to find him so open with the unhappy details of his life. His father had deserted him, his mother and his younger sister, Diane, not long after she was born eleven years ago. Their difficulty in making ends meet made them eligible for city-funded home relief, which supplemented an apartment in the housing project.

"How come you know so much about music?" Johnny asked, hoping to lighten the tone of the conversation.

"Music was the only subject I liked when I went to school."

"You don't go to school any more, how come?"

"I had to go to work, man." Bobby liked this Johnny kid so he opened up to him. "My mother drinks, a lot. When things got so bad that she couldn't handle a job, I quit school and went to work."

"That's rough. Where do you work?"

"Right here on Tremont at the Peter Reeves Supermarket. I stock shelves during the day. Two nights a week I deliver prescriptions by bicycle for Fleischmann's Pharmacy."

"Holy shit! Two jobs?"

"Gotta put food on the table, man."

Johnny waited outside the United Cigar candy store while Bobby went in for his cigarettes. He had a fresh one lit and in his mouth when he came out. On their way back to the project, Bobby went on with his story.

"But it's alright. Things will all change when I make it big," he said with confidence.

"Make it big doing what?"

"Singing of course. I told you I was serious about it."

"Got it all figured out, huh?"

"I know where I want my life to go if that's what you mean. I had a little duo going with another guy who worked with me in the store. But he moved away and that was the end of that."

They rode the small, square elevator of Bobby's building, to the fourth floor and walked down a narrow corridor where nine apartments branched off right and left. Bobby entered apartment 4D with Johnny close behind. Once inside, Johnny noticed that these rooms were smaller than where he and his family lived. Bobby's home lacked the warmth of his and, though neat and clean, it was sparsely furnished.

An entryway led to the living room. There, a young girl sat sprawled across a well-worn sectional couch. She'd been watching television but scampered into a seated position when she saw a new face in her home.

"That's my sister, Diane." It was the only introduction she got from her brother.

"Hi, Diane my name is Johnny."

"Hi," the girl said shyly. She was pretty, though appearing something of a tomboy.

Johnny followed Bobby as he walked down the tiled hallway. When he reached the entrance to the kitchen, he went inside. Johnny remained in the doorway.

Irene Vitale sat at a metal kitchen table pushed up against the only vacant wall in the room. A sink, refrigerator, oven and cabinets occupied the rest of the space. She was a short, gaunt looking woman with a vacant, disinterested look on her face. Her gray hair was disheveled and pulled back in a bun. There was a rosy glow around her nose and cheeks that wasn't caused by make-up or rouge. Johnny guessed that the ceramic mug she drank from didn't contain coffee. Beside the mug sat a large, glass ashtray nearly overflowing with dinched out cigarette butts and ashes. She cast a suspicious glance at the newcomer in her hallway.

"Ma, this is my friend Johnny." Bobby's reference to him as a friend made him feel good.

"How do you do, Mrs. Vitale?" Johnny said with respect.

"Nice to meet you dear," her response was somewhat slurred.

Bobby tossed an unopened pack of cigarettes onto the table, it slid across until the ashtray halted its progress.

"That's it till next payday, okay?" Bobby's scolding tone surprised Johnny.

"I get my check in a couple of days. I'll pay you back then."

"You don't have to pay me back. Just go easy on those that's all."

"I will, dear, thank you."

Bobby cocked his head to the side to indicate that Johnny should follow him. Once inside his room, Bobby closed the door.

"Pop a squat."

Johnny sat in the only chair in the room. It looked like it was part of the kitchen set. The room was small and square, furnished with a single bed, and a three-drawer clothes dresser with an oblong mirror attached. A crucifix hung on the wall over the bed and two other pictures adorned the walls. The air was stale from cigarette smoke.

Bobby set up a small, portable record player within a suitcase type carrier case. When he turned around he held a stack of forty-five's. He gave them to Johnny.

"You know the words to any of these?"

Johnny looked through the records, "This one, I guess," He gave it to Bobby.

"Alright, I'll put it on and you can sing along with it."

"Sing along with it? You mean out loud?" Johnny seemed shocked by the suggestion.

"What the fuck? Of course out loud!"

"I…I can't do that. I'd be embarrassed."

Bobby found that funny. "How do you expect to sing in the choir if you're embarrassed?"

"In the choir I don't have to sing by myself."

"Dufus! You're gonna have to sing by yourself at the tryout."

"Yeah, I know, but still…" Johnny was out of excuses. "…maybe if you sang it first?"

"I'm not trying out for anything," Bobby joked. "Okay, if it'll make it any easier for you, I'll do it first."

Bobby affixed a small, yellow plastic disc to the center of the forty-five so that it would fit properly over the nipple-like spindle on the record player. He turned the machine on, moved the tone arm to the beginning of the record, and lowered it. The four-inch speaker crackled and hissed before giving way to an instrumental introduction.

Bobby stood, raised his eyes to the ceiling and belted out the lyrics of the ballad in perfect unison with the singer on the record. His presentation and poise impressed Johnny. Bobby's voice was full and he exhibited great range. When the record finished Johnny felt like applauding, but didn't.

"Feel better now?" Bobby asked.

"Okay, but don't expect me to be as good as you."

"Oh, believe me, I don't. You ready?"

Johnny rose from the chair and took up position as his friend had done. Bobby started the record again and plopped down onto his bed. When Johnny opened his mouth, little came out.

Bobby laughed, "C'mon, c'mon that ain't singing, that's whispering! Open your mouth so they can hear you all the way up on Tremont Avenue!"

Johnny hesitated, and then composed himself enough to catch up to the lyrics being sung on the record. The two boys laughed together after it was all over.

"How was that?" Johnny asked.

"You sucked!" Bobby laughed.

"Aw, c'mon man. It wasn't that bad, was it?"

"All right, I take it back. But you need a lot of work, man. You were off key in a lot of spots. Oh, if anyone ever asks you again, you're a tenor."

"Is that good?"

"Well, I'm a tenor myself so I might be able to help you with some things. You wanna' try it again?"

Johnny thought for a moment, "Yeah, yeah I think I'd like to."

Before long, Johnny showed up at the Vitale apartment almost every day after Bobby got home from work.

Johnny never got to sing in the choir. His music teacher told him he sang too low for the open position and didn't pass the tryout. He was disappointed but it no longer mattered. By then, he and Bobby were close friends and singing together every day. Bobby taught him how to control his breathing and save his wind as he sang lyrics. They practiced harmony parts until they sounded quite good together. Bobby soon had an offer for his friend.

"Remember I told you I had that singing duo with that other guy?" he asked Johnny.

"Yeah, the one who moved away?"

"Right. Well I think maybe you and me, we could start up something like that again if you're interested?"

"You think I'm good enough?"

"Yeah, I think you got what it takes. It's like anything else, to be really good you gotta work hard…practice a lot. But, I'm telling you now, I'm gonna make it as a singer someday. If you're not going to be serious about this, don't bother."

"I'll tell you what," Johnny proposed. "I'll tag along until we figure out if we can really do this or not and then we can both decide okay?"

"Fair enough," Bobby replied.

They practiced every chance they got until their voices melded perfectly. To make sure they got every lyric to a song right they played and replayed records, pressing the speaker of a transistor radio tightly against their ears. They took turns singing lead on songs they both liked, and they stood in front of the mirror in Bobby's bedroom incorporating moves into their imaginary performances because, both boys agreed, teenage girls liked those moves.

♫♫♫♫♫

"Mrs. Yesso says he's a rebel and a dropout," Johnny's mother Rose told her son. She'd managed to corral him one afternoon before he had a chance to rush out of the apartment. Johnny was learning that adults had their own close-knit network to find out about things that were going on in the project.

"Mrs. Yesso is just an old busy body."

"You watch how you talk, Johnny," his mother warned.

"Why would she say anything about Bobby anyway?"

"You've been spending a lot of time down the block lately. I don't know many of the families down there, so I asked about him."

"Aw, Mom why did you have to do that?"

She'd done it out of concern for her son's well being but she couldn't convince him of that. She knew he felt it was just another instance of adults prying into his life

"I suppose Mrs. Yesso told you Bobby's mother was a drunk?"

"She said Mrs. Vitale had a drinking problem. She never said she was a drunk. Is she a drunk?"

"No!" he yelled loudly.

"Well, I don't think it's a good idea for you to spend so much time over there."

"He's my friend, Mom."

"You have plenty of friends right here in the court."

"Yeah and they're all such little angels, right?"

"That's not the point and you know it. Why don't you bring him over here sometime? That way I can at least meet him."

"Because we do stuff over at his house."

"What kind of stuff do you do there that you can't do here?"

"We sing."

"Sing? Sing what?"

"We sing along with records, sometimes even on our own."

"You can do that here, can't you? We have a nice hi-fi console in the living room."

"Sing in the living room? Yeah, right Ma."

"Your sisters have a record player in their room. I'm sure they'd let you use it."

"So Jackie and Tina can laugh at us?"

"Do you sing funny?" Rose asked with a smile.

"No, Mom."

"Then why would they laugh?"

"Because they're girls, that's why."

"It seems to me girls really go for singers. I used to go 'ga-ga' over Frank Sinatra when I was younger." Her comments had little effect on her son. "Johnny, I don't mean to tell you who you should be friends with, honey. Can't you just meet me half way on this?"

Her son had about run out of reasons for not introducing Bobby to his family.

"Okay, Mom…you win. I'll get Bobby to come over here."

"Soon?"

"Yes, Ma, soon."

Bobby was reluctant. But Johnny convinced his friend that to refuse his mother's wish would jeopardize their future plans.

That next week, Bobby bought his record player to Johnny's and they sang in his room.

Rose liked Bobby right away, finding him respectful and polite, not at all as she'd expected. She was sorry she'd listened to Mrs. Yesso's gossip and pre-judged the youngster. She wanted to make it up to him.

"Bobby would you care to stay for dinner tonight?" she asked.

"No, that's okay Mrs. Seracino. I don't wanna put no one to no trouble."

"C'mon man…stay," Johnny urged. "We can sing some more after we eat."

Rose wasn't about to take no for an answer. "You're not putting anyone to any trouble. I made enough ziti and meatballs to feed an army. And I baked a cherry pie. You're staying and that's the end of it."

"Well, since you put it that way, thanks," Bobby said.

When Johnny's father came home from work they all had dinner. Johnny and Bobby sang for another hour afterward. When it was time to go, Rose came out from the kitchen carrying a large bowl covered with aluminum foil.

"Bobby, I made up this dish of ziti for you to take home for your mother and sister."

"You didn't need to do that, I'm sure they both ate already."

"Actually I'm pretty sure there's enough food there for all three of you so why don't you save it for dinner tomorrow night? Just bring the bowl back when you're finished with it."

"I will, Mrs. Seracino. Thanks again."

Bobby hurried through the front door with Johnny right behind him. They scooted down the seven concrete steps to the lobby.

"I don't like taking this, man," Bobby pouted. "People know my old lady drinks and they think we need a handout or something."

"Hey, this ain't no handout, ok? My mom just wanted to do something nice that's all."

"I'm sorry Johnny. I know I can be a real asshole sometimes. You got a great family, man. Catch you later."

Chapter Twenty:

"Stardom"

Billboard Magazine's record charts for the week of October 8th 1955, saw the debut of several new artists.

One was Pat Boone, a twenty-one-year old singer who'd won top prize on both Arthur Godfrey's Talent Scouts and Ted Mack's Original Amateur Hour. Boone's hit, "Ain't That a Shame," was a cover version of a tune written by a Negro honky-tonk piano player from New Orleans named Fats Domino. Cover versions were R&B songs originally recorded by colored artists and re-done by white singers for release in northern or "white" markets. Some Negro groups also broke through. At number thirteen was a Los Angeles based singing group called the Platters with a haunting ballad, "Only You."

The newest addition of them all was a song that just managed to creep in at number nineteen. The song was "Move it on Over" by Teddy Boyette. It had taken a lot of people to get it there.

The initial pressing of the single called for five hundred copies. Half that number was shipped to Kentucky for Teddy to take out on the road. The rest were sold exclusively at the music store. After several weeks, all copies still on the shelves in the Bronx were sent to Georgia where they could catch up with the tour.

Joseph began to doubt his ability to push the song in New York. With so many people counting on him, he desperately sought out the one man who might have an answer.

Big City J. Munrow's popularity on the New York radio scene

had increased immensely. He was on the air six nights a week in the prime seven to eleven time slot. With strong backing by solid sponsors, his reputation and influence likened him closely to his main rival, Alan Freed.

"Are you telling me the kid singing on this record is white?" Munrow asked after listening to "Move it on Over," on the phonograph in his office.

"Yes he is, Jacob, as pure as the driven snow."

He played the song a second time.

"Let me hear the b-side," Munrow said. Joseph flipped the record over and played, "Within a Wooded Chapel" the ballad he'd written with lyrics adapted from one of Janet's poems. When the record finished, Munrow leaned in close as though sharing some dark secret.

"Do you have any idea what you've got here, Joseph?" He could barely control his enthusiasm and didn't wait for an answer. "You've got a fucking gold mine on your hands my young friend. Every record company in the country is looking for a white singer that sounds black. Somebody parents aren't afraid to let little Sophie and Aaron listen to on the radio. I'm thinking this kid of yours, this Teddy…Teddy…"

"Boyette," Joseph offered.

"I think he might be the answer. He's good looking right?"

"A living doll. Girls drool over him."

"Perfect."

"Then you'll play the record?"

"Play it? I'll play it until the grooves wear out!" Munrow exclaimed. "I'll see to it all the other jocks at the station play it. Shit, I'll see to it we make it our pick hit of the week."

Joseph was excited. "Jacob, I really don't know how to thank you."

"Oh, I do," Munrow already had a plan. "When can I get the kid on my show?"

"I'm not quite sure, Jacob."

Munrow threw the considerable weight of his celebrity around.

He was up and out of his chair, moving to sit on the edge of his desk. "Look, I want an exclusive on this kid…two weeks at least over the other stations…on this record and his next three releases."

"I'm appreciative, Jacob, I truly am but Teddy is out on tour. He won't be back until after Labor Day."

"Do you have another single you can line up for release…pictures…does the kid have a press agent?"

"We've got a bunch of songs we can choose from…no pictures, no press agent."

"Well, get some taken…head shots…shots of him signing autographs…and, girls, lots of girls. You should call an agency and get him signed. I'll give you some numbers."

"Yeah, I'll gladly do all that. But there is one problem, Jacob."

"How can there already be a problem?"

"We don't have any more records left to sell."

Munrow broke into a fit of laughter. "That's *not* a problem. In fact you can work that to your advantage. You see kid, when we start playing this record, people are gonna be screaming for it all over town. When they can't find it, they'll scream bloody murder. So do yourself a favor and put out a rush order for about ten thousand more copies. You're gonna need them."

"Ten thousand copies?" The number stunned Joseph. But he trusted Munrow's power and ability to influence the huge numbers of his teenage audience.

"And I want those exclusives Joseph. I want Teddy Boyette here, live, in my studio as soon as he gets back to town."

"You have my word on that Jacob."

Leo called the processing plant and ordered the additional copies of Teddy's record. He found it could take as long as a week before an order that big to be processed. Joseph believed the delay would fit right in with the plan Jacob outlined.

♫♫♫♫♫

The following Monday evening, everyone associated with

Chanticleer Records was in front of their radios at 7 pm for Big City Munrow's, "Night Flier" show. They joined the thousands of regular listeners, none of whom were aware that this would be a special night.

Like many of his contemporaries, Munrow adopted a loud, staccato style on his broadcasts. He hammered his listeners like a machine gunner, rarely pausing long enough between songs for commercials, time checks and jingles.

The pick hit of the week segment came twenty minutes into his first hour.

"Well, gang," Munrow's voice boomed, "This week's pick hit of the week is not just a new release, but it's a new release by a brand new artist, a great looking young cat named Teddy Boyette. His song is a cover version of a tune made famous by a Country Western singer named Hank Williams. But as you'll hear, his take on the tune will have you all reelin'and rocking." His voice picked up speed like an out of control locomotive. "So here it is, WNBA's pick hit of the week, Teddy Boyette and 'Move it on Over'!"

Even though they had heard the song dozens of times, Joseph and Janet understood they now shared the experience with people all over the tri-state area. What would the reaction be? How long would they have to wait to hear it?

At the radio station, Jacob Munrow played his role well. He waited fifteen minutes then announced that there had been several requests to play Teddy's song again. It wasn't true, but no one knew it except for himself. He played the song a second time.

An hour later he spoke of Teddy once more and played the b-side of the record"Within a Wooded Chapel." This time there *was* a legitimate response. Several people called in commenting on the ballad. Munrow had to keep the momentum going.

At 11pm when he handed the microphone over to Rich Rosen, the station's popular late night personality, he encouraged Rosen to keep pushing both sides of the record on his show, the Street Harmony Revue. By the time morning man Cal Coleman did his show, the pick hit had caught on in a big way. Requests for the song poured in.

Telephone orders for the record flooded the Bronx record store. More pressings had to be ordered. Leo rushed to make new deals with several local distribution outlets. The record soon found its way onto shelves of stores all over the city.

Soon it bubbled just below the Top Twenty.

♫♫♫♫♫

Teddy's return from his highly successful tour resulted in a whirlwind of activity. The three-week exclusivity agreement with J. Munrow on "Move it on Over" had passed. All the major stations in the entire tri-state area were now playing the record. By the time Teddy's on-air interview with Munrow took place, the single had broken into the Top 10 on many local charts.

At the last minute, Munrow suggested that Teddy might be more comfortable if Joseph sat in the studio with them. Though Joseph was nervous, he decided it might be a good idea. The interview was going well and they were just coming back on the air after Munrow played Teddy's new follow up single, another Rabinowitz/Cavelli composition, "Sweet Sensations."

"We're here now with rock and roll's newest singing star, Teddy Boyette. We also have his producer and the owner of Chanticleer Records, Mr. Joe Rabin live in the studio with us. Joe, you must really be proud of your new discovery?"

A long silent pause, known as dead air, followed. In the broadcasting business, dead air was something radio personalities dreaded. Munrow motioned frantically for Joseph to say something... anything.

"Why... a... yes, I am...very proud," Joseph stammered.

Joe Rabin?

His eyes begged Munrow for some kind of explanation. He didn't get one.

After the interview segment, Joseph and Teddy were shooed out of the studio by an assistant. They were taken to an anteroom where Janet, and Cap waited. They'd listened to the show thru speakers mounted on the wall.

"Where the heck did all that *Rabin* nonsense come from?" Janet asked.

"I have no idea."

"Maybe nobody paid him no mind?" Teddy suggested.

Cap knew better, "Son, I got a feeling folks in these parts pay real close attention to what that fella has to say. Fact is, that's what we're all banking on, ain't it?"

After the broadcast, Joseph confronted Munrow. The Deejay made light of the incident.

"That whole name game thing? What are you so pissed about? I did you a favor my young friend. In this business you gotta keep things simple...simple to say... simple to spell. How far do you think I'd gotten if I kept the moniker, Jacob Miliewski?"

The more Joseph thought about it, the more sense it made. He and Janet discussed his decision. "It probably means they'll start calling you Rabin as well," he warned.

"They can call *me* anything they want. But one thing is for sure, our kids are going to go by the name Rabinowitz and that's final."

Joseph agreed, but they both knew the matter wasn't closed.

♫♫♫♫♫

Dinner at his parent's home the next evening was to be a celebration for the success of the record release, but the mood was definitely chilled. After dinner with Janet and Myra in the kitchen, Joseph broached the subject with his father.

"You heard what happened during the interview on the radio? How they shortened my name?"

"*They* shortened it?"

"Yes, I had no idea Jacob was going to do that."

Then, why didn't you correct him? If someone misspeaks your name, you simply say, 'I'm sorry, but my name is Rabinowitz...' not, Rabin or whatever it was he called you. This radio person, this Jacob, he's Jewish?"

"Yes."

"So *he* changed *his* name as well? Perhaps he's ashamed of his name, his heritage. Are *you* ashamed of being Jewish?"

Joseph's heart quickened at the question, "No, Papa, that's not it at all."

"Do you intend to go on this way? To let yourself be known as Rabin?"

"I've been thinking about it and..." He couldn't continue. His father would never understand his reasoning. "It's an easier name for people to remember and to pronounce so for business purposes, yes I think I will."

Solomon's features froze like granite. He couldn't believe what he was hearing.

"Business purposes? You allow your success and your business purposes to take precedence over your good name? The Nazis tried to kill off our name once before. Is it your intention to finish the job they started?"

Old thoughts, long kept hidden, re-surfaced and spilled forth from Joseph. "I'm sure Jacob Miliewski had relatives murdered in the camps as well…relatives that didn't…didn't run away!"

As soon as the words passed through his lips he regretted saying them. The accusation struck Solomon harder than any physical blow.

"Run away?" He shouted the words back at his son. "Is that what you think your mother and I did? Because you've read books…seen films…you think you know what it was like in those days?" Solomon's eyes went vacant and his hands began to tremble. He then began a harrowing narrative Joseph had never heard before.

"My father called our family together. My mother prepared a supper, the best she could manage because Jews were not permitted to shop in the better stores. After we ate we talked about things… the taunting in the streets, the beatings. Our shops and synagogues were vandalized, and our property confiscated. The front door of our home was painted with the Star of David to mark it as a Jewish household."

The horror of the memories contorted Solomon's features. His gaze was trance-like, unblinking. "We knew things would only get worse and we'd all soon be in great danger. It was decided that some of us should try to escape."

Solomon wiped his brow and took a deep breath. He told of how his parents refused to desert their home. Solomon's brother Nathan was a doctor who would not abandon his patients. Nor would his other brother, Hiram, a teacher who felt obligated to remain for the sake of his students. "So it was left to your mother and I to be the ones to leave. We said goodbye to everyone, not knowing if we would ever see any of them again…" Solomon's anger flared once more. He stood, his fists clenched at his side, rage in his eyes. "… And we didn't see them, ever! None of them…because they were murdered…all of them murdered!"

"Stop this!" a shrill voice rang out from behind them. The startled men turned to see Myra standing in the doorway. She trembled, her eyes widened. Janet offered her a comforting arm, but she had more to say. "Wasn't it bad enough to have lived through it?" She asked Solomon who sank back into his chair. "Must we remind ourselves of such terrible things?"

Joseph tried to explain. "Mama, I'm so sorry. This is all my fault, I…"

"Not another word!" his mother scolded. "I won't have any more talk of such things in my home!"

"Come, Mama," Janet said as she gently turned her around. "Why don't you go and lie down? I can finish the dishes."

When Janet returned to the living room, Joseph and his father were sitting in silence. She guessed they'd said nothing to one another in the time she'd been gone. Solomon remained seated as the couple prepared to leave. Misty eyed, Janet kissed him lightly on the forehead before following Joseph out the front door.

They sat close together for the taxicab ride back uptown. "Things will be okay once he cools down," Janet assured him quietly.

"I don't know. We've had words before but never anything like that. I had no idea…"

"Of course you didn't Joseph. How could you?"

Her words did not console him. Despite his recent success, he'd once again disappointed his father.

♫♫♫♫♫

By Halloween, "Move it on Over" was number one on the Billboard charts. The flip side, "Within a Wooded Chapel" came in at number three. Teddy had a legitimate two-sided hit on his first single release. His follow-up, "Sweet Sensations" debuted at number eleven and began its rise to the top.

Leo worked a nation-wide distribution deal based on Teddy's appearances on television shows like the Ed Sullivan Show, the Milton Berle Show and Perry Como's Variety Hour. All the while, fan magazines clamored for pictures and interviews.

Teddy went back into the studio to lay down tracks for an LP and a Christmas album. A new tour was planned. Not just some regional jaunt, but a national tour going coast-to-coast to cover all the major markets.

Before going out on the road, Teddy had a chance for a short holiday visit home. He and Cap sat in a compartment of a Streamliner train looking out as the landscape sped by.

"Know what I wish, Cap?" Teddy asked.

"What's that, son?"

"I wish we could book us a show back in that town where that sheriff run us off."

"Castlehurst?" Cap remembered it well.

"Yeah, that's the one."

"Why ever would you wanna go back *there* for?"

"I just wonder what that sheriff would say about my music now?"

Cap chuckled. "Teddy, there's just some folks in this world never gonna stop bein' stupid no matter how much someone shows em' to be wrong. Most people just don't like change."

♫♫♫♫♫

On December 1st, 1955, a forty-two year old Negro seamstress named Rosa Parks boarded a bus in Montgomery, Alabama. Tired from a hard day at work, she paid her fare. In compliance with the local Jim Crow ordinance, she exited the bus and walked to the back to re-enter through the rear door. She took a seat two rows behind the last white passengers.

As the bus traveled along, other whites got on. Some found themselves without seats. The driver ordered four colored riders in back rows to stand and allow the white passengers to sit. Three of them complied. Rosa Parks remained where she was. The angry bus driver warned her that if she didn't give up her seat, he'd call the police and have her arrested.

"You may do that," Parks replied.

The bus driver made good on his threat.

At her trial, Mrs. Parks was found guilty and ordered to pay a fine for her act of civil disobedience. The incident came to the attention of the new Pastor of the Dexter Avenue Baptist Church in Montgomery, a man named Martin Luther King Jr. He helped organize a boycott of the Montgomery Transit System. For one of the first times in the history of this nation, a minority group banded together to assert their constitutional rights.

Chapter Twenty-One:

"Alexis Records"

"This record business is wide open for the taking." Richie Conforti told Phil Gambetta for about the millionth time. Phil was tired of hearing it. Richie leaned across the table at The Solare Italian restaurant in Brooklyn. His pencil thin, purple necktie nearly dragged across the plate full of linguini and red clam sauce in front of him. "These radio deejay's got every jig and guinea teenager in the country thinking they can be big stars."

"Jesus Christ, Richie, how many times I gotta tell you that it ain't me you gotta convince, man. I'm on your side just like always." Phil was annoyed that his friend was keeping him from his beef bracciole dinner. He managed to stuff a heaping fork full of food into his mouth before Richie had the chance to continue.

"But, if I already laid it out for Max Seiderman, why do I have to see the old man in person?" Richie persisted.

"Because Seiderman is just a middleman. You only met with him first to find out if your plan was worth bringing to the Don."

"So this meeting is a good sign, right?"

Phil swallowed hard. He waved his silverware in Richie's direction. "Is this scheme of yours gonna make money for the family or not?"

"Hand over fist, my man, hand over fist."

"That's all the Don needs to know. Now will you please let me finish my friggin' dinner?"

Later, the two of them sat on lush upholstered chairs in the parlor of Don Gugliemo Viola's sprawling Long Island estate. The room was furnished like a museum. Light sifted in through a small opening in a set of heavy deep purple drapes covering a set of patio doors that probably looked out onto the grounds.

They sprang to their feet when Don Viola entered the room.

Gugliemo Viola was seventy-three years old. His once commanding frame was now bent, gaunt and frail. His skin resembled old leather, withered and worn. What little hair he had was white and receded backward from his brow to the crown of his head.

He traversed across the parlor with a severe limp, making his way to the ornate sofa in the middle of the room. Another man followed, younger, muscular with threatening features. A trusted bodyguard Richie guessed, loyal and dedicated to protect his employer. Once the Don was seated, the bodyguard faded into the background remaining close enough to act quickly should the need arise.

Don Viola motioned for his guests to be seated.

"You are here on the recommendation of our good friend Max Seiderman. He speaks of you as a young man of intelligence and zeal and says you have an idea we might find profitable."

"Mr. Seiderman is most gracious." Richie accepted the compliment.

It was then Richie noticed it, the look in the old man's piercing eyes. It sent a bone chilling realization down his spine. He was about to propose a business partnership between himself and a very dangerous individual. Viola was a mobster, capable of ordering violence without mercy against anyone who crossed him or caused him displeasure. This was much more serious then selling magazine subscriptions. He needed this kingpin's connections, protection and his money if he wanted to operate within Don Viola's territory.

"Your idea has something to do with this new music that has the young people of this country acting wild and crazy?" the Don asked.

Richie began his well-rehearsed spiel outlining his plan. He spoke of how the organization could control every aspect of the business by setting up a record company, a completely legitimate enterprise. Then sign young talent to iron clad, long-term contracts taking advantage of the naïve youngsters forcing them to work for pennies. Their records would play in mob-controlled jukeboxes already in place in restaurants, pizza parlors, and diners, anywhere young people congregated.

Radio would be next. The Federal Communications Commission had strict rules pertaining to radio and television. So far the mob avoided trying to gain a foothold in those regulated areas. "Our people can get close to the most popular disc jockeys, offer them gifts, money to play the records *we* want played. The records are only the beginning. These kids will go out on tour - appear in our nightclubs and theaters. All of this will result in great profits for the organization."

Don Viola was impressed. But he had questions "How will you control these artists?"

"All any of these kids want is to be famous, have some money, and impress girls. They have no interest in the business end of what they do."

"But what of their parents? What if they express an interest?"

"I think most parents would be quite happy if their children were able to provide so much extra income for their family. I doubt there would be many questions."

The answer brought a smile to the Don's face.

"And, many of these singers are colored?"

" Yes," Richie answered.

"Many coloreds have developed a great love for 'babonia,' drugs." The Don emphasized his point by slapping the crook of his left arm with the fingers of his right hand. "We are quite able to feed their cravings." The Don rendered his decision. "I'm giving you permission to proceed with your plans. I'll see to it that ample funds are made available to you at once. From this point on you will have no direct contact with me. You will put yourself under the auspices of Max Seiderman. If trouble with the authorities ever arises, he is to be identified as your benefactor. Do you understand?"

“Completely. I’m most grateful for your confidence Don Viola.”

“May I ask, what will you call your record company?”

“Nothing has been decided as yet,” Richie answered.

The Don had a suggestion. “As a young man in the old country I once fell in love with a beautiful young woman in my town. Her family did not approve of me. I sometimes reflect on that lost love. Her name was Alexis.”

“Then we will call our company Alexis Records in honor of her.” Richie hoped this gesture might endear him to the old man. But there was no discernable change in his demeanor.

Don Viola rose from his seat to indicate that the meeting was over. The two young men stood and crossed the room. In turn, they each bent forward to kiss Don Viola’s hand as a symbol gratitude and respect.

“I wish you both luck in this new enterprise in the hope that it will be as profitable as you indicate it will be.” The Don offered before he left the room with his bodyguard close behind.

Richie and Phil got very drunk that night. They’d made it to the big time.

Chapter Twenty-Two:

"The Brill Building"

Teddy Boyette became the most popular rock and roll singer in the country. All his releases reached the top ten, many of them going all the way to number one. His records sold millions of copies nation-wide. Teen and fan magazines were filled with pictures and stories about him and he was also featured in mainstream publications like the Saturday Evening Post, Look and Life. He was linked romantically to female movie stars and debutants. Some were factual while others were mere publicity items. On tour it often fell to Cap to arrange for Teddy to spend time with some young woman who would be generously paid for her time and her descretion. Overall though, the life of a recording star could be a lonely one.

He wasn't alone in his popularity. RCA Victor signed a white truck driver from Tupelo, Mississippi named, Elvis Presley. Their similarity in style and appearance made them natural competitors fueling a publicity feud that bolstered sales for both. Other singers hot on his heels for spots on the charts were Carl Perkins, Gene Vincent and Buddy Holly.

The financial rewards benefited everyone. Teddy sent most of his money home. He offered to buy his parents a new house, but they declined. Instead Teddy arranged for massive improvements on the farm. He hired several hands to ease his father's burden.

Chanticleer Records also experienced a boom. Joseph signed two local black groups, the Windmills and the Reveres, both of whom achieved moderate chart success with their releases. He also brought in the Hollins Twins from Teddy's first tour, and a pioneering black guitar man out of El Paso, Texas, named Charles Bannister.

"Charlie's a buddy of mine from back in the day," Chanticleer explained to Joseph via phone when he called to ask for the favor. "His record company cut him loose some years back. You see, Charlie is a bit of a drinker. He found out I had a connection with Teddy and he prevailed upon me to ask you to give him a chance. But I warned him strong I weren't goin to do it if it put you at risk."

"That's no problem, Chanty," Joseph replied. "Have him give us a call and we'll set up a session for him."

Joseph's efforts were rewarded when Bannister's first release, a self-penned blues ballad, "Bare Legged Woman," broke into the national top ten despite some rather risqué lyrics: "*There's a bare legged woman hangin round my door. If she ain't after good lovin I don't know what she's sniffin round here for.*"

The only act to lag behind was the Pixies. Though the girls were now able to make records of their own they couldn't latch on to the right tune to propel them into the spotlight.

♫♫♫♫♫

"You want to sign Janet to a contract?" Joseph asked Leo after one of their regular morning meetings. "Why? She's my wife for crying out loud."

"She's also a songwriter…quite a prolific one I might add. Her name is on records that sell thousands of copies and we have nothing on paper to say that we ever paid her."

"That's because we never have paid her," Joseph said.

"My point exactly."

"She never expected to be paid for her lyrics."

"She's a truly singular woman, I agree. I'm happy for you. But, that won't do for an excuse when our friends from the Internal Revenue Service start looking around at tax time."

Joseph bowed to Leo's expertise in all matters financial and contractual.

"What do we have to do?"

"I'll open a separate bank account in her name. We'll deposit her royalties there. You can tell the little woman she can go out and buy a mink coat."

"She might like to have one of those new color television sets."

"Color television, another fad," Leo scoffed.

The little business in the Bronx had grown into a very big business, bursting at the seams. A change was needed. That change meant a move to Manhattan.

♫♫♫♫♫

The Brill Building was an art deco style office building located at 1619 Broadway near 50th Street. Named for the Brill Brothers, whose clothing store occupied the street level portion of the building. During the Great Depression, few businesses could afford to rent office space. In 1931, three music-publishing companies did so. Many companies followed until the Brill Building became the new Tin Pan Alley, a Mecca for the music business in New York City.

Chanticleer Records divided its operations on two full floors. Leo set up the business offices on one floor to house the accounting and legal departments, as well as executive offices and conference rooms. In time they added a mailroom and a typing pool and a bevy of Artists and Repertoire men who were assigned to discover and develop new talent and work with the acts through the recording process.

Joseph ran the creative department from the other floor. This was the blood and guts of the company. A series of cubicles partitioned off from one another, ran along both sides of the corridor. Each cubicle contained a piano and a table and chairs. Contracted songwriters and arrangers did their work there.

On any given day the halls would be crowded with artists and agents clamoring to get in to see Joseph or any of the other A&R men.

Further along were the rehearsal halls and recording studios. Studios A and B were of average size, equipped with the most up-to-date recording equipment. Studio C was unique. Custom-built by Mickey Christie, it measured thirty-five feet by forty-feet to accommodate a large number of musicians. The room was dubbed, the cave, because of its uncanny echo chamber, achieved this time by professional baffles and soundproofing instead of cardboard boxes and cut up rugs.

The control room was also oversized to house special equipment.

Chanticleer Records was one of the first companies to employ the use of an eight-track tape recorder. This machine captured up to eight sources of sound onto the parallel tracks of a special tape one inch in width. The tracks could then be re-mixed to highlight individual voices or instruments. Musician Les Paul invented the recorder. But it was Atlantic Record's sound engineer, Tom Dowd who modified the console. He replaced the cumbersome three-inch knobs with slide faders capable of moving in a linear fashion enabling engineers to control the input of each track.

♫♫♫♫♫

The record company's success allowed Joseph and Janet to move into a Fifth Avenue apartment closer to the Brill Building. Though she continued to write songs, Janet took great pride in her role as homemaker. She decorated the three-bedroom dwelling with tasteful, modern furnishings in soft earth colors and lots of hanging plants.

As was their custom, the couple discussed the more important matters of their life as they relaxed in each other's arms in their new queen-sized bed.

"The doctor says it probably has to do with all those x-rays you had in the Army after your accident." Janet spoke softly over the top of his head. It wasn't an easy thing to tell him and she felt his body go rigid when he heard the news.

Joseph was sterile.

He hardly remembered going for the test the week prior. Janet had suggested they see a doctor when she had so much trouble conceiving. He *did* remember canceling the appointment to get the results because he was busy at the studio. When he canceled a second time, Janet went alone. She now thought it just as well that he get the news from her.

"I used to joke with the doctors that I was gonna glow in the dark from all those tests." Joseph tried to make light of the situation. "Guess I wasn't far from wrong. I'm sorry sweetheart."

She kissed his head and held him closer. "Shhh, it's alright. It's not your fault."

"I know how disappointed you must be."

"It's only a temporary setback. We can always adopt a child."

"Sure. Sure we can." Joseph perked up at the idea. He turned around to face her. "We can adopt a whole bunch of kids."

Janet smiled at her husband's sudden surge of enthusiasm. "Why don't we start off with just one?"

"Yeah, I suppose that would be best." He reached for her, took her head in his hands and kissed her deeply.

Chapter Twenty-Three:

"The Du-Kanes"

Johnny got to the Vitale apartment a few minutes before six. He liked to be early for practice. They were back singing at Bobby's place. It was better this way, especially since their number had now swelled to five. Bobby's mother never complained. They called their group the Du-Kanes, something Bobby came up with. Johnny figured he'd had the name in the back of his mind for some time.

They sang with three other guys, Marty and Charlie, from the court on Johnny's end of the block. They weren't very talented but capable enough to sing some nonsense syllable background stuff. It bothered Bobby that they were more interested in hot rod cars and sports than singing. Johnny assured him they could be replaced when someone better came along.

The other new member was *very* talented. Tommy Gentile went to school with Johnny. He didn't live in the project but in one of the small private houses bordering the complex. Tommy also had aspirations of becoming a successful singer. There was another reason why Tommy's participation in the group was such a great asset, he owned his own sound system.

A present from his parents on his last birthday, the small public address system consisted of a portable amplifier and speaker, an RCA microphone, and a stand. With Tommy in the mix, the Du-Kanes had a distinct advantage over the other singing groups that seemed to be popping up all over. It also created a problem.

Tommy felt that because he owned the sound system it entitled him act like the leader. He pushed to sing lead on many songs and became quite critical of the others, a fact that didn't sit well with Bobby. Johnny, ever the peacemaker, preached patience for the time being.

Johnny handed Bobby two new forty-five records he'd bought.

"I don't know this one," Bobby said.

"That's Teddy Boyette's new single."

"My sister would dig that one. She's got a picture of the guy hanging up in the other bedroom."

Bobby wasn't a big fan of Teddy's. He found him too twangy and hillbilly. He preferred the tight harmonies of vocal groups like the Five Satins, who sang a ballad called, "In the Still of the Night." Johnny liked those songs as well.

Tommy soon arrived, ushered into Bobby's room by Diane. Marty and Charlie were late as usual. While they waited, Johnny wandered over to the open window that looked out onto Sampson Avenue.

"Our fan club out there?" Bobby asked with a grin.

"Yeah, they sure are."

Their status as singers brought with it increased interest from teenage girls in the project. Bobby liked to play the field. He flirted and made out with several of the neighborhood girls giving him a reputation as a playboy. Johnny was different. He'd caught the eye of Barbara Borelli, a pretty, brown-eyed girl with a budding figure. She lived on the second floor of Johnny's building. Her bedroom window was directly above his. The two spent many late hours talking to one another through their opened windows.

Though they never went out on a real date, they considered themselves going together. They walked to and from school every day, holding hands when they were sure no one would see them. Some Saturdays they'd join their friends and take in a double feature at the Interboro Theater, a place all the kids referred to as the itch. Afterward they'd go to Louis Pizzeria up the block. When they could, they'd sneak up to the roof landing of the apartment building to do some necking and petting.

Whenever the group got together, Barbara and a few other girls walked down the block and took up position against the bumper of a car parked outside Bobby's building. There, they could listen to the singing coming came through the speaker of Tommy's PA system.

Marty and Charlie had joined the others. They warmed up with an up tempo number they'd been doing for a long time. Tommy took charge, suggesting a song where he sang lead. He sauntered forward to hog the microphone. He snapped his fingers to indicate the proper tempo. Like obedient puppies, Marty and Charlie took up the beat. Johnny and Bobby exchanged annoyed glances before doing the same.

Tommy sang his tenor part. Bobby handled the background falsetto and Johnny alternately covered the baritone and bass line. When they reached the bridge of the song, a point where all five voices were to blend in tight harmony, the result was instead, badly off key. All five of them stopped immediately.

"That really sucked," Marty observed.

Bobby and Charlie burst out laughing which angered Tommy. He felt someone was deliberately sabotaging his song.

"What was that all about, man?" Tommy demanded.

"Don't look at me," Marty responded as he pointed to Charlie, "He's the one messed up."

"How much you wanna bet I didn't mess up?" Charlie flared out.

"I never liked that song anyway," Bobby added.

Tommy steamed. "Is that why you screwed up, out of spite?"

"Me?" Bobby quickly defended himself. "I didn't screw up and I don't do shit like that for spite. I ain't no kid!"

"All right you guys, cool it," Johnny halted the uprising. "It's no big deal, man, we'll just do it over again."

The tension was broken when the door to the bedroom opened slightly and Diane poked her head inside. She was frightened and shaking.

"Bobby, you better get out here quick. There's a cop at the front door."

The boys froze for a moment, "Did you let him in?" Bobby asked.

"No. I was too scared. I just saw him through the peephole."

Pushing his way passed the others Bobby hurried down the hall. Johnny followed, and Diane brought up the rear. The others remained in the bedroom.

"I'll get mom," Diane said, stopping at the other bedroom door. Bobby called back over his shoulder. "No stupid, leave her alone."

It was too late. She was already inside. There was another loud knock on the front door. Bobby muttered a curse word as he moved forward to answer it.

When he opened the door he found a tall, solidly built colored man dressed in the uniform of a Housing Authority Police Officer standing in the hallway.

"Something wrong?" Bobby asked.

"Are your parents home?" The policeman asked politely.

"My mother's asleep."

"I'm afraid I'm going to have to speak to her."

"Look, man, she's not feeling well. Can't you just tell me what you want?"

Bobby had no problem cracking wise with the housing cop. They didn't command the same respect real NYPD cops did. They were little more than private security guards hired by the project to patrol the grounds. They wrote summons for stupid violations like walking on the grass, riding a bicycle on the walkways or bouncing a rubber ball off the walls of a building. They weren't armed and didn't have the power to arrest anyone.

The young people in the project referred to them as "hip pockets" because the back pocket of their uniform trousers bulged from the thick summons book each of them carried.

Mrs. Vitale's voice called shrilly from back down the hall.

"Oh my God! What's wrong here? Robert...Robert, tell me what's wrong?" She was shaking and crying by the time she reached the front door.

"Good evening, ma'am. I'm sorry to have to bother you," the officer said.

"Oh, Robert don't leave the officer standing in the hallway where everyone can hear our business." She then addressed the officer directly. "Please come in."

"Thank you ma'am." After stepping inside the apartment, he removed his cap. Mrs. Vitale led everyone back to the kitchen. There, she had a seat and nervously lit a cigarette.

"Now, what seems to be the trouble officer?" she asked sending a thin stream of white smoke into the air.

"Well, ma'am, we've had complaints from some of the other tenants about all the noise."

"Noise? You mean the boys singing?"

"Yes, ma'am the singing, and the loud music."

"What?" Bobby responded angrily. "Who's complaining?"

"That doesn't make any difference, son. All that matters is that the office got several calls about loud, disturbing music coming from this apartment a couple of times now."

"Disturbing?" Bobby's mother sobbed through her cigarette smoke. "My son and his friends are just having some harmless fun. This is his home for goodness sake."

"I know how you must feel, ma'am," hip pockets said with what seemed like genuine regret. "Believe me, I'd prefer them doing stuff like this than to be out in the streets getting into mischief. But like I said, the other tenants…"

"What about us?" Bobby lashed out. "We're tenants. We pay rent for this dump too?"

"Listen, why don't you kids just call it a night and maybe next time you get together you can keep the noise down a little?"

"Yeah, sure… we'll whisper the songs."

The housing cop realized there was nothing he could say that was going to have much effect on this teenage boy, but he was concerned about the mother.

"Ma'am, try not to be too upset. Maybe something could be

worked out."

"I realize this is none of your doing officer." She told him as she slowly regained her composure.

"I'll be going now, and again, I'm sorry for this, folks."

"Goodnight officer," she said to him.

Diane showed the policeman to the door.

"Why don't you go back to bed, ma?" Bobby suggested.

"I'm too upset to sleep. I'm going to have a cup of coffee and sit up for a bit." Bobby felt pretty sure she meant she needed a drink. With his friends still back in the bedroom it wasn't a good time to argue with her.

With a tilt of his head he signaled for Johnny to follow him back to his room. The other three members of the group sat sullen and silent. Tommy had already packed up his gear.

"I guess we're done for tonight?" he asked.

Johnny nodded in reply.

"Man, I'd love to know who put the cops on us," Bobby exploded. He paced the floor, and then pounded the top of his dresser with his fist.

"What's it matter?" Marty threw in.

"I'll bet it was old man D'Ambrosio! Man if I was sure it was him I'd put a baseball bat through the windshield of that piece of shit car he drives," Bobby threatened.

"Yeah, and what happens when they drag your silly ass off to jail?" Johnny admonished his hotheaded friend.

"They gotta catch me first."

Johnny knew there was a bigger problem. "The thing is that now we gotta find somewhere else to practice."

With three of them living in the project, they were sure to encounter a similar fate if they sang in any of the other apartments. That left Tommy. When he didn't volunteer a possible solution, Bobby flat out asked him.

"How about you, Tommy, you got a basement in your house, right?"

The question caught the youth by surprise.

"Yeah, yeah sure. But my old man has his workshop and tools in the basement. He tinkers around down there a lot after work. He says it relaxes him. But I'll ask about it."

It was the type of answer Bobby expected of him. "Yeah, why don't you do that?"

"Okay, just let me know when we're going to sing again." Tommy seemed in a big hurry to get going. "Hey Marty, you and Charlie want to give me a hand with my stuff?"

"Sure, man. C'mon, Charlie let's split." The two of them helped Tommy gather his equipment and the three of them were ready to go.

"I'll walk you out," Bobby said before leading them down the hallway making sure they didn't linger near the kitchen and see his mother drinking. He seemed calm when he got back to the bedroom but Johnny knew he was still upset.

"We'll find another place to practice," Johnny assured him.

"Where, under an overpass somewhere?"

"There are lots of guys singin out on street corners all over the place, you know that."

"None of those guys got a chance. They ain't serious like we are. They're like the three assholes we sing with. None of them cares if we ever sing again."

"Marty and Charlie, yeah, you're right about them. But Tommy cares. He wants to make it big just like we do."

"Well, between you and me I wouldn't care if we lost him too." Bobby's remark bothered Johnny.

"The guy's a good singer. You gotta give him credit for that."

"He's too fucking bossy, Johnny. He's tried to take over the group ever since he joined up with us, pushes to sing lead on every song. We can sing rings around that guy, man."

"Maybe you can, but me? I'm not so sure."

"You ain't giving up on me are you Johnny?"

"No man, no way. I'm hooked. Just you wait. Our day will come. But have a little patience where Tommy is concerned. He could be a big help to us.

"I'm not real big in the patience department."

"No shit, Sherlock."

The two boys laughed

"You wanna stay?" Bobby asked.

"Nah." Johnny saw this as a chance to spend more time with his girlfriend. "Barbara is waiting outside. Why don't you come and hang out with us? Donna's with her." Donna had been Bobby's girl at one time. "You know she still digs you, man."

Bobby shook his head. "I'm not in the mood to deal with chicks tonight. You go ahead."

"You sure?"

"I'll just look after my old lady, make sure she doesn't get too plastered."

Johnny issued a short, unanswered good-bye to Bobby's mother when they walked by the kitchen on his way out of the apartment.

"Don't do anything I wouldn't do man." Bobby warned Johnny letting him out of the front door. Johnny smiled leeringly at his friend.

Bobby waited by the window in his room. He watched as Johnny met with the group of three girls waiting outside. He knew he'd tell them about what happened. Bobby lit a cigarette and flipped the extinguished match out into the night. He took a long drag and sent a funnel of smoke into the air that quickly disappeared.

From this vantage point he could look out beyond the suspension towers of the Bronx Whitestone Bridge. He saw the skyscraping buildings on the east side of Manhattan miles distant yet easily discernable by floor after floor of illuminating lights. That was where the answer to all his dreams of fame and fortune lay. The record companies, radio stations, bars and nightclubs where professional performers sang every night.

In daydreams, he envisioned the Du-Kanes right in the middle of all the bright lights and furious action. They would all be rich, rich enough for him to buy a house in the suburbs where Diane could have a big dog, romp around a huge backyard and swim in their very own pool. His mother could afford a good doctor, get well and live her life to the fullest.

It was all right there, right outside his bedroom window, just out of reach – for now.

♫♫♫♫♫

Barbara Borelli was happy that the housing cop put an early end to the practice. The idea that the Du-Kanes were becoming popular bothered her. She worried other girls might chase after Johnny. She longed for a time after they graduated high school and Johnny would have to go out and get a real job. Then he'd forget all this singing stuff and settle down with her to raise a family. She would do everything she could to hold on to him.

After they reached the court, Donna and Marianne, the two girls walking along with them, giggled to one another.

"C'mon Marianne," Donna kidded, "Let's leave these two love-birds alone. Johnny won't let anything bad happen to her."

When the girls were gone, Johnny and Barbara sat together on a wooden bench in front of the buildings. Johnny was quiet, still upset about the abrupt end to the rehearsal. Barbara was sure she could brighten his mood.

"I copped the key to the carriage room from my mom's pocket book," she whispered.

"You did?" Johnny was surprised. "What'd you do that for?

"What do you think for, numb nuts?" She punched his arm.

"Holy shit. That's naughty."

"C'mon, let's go."

The basement under every building in the project was accessed by a long ramp that sloped downward from street level. Inside were several large rooms mostly off limits to tenants. There, the boilers for heat and hot water were located, so was the incinerator room where the trash was burned. Adult tenants were issued keys to a basement room they called the carriage room. Tenants used it as storage space for carriages, baby strollers and bicycles so they wouldn't have to keep them in their apartments. The basement also served as a civil defense shelter. In the event of a nuclear attack, tenants could gather there for protection.

Once inside, Johnny and Barbara were assured of privacy but they'd have to be careful not to be seen. They waited at the top of the ramp behind a brick wall about waist high. When the coast was clear they scooted down the ramp on the balls of their feet. Certain they hadn't been detected they entered the basement and closed the door behind them.

The cellar was in total darkness and smelled bad. They felt their way along a cinderblock wall estimating the distance to the carriage room door. Using the key she'd swiped from her mother, Barbara unlocked the door. They both slipped inside. There were no windows in the carriage room so it was safe to flick the switch turning on a bank of overhead fluorescent lights.

There, amid the clutter of stored possessions a disassembled baby's crib and mattress rested against one wall. The mattress would suit their purposes quite nicely.

"Let's lay that mattress out on the floor," Johnny said. "But be careful honey there might big some big ass cock roaches or rats down here."

Barbara scowled at him. "Johnnyyyy!"

He took her in his arms and kissed her. They fumbled with one another's clothing as they eased themselves down to the floor in a naked mass of flesh. The mattress provided enough comfort to allow them to fully concentrate on what they were doing. Barbara was prepared to go all the way. She wanted this to be a moment she'd always remember.

Their young emotions overwhelmed them. They explored one another as never before. Johnny positioned himself between Barbara's legs. She hesitated long enough to ask.

"You won't forget to pull out, right?"

"Don't worry baby, I won't," he assured her.

Chapter Twenty-Four:

"The Community Center"

The weeks that passed yielded no solution in finding another place for the Du-Kanes to practice. They tried using the loading dock out behind the Peter Reeves Supermarket where Bobby worked. City cops chased them out of there on several occasions. A brute of an Irish cop named Flaherty promised the next time he caught them, someone was going to get run in.

This second brush with the law proved too much for Marty and Charlie and both boys quit the group. Tommy also became frustrated because they couldn't use his sound system. He often came up with some lame excuse for missing the now infrequent sessions.

Summer was almost over. It would soon be too cold to practice anywhere outdoors. A bit of luck came their way when a new kid moved into the court. Kenny Liebermann was a tall, lean kid about a year younger than both Johnny and Bobby. He had a deep bass voice and was invited to join the Du-Kanes almost immediately. He had a friend from school, Hector Torres, a wiry, light skinned Puerto Rican who also loved to sing. After coming around once or twice, he too was asked to come aboard. The new voices fit well into the mix though Tommy offered more than a mild protest about singing with Hector.

"I really don't dig the idea of singing with some spic," he complained.

Bobby made it plain to him that neither he nor Johnny cared about his bigoted opinion. Hector remained and they were five again.

♫♫♫♫♫

Hip pockets returned to the Vitale apartment. After assuring Mrs. Vitale that the boys weren't in any kind of trouble he left a written message asking that Bobby and the rest of the group meet him at the project's Community Center Building later in the afternoon.

The Community Center was located on the ground floor of a seven-story apartment building on the opposite end of the project several blocks from the court. The building also housed the rent and administrative offices of the housing project. It provided an indoor facility where tenants and their families could congregate for recreational purposes. There was a large indoor gymnasium area with a hardwood floor where basketball backboards and hoops were set up. The area could also be outfitted with a net for volleyball. Beyond a cinderblock wall at the far end of the gym stood an open area with cafeteria type tables and chairs. Teens and smaller children, played board games, ate snacks or simply sat around talking.

When the Du-Kanes arrived for their meeting, several young girls gathered at the tables. They set up a record player and cleared an area where they could dance.

Hip pockets showed up with another man, a schoolteacher type, dressed in a tie and sweater. He wore glasses and carried a clipboard with papers on it.

"I'm glad you boys could make it," hip pockets greeted them. "This here is Mr. Fillmore. He runs the Community Center."

Johnny shook the man's hand, the others merely waved or grunted a greeting his way.

"Glad to meet you guys," Mr. Fillmore said in an authoritative yet friendly way. "Officer Davis here tells me you boys have a bit of a problem? If you follow us downstairs, there's something we'd like to show you."

With Fillmore leading the way, they walked through a doorway to a metal staircase, taking them to the lower level of the building. There, they waited while Mr. Fillmore used one of the many keys on his key ring to unlock a door that opened up onto a long corridor with rooms on both sides. He led them part way along the corridor before stopping to unlock another metal door. He flipped on the light switch to reveal a small classroom. They went inside.

"We use these rooms for arts and crafts and stuff like that for kids after school," hip pockets explained. He sat on one of the several wooden tables placed around the room. "It ain't much, but I think it'll serve your purpose. You can use this room to practice in from four to six every weeknight. That way you won't be bothering any of the other tenants. All you gotta do is keep it clean and not wreck anything. That means you pick up your cigarette butts after you... you don't bring any girls down here...and you never do no drinkin, ever. You understand?"

The five young boys were stunned.

"What's the catch?" Bobby asked.

"Fuckin Bobby, why do you always have to question everything?" Tommy chastised him.

"That's all right," hip pockets responded. "I can dig where he's coming from." He moved to the other side of the room and addressed Bobby directly. "You can't quite figure out why some colored cop would want to do something for you and your friends, right?

Bobby shrugged his shoulders in reply.

"Fact is your mama didn't lie that first time I came to your place. You boys coulda' been out getting into some real trouble if it wasn't for your singing. Chasing after you for that would only make my job harder and I got no desire to do that. So, I asked Mr. Fillmore if you could use one of these classrooms."

"Officer Davis went to bat for you boys," Mr. Fillmore felt obliged to say. "We don't usually let anyone use these rooms in the evening. You can talk it over amongst yourselves, but in my opinion you'd be foolish to turn it down. We'll be upstairs in my office when you're ready. Just remember we close up at six."

With that Fillmore and hip pockets left them alone in the classroom. The boys waited until they were sure the two adults had indeed gone back upstairs before any of them let out a breath. Bobby broke the silence by clapping his hands together has hard as he could. The sound reverberated all around them.

"You think there's very much for us to talk about?" he asked.

As Fillmore and the housing cop named Davis sat drinking coffee in the Community Center's office, the faint sounds of singing filtered up from the classrooms below.

"Sounds like them boys are gonna take you up on your offer," Davis said.

"You know, they sound pretty good."

"And they'll get better as they go along."

"You think they appreciate what you've done for them?" Fillmore asked.

"They're a bunch of teenage boys. They wouldn't let on even if they did."

♫♫♫♫♫

The opportunity to practice every night at the Community Center paid off. The Du-Kanes grew into a tight knit, cohesive singing group. Bobby worked out some simple dance moves giving them a professional look. Kenny proved to have additional talent when it came to arranging some of their material. He'd come up with some older standard tune and adapt it into a distinctive new arrangement only the Du-Kanes featured.

They expanded their domain by singing at local school dances and parties. They were paid for some of these performances, not a lot but enough to buy matching yellow button down shirts, thin black ties and vests to wear when they sang. One of the neighborhood girls took pictures of the group. Soon, lots of kids had photographs of the Du-Kanes posed on the rocks at Ferry Point Park beneath the Whitestone Bridge.

Barbara's jealous worry turned into a legitimate concern. The group took part in a neighborhood Battle of the Bands, competition put on by a local movie theater. Several groups performed, without pay, in between showings of a horror movie. The Du-Kanes won the contest easily. They were all excited about the first prize, the chance to cut a demo for a record company in the Brill Building in Manhattan.

This led a confrontation between Tommy and the others.

"I want it made official. I'm the lead singer of this group nobody else."

His demands shocked the others.

"Are you fucking crazy or what?" Bobby asked in total disbelief.

"I'm the best singer out of all of us, we all know that."

"Man, you really are something," Bobby came right back at him. "We all do our part to make this group work."

While the rest of them kept silent, Tommy kept on the offensive.

"You really think you guys would ever get anywhere without me? If those demos we cut pan out, that company is gonna sign us. We need a leader. I figure I'm it."

Johnny couldn't keep quiet any longer.

"Hard work got us where we are, Tommy. It isn't fair to put anyone ahead of the group."

"What would you do if I decided to quit?" Tommy threatened.

"Know what? You don't gotta worry about quitting. Bobby and me started this group. We get to say what's what and why…you're out Tommy!"

His actions brought startled looks from the others. Bobby's became a proud smile… Tommy's, an open mouthed stare.

"You're joking, right?" Tommy wasn't yelling anymore.

"No joke, man. You're out of the group." Johnny stood firm.

"You other guys feel the same?" Tommy's question went unanswered. Even Bobby remained silent. Tommy hung his head but lingered for one last parting shot. "You guys are gonna be real sorry about this."

Tommy stormed out of the practice room leaving the others in stunned silence.

"I can't believe you fired the fucking guy," Bobby said.

"Do you think I did the right thing?" Johnny wondered out loud.

"Absolutely," Kenny responded.

"It was bound to happen sooner or later, man," Hector added.

They sat and discussed their situation deciding to eliminate some of the songs Tommy sang. Practice sessions were now spent re-working the harmonies with the remaining four voices. Johnny and Bobby were strong tenors, quite capable of alternating lead vocals. Bobby would add a dynamic falsetto to support the lead voice, above the background harmony or to provide fade-outs and trail offs for many ballads. Hector supplemented the background harmony with whichever of the tenors wasn't singing lead. Kenny's strong bass line acted as part of the harmony running under the lead voice. They were back on track.

Chapter Twenty-Five:

"Tragedy"

In the summer of 1956, a young disc jockey in Philadelphia named Dick Clark became the host of a televised afternoon dance party show called "Bandstand." It proved successful in part because of Clark's uncanny understanding of his teenage audience and his non-threatening demeanor. The show featured local boys and girls, neatly dressed and well-behaved dancing to records he played. His sponsors sold toothpaste, hair cream and acne medication. Kids watched the show religiously to see the latest fashion, learn the newest dances and hear their favorite singers and groups.

Many featured entertainers went on to even greater popularity after being on the show. The formula worked so well that one year later, the ABC television network took the show national. It premiered under a new name, "American Bandstand," and aired five afternoons a week from three o'clock to four thirty. Clark, realizing the importance of his national broadcasts, went to great expense to snare Teddy Boyette as one of his first guest stars.

The singer thrilled the audience by lip-synching his way through his current number one single and previewing his next upcoming release.

Afterward, Clark conducted an interview seated next to Teddy on a grandstand bench located in the middle of the studio audience. Girls giggled with excitement at being so close to their teenage idol.

"Teddy, you are without a doubt the most popular rock and roll singer in America today. But, how do you feel about the other guys, your competition, so to speak, Elvis and Buddy Holly and the others whose style is so similar to your own?"

"Well, I don't lay claim to owning this type of music." Teddy hated being asked to compare himself to other popular singers. He worried his answer might make him appear conceited or snobbish. But, he was polished enough to know that if he simply flashed a snarly, sexy grin, he could stall long enough to come up with an answer that wouldn't embarrass him.

"Those other fellas love rock and roll just like I do. I listen to their songs and I enjoy them just like any other fan."

"Now, Elvis is making movies. They say he's going to be a big star. Is that what the future holds for you, Teddy, you going to make movies?" Clark asked.

This was a much easier question for Teddy.

"No. Elvis is welcome to all that as far as I'm concerned."

The host and the studio audience erupted into laughter. Dick Clark had one more question.

"Okay, no movies for you. But, seriously Teddy, where would you like to be in say… five or ten years?"

Teddy thought for a moment, no stalling sexy smiles now, just a straightforward, honest answer. "Well, if I'm lucky enough that my records are still selling, I'd like to keep on singing I suppose. But I would like to be able to slow things down a might, not have to work as hard as I do now. That way I could have more time for myself, settle down, raise a family." Then, came his famous smile. "I guess I'd just like to have a normal life, if I could."

After his guest shot on American Bandstand Teddy went back on the road for a short series of shows in Pennsylvania, Ohio and Indiana.

♫♫♫♫♫

Leo received a Western Union telegram from Cap that required Joseph's approval. He found him in "the cave" laboring over a cut for Charles Bannister's new Blues album.

"Cap wants to extend Teddy's tour a few days and come back through Florida." He handed the wire to Joseph who read it for himself.

"Does he realize Teddy needs to be back in town for the Sullivan show on the nineteenth?"

"He does. He's pretty sure he can do it if he charters a plane."

"A plane? You okay with that?"

"Teddy's numbers are down a bit in Florida. A few shows there can only help business."

"Okay. Tell him to set everything up. But he has to make sure he has Teddy back here in time for the Ed Sullivan show."

♫♫♫♫♫

At seven in the morning, the phone rang in the Rabinowitz' apartment. Half asleep, Joseph rolled over to the nightstand on his side of the bed. He picked up the receiver.

"Hello?" he said in a half stupor.

It was Leo. He offered no greeting. "Teddy's plane has been reported overdue in Sarasota."

"What?" Joseph sat up like a shot. He really didn't need to hear the words again, but he did need a few seconds to clear his head of sleep and gather his thoughts. "Is there bad weather down there, maybe the plane got diverted?"

"Clear skies all across the state and they've lost radio contact."

"Where are you?"

"On my way out the door to the office."

"I'll meet you there as soon as I can."

Joseph hung up the phone. He rolled over to find Janet awake, lying on her side, looking at him. He quickly relayed the bare details of the call, and then leapt out of bed. Janet rolled onto her stomach, folded her arms under her head and lay motionless, too numb to react in any other way. Minutes later Joseph stopped by the bed long enough to kiss her.

"I'll call you as soon as I know anything more."

Once she heard the door close and lock behind him, the first tears leaked from her eyes, and trickled down her cheeks until they were absorbed in the fabric of her pillowcase.

By the time Joseph got to the office, there was more grim news.

According to a radio bulletin out of Florida, a witness reported seeing a small plane on fire and trailing smoke go down in the Everglades earlier in the morning. The pieces of a disastrous puzzle began to fall into place.

"Where are we getting our information from?" Joseph asked.

Tom Merriman, the company's chief A&R man answered. "Harry Reed, he's the morning man for a station in Fort Lauderdale, he's been following Teddy's tour. He was at the airport when the plane took off. When he heard it was overdue he contacted us. I called Leo first and he told me he'd give you the news."

"Okay. Get back to that guy. Tell him to stay on it. Set up an open line if you have to. I don't want any more bad news leaking out."

"Yes sir," the A&R man replied.

A short time later, Leo arrived from Scarsdale. Other employees were arriving at the offices. The ominous mood they found made it impossible to work. Many gathered around in front of their cubicles or offices hoping for a miracle.

As the morning turned into an agonizing afternoon more news filtered in, none of it good. Newswires around the country had picked up the story. Those that weren't getting information from Florida flooded the Brill Building switchboard for some kind of statement.

Joseph ordered the publicity department to draft something. By late afternoon the company issued a statement:

At this time, we at Chanticleer Records can only say that we have no additional or independent information regarding the tragic events unfolding in Florida. Our prayers and hopes are that rescue teams will locate the plane and survivors. We ask that all of Teddy's fans and friends join us in that hope."

Those words were true at four o'clock but by five they were being contradicted by a television report being broadcast live from the scene in Naples, Florida. The entire staff huddled around a TV in the reception area. They watched the image of a tired, somber looking Florida State Trooper as he was being interviewed.

"The area where the plane was seen going down is in a thick swamp which is almost totally inaccessible except by airboat or other small water craft. We do have a couple of helicopters from the naval base searching from the air but once it gets dark those efforts will be severely hampered."

"So you don't think any survivors will be found until after daylight tomorrow?" the interviewer asked.

The State Trooper took a deep breath. "Mister, that plane has been down in the swamp all day. We have reports that it was on fire before it crashed. But we also know it landed in the water 'cause there's no smoke plume to help us find it. Now between the fire, the impact and the snakes and gators…well I don't hold out much hope we'll find anybody alive in there at all."

"Jesus Christ," Joseph heard someone say from behind him.

Those were the only words anyone uttered out loud. The gruesome images painted by the State Trooper's comments sickened everyone. Some female staff members sobbed. Others had seen and heard enough and wandered away from the area.

Joseph buried his head in his hands but his shoulders and body shook with emotion. Leo was able to hold things together and finally got Joseph to go back to his office. He remained there with the door closed. Leo had members of the publicity department station themselves at the elevator banks with orders not allow any members of the press access to the offices for any reason whatsoever.

A couple of staff members monitored the television until the networks signed off for the night. There was no further information to learn. Sometime in the middle of the night, the open phone line to Florida was disconnected. No one sought to re-establish it.

Janet waited up until three o'clock in the morning. Joseph never called. She'd seen the interview on television so she wasn't surprised. She cried herself to sleep some time later.

It rained all that next day in New York City. "Heaven's tears for Teddy Boyette," some quick thinking radio personality called it. Later in the afternoon, in a nationally televised broadcast, a Federal Aviation Agency official issued a statement.

"At approximately five-thirty yesterday morning, a twin engine Apollo HP-30 charter aircraft crashed in the Florida Everglades at a point some twenty miles south of the city of Belle Grade. There were no survivors. Taking into consideration eyewitness accounts of a ball of fire and a trail of thick, black smoke falling from the sky, our preliminary ruling is that mechanical problems or engine failure caused the crash. Burned remains found at the crash site indicate that all on board were killed either before or directly upon impact. While no positive identification of the remains could be made, an official at the flight's point of origin, verifies those on board as being: Mr. Elias Bowie, age thirty-five, a pilot for the Capitol Air Charter Service; Mr. Teddy Boyette, age twenty, rock and roll recording artist; Mr. Marlon "Cap" Stewart, age forty-five, Mr. Boyette's personal manager and confidant; Michael Farmer, age twenty-two, Peter Simms, age twenty-one and David Coleman, also twenty-one, all of whom were musicians in Mr. Boyette's band."

It was a clear, concise report but it didn't begin to scratch the surface of the impact the event had on the youth of the nation.

Memorial services and candlelight vigils were held in big cities and small towns everywhere. Teddy's parents and Chanticleer flew to New York to be among the celebrities, dignitaries, and fans that viewed an empty, closed coffin at a wake held at the Frank E. Campbell Funeral Home on Manhattan's Upper East Side.

A huge throng gathered both inside and outside St. Patrick's Cathedral on the day of his funeral. Afterward, the coffin was loaded aboard a train at Grand Central Station for the trip back to Kentucky. Thousands lined the railroad's right of way to watch the train as it went by.

The coffin was buried on the crest of a knoll on the Boyette's farm. But, every night thereafter, groups of teenagers would sneak onto the property and sit vigil at the grave. They'd light candles, leave flowers, hand written notes or cards as well as dozens of stuffed teddy bears. Local police feared the possibility that someone might go so far as to desecrate the grave. They managed to convince the family to move the coffin to a more secure cemetery in Radcliff. The town donated a marble headstone in honor of its favorite son.

For Joseph and Janet, the mourning period following Teddy's death proved long and difficult. Janet was unable to write and Joseph spent an inordinate amount of time away from the studio. She overheard one side of a telephone conversation Joseph had one morning. She approached her husband after he angrily hung up the receiver.

"Leo?" She asked, making an assumption, which proved erroneous.

"No, that was Mickey, reminding me I have a business to run."

"I always said you were indispensable," Janet kidded him. She could alibi her own actions but if Joseph shut down, it could prove disastrous for a great many people. "It's been two weeks already, Joseph."

"First, your brother Danny and now Teddy. Janet, I'm twenty-two years old and I've lost the two closest friends I've ever had."

"There's nothing you could have done about any of that."

His sense of guilt went very deep. "Maybe we worked him too hard, pushed him into doing those extra shows in Florida."

"Singing was Teddy's life. He loved doing it and millions of people loved hearing him. He was more than just a *singing* star. He was like a *real* star burning bright in the sky until one day he exploded and became a comet hurtling across space with a sparkling light trailing behind. Then in a flash he burned out and was gone. I think that's the way I'd like to remember Teddy. And, you know what happens when a comet burns out don't you? You search the sky looking for another one. Where will you find your next comet, Joseph?"

♫♫♫♫♫

On October 5th, 1957, nearly thirty million television viewers received shocking and disturbing news from Douglas Edwards, the even-toned anchorman for the "CBS Evening News."

The Russians had launched the world's first artificial space satellite, Sputnik, which beeped its way in an orbit around the earth every ninety-eight minutes. The spacecraft's innocent sounding name freely translated as "fellow traveler." The ominous reality of it was that the rocket used to propel Sputnik into space was originally designed to carry a nuclear warhead.

The Soviets had created an Intercontinental Ballistic Missile, capable of delivering a bomb halfway around the world in less than an hour.

Democratic Senator Lyndon Johnson from Texas aptly described the situation. "Soon the Soviets will be dropping bombs on us from space like kids drop rocks on cars from freeway overpasses."

It became the top priority of the U.S. government to surpass the Russians in developing a space program. Several months later, the National Aeronautics and Space Administration was established. NASA began a long-term civilian and military space research program. A new era dawned. Many referred to it as the race for space. Others dubbed it the Arms race.

Chapter Twenty-Six:

"The Big Break"

The recording industry grew to such huge proportions that a nation-wide organization made up of performers, musicians, recording engineers and other professionals became necessary. The National Academy of Recording Arts and Sciences formed with its members dedicated to improving and developing the state of the recording industry.

Another trade organization, the Recording Industry Association of America, known by the initials RIAA, began in the collection, administration and distribution of royalties based on the certification of national sales for single records and albums released in the United States.

Early in 1958, the organization decided to present an award in the form of a gold record to any song selling one million copies. On March 14th, Perry Como's single release "Catch A Falling Star" became the first record ever to receive that award.

Five days later, as a result of the draft, Elvis Presley entered the U.S. Army.

♫♫♫♫♫

Bobby had looked for Johnny all over the neighborhood. He had big news. He finally found him leaning against the fender of a car parked outside the Pizza Shop on Tremont Avenue. From the way he stood, Bobby figured he'd been listening to the radio that day too.

Johnny hardly looked up as Bobby approached.

"Hey, man, I guess you heard?" Bobby asked.

"Heard...heard what?" Johnny answered, leaning back, laying the palms of his hands on the hood of the Lincoln for support.

"The song...on the radio."

"I don't know what the fuck you're talking about, man."

"Tommy Gentile has a song on the radio." The news clearly surprised Johnny. He looked at Bobby and shook his head. "They played it a little while ago on WABC. I didn't catch the name of it but I heard the deejay say Tommy's name sure as shit."

Though neither of them knew the details yet, Tommy had somehow come to the attention of Alexis Records. He cut some demos, signed a contract and soon released a single called "I Was Wrong." The tune was just now breaking onto the charts. Of course there'd been considerable help in getting it there. Pressure tactics exerted on jukebox companies to put the record in their machines even though radio airplay didn't warrant such a move. Deejays were "encouraged" to play the record often. Record stores were overstocked with Tommy's release and other Alexis' titles along with the warning that no returns would be accepted.

"I'm surprised he hasn't come around to brag about it," Bobby spewed, "Man, if he does that I'll knock a few of his teeth down his throat. We'll see how pretty he sings after that." When he realized his tirade had no effect on Johnny, he guessed something else was bothering him. He leaned on the fender next to his buddy. "Hey, man if you didn't know about Tommy's record what is it that's got you so bummed out?"

"Barbara's knocked up," Johnny's voice quaked with his admission.

"Holy shit!" Bobby's words tumbled out of his mouth one syllable at a time. He stood straight up as though he wanted to run off someplace. He went only a few feet before turning to face his troubled friend. "I thought you said the two of you were being real careful?"

"Well, I guess we weren't careful enough."

The ease with which the two of them were able to steal away to the basement and have sex made them careless. A miss-calculation on Barbara's part proved disastrous.

"What the fuck are you guys gonna do now?" Bobby asked.

"There's not much choice is there? I gotta do the right thing here."

"Get married? Shit, you guys don't finish high school till June!"

"I guess Barbara's gonna have to drop out. But me, I gotta finish. I won't get any kind of job without a diploma."

There it was, a reality neither of them wanted to discuss would soon play out. Bobby tried to be supportive but he found himself giving in to his selfish motives. The responsibilities of marriage, fatherhood and a full time job probably meant the end of Johnny's singing career and the end of a dream the two of them shared.

In the days that followed, Johnny and Barbara bore the brunt of the repercussions their actions heaped upon them. Disappointment, shame, and anger rocked both households, as did pointless lectures about how they'd both ruined their lives.

Barbara felt guilt, guilt she'd never reveal to anyone. It wasn't that she got pregnant on purpose, planned it, or plotted it. But guilt because she'd long ago decided that she didn't care one way or the other.

Johnny suffered deep regret. His life had taken a drastic u-turn. He was forbidden to continue with the *nonsense* of becoming a singer.

Barbara dropped out of school. She and Johnny were married before a justice of the peace. They continued to live apart, with their families, at least until Johnny graduated from high school and got a steady job.

♫♫♫♫♫

"You promised that song to us, Joseph," Evie fumed when Joseph told them that he'd cut a song called, "When She's Around," from the session the Pixies were about to begin. Evie liked the song, all the girls did.

They sat in Joseph's office discussing the matter. Both Roberta and Althea were uneasy with the way Evie spoke to him.

"I don't *promise* songs to anyone, Evie," Joseph shot back at his singer, "I assigned it to you. But now I've had second thoughts. Besides, I don't have to explain myself to you. I'm the boss, remember?"

The company had released a string singles by the Pixies but none of them came close to breaking into the top ten. It was difficult for a female group. A vast percentage of the record buying public was girls and they bought records made by boys.

"So what are we supposed to do, sing background for the rest of our career? Settle for five words on the back of everybody else's album, 'background vocals by the Pixies?' I don't like being kept in the background, Joseph, singing or otherwise."

That remark was most scathing. "Would you girls give Evie and me a few minutes?"

Roberta and Althea rose without a word and walked out of the office.

"What was that last crack supposed to mean?" Joseph asked, not really needing an answer. Evie just shrugged her shoulders and looked away. "All that was a mistake," he continued, "we agreed about that."

It went back to the time when he found out he was sterile. His feelings of inadequacy, pride and ego got the better of him. He needed to prove something to himself. In a weak moment, he strayed.

Evie was a logical choice and a willing participant in his indiscretion. But, she had an ulterior motive, her career. When it became apparent that Evie might use their brief affair as leverage in a business sense, he ended it. He hoped that wasn't what she was doing now.

"Don't worry Joseph, I'm not going to blackmail you or anything.

I'm upset about the song, that's all."

"It's just a song. There'll be others."

But it wasn't *just* a song and Joseph knew it. The lyrics were the best Janet had written in a long time. Harmony was a vital key and a girl group wasn't going to cut it. Neither were any of the male groups currently in the Chanticleer stable. He had to find fresh, new voices.

Joseph and Curtis spent long hours mulling over dozens of recent demos. Part way through the stack Joseph heard something that caught his attention.

"There's something about this group…who are they?"

Curtis referred to the information sheet attached to the sleeve of the demo recording. "Four guys from the Bronx. They call themselves the Du-Kanes. They won a battle of the bands contest a while back. Cutting the demo was first prize."

"The Bronx, our old stomping grounds, bring them in."

♫♫♫♫♫

The Du-Kanes had vivid recollections of their previous visit to the Brill Building. Filled with the excitement of winning first prize in the local talent contest, they were certain this was their big break for stardom. However, upon their arrival, they were treated with little fanfare or importance.

A young, assistant producer barely older than themselves rushed them into a rehearsal hall where they sat in an assembly line with four or five other groups of singers, each awaiting their turn to cut demos. They recorded three takes of a popular ballad accompanied by piano and a drummer. They were sent home with the promise that someone from the company would contact them if there were any interest.

That was the last they heard about it, until now.

Bobby, Kenny and Hector sat huddled together in a booth in

Jim and Nellie's ice cream parlor on Tremont Avenue, the jukebox blared behind them. Bobby kept peering out the plate glass window into the dwindling daylight.

"Maybe he ain't coming?" Kenny said.

"He'll be here, don't worry," Bobby assured him. But he couldn't really be sure. He'd told Johnny about the important meeting when he spoke to him earlier over the phone. Johnny was quite non-committal.

"You didn't tell him what it was about?" Hector asked.

Bobby shook his head. He feared Johnny might not show up if he knew the reason. Bobby's eyes brightened when he saw Johnny's figure approach. "He's here."

Johnny joined his buddies in the booth amid greetings and pats on the back.

"How's work?" Bobby asked.

Johnny frowned and shrugged. After graduation he'd taken a job at the Ninth Federal Savings and Loan branch in the neighborhood. "I'm a fucking bank teller. Could it suck any worse?"

The others laughed.

"Well, buddy boy, I got some news that just might perk you up," Bobby beamed as he leaned in closer to the table, "I got a call from Chanticleer Records. They want us to come down for a meeting."

He didn't get the reaction he expected from his best friend. "Now, after all these months? What could they possibly want now?" Johnny asked.

"Shit. It's obvious, ain't it? They want to sign us up."

Johnny shook his head. "It's too late for anything like that, Bobby."

"Whaddaya talkin' about?" Kenny blurted out, "Why too late?"

"I mean it's too late for *me.* You guys wanna go down there and take a shot you go ahead. Don't let me stop you."

"No, no, man," Bobby argued, "We ain't doin' nothing without you, Johnny."

"That's bullshit. We got along without Tommy Gentile, you can get along without *me* now. Me and Barbara are gonna be getting our own place…I got a kid on the way…my old man would drop a chunk of marble on my head if I even *talked* about singing again."

"So don't talk about it," Bobby reasoned, "Listen fathead, you done everything your parents demanded that you do, you quit singing, got a job. What harm would it do if you went downtown with us Friday and listened to what the record company people have to say?"

Bobby made sense.

"I gotta work Friday." Johnny made one last excuse.

"So play hooky."

"Play hooky from work?"

" Ya' done it enough during high school didn't you?"

There was no more to be said. The four friends celebrated with egg creams and malteds.

♫♫♫♫♫

Curtis Tinnsley greeted the four singers when they arrived at the record company. They soon realized this visit would be quite different from the last when they were taken to the executive suite of offices and put them in an anteroom to wait. Gold records adorned the walls along with pictures of people like Teddy Boyette and other successful Chanticleer artists. The boys remained quiet and nervous.

When Curtis returned he brought them into Joseph's office. They seemed impressed and intimidated. After introductions they sat at a conference table. Joseph got straight to the point.

"That demo you made for us a few months back was anemic," Joseph told them.

The boys sat quietly, their earlier confidence shattered. Johnny especially now felt this trip had been a waste of time.

But the music executive had a plan. "I *do* hear something in your style that I like very much. I have a song. Musically and lyrically it's probably the best thing my wife and I have ever done. It's got the potential to be a monster hit and I think you guys can make it happen."

This time, they were unable to control their emotions.

"Oh wow," Kenny uttered.

"Thanks, Mr. Rabin," Johnny gushed.

"Yeah, man, thanks," Bobby said.

Hector just gasped and put his hands to his face to stifle a shout of glee.

They spent the latter part of the day discussing the terms of a contract. Bobby, Kenny and Hector would take theirs home for their parents to sign. Johnny had concerns.

"Mr. Rabin, I might have a problem," he explained.

♫♫♫♫♫

By now, Joseph had become quite adept at convincing parents to allow their offspring to sign a recording contract. At least in the case of the Seracino's it involved a delicious home cooked Italian dinner at their home. Over coffee and dessert Joseph spoke to Dominic, Rose and Johnny's wife Barbara. He outlined a plan that provided a substantial monetary advance and weekly salary that would go a long way to pay for Barbara's medical expenses and the things she'd need throughout her pregnancy. Johnny signed his contract at the dinner table.

Barbara pretended to be happy for him. She said all the right things and outwardly offered her support. Inside, old fears re-surfaced. She'd calculated every move in guiding Johnny into a quiet home life. No spotlight. No screaming female fans. No thoughts of fame and fortune to distract him. Now she wondered if all her manipulations and sacrifices had gone for naught.

Chapter Twenty-Seven:

"Genius at Work"

By re-working the lyrics and changing the gender pronoun from male to female, the title of Joseph's new song went from "When She's Around" to "When He's Around." The subject matter was standard, revolving around a young couple in love. But at times, the male protagonist senses a change in his girlfriend's mood, a distance that comes over her whenever her former boyfriend is around them. The haunting lyrics Janet wrote hinted that the girl wasn't totally over her past love and has doubts. Her boyfriend questions her attitude – 'I feel when you see him – that he is the real one – and your heart will no longer be mine.'

The song was foreboding in tone and tempo. It began slowly like an aria from some romantic grand opera, and then gradually built to a thunderous crescendo finish. The first time Joseph played it for them on a piano, they were confused at Joseph's insistence that Bobby sing the first verse in a lower baritone range rather than his natural tenor.

"I sound like I'm singing at the wrong speed," he told Joseph.

"This tune takes time to build," Joseph explained, "I know you can't hear it now, but when we get into the studio you'll understand. It'll all come together, you'll see."

Step by step they learned the intricate arrangement of the song. The material stretched their vocal abilities to the limit.

Joseph planned to record the song in separate sessions. During the first two he'd work with the musicians on the instrumental tracks.

He gave Curtis a list of the instruments and musicians he required. It was truly staggering.

"You know you're about three guys short of a symphony orchestra, don't you boss?" his musical director noted.

Curtis was right. There were close to a dozen musicians and background singers on the list. Four guitars, a baby grand piano and organ, two complete drum kits as well as kettledrums, bongos and other percussion equipment supplemented by horns and a full string section. Mickey and Tom Dowd again updated the eight-track console. They wired in limiters and equalizers to monitor and control each instrument. This created a mass of wires and cables that snaked along the floor in every direction.

Joseph spoke to his small army over the talk back microphone in the control room. "Okay, folks I know it's tight in there so let's just make the best of it. The charts you have in front of you are very specific and I want this song done note for note. That means no jam session riffs, nothing that isn't on the page."

Mickey spoke to them next. "Ok, this will be 'When He's Around,' take one."

He gave Curtis his cue. The musical director raised his hands to direct the orchestra. Three bars into the song, the string section, which was to have softly eased their way into the first movement, came in too abruptly and much too loud. Joseph's voice intruded over the proceedings. "Listen people, those first notes are supposed to underscore the lyrics not launch them into the stratosphere. Do it again, please."

And so it went. Take after take spoiled by amplifier feedback, missed cues or the failure of someone to convey the right emotion or piece of perfection that until now existed only in the producer/composer's mind. It seemed an impossible task, but still, Joseph drove them on. He ignored the union mandated three-hour limit on recording sessions, promising bonuses on top of the overtime.

They finally paid attention to a thin, blonde violinist who brazenly stood to declare.

"If we don't stop soon, I'm gonna pee right in this chair."

♫♫♫♫♫

On the morning the Du-Kanes joined the orchestra in the studio there was a sense of excitement and anticipation. Many of those associated with the sessions realized something magical was happening. Joseph positioned Kenny and Hector behind a baffle at one end of the studio, alongside the Pixies and several other background singers to form a choir of voices. A large GE microphone on a boom extended above their heads. He then took Johnny and Bobby to the opposite end of the studio where they too stood behind a baffle, each of them on either side of an RCA 77-A multi-directional microphone. There, Joseph gave them last minute instructions.

"Just remember everything I told you, soft and slow at first and then you begin to build. Heading into the middle section you alternate the lyrics, Bobby first and then you Johnny, point, counterpoint sometimes only one word each…got it?"

"Yeah, Mr. Rabin, we won't let you down," Bobby told him.

"I know you won't fellas, just give it all you've got no matter how long it takes."

Despite the assurances, when the session began there were flaws and re-takes made necessary by the young vocalists or the musicians.

Finally, Bobby got them soulfully through the first verse. His voice, rich in tone and timbre, traversed the lowest end of his vocal register intoning the woeful lyric that lamented the male lover's plight. The song was borne along by a strong, throbbing backbeat of drums and percussion. A harmonic vocal whisper ushered them into the first chorus.

Kenny, Hector, and the other background singers blended with the string section that was now, note perfect. They provided an underlying musical wave that propelled them crashing forward. Then, back like the ebb tide, the choir drifted into the background for a second verse. Johnny took over the lead as the wave once again gained momentum, to repeat the chorus.

Now it was on to the middle section. More than just the standard musical bridge linking the verses, this was Joseph's masterstroke of an idea. As Curtis called for quiet from all except the bass guitarist playing a single note pattern of C, A-minor, F, and G, Bobby and Johnny prepared themselves for the point-counterpoint exchange of lyrics Joseph had pounded into their heads. They fed off one another's energy. Bobby's growling tenor answered by Johnny's wailing falsetto. The intensity of the music increased.

Violinist's fingers plucked eighth notes while percussionists used tambourines, cowbells, sleigh bells or simply drumsticks on wooden blocks to accentuate the beat. Kettledrums rolled like thunder, rim shots on snare drums or tom-toms punctuated every line, cymbals crashed.

Curtis unmercifully drove the orchestra to a point of frenzy. Joseph was on his feet in the control room completely immersed in the magnitude of what he was hearing. He bounced on his tiptoes, hands raised above his head like a cheerleader at a football game.

Mickey's eyes darted back and forth across the soundboard watching the needles of the level meters. He hurried to adjust any that seemed close to crossing into the red, which could distort the sound and ruin the take.

Things in the studio were at a fever pitch. Voices strained to hold notes, fingers ached on strings, and breath grew short playing horns. Curtis glanced over his shoulder looking for direction from inside the booth. Joseph nodded his head and the musical director froze his arms high in the air signaling the musicians and singers to hold for one last note. When the crescendo was finally reached, the studio fell into a stunned silence save for the audible release of tension felt by many.

"I assume you don't want another take?" Curtis asked Joseph who stood on the other side of the glass looking at him.

Joseph keyed his mike, "No. That'll do it."

"What was the time on that, Mickey?" Curtis asked.

"Three minutes and fifty seconds," Mickey answered.

His response brought a murmur of whispers and gasps from the musicians. Curtis dismissed them. "That's all for tonight boys and girls. I thank you very much."

"No radio station in the country is going to play a record that long," Mickey said after Joseph finally sat down.

"Put the running time down as three minutes, five seconds," Joseph told him.

"What?" Mickey asked.

"Invert the seconds from five-zero to zero-five."

"You don't think somebody's gonna notice?'

"It's too fucking long," Curtis offered before he'd even come halfway through the control room door. He wiped sweat from his head with a towel.

"Don't worry. We just fixed that," Mickey said.

"Huh?" Curtis was confused.

Joseph and Mickey just laughed.

Back inside the studio, musicians and singers were abuzz with what they'd accomplished. Some gathered around the members of the Du-Kanes to congratulate them on their performance. Bobby made eye contact with a young, black girl standing off to one side. It was Evie Rhodes. She smiled at him and Bobby eased his way over to her.

"Hi. You were one of the backup singers weren't you?" Bobby asked.

Being called a back-up singer melted the smile from Evie's face but she had no desire to spoil the moment so she let his comment pass.

"I'm Evie Rhodes. I'm the lead singer of the Pixies."

"Oh yeah? I've heard some of your records. You're real good. My name's Bobby." The boy redeemed himself.

"You guys were great in there."

"Thanks. It's a terrific song."

Evie couldn't resist the temptation. "Would it surprise you to know that at one time Joseph was going to give that song to us, with different lyrics of course?"

"I had no idea. I'm sorry about that, Evie." Bobby felt guilty.

"No…no, don't apologize. Joseph thought it would be better for a guy group and judging from the way things went today I suppose he was right."

"Is he always right?"

"M'mm, most of the time. But don't ever tell him I said that."

"He'll never hear it from me," They both giggled. "Do you suppose we'll ever get the chance to work together again?"

"Maybe. That's usually the way things work around here."

"And even if we didn't, I suppose we're bound to run into one another from time to time?" He was flirting.

"Oh, I'm sure of that," she countered.

♫♫♫♫♫

Despite the fictional running time applied to "When He's Around," many radio stations balked at playing it. The record buying public loved it.

Billboard Magazine had expanded their pop chart to include the top one hundred songs of the day. "When He's Around," entered the chart at number fifty-one. Five weeks later it broke into the top ten before topping the chart at number one, where it remained for three weeks. It was still working its way down the chart when the DuKanes follow up hit, "Bouncing a Kiss off the Moon," hit number one.

The group became an unqualified success. Many more days of hard work went into the sessions that produced their first LP. Three consecutive single releases all penned by Joseph and Janet went to number one. The album also contained two cover versions of show tunes from the forties, two upbeat blues numbers and three throw away ballads. One of the ballads almost cracked the national top ten, much to everyone's surprise.

Royalties and residuals soon made it possible for the Vitale and Seracino families to move out of the project. Bobby bought a small wood framed house in Silver Beach, a semi-private community located on the water. Johnny set his family up in a two-story brick dwelling in the Morris Park section of the Bronx. His parents and two sisters occupied the main floor while he and Barbara moved into an apartment downstairs.

In November, their first child, a son Steven, was born. Eighteen months later their daughter, Marie, followed.

Chapter Twenty-Eight:

"Payola"

Avid followers of rock and roll music moved into a new decade. Many put high school behind them to enter the work force. Allowances were replaced by weekly paychecks. Spare pennies grew into extra dollars. They spent those dollars on the latest fashions, the hottest new cars and of course, music and records.

Other rock and roll fans walked the hallowed halls of higher learning, their rebellious attitudes further fueled by the members of the beat generation, a term used to describe a new sub-culture built around the ideology of authors Jack Kerouac, Alan Ginsburg and William S. Burroughs. Known as beatniks, they advocated an anti-materialistic attitude that stressed the exploration of one's inner self. Beatniks were liberal in their politics supporting civil rights and desegregation. They were also open with regard to sexual behavior and the use of recreational drugs, most especially, marijuana.

They had their own fashion look. Men wore turtleneck shirts, berets, and sported goatees. Women dressed plainly in leotards or shapeless sack type dresses. They kept their hair straight and unadorned, often going out in public without any makeup. Musically they supported jazz combos or even a simpler blend of bongo drums and flutes. This music played as background for poetry readings in small urban coffee houses beatniks frequented. They embraced a nation-wide revival of American folk music and attended shows called Hootenannys.

But the new crop of high school students still supported singing stars and groups like the Du-Kanes that scored top ten hits with almost every new release. But there were indications that rock and roll was losing its edge.

Teddy Boyette was gone. So were Buddy Holly, Ritchie Valens and J.P. the "Big Bopper" Richardson, all killed in another airplane disaster in Iowa. Little Richard walked away from his singing career to become a preacher. Scandals involving underage women cast a cloud over the reputations of both Jerry Lee Lewis and Chuck Berry. Elvis Presley was overseas in the Army.

They were replaced by a bevy of clean-cut, inoffensive, white performers like Bobby Rydell, Paul Anka and Fabian. All enjoyed hits on the national charts. Tommy Gentile led a similar contingent of hit makers for Alexis Records.

Not everyone welcomed the new genre with open arms.

The American Society of Composers, Authors and Publishers, or ASCAP, began to fear losing its stranglehold on the music industry to its main rival Broadcast Music Inc, or BMI.

ASCAP, the more established music-publishing house, employed strict membership requirements and did not embrace independent record labels, R&B music, or rock and roll, the way BMI did. They desperately sought some way to tarnish the music millions of teenagers loved.

The year before, television was rocked with scandal. Certain contestants on some of TV's most popular quiz shows were provided answers to questions prior to airtime. Some were even coached on how to best dramatize their response. A House Legislative Oversight Committee formed in Congress. They conducted an extensive investigation, grilling network executives and former contestants. Soon, they uncovered enough evidence to prove that some of the shows were rigged. The networks tried to alibi their way out claiming the quiz shows were considered dramatic entertainment and should not be held to such a high standard of honesty. The committee disagreed. Quiz shows ratings plummeted. Many were cancelled.

Fueled by this success against corrupt broadcasting practices,

ASCAP urged Washington to broaden its investigation to include radio. Disc Jockeys became the prime targets. The accusations were that record company executives paid radio personalities to play their records on the air.

A new word entered the vernacular, a contraction of the words *pay* and *victrola*: Payola.

In all, some twenty-five deejays and executives found themselves questioned at the hearings. When they were called to testify, Joseph and Leo opened the company's book for official scrutiny. Leo's meticulous accounting of every penny earned and spent, as well as the ability of both men to answer every question put to them impressed the Congressmen. Chanticleer Records received a clean bill.

♫♫♫♫♫

Phil Gambetta strolled through the lobby of one of the finer hotels in midtown Manhattan with a gorgeous, provocatively dressed young, blonde party doll on his arm. They turned the heads of men and women alike as they walked along a plush, lavender blue carpet to the bank of hotel elevators. They took the next available car to the penthouse floor without exchanging a glance or a word between them.

Phil was still the number two man at Alexis Records, holding the official position of Vice President. Normally, an errand such as this was assigned to an employee of much lower rank but Richie Conforti made it clear to him how important this job was. Phil assured Richie he'd take care of it personally. Exiting the elevator, Phil and his buxom companion stood outside the door of one of the two rooms on the floor. Phil knocked softly on the rich wood. Seconds later the door flew open to reveal the occupant, a tall, gaunt looking man wearing a dressing gown and rimless glasses. Strands of hair from his embarrassingly bad comb-over flew up from the slight breeze created by opening the door. His leering gaze fixed immediately on the blonde's deep cleavage.

"Mr. Bertram, my name is Phil Gambetta. Richie Conforti from Alexis Records sent me. This here is my friend, Jo-Ann."

"Hello, Jo-Ann." Bertram tried being sexy and flirtatious. He stepped aside to allow his visitors to enter. Phil looked around, surveying the lavish surroundings of the suite. An ice bucket containing an opened bottle of expensive champagne sat on a room service cart. Another empty bottle lay on the floor. The remnants of a thick T-bone steak and a partially eaten baked potato were also in evidence.

"I hope you're finding everything to your satisfaction?" Phil asked. He couldn't help but think to himself what a pretty penny all this must be costing the Record Company.

"Why yes I am. Thank you very much indeed."

Phil reached into his inside jacket pocket and produced a white, business sized envelope expanded to the thickness of about one inch by whatever it contained.

"Mr. Conforti also wanted you to have this," he said as he handed the envelope to Bertram. "Perhaps you'd like to take Jo-Ann out on the town, see a show? Then again, maybe just order up some more room service?"

"I think we'll just go with the room service. I have a rather early flight back to the Capital tomorrow. That is of course, if that's all right with you my dear?"

"Sure, whatever you say sweetie," came Jo-Ann's sultry reply. "You're so cute. We can have our own little party right here, just the two of us."

"We'll have a car take you to the airport in plenty of time," Phil assured him.

"That's very kind. Please assure Mr. Conforti that he has nothing to be concerned about."

"He'll be happy to hear that, I'm sure." The two men shook hands and Phil let himself out of the suite. He smiled as he made his way back to the elevator. He liked Jo-Ann and didn't envy what she had to endure for the cause. But then, he thought, what the hell, she wasn't anything more than a common tramp. Besides, she too was being well paid.

♫♫♫♫♫

The following Monday morning, U.S. Congressman Stanley Bertram from the state of Delaware was back in Washington DC in his capacity as co-chairman of the House Special Committee on corruption in the recording industry. The report on his recent findings indicated there was no need to call anyone from Alexis Records to testify before the committee. Payola was indeed everywhere.

The attention of the investigations soon fell on the two top disc jockeys in the country, Dick Clark and Alan Freed. Clark testified that he became involved with outside interests associated with the recording industry solely for the tax advantages they provided. He denied accepting any monies or gifts, but admitted to divesting himself of whole or part interest in thirty-three companies, after the Payola issue surfaced. This accounted for over twenty-seven percent of the records he played on American Bandstand. While his admission did not exonerate him, he escaped the hearings with his reputation intact.

The same could not be said about Alan Freed. Though granted immunity, Freed refused to admit to any misconduct. Clearly, he was prepared to be the scapegoat and take the fall.

In May of 1960, a New York Grand Jury handed down misdemeanor indictments charging Freed and seven others with receiving over $116,000.00 in illegal gratuities. Freed was soon fired from both WABC-Radio and WNEW-TV. The man credited with coining the term “rock and roll” was through in the music business.

Chapter Twenty-Nine:

"Camelot"

The international and political situations facing Americans in the new decade were tenuous to say the least. In the tiny Caribbean island nation of Cuba, a rebel leader named Fidel Castro overthrew the cruel and corrupt regime of President Fulgencio Batista, backed with weapons and funding provided by the United States. However, not long after taking power, Castro's reforms set about to seize many American owned interests on the island. In response, the United States reduced the import quota on Cuba's most vital trade commodity, sugar, by seven million tons. However the Soviet Union stepped in and bought the sugar, initiating a friendly trade policy between the two countries, which angered Washington.

"What makes you think he won't win?" Janet asked after dinner at Joseph's parents home.

Joseph quickly answered, "Because he's too young, he's Catholic and the country doesn't need a change in political policy with the Russians practically camped on a beach in Cuba."

"And his father is a crook," Solomon offered his opinion. "A bootlegger from way back. I'll bet you his son doesn't even get the nomination."

Joseph shook his head.

"Well, I disagree with you there, Papa. He's the only real candidate the Democrats have. He'll get the nod at the Convention."

They were discussing the upcoming Presidential election and the front-runner of the Democratic Party, a charismatic young Senator from Massachusetts, John Fitzgerald Kennedy.

"We'll see about that," Solomon replied between bites of pot roast. "If Eisenhower wasn't forbidden by law from running for a third term, he'd win again in a landslide. He was a great general…a war hero. That's the kind of man we need running the country, not some glamour boy."

"Senator Kennedy was a hero in the war too, Papa," Janet defended her choice.

"Yeah, he had a P.T. boat shot out from under him," Joseph teased her about Kennedy's naval war record in the Pacific. Kennedy commanded a Motor Torpedo Boat that was sunk by the Japanese. He was honored as a hero for orchestrating the rescue of himself and his crew from a desert island. Janet sought an ally.

"What do you think of Senator Kennedy, Mama?" She asked Myra who seemed surprised that someone would ask her opinion on such a subject.

"Well, he's a handsome man and his wife is very beautiful."

Solomon scoffed, "Wonderful qualification to run the most powerful nation on earth."

"Yes, he is very handsome," Janet pressed her, "but will you vote for him?"

"Vote? Oh my goodness dear, I've never voted for anything in my life."

The men at the table laughed. Janet didn't continue the conversation.

Later, when the women were alone in the kitchen, a feeling of melancholy washed over Janet. Joseph had purchased a home for them in Florida and they were moving there in several weeks.

"I'm going to miss you Mama," Janet said.

"Oh, my dear, we're going to miss you as well. But you'll have plenty of chances to come and visit. Maybe leave New York for the entire winter, lots of people do that you know."

"That's a wonderful invitation, but I don't think Joseph would be interested in taking so much time away from the company."

"He works too hard, my son."

"Yes he does. But things change so quickly in the record business these days, it takes so much effort just to keep up."

"Hmm, there are other things he could be putting extra effort into."

Janet knew what her mother-in-law alluded to, but Myra didn't take it any further and she was grateful for that. Right or wrong they never told Joseph's parents about his being sterile. Janet knew they were disappointed about not having any grandchildren. Thinking of it now she couldn't remember the last time she and Joseph even discussed adopting a child. It was as Myra had said, her son worked too hard.

"Come, sit with me," Myra intruded on her thoughts. "Let's leave the talk of moving, and Florida, to the men and you can tell me all about this Senator Kennedy you like so much."

Janet smiled and happily did so.

A short time later, Joseph called for his car and driver.

♫♫♫♫♫

"I'm going to make a contribution to Kennedy's campaign." Her comment on the ride home came out of the blue. "I've also called and offered my services as a volunteer."

"You're really serious about this, aren't you?"

"Yes I am. Do you mind?"

"Not me. I'm impressed you feel so strongly about the election. I just think you're backing the wrong guy, that's all."

"And I can't believe *you're* for Nixon."

Joseph chuckled, "To tell you the truth sweetheart I'm not really for either one of them. After all this Payola nonsense, I've just kinda had my fill of Congressmen and Senators and all this political stuff."

They had sex later that night, *married sex* Janet called it, quick, sanitized and unfulfilling. Joseph took the time to wash up and shave afterward so he wouldn't have to do so in the morning. As she lay in bed listening to the water running in the shower, she couldn't help but think how she missed the cuddling and holding, the feel of his breath on her cheek to comfort her. While he worked in the studio, long nights alone were an all too common occurrence. She hated the distance that had recently come between them.

There had been rumors about other women, Evie Rhodes in particular. But she refused to lend them any credence. She longed for something to come along to divert her attention from her marital problems.

♫♫♫♫♫

On the day after Myra and Solomon left for Florida, Janet got a call from the Kennedy people. Their background research revealed her notoriety as a successful songwriter. Someone offered her the opportunity to write a campaign song for the Senator. She readily obliged. With Joseph's wholehearted support she agreed to turn over all royalties from the song to Kennedy's political campaign.

In return, they invited Janet to the July Democratic National Convention held in California. There she met the candidate and his family. Frank Sinatra sang the song she wrote at a gala ball given on the night Kennedy won the nomination to run for President.

Janet spent long hours as a volunteer at Kennedy's New York headquarters. She saw less and less of Joseph, only now she found *herself* to be the busy one.

♫♫♫♫♫

Since its inception, rock and roll music always had a massive impact on the dance culture. Many youngsters, especially males, preferred slow dancing to ballads and love songs. These dances were called the fish and the grind where boys were said to shine their belt buckles by pressing against the bodies of their female partners.

But the most popular dance of the day was by far the Lindy Hop, a dance comprised of intricate moves, turns and flips with names like the whip, hijack and the windmill. The dance derived its name from the famous aviator, Charles A. Lindbergh, nicknamed Lindy, who made his historic solo flight, or *hop*, across the Atlantic Ocean from New York to Paris in 1927. The dance itself had undergone several name changes over the years eventually known as, the jump, jive, boogie-woogie, and the bop.

New dances started cropping up all over the country. Cameo-Parkway Records in Philadelphia signed a new artist named Ernest Evans. A chance meeting at a recording session saw Evans introduced to Dick Clark and his wife, Barbara. On learning that his boss at a local produce market had given Evans the nickname Chubby, Barbara Clark suggested a new stage name for the singer. She reasoned, if there could be a Fats Domino why not a Chubby Checker? The big break in his singing career came when the record company gave him a Hank Ballard tune to record called the "Twist."

The tune was catchy, Checker's performance exuberant, and the dance easy to learn. One simply mimicked the action of putting out a cigarette with the balls of your feet, at the same time, swinging your arms and hips from side to side in a twisting motion as though drying your backside with a bath towel. Soon everyone was twisting the night away in malt shops, sock hops, and even posh nightclubs.

Follow-up songs and variations soon populated the record charts as companies created a new batch of dance moves and singers generating millions of dollars in revenue.

Ironically, Leo Klein came up the idea for the dance that would represent Chanticleer Record's entry into the dance craze mania.

♫♫♫♫♫

"We can call it the Caterpillar." He pitched the idea at a meeting of executives one morning as they discussed possibilities. Leo rarely ever made a suggestion with regard to creative content, so his idea caught everyone off guard. His younger partner wondered if he should take the suggestion seriously.

"And just how do you do this – Caterpillar?" Joseph wanted to know.

Overcome with embarrassment that he must demonstrate his idea to the others, Leo timidly rose from his chair. He fumbled through movements clearly making them up as he went along.

"Well, you can just sort of stand in the middle of the dance floor with your arms out, bent at the elbow like the legs of a caterpillar…"

"Maybe snap your fingers a little?" Mickey jokingly interrupted.

"Yes, certainly," Leo took it as a serious suggestion, "snapping your fingers is fine. Then you would just kind of wiggle your ass back and forth sort of in a slinky motion."

"Do you get to move your feet at all? It *is* a dance, remember?" Curtis commented stifling a grin. Leo knew all the others were ribbing him.

"Of course! You can do some turns, slink around the floor… whatever a caterpillar does for Chrissake!" Leo shouted.

"You think we could get away with something like that?" Joseph asked Curtis.

"Maybe with some refinements here and there."

"Of course it needs some refinements," Leo chimed in, happy to sit down again.

"Who do we give it to?" Curtis asked.

"A girl group," Mickey offered after Leo's demonstration.

"Definitely," Again, Leo whole-heartedly agreed.

"The Pixies?" Curtis opted. "It could be just what they need to put them over the top."

"I agree. I'll work up some lyrics and charts and have it all ready for you by tomorrow morning," Joseph told him.

"Another all-nighter?" Leo asked with some concern.

"Looks like it," he replied.

"Do you really think it was such a good idea?" Leo asked.

"The best idea we've had around here since…coonskin caps," Joseph smiled.

Two days later Joseph ran through a rough arrangement of the perky little tune for the Pixies in one of the rehearsal halls.

"Is that the best you can offer us, Joseph…'the Caterpillar'?" Evie wasn't impressed.

"I didn't come up with it. Leo did," Joseph smiled.

"Mr. Klein? Mr. Klein wrote this song?"

"No, I wrote the song. Leo invented the dance."

"I don't like it," Evie pouted.

"Oh, come on," Althea challenged "Why do you have be so damned contrary?"

"Yeah, Evie. The tune is real catchy. I'll bet we could work up some real good dance movements to go with it, couldn't we Mr. Rabin?" Roberta asked.

"Absolutely! The steps, the choreography…I'll leave all that up to you girls. I want you to have fun with it."

Evie wavered but she had conditions.

"Would it be too much to ask for a nice, slow ballad for the b-side?"

"Did you have something specific in mind?"

"There's a song from Janet's catalog, 'Seven Ways to Sunday'?" Evie said without hesitation.

Janet wrote the song for Teddy but he didn't live to record it. Evie asked for it once before when things between she and her boss were different. He refused her then and he thought badly of her to ask again now.

"Okay. It's yours," then he stressed, "On the B-side."

"Okay, girls," Evie preened, "Let's go find us a full length mirror and see if we can learn to shake our asses like caterpillars."

♫♫♫♫♫

The Presidential Election of 1960 would be unique in several ways. With Alaska and Hawaii joining the union the year before, a total of fifty states would now participate in the voting. Television would also play a major role in politics for the first time. Three televised debates took place between the Republican candidate and current Vice-President, Richard M. Nixon, and the Democrat candidate,

John Kennedy.

Nixon did not come across well on TV. He appeared frumpy, wrinkled with a constant sourpuss and five-o'clock shadow. He refused to wear any stage make-up. The heat from the studio lights made him sweat, and he looked nervous. Kennedy, on the other hand, seemed to love the camera. He was impeccably dressed, every hair on his head in place. His broad smile exhibited confidence and control as he wooed the nation-wide audiences. The candidates' political platforms and campaign promises took a back seat to the visual impact put forth on the tube.

John F. Kennedy was elected the thirty-fifth President of the United States on November 6th, 1960. But his triumph wasn't a decisive one. His margin of victory was ever so slight, a mere 49.6 to 49.3 of the popular vote, leaving the nation clearly divided.

The election result pleased Janet. She and Joseph were invited to attend Kennedy's inauguration in Washington DC where they heard the world leader chart a new and dynamic course for the nation, a fresh "new frontier" with big ideas and an open declaration to citizens young and old, black and white, rich and poor: "Ask not what your country can do for you: ask what you can do for your country."

Thus began a time of optimism and confidence that the nation was in the hands of a leader that would propel Americans to a new level of greatness. The era soon came to be known as "Camelot."

Chapter Thirty:

"Gerde's Folk City"

On January 30th, 1961, "Will You love Me Tomorrow?" by the Shirelles became the first single recorded by a girl group to reach number one on the Billboard chart. Three weeks later the Pixies made it to the top thanks to their two-sided runaway hit, "The Caterpillar" and "Seven Ways to Sunday." Chanticleer Records now had a solid one, two punch with the Du-Kanes and the Pixies performing at the top of their game. Singles and album sales over the next few months kept cash registers ringing all across the country. The girls began making regular appearances at Palisades Park, an amusement complex in New Jersey. The shows were hosted by popular WABC radio personality Bruce "Cousin Brucie" Morrow. And, while Joseph and Leo made plans to send both groups out on a massive tour, the world adjusted to the new era.

The Russians had once again taken the lead in the race for space. They launched a rocket powering a spherical module dubbed Vostok 1 that carried the first man into space. Cosmonaut Yuri Gagarin flew in an orbit 187 miles above the earth for ninety minutes.

Weeks later, millions of television viewers watched as the U.S. manned space program made its first attempt to get off the ground. Seven astronauts were culled from a field of some seventy test pilot candidates. After undergoing a rigorous program of physical training and mental examinations they became known as the Mercury Seven Astronauts. U.S. Naval Commander Alan B. Shepard would pilot the first manned mission called Freedom 7. On the launch pad atop a Redstone rocket, he was heard to say, "Please dear God, don't let me fuck up."

Minutes later he launched into space for a twenty-minute sub-orbital flight before a helicopter recovered his capsule in the Atlantic Ocean.

♫♫♫♫♫

A yellow cab pulled up in front of 11 West Fourth St. in the heart of Greenwich Village, an area becoming well known as a bohemian meeting place for students, artists, and musicians seeking to embrace an emerging folk culture. Janet and Linda stood on the curb after the cab pulled away.

"This is it?" Linda asked, with more than a hint of disappointment in her voice.

"Uh-huh," Janet said.

The canopy that extended to the curb identified the place as Gerde's Folk City. Months before it had been an Italian restaurant, one she and Joseph often frequented. They'd become acquainted with the owner, Mike Porco, a gentlemanly Italian immigrant. When business began to sag because of the influx of beatniks and folksies into the area, Porco took on new partners. Together they transformed the place into a showcase for new talent.

When Porco called and invited them to come to see his latest discovery, Janet felt obliged to attend. She knew Joseph would be too busy so she asked Linda to go along. Her friend reluctantly agreed.

Inside the doorway to the club, the owner greeted them.

"Ah, Mrs. Rabin, thank you so much for coming," Porco said as he took Janet's hand. He spoke broken English with a quaint European charm.

"Thank you for inviting me, Mike. This is my friend Linda."

He turned his attention to her and repeated the handshake gesture with a genuine smile. "Very nice to meet you Miss, welcome to my place."

"Charmed, I'm sure," Linda replied.

"Let me get a table," Porco continued, "We get busy so early these days."

He led the two women into the tight quarters of the club, scarcely thirty-five feet across and fifty feet deep. The red-checkered tablecloths were holdovers from the restaurant days. The walls were painted maroon. A small raised platform serving as a stage stood against a far wall. Porco brought them to a table that would offer the best view of the show. He pulled back both chairs for the women and then sat to join them.

Porco said, "I want you to see a boy named Alan Thomas. He showed up here one Tuesday night, that's the night we have our Hootenanny show."

"For new talent?" Janet said.

"That's right. He worked his way across the country from the Midwest and told me he wanted to sing. But, you see, he's underage and can't sing in public. So, I took him down to the musician's union and they say he can't join unless his parents sign for him. Alan tells them he's an orphan and he don't have any parents, so I end up signing to become his guardian."

"He must have really impressed you for you to go to such lengths for him," Janet said.

"Impressed isn't the word," Porco explained, "He's become a huge hit in the place, packs them in every time he sings. So much that I'm having him open for Clifford Lee tonight."

Janet knew Lee to be one of the foremost names in the folk/blues scene. "I'll look forward to seeing him then."

Her comment made Porco smile.

"I know both you ladies will love him." He then stood and called out to a waitress, "Oh, Carol?" A pretty waitress hurried over. Her boss gave her explicit instructions. "Bring these ladies anything they like, on the house."

"Oh, really, Mike, that's not necessary," Janet protested.

"Please, it's my pleasure. I'll join you again at intermission." He bowed and hurried off.

Janet ordered an espresso coffee and Linda, a glass of wine.

After the waitress left Janet leaned across the table.

"You could at least *pretend* you don't mind being here."

"I don't know what you see in this place, it's so seedy and dirty. My dress is gonna smell of cigarette smoke," Linda complained.

"Mr. Porco is my friend. Besides, this is where all the hip people meet these days."

"Yeah? Well, the Copa is hip enough for me."

"They don't smoke cigarettes at the Copa?"

Linda tsked.

As show time rolled around, the club became crowded with patrons, a mixed bag of people, with attire ranging from casual to business and evening wear.

The announcer's voice addressed the crowd, "Ladies and gentlemen, welcome to Gerde's Folk City. Lets have a warm round of applause for Alan Thomas."

The crowd greeted the young singer with loud clapping and a chorus of whistles. It was obvious many had already seen him perform. The singer stood alone on stage. He was short of stature, with a thick tussle of unkempt brown hair. A six-string acoustic guitar hung around his neck, along with a metal brace holding a harmonica, which sometimes obscured the view of his face. He did not make a good first impression dressed in a wrinkled work shirt, black slacks, and dirty deerskin boots.

All that changed when he began to sing. His voice came across nasally, almost monotone, but the real impact came from the lyrics. Thomas sang a few familiar songs by the likes of Pete Seeger and Woody Guthrie, about migrant farm workers of the Great Depression, work camps, and hobos riding the rails.

He moved on to his original compositions. Some had poignant, poetic words that touched the heart, others were hard and brutal, and their real meaning lost on those hearing them for the first time. No syrupy teenage love songs or songs about dancing the twist, instead his songs were about picking fruit for pennies under a hot sun and other timely topics.

Thomas left the stage to a great ovation. Janet stood, as did many others. Linda remained seated.

"What did you think of him?" Janet asked.

"He's different," Linda replied with a disinterested shrug.

Mike Porco soon returned to the table with Alan Thomas in tow. After a polite introduction, the men crowded into two empty chairs. Up close, Thomas seemed shy and younger than his onstage persona. He smelled of perspiration. Linda did her best to move away from the scruffy singer.

"Mrs. Rabin's husband owns Chanticleer Records," Porco said.

"Yeah, I've heard of it." Thomas seemed unimpressed.

Porco went on, "She's a famous songwriter as well."

"I know *that* too," his compliment sounded sincere.

"I tell you, Mrs. Rabin, I got a feeling about this boy. Do you think your husband might be interested in giving him a tryout?" Porco pressed her.

The young folksinger got embarrassed, for himself and the woman. His mentor's question had put her on the spot.

"Well, Joseph is always looking for new talent and isn't above taking risks," Janet said.

"Yeah, I guess signing a guy like me *could* be risky," Thomas replied.

"Why is that?" Janet asked.

"Look, Mrs. Rabin," he took charge of the moment. "It's not like I don't appreciate what people like you and Mike are trying to do for me, I do. But, you both gotta realize, I'm gonna sing and play my songs the way I want. I ain't gonna be a whore for nobody."

"Alan, watch how you talk!" Porco bristled with anger.

Linda just rolled her eyes at the audacity of the sweaty, smelly punk. Only Janet remained calm.

"That's okay, Mike, Alan is entitled to his opinion," she said.

Until then, Thomas had reminded Janet of Teddy Boyette with his deep passion for his music. Now, she recognized the sharp contrast between the two singers. Teddy was innocent. All he ever wanted to do was make his fans happy. Alan Thomas wanted to make people think. He had a message he wanted to deliver to his audience whether they wanted to hear it or not.

"I can't guarantee you anything, Alan," Janet concluded. "My husband runs the business and ultimately it's his decision. But, I'll get you in the door if that's what you want?"

"That's what he wants," Mike Porco answered for him. "Right kid?

"Okay, Mike, whatever you say."

♫♫♫♫♫

Alan Thomas auditioned seated on a stool in a rehearsal hall at the record company. Joseph and Curtis sat nearby. Mickey, Janet and Mike Porco sat further back. When Thomas finished, Joseph was quite cordial.

"Thanks a lot, Alan, I enjoyed that a great deal." He stood and called to his wife. "Janet, why don't you take Alan and Mike for a cup of coffee?"

"Sure thing. C'mon, Alan, this way."

Thomas put his guitar down and walked past the executives without so much as a casual look. Mickey stepped forward to join Joseph and Curtis.

"Well?" Joseph asked his musical director.

"I don't hear no top forty hit songs in that batch," Curtis replied.

"Me either," Joseph said, "He's got something though, hard edged. Folk fans dig that."

"Do you think he ever smiles?" Mickey asked.

"He doesn't need to smile. It detracts from his personality," Joseph answered.

"What personality?" Mickey's comment made them all chuckle.

Joseph had an idea. "Maybe we could come up with a different way to market him."

"How so?" Curtis asked.

"Suppose we work backwards with this kid. Like you said, he's not going to have a hit single with the stuff he does. So why bother trying to do a single at all? Let's record a whole album and introduce him that way."

Curtis liked the idea. "He already has a strong fan following. An album might sell better anyway."

"It could be fun working in a studio with just one guy instead of twenty," Mickey joked.

"What if we don't bring him into the studio at all? Suppose we record him doing a live show in a club?"

"Mike Porco's place?"

"Why not?"

Curtis chimed in, "That way we get the full impact of him performing onstage, fan reaction, the whole bit."

"Let's get him signed up," Joseph said.

Once he had signed contracts, Joseph told Alan about doing a live album. The singer was delighted. Joseph would allow Alan to pick all the songs he would perform. Mike Porco graciously agreed to use Folk City as the venue. Mickey looked the place over to work out the logistics necessary for doing a live recording. Joseph even suggested that Janet work along with them to get everything set up.

♫♫♫♫♫

Several weeks passed. Joseph became heavily involved in planning the nation-wide summer tour for the Du-Kanes and the Pixies.

Curtis knocked on the open door of Joseph's office and poked his head in. "Got a minute for me?" he asked.

"Barely," Joseph answered. He hoped Curtis would take the hint and go away, but he didn't. He came in and sat down. He held a batch of music charts in his hands.

"Alan Thomas finally gave me the lineup for his live LP," He told Joseph.

"That was nice of him. The session is only three days away." When Cutis didn't respond, Joseph gave him his undivided attention.

"Is there something wrong?"

"Not really, but take a look at this list. It's pretty interesting."

He handed one of the music charts across the desk for Joseph to look at.

It was for a song called, "Storming a Greyhound." It listed the composers as, Alan Thomas and Janet Cavelli.

"Did you know anything about this?" Curtis asked.

Confused, Joseph shook his head. "I don't think so. I mean, she may have mentioned something to me about it…I've been busy with all this other stuff. But, no, I don't think she did. Is it any good?"

"It's very political, Joe. Probably gonna cause a big stir. But it's in line with the rest of Alan's stuff."

♫♫♫♫♫

Janet was surprised when Joseph got home. She hadn't expected him so early. She heated a plate of leftovers and sat with him at the table while he ate. After he was done, he asked her about the song she'd written with Alan. She seemed surprised by the question.

"How did you know about that?" she asked.

"He's going to record it on his LP."

His response surprised her. "He is?"

The two of them had hastily composed the tune based on news accounts of an incident about a group of Freedom Riders in Alabama. The Freedom Riders were integrated groups of protestors traveling throughout the south, usually by Greyhound bus, to take part in sit-ins, promoting the desegregation of waiting rooms in bus stations and train terminals. On this particular occasion, one bus was forced off the road, had its tires slashed and windows broken. The bus was then fire bombed and the riders beaten by angry whites.

"I had no idea he planned to do that. I'm sorry," Janet said.

"No need to apologize. I just didn't realize you'd taken such an interest in him."

"I guess I feel that in some way, that he's *my* discovery," She felt awkward explaining. "He has plenty of material. If you don't want him to record the song, then just tell him so."

"I doubt that would go over very well with him, do you?" he asked with a smile.

"Probably not," she answered.

There was another reason Joseph was agreeable to let Alan record the song. "Storming a Greyhound," was an intense, angry piece, just the kind of song to stir up controversy and catch everyone's attention, just the kind of song to sell millions of copies.

♫♫♫♫♫

"So, I made the record man jealous? I'm impressed," Alan said to Janet the next day at the rehearsal at Folk City.

The arrogant tone in his wisecrack angered her. "Why didn't you tell me you were going to put that song on the album?"

"I thought it would be a nice surprise. Sort of my way of thanking you for getting me this break," his explanation didn't sound sincere. "Listen, Janet, the lyrics you wrote for that song were terrific. That's the kind of things you should be doing, not that trite, lollipop crap you've been doing up till now."

"That *crap* as you call it, has sold millions of records," Janet pointed out.

"There's more to music than selling records and making money. Music can help make changes in the world. *You* can make those changes."

He moved uncomfortably close to her until she could feel his breath on her cheek. Their familiarity with one another seemed a natural progression but she never expected anything like this. She averted his gaze and walked away.

Alan's live show proved to be an unqualified success. Celebrities and fans alike packed Folk City. The singer performed flawlessly and with great confidence. Reviews in the press varied depending on which publication you read. The Village Voice, issued words of glowing praise, while confusion and indifference blared from the pages of the New York Times.

Chanticleer Records released the album, "Alan Thomas: Live from Folk City." It sold like wildfire. From that point on, an A&R man from the company was at a table in Mike Porco's club every night looking for new talent.

♫♫♫♫♫

The tour that took Chanticleer Records two top groups out on the road began when they appeared together on the Clay Cole Show, a New York based television dance program. Then it was on to Philadelphia, Pennsylvania where the Du-Kanes made their fourth appearance on "American Bandstand," and the Pixies, their first. They played two live stage shows receiving third and fourth billing behind Chubby Checker and Bobby Rydell.

The Du-Kanes overshadowed Rydell's performance, but they took a back seat to the explosive twist master. Bobby managed to garner free publicity when photographers snapped pictures of him after he wandered onstage during Checker's encore. The coverage made the New York papers much to the glee of Leo and the advertising department. The headline read "New York vs. Philly Twist off."

Publicity was something Bobby and Evie made sure to avoid when they stole away all three nights for a rendezvous at a small roadside motel off the Pennsylvania Turnpike. Their flirtations had grown into a deep romance kept secret because of the obvious racial implications.

The groups boarded a train in Philadelphia but parted company a short time later. The Du-Kanes went to Washington DC as the Pixies continued on to Florida. The boys did a show in the nation's capitol before a bus ride to Virginia Beach, Virginia. There the group headlined for the first time.

A long drive through Tennessee saw a series of one nighters in Knoxville, Nashville, and on into Memphis. The significance of their stop in that city was not lost on them. At a press luncheon they met Artie Franklin, the very same record executive that booted Teddy Boyette out of his office almost a decade earlier. They appeared as in-studio guests on deejay Rufus Thomas' radio show on WDIA, radio and headlined three sold out concerts.

Several days later they were in Dallas, Texas. The Du-Kanes performed there and in Fort Worth, Abilene, and finally Lubbock, the birthplace of Buddy Holly. From Dallas they hopped a Boeing 707 jet aircraft for a flight to Los Angeles, California.

The group would spend ten days in California. The first two set aside for a well-deserved rest from performing. Hector and Kenny went on a tour of movie stars homes in Beverley Hills and enjoyed a day of fun at Disneyland. Johnny and Bobby were content to relax on Malibu Beach taking in the sights and sounds of the Pacific Ocean. The beaches were crowded with people of all ages and there was no shortage of gorgeous girls in bikinis.

Johnny exercised a married man's prerogative of girl watching. He was surprised to find Bobby's attention diverted from the bikinis to another activity taking place out in the water.

Several young men were surfing, a popular though somewhat dangerous sport where individuals rode a banana shaped board seven to ten feet in length made of balsa wood or fiberglass. They sought to catch a wave, jump to their feet, and ride in the curl as it broke toward shore.

"That looks like fun, don't it?" Bobby asked.

"I guess so, if you have a death wish."

"I gotta try that man." Bobby jumped to his feet kicking up sand doing so.

"What the fuck…!" Johnny protested.

Johnny watched Bobby approach a group of young men and women working on their surfboards. He could imagine Bobby using his gift of gab to convince one of the surfers to let him use his equipment. Eventually Bobby and one of the other boys shook hands, grabbed two boards and headed into the water. Johnny got to his feet and hurried to the spot where the other surfers stood.

"You're friend's got balls, man," a tall well-built blonde boy told him, "He says he's never done this before?"

"That's right. I don't even know if he can swim," Johnny replied.

"Holy shit!"

Bobby's first attempt almost drowned him. He paddled hard to match the speed of the wave he'd chosen. When he tried to stand, he lost his balance and tumbled into the water. The riderless board flew into the air and flippded over several times.

"That's a real bad wipe out," one bikini-clad girl said. Johnny became concerned.

Two less severe falls followed, but on his next try Bobby managed to stay on his feet and ride the wave. Johnny and the others raised a cheer. When Bobby returned to shore the California kids invited the New Yorkers to a beach party. After sunset they built a bonfire, roasted hot dogs, and drank beer. When someone brought out an old acoustic guitar and strummed some tunes, Johnny and Bobby harmonized along with them. They didn't tell their new friends that they were famous rock and roll singers. That night they got a ride back to their hotel with one of the surfers.

They went back to work doing radio and television spots before headlining at a concert at the Civic Center in Los Angeles. Their opening act was a local guitar band, three brothers, their cousin and a schoolmate. The group called themselves the Beach Boys. They performed in white pants and candy-striped shirts, their act made up of cover versions of songs by groups like the Four Freshmen sung in tight, barbershop type harmony. They also did some original compositions about surfing and hot rods. The local audiences were quite partial to their hometown boys, but when the Du-Kanes took the stage, they easily won over the crowd on their way to three well-deserved encores.

The itinerary for the homeward bound leg of their journey had them flying to shows in Kansas City and St. Louis, Missouri. Then, back aboard a bus to Chicago, Illinois. There they came to know a young, black entrepreneur named Malcolm Brown. Brown had achieved success with an independent record company he'd started called, South Side Records.

There was a similar story at their next stop in Detroit, Michigan. A former auto assembly line worker named Berry Gordy bought three wood framed buildings in a residential area on West Grand Boulevard. He started his company, Hitsville USA, with eight hundred dollars he'd borrowed from members of his family. Berry recorded much of the untapped black talent in the area. He struck pay dirt when he signed a group called the Miracles, fronted by a talented songwriter and performer named Smokey Robinson. The group had a massive hit with a song called "Shop Around."

The Du-Kanes took second billing to the Miracles for two shows in Detroit before moving on for one last stop in Cleveland, Ohio. They'd been on tour almost the entire summer. Their nation-wide success put them on top of the world, a world that was in the process of turning itself upside down.

♫♫♫♫♫

For some time President Kennedy's closest advisers urged him to take a more active roll in its dealings with the tiny Southeast Asian nation of Vietnam. In the past ten years the region had been divided by communist rule in the north and a democratic regime in the south. But the situation in Cuba made Kennedy cautious with his foreign policy. Those closest to him recommended combat military support, instead Kennedy sent three thousand military advisors to help train the South Vietnamese Army.

Chapter Thirty-One:

"Guided Missiles"

In the summer of 1962, the United States, Great Britain and France financed a multi-national project commissioning NASA to launch a satellite into permanent elliptical orbit around the earth. The satellite, designed to transmit telephone calls and live television broadcasts around the world, was called Telstar.

The voice on the telephone surprised Janet.

"Hello, record lady." It was Alan Thomas.

She'd managed to steer clear of him in recent months. He had a busy schedule of appearances on the college campus circuit up and down the east coast. After exchanging pleasantries with him, he got down to the reason for his call.

"I've been invited to Norman Mailer's place for a party tonight. I wondered if you'd like to come along?"

She knew Mailer as a best-selling author famous for counterculture views.

"I don't think that's a very good idea, Alan," she replied.

"You gonna pass up the chance to meet Norman Mailer?"

"I'll have to think about it. If I decide to go I'll call you back, okay?"

"Okay, great."

They'd barely been disconnected before Janet called Linda and told her about the conversation.

"I can't believe the balls on that creepy little bastard making a pass at you like that," Linda said angrily.

"I don't know, maybe I'm making too much of it?"

"Too much of it my ass! That horny little bugger wants to get in your pants for sure!" There was a long pause on the phone. "Don't tell me you're even considering going to this party with him?"

"To Norman Mailer's? Of course I'm considering it. It beats sitting at home here all by myself. Unless, of course *you* want to take in a movie or something?"

Linda was quick to answer. "Oh no, sweetie, not tonight. Mickey has a table reserved at the Copa for Bobby Darin and I ain't missing that for nobody."

"I can't say I blame you."

"Janet, just promise me you won't do something stupid honey, okay? If you go to the party with that asshole and some reporter or columnist sees you and takes a picture, it'll be splattered all over the papers and Joseph will find out for sure." Then Linda chuckled. "Hey, maybe that wouldn't be so bad. I'd love to see Joseph kick that punk's ass from one end of Central Park to the other."

They both laughed.

After she hung up, Janet stood by the telephone table for a long time. The image Linda planted in her mind took shape in an odd way. There was Joseph, her white knight mounted on his steed doing battle with Alan, a dark knight all in black, jousting for the hand of their fair lady. She dismissed the daydream. Perhaps in the past that might have been so, but now in the reality of her situation, she had doubts. Janet decided she desperately needed to soak in a tub full of bubbles.

♫♫♫♫♫

A U-2 spy plane flying over Cuba photographed what experts believed to be rocket-launching sites under construction. The Soviet Union had been providing Castro's regime with arms and defensive weapons. When questioned by Kennedy about the missile sites, Soviet Premier Nikita Khrushchev insisted the construction was solely for the purpose of contributing to Cuba's defensive capabilities. Kennedy wasn't convinced. He put the country's military on high alert and ordered more U-2 flights.

Weeks later, new photographs showed that the missile sites could indeed be equipped with mid-range ballistic missiles and outfitted with nuclear warheads capable of reaching targets within the United States. But there was no sign of the missiles themselves. The government was convinced they hadn't yet been delivered and became determined to keep them from arriving.

Kennedy decided to go public. On the evening of October 22nd, he addressed the nation in a news conference. The leader who'd smiled so beamingly so many times before in his televised speeches wasn't smiling on this occasion. With a grim, somber demeanor he used enlargements of U-2 photographs to show the public the launching sites. He stated that intelligence reports confirmed that nineteen Soviet ships were currently en-route to Cuba. A number of them carried nuclear warheads.

"It shall be the policy of this nation…" Kennedy intoned, "…to regard any nuclear missile launched from Cuba against any nation in the Western Hemisphere as an attack by the Soviet Union on the United States, requiring a full retaliatory response upon the Soviet Union."

He further announced a naval blockade of the waters surrounding Cuba. Kennedy ordered U.S. warships to stop and board any Russian ships for the purposes of inspecting their cargo.

The world now stood on the brink of nuclear war.

♫♫♫♫♫

"We're fine, Joseph, just fine," Solomon Rabinowitz told his son when they spoke on the telephone the next day. Joseph was concerned about his parents living in a house off the intercostals causeway near Miami Beach, Florida. While he never once mentioned the missile crisis or Kennedy's speech, he knew his father was aware that this was more than a social call.

"Say hello to your mother," Solomon instructed him.

"Hi, Mama," Joseph said as pleasantly as he could when Myra got on the line. Janet stood close by trying to hear both sides of the conversation.

"The whole world has gone crazy, Joseph," his mother told him sounding more angry than frightened.

"I know. All we can do is hope that Kennedy and Khrushchev keep their wits about them and somehow back away from this."

"We can do more than that, Joseph. We can pray. We can all pray very hard."

That solution didn't lessen Joseph's concern. "I'm going to put Janet on the line Mama."

He handed the receiver to his wife then stepped away to give her some privacy.

"Hello, Mama," Janet said, smiling in the comfort of hearing Myra's voice.

"Hello, my dear. How are you holding up during this awful time?"

"We're okay. It's just so weird here. The whole city seems to be holding its breath waiting for something bad to happen. Everyone is glued to their TV sets waiting for news." After a long pause Janet covered the mouthpiece and spoke to Joseph. "She says we should all pray." Joseph simply nodded.

The two women spoke for a few minutes more before Joseph took the receiver. He told his mother he loved her, and then hung up.

He told Janet that he had to go back to the studio. After he'd gone Janet sat on the couch and cried. She recalled a time when he never would have left her alone. How he would have remained there by her side to comfort her, assure her that her he-man would protect her from any harm. Instead she sat alone with the fear of the television broadcast interrupted by a news bulletin. The shrill beeping of the emergency alert system might sound, sending her down to the air raid shelter in the basement of their building. There she'd wait for an all-clear signal or bombs to fall.

The situation came to a head on October 26th when the United States Navy boarded the Russian freighter Marluca. When no weapons were found, the ship continued on to Cuba. The action convinced the Russians that the Americans were prepared to enforce the blockade. Castro sent Premier Khrushchev an impassioned plea to allow nuclear missiles to rain down on America. But the Russian leader had no real desire for such a confrontation. He ordered any ships carrying weapons to reverse course and head home.

The two nuclear powers negotiated a deal that would see the dismantling of the missile sites in Cuba and a guarantee that the Russians would no longer send any more offensive weapons to its Latin American ally. In return, the U.S. would soon abandon missile sites they had in Turkey. The crisis in Cuba was over.

♫♫♫♫♫

Janet spent the morning with Joseph at the studio putting some finishing touches on the latest batch of songs they'd written. The Pixie's had several slated for their new album. Joseph had been called away to take a phone call. When he returned, he was visibly angry. Leo followed behind him. He too was upset.

"What's wrong?" Janet asked.

"It seems our friend Alan Thomas has taken a powder," Joseph said.

Janet looked to Leo for some sort of explanation. "He didn't show up for his show in Connecticut last night," Leo said. "He left a note with our A&R man. He says he can't sing and make records for a company that supports this country's policy to bully a small Latin American country. He says he's going to live and work in Cuba."

"Whaaat?"

"Did you know anything about this?" Joseph asked her.

"Me? Certainly not!" Janet didn't like the accusation. "I haven't heard from him in months." She didn't say why.

"The guys a nut," Leo added.

"He's more than a nut. He's an ungrateful little bastard! I'll sue the son-of-a bitch! When I get through with him he'll be singing in the streets with a tin cup."

Janet had never seen her husband so angry. It frightened her.

"I'll hire an investigator. We'll find him before he can skip the country," Leo tried to be re-assuring. But it was to no avail.

Thomas somehow avoided detection. No one could verify if he ever did manage to reach Cuba. That was just fine as far as Janet was concerned.

♫♫♫♫♫

Not long after Telstar became operational, an avid space buff and record producer in London, England named Joe Meek came up with an infectious melody line and hard driving beat that he transformed into a song he called "The Theme From Telstar." He gave the song to an instrumental group he'd formed, the Tornadoes. After the initial session, Meek shortened the name to "Telstar." He also added several special effects to further fill out the sound. By overdubbing the melody track using a Clavioline, an electronic keyboard, the song took on an eerie, spaced out sound. The record zoomed to the top of the U.K. record charts. Then, in December 1962, the Tornadoes became the first English rock and roll group to top the American charts. "Telstar" remained there for three consecutive weeks.

Greatly influenced by radio broadcasts, records, and films imported from America, British teens became familiar with the work of Teddy Boyette, Elvis Presley, Bill Haley and Chuck Berry. A huge rock and roll market emerged in Great Britain.

Unlike their more affluent American cousins, aspiring musicians couldn't afford musical instruments so they formed skiffle bands. The term skiffle dated back to the early 1900's defined as good time music utilizing simple, homemade instruments like a washboard, whistle jug or kazoo, to create its unique sound. If you added a guitar or banjo to the razzle-dazzle mixture, you had the makings of a real skiffle band.

One such Liverpool skiffle band called themselves the Quarrymen. The group honed its craft playing long hours in raunchy strip clubs and beer halls in Hamburg, Germany. They signed as a back-up band for singer Tony Sheridan, using the name of the Beat Brothers. They performed behind Sheridan in many appearances and in the summer of 1961 they recorded a song called "My Bonnie," released on the Polydor Record label in October attaining some moderate success both in Germany and back home in England.

The record came to the attention of Brian Epstein, the proprietor of the North East Music Store, a business venture his family owned. He discovered that the band no longer provided back up for Sheridan and had changed their name to the Beatles.

They played to packed houses of frantic fans at the Cavern Club, a dank subterranean Jazz Club that had become a haven for the local music scene. On seeing them there, Epstein recognized their raw talent gave them the potential to become something special. He signed them to a five-year contract as personal manager. Under Epstein, the Beatles developed a new and refined look and style, wearing matching suits and adopting uniform pageboy haircuts.

After rejections by several major record labels, Epstein had the group audition for George Martin, the head of EMI's Polyphone Records. Martin signed them to a one-year contract with a royalty payment of one farthing per record, amounting to one quarter of a penny for each of them. Martin made some further refinements and a personnel change at drummer. He guided them as producer to three hit singles and an album, which hurled them to star status as they toured all over England.

Vee-Jay Records, a popular R&B label based in Chicago acquired the US rights to early Beatles songs as part of a licensing agreement they had with several other EMI performers. They released the Beatle's single, "Please, Please Me," and placed the record into the rotation at the City's top radio station WLS in February 1963. It failed to impress anyone. When Dick Clark featured another of their singles, “She Loves You,” on American Bandstand later that summer, the audience laughed and ridiculed the act because of their offbeat hairstyle. In New York City, popular radio deejay, Murray the K, played the song on his 1010 WINS record revue in October. Once again it garnered little response.

It appeared American audiences had little interest in these four mop top, faggy looking performers from Liverpool, England.

Chapter Thirty-Two:

"Goodbye"

In Dallas, Texas, on November 22, 1963, at 12:39 pm, CST, the Top 40 radio station KLIF was playing "I Have a Boyfriend," by the Chiffons. The song was cut off mid way thru. At the same moment, television viewers across the country were annoyed when the CBS-TV network interrupted the popular soap opera, "As the World Turns." A printed "BULLETIN" placard appeared on-screen because CBS didn't have a camera warmed up in their newsroom in New York. The voice of news anchorman Walter Cronkite followed.

"Here is a bulletin from CBS news in Dallas, Texas, three shots were fired at President Kennedy's motorcade in downtown Dallas. Reports say that President Kennedy has been seriously wounded by this shooting."

Cronkite repeated the details, advising viewers to stay tuned to CBS for further reports.

Twenty minutes later he returned, this time on-camera while frantic employees monitored the wire service tickers in the background. Cronkite continued to report on whatever random, sketchy details he had. At 2:38 pm EST, someone handed the anchorman a piece of paper. He put on his glasses, read the note, and then looked into the camera.

"From Dallas, Texas, the flash, apparently official..." he proceeded to read the note, "President Kennedy died at 1 pm central standard time, 12:00 eastern standard time..." His eyes glanced up at a clock on the wall, "…some thirty-eight minutes ago."

Visibly shaken, he fought to keep his composure. His demeanor reflected the sadness felt by millions around the country.

Less than two hours later, police arrested a suspect, a meek, frail looking ex-Marine named Lee Harvey Oswald. He worked in the building where the shots were fired. During his escape he'd shot and killed a Dallas police officer. Several witnesses saw him enter a nearby movie theater where authorities apprehended him.

During the flight that brought Kennedy's body back to Washington, Vice-President Lyndon Baines Johnson took the oath making him the thirty-sixth President of the United States.

♫♫♫♫♫

Like millions of others, Janet Rabinowitz followed the events of the next three days in a trance-like state. The sight of Kennedy's widow Jackie, her raspberry colored suit and legs stained with the blood and brain matter of her beloved husband was seared in her memory. Two days later, the alleged assassin himself was killed while in police custody in the basement of the Dallas Police Headquarters, meaning that perhaps the motives behind the assassination might never be revealed.

Saddest of all was the live broadcast of President Kennedy's State Funeral in Washington on Monday, November 25th. A solemn high mass took place at St. Matthews Cathedral attended by 1,200 family members, dignitaries and heads of state from all over the world. The flag draped casket was placed onto an Army caisson drawn by six white horses for the procession to Arlington Cemetery. As it passed the point where the Kennedy family stood waiting, the President's son, John F. Kennedy Jr. saluted the casket. It was the boy's third birthday.

♫♫♫♫♫

Many marriages are over before they end. Janet knew that when she told Joseph of her plans to leave him. He initially took it to be an over-reaction to the assassination. He believed seeing the former first lady, no longer radiant and elegant, was too much for Janet to handle. To a point, his opinion had merit.

Janet did draw such a comparison, though certainly to a much lesser degree. While Jackie Kennedy personified a shattered, tortured widow retreating into her grief and loneliness like any other normal woman, Janet's decision was more personal.

For ten years she'd dedicated herself to her own personal hero. She'd been his friend, lover and wife. She supported his dreams and sacrificed to help make them come true. In business she'd become his collaborator and confidant. She still believed that if there was a mistress, it was the music business. The pressures he faced every day at work pushed the concept of family life into a corner of his consciousness that had become minute. They came to live in two different worlds.

She'd made frequent attempts to have a life of her own. She had friends, Mickey's wife Linda, and others but Janet found them to be a flighty bunch prone to spending the afternoon drinking martinis, going to the beauty parlor, and nightclubbing whenever possible. Janet needed more. She thought for a time of joining the Peace Corps, a civilian, volunteer program Kennedy started in 1961 that sent qualified men and women to needy nations around the world to educate and train its citizens in the ways of government, agriculture and information technology. But now, with Kennedy gone, her interest in politics waned. His successor might prove to be a great leader but Johnson wasn't a young person's president. The perceived utopia of Camelot disappeared. Janet longed for the days when she and her husband would lay naked in their bed with a quart of butter pecan ice cream and one spoon.

The announcement that she was leaving him stunned Joseph. He sat with his eyes in a vacant stare, his mouth agape. There was a knot in the pit of his stomach and his body began to shake as Janet came to the conclusion of her argument.

"I just don't have a place in your life anymore Joseph," she told him through tears.

"You're my wife. Of course you have a place in my life Janet. I know things haven't been easy lately. I've been distracted. But you can't leave me. We can go to a marriage counselor...there's still time...we can adopt a child."

"You can't find time to come home for dinner at night, when would you find time for a marriage counselor or to be a daddy? I don't want to have a child just to keep me busy, Joseph. That's *not* what this is all about."

"Just, promise me you won't do anything rash. We'll fix this sweetheart. I know we can fix this."

After a few weeks and many tearful pleadings on his part, nothing was fixed. With great reluctance Joseph accepted the idea of a life without the woman he loved. He spoke of things he dreaded.

"We'll need to get lawyers, draw up papers and all that," he told her.

"I think we can come to agree on most things. I'm going to Reno. It wouldn't take very long that way and we wouldn't need to go to court."

It surprised Joseph at just how well she had all the details worked out. Reno, Nevada had become the quickie divorce capital of the world. The cost and requirements to dissolve a marriage there were most lenient. Divorce ranches located there, provided people with a place to stay while fulfilling the six-week residency requirement.

"There's alimony and stuff," Joseph reminded her.

"I don't want very much, Joseph, really. There's plenty of money in that account you set up for me, all the royalties from my songs. That's more than enough."

"I'll put some of my things together and move into a hotel downtown for now."

"No, Joseph I don't want you to do that. I spoke to Linda, she says I can stay in their guest room until I'm ready to go to Reno."

"She didn't know about this beforehand, her and Mickey?"

"No, sweetheart, nobody knew until after I told you."

It relieved Joseph to hear that but still, he was puzzled. "But, why stay there? I have to move out of here sooner or later, don't I?"

"I'm not going to stay in New York, Joseph. I'm going away."

"Away… away where?"

"England, I think."

"Jesus Christ, Janet," Joseph exploded. "What the hell are you going to do in England?"

"I'm going to visit all those wonderful castles I used to dream about when I was back in Cleveland, take tons of pictures. Maybe I'll put them all in a book with some new poems."

"Camelot all over again, huh?" His sarcasm hurt.

"I can remember a time when you would have thought that the idea was kinda neat."

It was just another example of the distance between them.

"I'm sorry, Janet."

"It doesn't matter anymore." It was difficult to accept that now every conversation they had upset one of them.

When Janet returned from Reno eight weeks later she and Joseph were divorced. She put the things she wanted from the apartment into storage and made her plans to leave the country.

Joseph immersed himself in his work even deeper than anyone could ever imagine. Those closest to him at the company saw the changes in him almost immediately.

♫♫♫♫♫

On December 26,1963, WMCA-Radio in New York City played the Beatles first single record release on their new label, Capital Records, "I Want to Hold Your Hand." It became an instant hit.

The other two major radio stations in the City, WINS and WABC also picked up the tune and its popularity quickly spread to other markets across the country. Suddenly, the band American teenagers shunned months earlier caught on like wild fire. The record sold one million copies and reached number one on the U.S. charts on January 16th, 1964, leaving the public hungry for more.

Chapter Thirty-Three:

"Yeah...Yeah...Yeah"

Traffic on the Belt Parkway was backed up for miles outside Kennedy Airport in New York City. The International Transportation complex located on the Brooklyn/Queens border was renamed from Idlewild Airport just three weeks after the President's assassination. New Yorkers had already shortened it to JFK. The Cadillac Coupe Deville leased by Chanticleer Records took Joseph and Janet to the airport.

She'd tried to convince him there was no need to accompany her, but of course, he'd insisted. Now, stopped dead in this traffic jam two miles from the airport exit, he became antsy.

"What's with this traffic, Tommy?" His regular driver a former cab driver knew the city streets quite well.

"I don't know, Mr. Rabin. It ain't rush hour. Maybe there's an accident up ahead or something."

"We have plenty of time, Joseph," Janet assured him.

"Yeah, I know, but you have to go through customs and everything."

"We'll be fine." Janet knew her departure would be an emotional nightmare. To have it rushed now would only make matters worse.

When the car finally approached the terminal building, the reason for the long delay became clear. Wooden police barricades were in place to hold back a tremendous crowd of young people lining both sides of the road leading up to the Pan American Airlines Terminal. Joseph now realized what all the commotion was about.

The Beatles were arriving for their first scheduled American appearances. The crowd consisted of screaming, teenagers dressed in heavy coats, wool hats and scarves to brace them against the frigid February weather. Many carried homemade cardboard signs and placards expressing adoration for the group or its individual members, Paul McCartney, John Lennon, George Harrison, and Ringo Starr.

"This is unbelievable, huh?" Janet asked.

"A few months ago nobody knew who these guys were. Now look."

Tommy brought the car to a halt at the terminal's entrance. As Joseph and Janet got out they became aware of further bedlam. More Beatles' fans were up on the roof of the terminal building.

"There must be thousands of them," Janet observed.

"With everything else that's been going on, I completely forgot about these guys getting in today."

Joseph motioned to a red-capped baggage handler who quickly guided a metal baggage cart in their direction. Tommy and the red cap removed Janet's baggage from the Caddy and onto the cart.

"Flight one twenty-four, please," Janet instructed the red cap as Joseph gave him a tip. He then took Janet's arm to lead her into the terminal building.

The din from the roof became a muffled hum. Joseph maneuvered Janet off to one side to get as much privacy as they could in their final moments together. Janet became anxious. He wanted to accompany her to her departure gate, but because of the heightened security, police would only allow ticket holders to proceed any further.

It was time to say goodbye. "Joseph, I really should be going."

"This isn't the way things were supposed to be, Janet," His voice cracked with emotion.

Her own reply had to navigate a lump in her throat. "I'll write to you."

"Letters? That's how we got started in the first place."

Janet knew what he meant. She leaned forward and gave him

one last kiss on the cheek. Then she turned and hurried off. Joseph watched until the sight of her walking away became too painful. He went outside to find Tommy leaning against the Cadillac.

"You think these guys from England got any chance of making it big?" Tommy asked.

"Hard to say." Joseph answered half-heartedly, happy for the opportunity to get his mind off his situation. "They're signed to be on the Ed Sullivan Show three times."

"Ah, if you ask me they're just a fad," Tommy said. He opened the rear door of the car.

"That's what Leo says."

"Yeah, that Mr. Klein is a real smart man."

Joseph got into the car. Tommy closed the door behind him.

"You going to the office, boss?" Tommy asked after getting back behind the wheel.

"No. Take me home."

It was easy for Joseph to dismiss the clamor he'd witnessed. The Beatles, the music business, all of it took a back seat to the sadness invading his personal life. He didn't say another word on the drive back to the city.

♫♫♫♫♫

Approximately forty percent of the American population watched the Beatles perform on the Ed Sullivan Show two nights later. Their subsequent appearances brought in similarly staggering ratings numbers. The group was fast becoming a worldwide phenomenon. A two-year backlog of recordings from the U.K. provided American radio stations and record distributors with a treasure trove of material that swamped the airwaves from coast to coast.

By Spring, the Beatles accomplished the unprecedented feat of having five of their singles occupy the top five spots on Billboard Magazine's Hot 100 List, fourteen singles on the list overall. A stunning sixty percent of all records sold in the United States were Beatles records. They called it, "Beatlemania."

It didn't end with the Beatles. Other groups from England, the Dave Clark Five, Gerry and the Pacemakers, and the Rolling Stones, followed them to perform on American television and stages. They were self-contained bands, playing their own instruments and in many instances writing their own songs.

It became a veritable British invasion of talent. An invasion the American music business was ill prepared to handle.

It wasn't just the music business that felt the effects of the British onslaught. English clothing designers like Mary Quant were having a huge impact on fashion trends in America. She introduced young women to the miniskirt, worn tight around the body with a peek-a-boo hemline rising a scandalous six full inches above the knee. There were also tall, vinyl go-go boots in outrageous colors accentuating the exposed thigh, raising a ruckus around the world. Women took to wearing their hair in a bouffant style. Many men abandoned the flattop crew cut look top sports figures wore. Instead they went for the pageboy "Beatle cut" with long sideburns and a length that ran down beyond the back of their shirt collar.

♫♫♫♫♫

Bobby Vitale skulked like some common criminal in the darkened doorway of a dress shop on W. 48th Street. The closed storefront offered a good vantage point for him to observe any activity in front of the Alva Hotel across the street. He'd been there for several hours, waiting, watching, and needing to have his suspicions verified.

He dropped his cigarette butt on the ground at his feet. It landed amid a dozen others he'd similarly disposed of during his vigil. Bobby pulled the collar of his dark tweed coat tightly around his body. He was about to reach for another cigarette when he spied movement inside the hotel's revolving door. He pushed further back into his hiding place.

His keen eyes focused on the images of a man and a woman

coming out of the hotel to the sidewalk. It was Joe Rabin and Evie Rhodes. The anger that swelled in him boiled the blood in his veins.

He watched the hotel doorman raise his hand hailing a vacant taxi from a sea of yellow cabs, cruising the mid-town area. One pulled up to the curb. The doorman opened the door allowing Evie to enter. He then repeated the ritual putting Joseph into a cab of his own.

The entire event took place in a matter of moments. It replayed in Bobby's brain like a scratch on a vinyl record makes a phonograph needle skip, repeating the same thing over and over. Seeing Evie with Joseph together answered the question as to why she hadn't returned his phone calls. There'd always been a no strings attached element to their secret love affair, but Bobby had fallen hard for Evie. She'd become cold and distant to him in the months since Joseph's wife left him. Evie was an ambitious little vixen, willing to do whatever it took to keep her name in the limelight even if it meant screwing her boss in a seedy hotel room on the wrong side of Broadway. Bobby stepped out of the shadows and hailed another yellow cab. He got in and shouted his destination to the driver.

"Take me to the Peppermint Lounge."

No directions were necessary. The Peppermint Lounge was the hottest new nightspot in town. There, Bobby would find fans and hangers on eager to buy him drinks. He'd have no problem picking up some female rock and roll fan to sleep with. Such were the perks of being a singing star. But it wouldn't make him happy.

By July 4th, the day Americans celebrated their independence from British rule, more than half the songs on the U.S. record charts were by English artists. The takeover was so overwhelming that many independent labels closed. Record sales by American performers dropped off dramatically. Singles and LP's were returned by the caseload.

♫♫♫♫♫

Lyndon Johnson's "Great Society" legislation achieved much success in the area of domestic reform. Despite all that, his efforts met with intense, sometimes violent resistance.

Three young Civil Rights workers, two white and one black, were kidnapped, murdered and buried in an earthen dam in Mississippi. Not all black leaders adopted the same non-violent approach preached by men like Dr. Martin Luther King Jr. in achieving and maintaining their civil rights. Malcom X, a highly influential religious leader from the Nation of Islam portrayed white men as devils. He advocated violence if necessary in order to put blacks on top of the social order of things. Many whites viewed this as a call to arms for a black revolution. There were race riots taking place in major cities and small towns alike.

Johnson's foreign policy, especially in Southeast Asia was also on shaky ground. In early August, North Vietnamese gunboats attacked the naval destroyer, USS Maddox, on patrol in the Gulf of Tonkin. This unprovoked attack led Congress to pass the Gulf of Tonkin Resolution, allowing Johnson to retaliate without a declaration of war.

He ordered the Air Force to commence a campaign for the aerial bombing of North Vietnamese military targets dubbed "Operation Rolling Thunder." But Johnson needed to be cautious in an election year. The weight of his decision to begin the bombing could easily jeopardize his position as a peace candidate. His Republican opponent, Senator Barry Goldwater from Arizona, was already viewed as a warmonger. He threatened that if elected, he'd use Nuclear weapons against the Asian nation as well as send US combat troops to fight in Vietnam, something Johnson promised to avoid. This combined to lead Johnson on a landslide victory in the 1964 Presidential election.

Chapter Thirty-Four:

"Return To Sender"

After watching Johnson's Inaugural Ceremony on television Joseph he got a phone call from a reporter at the New York Daily News asking for a comment on a story that would be running in the paper the next day.

Alan Freed had died in a hospital in Palm Springs, California at the age of forty-four. The cause of death, Uremia and Cirrhosis of the liver, diseases related to severe alcohol abuse.

The news shocked Joseph. He thought for some time, before speaking.

"Alan Freed was a pioneer in the music business. As a disc jockey and producer he inspired us all. There'll never be anyone else like him. He'll be sorely missed."

A pause followed on the other end of the line before the newspaperman asked. "Yeah, that's all well and good. But then he got caught up in that Payola scandal years back and that ruined him right? What do you have to say about all that?"

Without another word, Joseph hung up the receiver. He regretted not blasting the reporter, to tell him off in no uncertain terms for trying to paint the passing of such a great man in such negative colors. Freed deserved better no matter how he ended up. But the music he loved faded from the consciousness of today's youth. Maybe in his last days of ill health, Freed too recognized that fact and didn't want to be around to see the worst that could happen.

♫♫♫♫♫

The intercom on Joseph's desk buzzed, annoying him as he made his way through a mountain of paperwork. He wanted to ignore it but the noise didn't stop.

"Yes?" he finally replied with a flick of a switch.

"Ronnie McGinnis from accounting is out here. He says he needs to speak to you," his secretary said from her post just outside his door.

"Where's Leo?" Joseph didn't disguise his displeasure in his tone.

"He says he needs to speak to you personally."

"Okay. Send him in." Joseph continued working as the young, neatly dressed accountant entered the office and closed the door behind him.

"I'm really sorry to bother you, Mr. Rabin, I know how busy you are."

"That's all right, Ronnie," Joseph looked up from his work and saw that the thin, collegiate type had a look of great concern on his face. He carried a large mailing envelope. Joseph felt certain the contents contained the reason for this visit.

"Why don't you go ahead and tell me what's on your mind?"

"This came in the mail the day before yesterday." He handed the envelope to Joseph who inspected it. The envelope was addressed to the record company. It was open. "It's all returned mail," the accountant said.

"Returned? Returned from where?" Joseph asked. He spilled the contents of the envelope out on his desk to reveal dozens of smaller business envelops now in a pile in front him.

"Radcliff, Kentucky."

An uneasy feeling washed over Joseph when he heard those words. He picked up one of the smaller envelopes and read the name that appeared in the plastic film window: McKinley Williams... Chanticleer's real name.

"These look like..." Joseph started to say.

"Royalty checks. They date back to nineteen fifty-nine."

"And, none of them were opened?"

"One of them was." Ronnie moved forward to show Joseph a

letter that came with the larger envelope. By this time Joseph had difficulty concentrating.

"That letter is from the Hardin County Police Department. It says they found the envelopes in a drawer of the decedent's home. They opened one to see if they were important."

The word *decedent* cut through Joseph's flesh like a spear.

"I'm sorry to be the one to tell you. All of us around here know what that gentleman meant to you." Ronnie saw that Joseph wanted more than just condolences. He went back to the facts of his report. "Apparently he died of natural causes several weeks ago. He didn't have any family and the authorities weren't able to find any sort of will. The police sent all these back when they discovered they were checks."

Still quite stunned, Joseph stared passed the accountant. It was as though an old time movie was being projected on the beveled glass of his office door. There, flashback images of Kentucky, his days the Army, the accident that nearly killed him and the kindly old black man with a guitar played out. The sound of Ronnie's voice brought him back to reality

"I kinda went over Mr. Klein's head with this, but I thought you would want to know."

Joseph suspected there was more to it than that. Maybe the young man sought some sort of job security by making an end run around Leo. One thing was certain though, Leo was indeed the one to fill in more of the blanks.

"That's okay, Ronnie. I'll take it from here. Thanks for letting me know."

The young man didn't respond. He obviously expected more for the information he'd revealed but he wasn't about to push his luck. He simply backed out of the office.

Joseph sat in silence for a few minutes, anger now replacing sadness. He scooped the checks back into the larger envelope, stepped out from behind his desk, and left his office. He started down the corridor.

Leo's secretary Lucille, a short, stout woman of about fifty smiled as Joseph entered from the hallway. She sensed a problem when he didn't smile back.

"Is he in?" Joseph asked curtly.

"Yes, he is, Mr. Rabin."

"Go get yourself a cup of coffee, Lucille."

"Mr. Rabin?

"Now Lucille!"

Realizing it was an order and not a suggestion the secretary got up and hurried out of the office. Joseph didn't bother to knock on the inner office door, but merely pushed it open and walked right in. Leo was startled as he looked up from his adding machine.

"Something wrong, Joseph?" Leo asked with concern. His partner moved forward and dumped the contents of the large envelope onto Leo's desk. Leo picked one up and looked at it, just as Joseph had done earlier.

"Chanty's checks," Joseph blurted out. "He's dead."

Joseph's blunt announcement got the reaction he wanted. Leo sat open mouthed, leaning back in his chair, removing his glasses.

"I'm so sorry to hear that. When did it happen?" The sincere regret in his voice softened Joseph's tone.

"Weeks ago is all I know," Joseph hung his head and folded his arms in front of him. He turned and paced to the door and then back again. He motioned toward the envelopes on the desk. "You never agreed with me about sending him that money, did you?"

Leo fully understood the question. After Teddy's death Joseph instructed Leo to send a small portion of his own composer's royalties on Teddy's songs to Chanticleer.

"That's right," Leo felt comfortable defending his position but he disliked the tone and the accusation. "Our contractual responsibility is to Teddy's parents as executors of his estate, no one else."

"I didn't give a damn about our responsibility. I wanted Chanty to have that money."

Leo raised his voice. "And he got the money!" He stood and passed his hand over the evidence that proved what he said was true "He got every penny of it. Is it my fault he chose to wallpaper his place with it?"

Leo's remarks took some of the wind out of Joseph's sails. Yet there remained a personal detail Joseph wanted answered.

"But all this time, all these years? The checks weren't cashed. The money was never paid out of our accounts. Leo, you had to know about this. How come you never told me?"

Leo lowered his eyes to elude Joseph's demanding stare.

"You always said you wanted no part of the company's accounting procedures."

The answer was nowhere near good enough. Joseph's anger rose again. "I had no interest in our accounting procedures because I trusted *you* with all that!"

His integrity now questioned, Leo took offense. He leaned across the desk putting himself directly in Joseph's face.

"You say you can't trust me? You think you can come in here and shout at me like I was one of your teenage singers? Do you forget who I am?" Joseph backed away like a scolded puppy. Leo wasn't finished, though now he spoke more calmly. "If I didn't love you like a son I'd tear up our contract and walk out that door. I'm sorry about Chanticleer, Joseph, I truly am, but I'm not the enemy. If you want me to clear out I will."

"No, that's not what I want. I need you now more than ever," Joseph answered sheepishly. He slumped down into the chair on the opposite side of Leo's desk. "I'm sorry, Leo."

"If you wish, I'll contact the authorities in Kentucky, see if I can find out anything more about what happened, what arrangements were made?"

"I'd appreciate that Leo, thank you," Joseph stood and left Leo's office.

On his way back down the corridor he cursed himself for the harsh words they exchanged. For a brief moment Joseph had indeed forgotten to whom he was talking. Leo Klein, the man whose trust and generosity made it possible for him to get into the music business in the first place. Through all the years of success and good fortune he couldn't remember the last time he outwardly thanked his older and wiser partner. Now, with their business on a downward spiral he attacked his friend, accused him of terrible things. Joseph truly hated the person he'd become.

♫♫♫♫♫

Leo's inquiries to the police in Hardin County met with vague details and little information regarding Chanticleer's last days. That prompted him to take greater pains to find out exactly what happened. A telephone call to Teddy's family yielded little more. They'd seen or heard less and less from their son's good friend in recent years. George Boyette assured Leo he'd personally look into things. His subsequent report revealed some troubling facts.

Lester, the mechanic at the service station told George that Chanty had become involved in the local civil rights movement, an avid follower of the Reverend Martin Luther King Jr. He participated in the march on Washington DC in 1963. As part of over 250,000 people who stood at the Lincoln Memorial he'd listened as Dr. King delivered a speech that included the inspirational refrain, "I had a dream…."

This put him at odds with the citizenry of Radcliff. Locals boycotted his business to the point where the service station closed down. There were reports that he'd been set upon and beaten by roughnecks on at least two occasions.

Lester found him dead on the floor of his house about a month ago. Since there was no sign of foul play, no autopsy seemed necessary. Lester also told the Boyette's that he was buried in a local black cemetery on the poor side of town with only a wooden cross to mark his grave.

The report sickened Joseph. The company sent the Boyette's enough money to have the body exhumed and moved to a more fitting resting place. A headstone placed at the new gravesite read:

McKinley "Chanticleer" Williams
A Mentor and Friend
He Loved Music, Freedom and His "Senorita"

Chapter Thirty-Five:

"You Don't Own Me"

President Lyndon Johnson came to realize that sometimes, the promises you make turn out to be impossible to keep. In the first week of May 1965, a contingent of some 35,000 U.S. combat troops deployed to Vietnam. By summer that number swelled to 125,000. The military draft increased from 17,000 to 35,000 men per month. The male youth of America, culled primarily from working class families and minorities, were destined to become infantry riflemen fighting in the jungles of Southeast Asia.

The turnaround Joseph Rabin needed so desperately to save his company never materialized. In fact, things got worse. British bands continued to come ashore to dominate the record charts. Female artists like Dusty Springfield, Petula Clark and Cilla Black joined groups like Herman Hermits and Freddie and the Dreamers in the next wave. A male torch singer from Whales, Tom Jones gave Elvis Presley a run for his money, driving female audiences to such frenzy that they regularly tossed their underwear onstage wherever he performed.

Only a handful of American artists managed to get it together and compete at top levels. The Beach Boys from Southern California with their surfing and hot rod tunes remained strong. In the East, groups like Jay and the Americans from Brooklyn and the Four Seasons out of New Jersey specialized in tight harmonies and message songs about love on the wrong side of the tracks that appealed to many fans.

Because black audiences didn't fully embrace many of the predominantly white British invaders, Berry Gordy's Motown label featuring acts like the Temptations, the Four Tops and a female singing trio, the Supremes were consistently in the top five. Malcom Brown's South Side Records in Chicago and Stax Records out of Memphis also prospered during this period.

"What are we going to do?" Leo asked Joseph at a closed door meeting when it became clear that the company would finish in the red for yet another consecutive fiscal quarter.

"I wish I had an answer for you, Leo, but I really don't," The creative genius and tower of strength behind Chanticleer Records seemed to have lost his edge.

"In that case, I'm afraid we'll have to cut some corners around here," Leo warned.

"Fire people?"

"It could come to that. There are some contracts coming due. We can try to renegotiate for better terms or just not renew them at all."

"Shit."

"There's another option. We can sell off the contracts. Alexis Records has made several offers to buy out any we wish to divulge ourselves of."

"Those gangsters?" Joseph knew Richie Conforti's reputation and crooked business practices. "No. You're free to entertain offers from any other label but not Alexis!"

"As you wish. But this is all still a temporary fix. Joseph if things don't get better soon…" Leo didn't need to finish the sentence.

Joseph believed he had one last card to play. The last bright spot in the Chanticleer stable of performers was the Pixies. As long as they held their ground on the charts Joseph felt he could keep the company's head above water. He learned that concert promoter Sid Bernstein was looking for a female act to accompany the Beatles when they opened their next US tour in the summer. Joseph decided he'd lobby hard to get the Pixies that job.

♫♫♫♫♫

All four of the Du-Kanes complained about the new hairdos and Carnaby Street wardrobe Joseph had them wear at the photo shoot for the cover sleeve of their next single. They relented only after he told them the importance of this change in appearance. If the new single failed to do well, there would be no album release for the first time in seven years.

"I feel like a fucking hairdresser in this getup!" Bobby complained loudest during a break at the photographer's studio. The double-breasted suit jacket he wore had wide lapels, pinstripes and bellbottom trousers. His tie, several inches wide had a thick, strangling knot.

"You do look kinda sweet there, Bobby boy," Hector kidded him.

"Up yours!" Bobby flipped the middle finger of his right hand up at his singing mate. Hector laughed at the obscene gesture.

"Can you please tell me why we have to dress like this? How is all this gonna help us sell records?" Bobby asked Johnny.

"Joe thinks maybe we can get some new fans if we look more like the Brits."

"He's such a fucking bullshit artist, man! All he gives a rat's ass about is the goddam Pixies and pushing their stuff. He's probably banging all three of them by now."

Bobby's angry rant was lost on the rest of the group who were all unaware of the secret Bobby knew which still had him festering.

"The girls are the only act on the label making any money. You can't blame him for focusing on them."

"I blame him for a lot of things."

"Shit, Bobby how can you say that, man? Where would we be without Joe Rabin?" Kenny chimed in.

"Well, if you ask me, he's just hanging us out to dry. He's got us dressed us up like a bunch of organ grinder's monkeys. That's supposed to change his luck? He's an asshole."

"No, you're the asshole Bobby!" Hectors Puerto Rican blood boiled.

"Fuck you!" Bobby yelled.

When Hector lunged toward Bobby, Johnny stepped between them.

"Take it easy you two! You mess up these fancy threads we're wearing and there'll really be hell to pay."

Both boys backed off. Bobby bolted for the back door of the studio. Johnny headed after him as Hector called out, "I'm telling you Johnny, I'm fed up with that guy mouthing off all the time!"

Johnny found Bobby in the alley outside the building. He leaned against the wall puffing on a cigarette.

"You gonna tell me what it is that's eating at your gut?" Johnny said.

"I told you, Johnny, it's these…"

"It's not the clothes, man, we both know that."

"It's my mother," Bobby confessed. "She's finally gone off the deep end, man."

Great frustration showed in his voice as he spoke. His success as a singing star allowed Bobby and his family to vastly improve their lives and for a time it was all good. His mother cut back on her drinking, but her lack of social skills kept her home most of the time with Diane acting as babysitter. With Bobby out on the road so much it was just a matter of time before the drinking started again accelerating beyond the point it had ever been.

"She doesn't know who or where she is half the time. The doctor says it's the DT's… says she's got to go into a home, constant care. That's gonna cost me an arm and a leg."

"You got the money for it though, right? You've been saving up?"

Bobby's answer didn't really surprise Johnny. "I've blown most of what we make on booze and broads. Whatever's left won't last very long. Then I'm up shits creek."

"I suppose I could help you out some," Johnny offered, not really knowing how.

"I appreciate that, man, I really do. But you got problems of your own, a wife, two kids, that big house with your in-laws. You just better hold on to what you've got and not worry about me. I'll manage, sell the house, and get a smaller apartment somewhere."

"What about your sister?"

"She's going to live with my aunt upstate, go to college up there. She'll be better off." Bobby even managed a smile he hoped would satisfy his best friend.

"Things will be fine. Rabin will come up with something," Johnny assured him.

Bobby's smile turned into a sarcastic smirk. He put his arm around Johnny's shoulder as if to impart some wise, fatherly advice.

"Listen, man, Chanticleer Records is going down like the Titanic. These English groups are killing us and there's nothing you, Joe Rabin, or me can do about it."

♫♫♫♫♫

Fifty-six thousand people attended the Beatles' outdoor concert at Shea Stadium, in Flushing, New York. The Vox Amplifier Company had special 100-watt speakers made for the event. When it became apparent that they were still not loud enough for the artists to be heard over the screaming fans, someone decided to employ the Stadium's Public Address System. This system wasn't designed for use by singers or musical instruments. The resulting sound reverberated through the cavernous ballpark and right back to the performers onstage. At one point, John Lennon, playing an electronic organ on one number became so frustrated that he pounded on the keys with his elbows, smiling at his band mates as he did so.

The Beatles were onstage for a scant thirty-five minutes performing just twelve songs. There had been several opening acts before them. The Pixies were not among them. Despite his best negotiating skills, Joseph couldn't secure a spot for his female artists on the tour. Obviously, promoters were playing hardball, trying to get Chanticleer's top talent at bargain basement prices. It was a major setback.

He did manage to get the girls booked on a series of shows in the

Chicago area headlining for some of South Side Records stable of artists. Malcom Brown who owned South Side was also facing some serious financial hardships. He thought the Pixies could help put the shows over. Joseph agreed.

The concert tour lasted three weeks. When the group returned to New York, Evie wasn't with them. Remaining loyal to a family member, neither of the other two other girls proved forthcoming about what happened. Phone calls to Malcom Brown went unanswered.

When the singer did show up several days later, she requested a private, after hours meeting with Joseph.

"We were worried about you," Joseph told Evie quite calmly.

"I'm a big girl, Joseph," She enjoyed playing cat and mouse with him.

"There were concerns. Insurance-wise and things like that."

"Did you reach out, try to find me?" It became a verbal fencing match, each of them parrying, seeking an opening.

"We found out you and Malcom Brown were becoming something of…an item?"

"We had dinner together a time or two, went to a party here and there. He's a good man, doing a lot of good things for the black community in Chicago."

"I'm well aware of that."

"Is it that maybe you're a little jealous of Malcom?"

Joseph scoffed at the idea. "Only if he's trying to steal the group away from us."

"I should have known your interest in all this would be strictly business."

"We've been down this road a couple of times already, Evie." He wanted her to get to the point, which made her angry.

"Then you might as well know that Malcom did in fact make me an offer. A very generous one at that."

The conversation now lost all sense of lightheartedness.

"Maybe we should put the rest of this off until tomorrow, when Leo can be here."

"Suppose we just leave Leo out of this particular negotiation?"

"Why?"

"Because I want you to hear what I have to say without anyone else around. I think we can work this out Joseph, just you and me. Leo isn't aware of what we shared," She tried to personalize things.

"None of that can play into this, Evie. Just tell me what it is you want."

Her demands rolled off her tongue as easily as the lyrics to any of her hit songs. "I want to change the name of the group. I want my name out front, Evie Rhodes and the Pixies, and I want full approval of all the songs we do from here on," she paused, but Joseph sensed she had more to say. "I also want a bigger royalty share than the others, and I want to record a solo album."

"None of that is going to happen, Evie." Joseph responded without hesitation.

"Why not?" It angered Evie that he would dismiss her so quickly out of hand.

"What do the other girls have to say about this?"

"It doesn't matter what they say. They've been riding the hem of my skirt for years now and we both know it."

"But they're family. Althea is your sister for Chrissake!"

"We're not Siamese twins…not joined at the hip or anything like that."

"The answer is still no," Joseph said firmly.

"I'm not taking no for an answer."

"You're still under contract, Evie, two more years."

"We may have a contract, Joseph, but you don't own me! The way things are going around here, this company might not be around for another two years. Without me, maybe not even one. I'm all you've got left." She reveled in the facts she knew to be true. "Contracts can be broken. They have some pretty good Jewish lawyers in Chicago too, Joseph."

Leo's territory.

"If you haven't already done so, hire one," He challenged. Evie glared at him.

"They say you don't know what you've got until you lose it. I hope you remember that Joseph," she said.

Evie stood and walked out of the office at a defiant gait. Joseph sat there for a long time. He could now clearly see the writing on the wall. Leo might well argue that without Evie, the company was doomed and they should give in to her demands, but Joseph would refuse to be bullied. He was tired, robbed of the strength to withstand a lengthy court battle especially when he couldn't be sure what personal issues Evie might dredge up for public scrutiny.

He called Leo at home and relayed the gist of his conversation with Evie.

Leo's response was somber in tone. "I'll call my brother-in-law, the lawyer. This is very bad Joseph."

Chapter Thirty-Six:

"Dark Days"

Richie Conforti and Phil Gambetta walked into Decades, a hot new nightspot in New York, catering to the in crowd. The maitre'd made his usual fuss. He ushered the two men to a table where the rest of their entourage, seven men and women dressed in their finest club attire were already seated. The man pulled out a chair to allow Richie to sit, but the executive froze for a moment. His gaze fell upon a table in the corner of the restaurant some distance away. There, Tommy Gentile sat in a booth with a beautiful, very young girl on either side of him.

Tommy noticed Richie glaring at him. The sight of his boss made him squirm a bit. The effects of the liquor he'd consumed made him arrogant enough to raise his cocktail glass in Richie's direction in a mock toast.

"What's he doing here?" Richie asked.

"He was here when we arrived," one of the men seated at the table answered.

Phil leaned forward and spoke quietly, "You want me to have Mario toss him out?"

Richie frowned. "Toss him out? Certainly not. The young man is a celebrity after all. In fact we should go over and say hello."

He motioned for Phil to follow. The two men made their way across the room until they stood at the curved booth where Tommy sat with his lady friends. Tommy seemed uncomfortable.

"Good evening Tommy, having a good time?" Richie asked him.

"Oh, absolutely the best, thanks to Phil. Did he tell you, we had a meeting at the studio today? He let me know point blank how disappointed you guys were about the tracks for my new album. He practically told me the original songs I wrote sucked."

He was getting loud. Richie didn't like that.

"Now, now. There's no reason to raise your voice. We can all hear you."

Tommy obediently adjusted his tone. "He made it up to me though, fixed me up with these two beautiful young girls, even told me to go out and have a good time."

"I didn't expect you to go on some drunken binge," Phil said.

"I'm not drunk. Hell, I'm just a little out of practice. Gimme another hour, I'll be fine."

The years of stardom had changed Tommy. Since his days with the Du-Kanes he'd enjoyed a long series of hit records as one of Alexis Records top names. The company drove their performers hard, applying great pressure to succeed and pressure to earn. If any of them dared complain about the long hours and sleepless nights in the studio or out on the road, they were given pills, uppers to keep them going and downers to make them sleep. Like so many others, Tommy grew dependant on the drugs and the alcohol. Several times during his career he'd entered recovery clinics to deal with his addictions. He'd been clean for months…until tonight.

"Tommy, do you think we could have a word with you privately?" Richie asked.

"Sure, you're the boss," Tommy fumbled through his pants pocket producing several crumpled bills. He tossed them on the table. Then he spoke to one of his companions. "Why don't you and your friend go see if they have a candy machine outside somewhere?"

The girls picked up the cash and wiggled their way out of the booth heading off toward the entrance of the club. Richie and Phil sat in their places but didn't cozy up to Tommy the way the girls had.

"You know, Phil, I'm not exactly sure about this but I don't think either one of them two chicks is old enough to be in this place" his wisecrack annoyed Phil. Richie tried to keep things in check.

"Now, Tommy, we're all friends here."

"Really?" Tommy quipped back at him. "Is that what we are, just three old buddies?"

"I would find it quite troubling if you no longer thought of me as a friend, Tommy," Richie said quite sternly. Tommy took the hint and grew silent. He'd pushed Richie as far as he would go. "I heard the master of your album myself. It's not that we feel your songs are bad per se. We just don't think they're commercial enough to put out. You're successful because you sing about the things young people understand, love, and romance. Your audience is made up beautiful young women like the two you have here with you tonight. They worship you. You make their panties wet and I envy you that. But these new songs…songs that protest the war and criticize the government, that's not what we promote at Alexis Records."

It was a convincing spiel with Richie fully expecting Tommy to surrender to his wishes the way he always had. But the singer managed one last bit of resistance, however weak.

"I just thought…I mean…isn't time I grew up…got out of that pimply faced mode and sang about things that really matter? You guys sit up there in your ivory tower and make all the decisions for me."

"That's because we know what's best for you. Now, I'd invite you and your two friends to dine with us but I don't think there's enough room at our table."

"That's okay Richie. I better get them home. It's a school night."

Richie smiled at the comment. He and Phil got up from the booth allowing Tommy to slide along the vinyl upholstery.

"Goodnight, Tommy," Richie said as Tommy walked by, his head hung down.

"Goodnight," Tommy muttered as he left.

"What are we going to do about that little punk?" Phil asked quietly.

"Relax. After tomorrow our friend Tommy becomes very expendable. Come, our guests are waiting."

They walked back to the table where the rest of their party waited. Everyone seemed to be having a good time. Richie wanted to get into the spirit.

"Mario!" He called out to a waiter who reported to the table in a flash. "Bring more champagne and keep it coming. Tonight there is great cause for celebration!"

And indeed it was. In the morning, Richie and Phil would attend a meeting to sign papers buying out Chanticleer Records, lock, stock and barrel.

♫♫♫♫♫

Negotiations had been ongoing for weeks. Joseph despised the idea of selling out to Conforti's bunch. But there was no choice. He'd waited too long to act and Alexis Records was the only company willing to give them decent terms. Joseph and Leo believed that once the mob run company made their desire to acquire Chanticleer Records widely known within the industry, no other company would dare engage them in any kind of bidding war.

Two attorneys represented Alexis Records interests. They were older Harvard types dressed in expensive Brooks Brothers suits exuding confidence with every stroke of the pen.

They faced off against Leo Klein's brother-in-law Norman Klapish, a fresh faced, stocky man in his mid-thirties. He wore an off-the-rack suit from Robert Hall's Clothing Store. His hereditary receding hairline and bespectacled demeanor may have betrayed his City College education, but it also camouflaged his ability and tenacity in reading through the small print and the little things that could mean a lot in negotiations such as this. He'd been the company's lawyer since the very beginning. He now also represented many recording artists and several other independent labels. He wasn't about to fall prey to any of the tactics the opposing side tried to ram down his throat. Joseph and Leo came away with a generous settlement leaving both men financially set from royalties for many years to come.

But, in the end, Richie Conforti got exactly what he wanted. All Chanticleer artists currently under contract now worked for Alexis Records. This included the Du-Kanes and the Pixies, though without Evie Rhodes who made good on her threat to abandon the group and go to Chicago. They also acquired all recording equipment, hardware, musical instruments and office furnishings, which they intended to sell at auction.

Principals from both sides sat across from one another at a conference table in the Brill Building to sign off on the deal. At one point, Joseph looked up from the contract. He'd come across something that prompted a question.

"It says here you have the right to re-open contract negotiations with all the artists at the end of the calendar year. That's just six weeks away. It was my impression that you were to honor all existing contracts until they expired?"

Norman removed his eyeglasses and laid them on the table. Joseph knew this to be a pre-arranged signal the attorney worked out that meant that he or Leo should stop talking. This way, the opposing side would not discern any sign of disagreement in their camp. Joseph heeded the signal and Norman explained.

"Mr. Rabin that was a proviso we agreed to in consideration of the fact that Mr. Conforti will allow you to retain the rights to the name of the company and its logo in any business endeavor you may choose to undertake in the future," Norman put his glasses back on.

"I see," Joseph replied, "Thank you for reminding me of that Norman."

Breaking the news to the employees and the artists proved the most difficult part of it all. Leo took care of the office staff, explaining the stark realities leading up to the buyout. The company gave everyone two weeks pay and thanked them for their hard work and loyalty.

The two lead singers of the Du-Kanes saw things differently. Bobby viewed it as a betrayal and accused Joe of selling them out.

Johnny, though greatly disappointed by the move fell short of heaping all the blame on Joseph's shoulders.

♫♫♫♫♫

Four friends, who'd put together a record company in the basement of a record store in the south Bronx, gathered for lunch on their last day at the office. Joseph, Leo, Mickey and Curtis spent a long time reminiscing about happier times. Then, the topic of conversation turned to the future.

"What are you planning to do now, Leo?" Mickey asked.

"I'm going to retire to Florida. My wife has been after me to do so for a long time now. So, I guess I'll sit on a beach somewhere and get skin cancer from the sun." The four of them laughed. "What about you boys?"

"Me and Curtis have talked it over. We're gonna sit in the sun too but out in California. Phil Spector is doing some interesting things with music out there," Mickey answered, and then spoke to Joseph, "You should come with us, Joe."

"No, no thanks," Joseph replied. He knew Phil Spector to be a highly successful if somewhat eccentric record producer. "Phillie and I wouldn't make a good mix. No, I'm through with the record business."

"Don't let him kid you boys," Leo warned, "It's in his blood. Six months from now he'll latch on to the next big fad and he'll be back on top. Just you wait and see."

"Nah. It wouldn't be the same without you guys to share it with."

His response struck an emotional chord with the others and they were all quiet for a moment until Mickey broke the silence.

"I left some boxes in your office for you. Your secretary was still packing up some of your personal things."

"Yeah, some photos, gold records and stuff. What's in the boxes?" Joseph asked.

"Tapes from the Bronx days, just some of the stuff we

experimented with back then. I didn't want Conforti's goons getting them."

"Thanks, Mick. I appreciate that."

Mickey and Curtis prepared to leave.

"I'll have Linda give you a call and we'll get together for dinner?" Mickey said.

"Sure thing," The two friends shook hands, "So long, Curtis."

"I'll see you around, Joe," his musical director said as he and Mickey walked away from the table.

Joseph and Leo walked together to the coat check counter where Joseph helped Leo put on his heavy overcoat.

"What I said before," Leo began, "About the next new fad? When you find out what it is, give me a call. I'd be happy and proud to share it with you."

"Thank you my friend," Joseph said. It was a bittersweet moment of parting. They'd shared great success and endured failure over the years. "I couldn't have done any of this if it wasn't for you."

"No, Joseph, it was your dream. I'm just glad you let me come along for the ride."

♫♫♫♫♫

Tommy pulled the Cadillac in front of Joseph's building. The doorman opened the door for Joseph.

"There are some boxes and things in the trunk," he told the doorman. "Will you get a dolly or something and have them put in the basement for now?"

"Certainly, Mr. Rabin," the doorman answered.

Joseph handed the man a tip.

"Will you be needing me in the morning, boss?" his driver asked.

"You mean I still own this heap?"

"Till the end of the month as far as I know."

"I'll call you if I need you, Tommy."

"Have a good night, Mr. Rabin."

Joseph didn't answer. It hadn't been a good day so it couldn't possibly be a good night.

Once inside his apartment, he poured himself a drink, kicked off his shoes, loosened his tie and shirt collar and got comfortable on the couch. He turned on the table radio next to him. Radio personality, Dan Ingram was on the air. Before long, Joseph noticed that the song playing, "Everyone's Gone To The Moon," sounded funny.

Ingram noticed the same thing. In a minute he commented on the situation. "Everything sounds like it's playing in slow motion. I don't know what's going on." He went on to mention that the lights were getting dim in the studio. After introducing the 5:25 pm Action News Report, the station faded off the air entirely.

Joseph found himself sitting in the dark. He stood and felt his way across the room to a window and peered outside. Except for the headlights of the traffic below, it appeared the entire city had gone dark, locked in the grip of some sort of massive power blackout.

The irony wasn't lost on him. He turned, fumbled his way to refill his drink and plopped on the sofa. He was alone on one of the darkest days of his life.

Chapter Thirty-Seven:

"1-A"

The booming automobile industry brought about a demand for improved technology in the music business. American drivers, most especially cross-country truckers, wanted to play their favorite recording artists in their vehicles. As early as 1962, a flamboyant television pitchman and inventor, Earl "Madman" Muntz developed a plastic 4-track tape cartridge that played standard ¼ inch recording tape around a single reel in a continuous loop. He dubbed his player the Stereo-Pak and at first they were custom additions in luxury cars driven by the like of Frank Sinatra, Dean Martin and Lawrence Welk. Soon after, Bill Lear, the inventor of the Lear business jet airplane, came up with his own version of the player that used 8 tracks. Drawbacks on both versions were that the tapes could not be re-wound.

By 1966, the Ford Motor Company introduced a built-in 8-track player as an option in all their vehicles. The backing of this major automaker spelled great success for Lear, and oblivion for Muntz' 4-track Stereo-Pak.

The full impact of the Alexis Records takeover did not manifest itself until after January 1966. Richie Conforti and his executives exercised the stipulation to re-negotiate the contracts for former Chanticleer Records artists, none of which worked in the performer's favor. Royalty and personal performance fees were cut. Tours became longer in duration often accompanied by a brutal travel schedule.

Don Viola's international contacts enabled the company to sign some overseas acts to import into the American concert circuit and recording industry. These acts were mostly second rate but when headlining a bill with some well-known names like the Du-Kanes or the Pixies, it helped in some small part to extend the popularity of the Americans. However, for some, it merely made them expendable.

Tommy Gentile never got over the anger he felt when his bosses ultimately insisted he cut his original socially relevant songs from his latest album. The record label then inflicted a type of banishment, sending him out to appear on the bottom third of a bill touring Texas and Louisiana. Tommy became despondent and relapsed to his addictive ways.

The details of the events that occurred after a performance at the Civic Auditorium in Houston, Texas, were derived from eyewitness account, primarily, those of a man named Duke Roberts who worked for Alexis Records. They became the official record.

According to Roberts, he, Tommy, and a local musician, along with two unidentified females were together in a backstage dressing room. They'd all been drinking heavily with a variety of drugs present when Tommy allegedly announced, "Let's have a party!"

He produced a .45 caliber pistol from his dressing table, removed all but one of the bullets and spun the cylinder. He put the gun to his head and pulled the trigger. The bullet killed him instantly.

Tommy's funeral proved to be major public relations affair. Hundreds of fans, music industry people and celebrities attended, including all four members of the Du-Kanes. A single from Tommy's last album, released posthumously went to number one on the charts.

Soon after, rumors surfaced from one of the females present in Tommy's dressing room. She debunked the "Russian-roulette" story and said Duke Roberts murdered Tommy after the two others had passed out. The woman refused to go to the authorities and no investigation followed.

♫♫♫♫♫

The spotlight also faded for the Du-Kanes. Their long string of hits ended when their two most recent singles failed to make it into the Top 40. They too went on the road, appearing as an opening act for a band imported from Dublin, Ireland, called Bailey and the Shamrocks. They were appearing in Pittsburgh, Pennsylvania at an arena that housed that city's minor league hockey team.

A din of applause followed the Du-Kanes off stage, but they all knew the ovation wasn't for them but in anticipation of the Irish headliners to follow. Johnny and the others were angry when they got back to their dressing room.

"I've had it!" Bobby yelled as he ripped his clip-on bowtie from his shirt collar and bounced it off the dressing table. "Did you hear those assholes out there? Some of them actually booed us, man, booed us from the very start of our set!"

"We want Bailey…" rang out through the rafters. They tried to keep it professional, but it became embarrassing. Johnny raised his hands and with a forced smile, practically begged the crowd to settle down. "Bailey and the guys are back there getting ready to come out and play for you so just give us a chance, okay?"

It did no good. The group went on to perform an already shortened set list without any of the usual banter or byplay they'd normally share with an audience. The crowd noise had such an effect on their backup band that they missed several cues making the performance sound sloppy and ill prepared.

"I'm telling you, Johnny, I'm not doing this anymore, man!" Bobby continued his rant. "On our worst fucking day we're better than those mick bastards!"

"That's right!" Hector spoke up from across the room. He and Kenny sat on a tattered sofa in the cramped dressing room. "I heard them guys rehearsing…they can't harmonize worth a shit, man."

"Yeah, but none of that matters cause nobody can hear them

over all the fucking screamin' the audience does," Kenny offered his opinion. "All they gotta do is stand out there and strum them guitars and beat the drums. Nobody's gonna even think twice about it."

"I'm done, man, no more," Bobby punctuated the conversation.

"Bobby, we got a contract. We can't walk out on that," Johnny reminded him.

"Ah, piss on their contract. That's all just record company bullshit. First, Joe Rabin sells us out to these gangsters and then *they* work us to death and rob us blind. They can stick their contract up their ass as far as I'm concerned."

Hector and Kenny chuckled. But Johnny knew full well that if Bobby made good on his threat there would certainly be consequences. He reminded his three friends that what cards the record company didn't hold in their hands, they hid up their sleeves.

"Have you guys forgotten about the deferments?" His comment silenced everyone. They remembered well the pep talk from Phil Gambetta just days after they signed their new contracts. He told them of the connections the record label had with local draft boards. As long as the young men towed the line and followed the rules they'd all be kept safe from, as he put it, "*...acquiring a taste for fish heads and rice*."

Many Americans were bothered by the nightly televised images of dead soldiers being loaded onto helicopters for shipment home from Vietnam. They came to question the government's involvement in an unpopular war. The management at Alexis Records was quick to employ this fear tactic on the young men who worked for them.

♫♫♫♫♫

The performers had about two hours of free time before boarding the tour bus for the late night trip to their next scheduled show in Buffalo, New York. Hector and Kenny opted for dinner at a local diner. Johnny and Bobby walked the quiet streets alone. They'd gone several blocks without saying a word and then Bobby opened up.

"I'm serious about not doing this anymore, Johnny."

"You gonna call it quits, give up on our dream?"

"Our dream has turned into a fucking nightmare. Nah…we shot our load, Johnny. It's all over now. I figure this is as good a place as any to make my move."

"Move? What move? What are you talking about?"

Bobby had a plan. He knew the drive to Buffalo would take all night. If he could find a way to keep from getting on the bus he might not be missed until morning.

The bus was parked in a large area across the street from the arena where the show had been staged. The tour manager representing Alexis Records was a most unpleasant individual named Al. His primary duty was to make sure the entire entourage got from point A to point B without a hitch. Like most flunkies, Al catered to the needs of the headline act and treated the rest of the performers with great disdain. Little more than a school bus monitor on travel days he was often lax in his duties. Bobby counted on that, as he and Johnny were the first to report to the bus.

"Hey, Al, man, I'm gonna hop the bus early," Bobby told him, "I feel like shit and I want to stretch out in the back and catch some z's, okay?"

"It's up to you. Don't breathe on nobody. We don't want to start a friggin epidemic."

"Yeah, alright, I'll tape my mouth shut. You riding the bus with us tonight?"

"Hell no. I'll be in the limo with the Irish and the good booze," Al chuckled.

"Lucky bastard."

"Yep. Rank has its privileges."

Al moved off to oversee the work of two men who were putting baggage and other equipment into the storage areas beneath the chassis of the bus. Johnny and Bobby went onboard but remained close to the front doors. With Johnny acting as lookout, Bobby waited until Al's attention was diverted before stepping behind Johnny and then, using the bus to shield his movements, he ran off in the opposite direction disappearing around the nearest corner. Certain that his friend had made a clean getaway, Johnny walked partway down the aisle and sat down.

A short time later everyone else crowded onto the bus. Al failed to make an accurate head count as he stood next the driver and called out, "Whoever's not here, raise your hand!" It was a lame joke, gone stale by this time and everyone was sick of hearing it. "Everybody here?" This time he wanted an answer.

"Yeah," Many replied. But Al didn't bother to confirm the information.

Hector, was now seated across the aisle from Johnny and noticed Bobby wasn't in his usual spot next to his best friend. He leaned over his armrest peering to the back of the bus. He then looked quizzically at Johnny who tried to ignore his scathing glare.

Once they were on their way to Buffalo, Johnny recalled more of the earlier conversation he'd had with Bobby.

"Say you don't get on the bus, what then?" he'd asked his friend.

"I'll make way down to Virginia."

"You think you can hide out in Virginia?"

"I'm gonna hide out in a place where nobody can do nothin even if they did find me…I'm gonna join the Navy."

"The Navy?"

"Yep, I can sign up and they can process me in right there."

Johnny knew there was no use in arguing. Bobby had made up his mind.

On a dark street in Pittsburgh, best friends bid one another goodbye. They'd been through a lot together, happy times, difficult times, days of hard work and days of fun and laughter. Sitting there now with the empty seat beside him, Johnny found it impossible to believe that he'd never see his friend again. But at that exact moment he couldn't really be sure.

Johnny glanced over toward Hector who was by now quite antsy. The Puerto Rican glanced back over his shoulder then got up and walked to the rear of the bus. Johnny sensed he was looking for Bobby. When he returned to his seat, he leaned across the aisle.

"Bobby is gonna fuck us all up ain't he Johnny?" he whispered.

"It's not for me to say," Johnny had no real desire to lie to his friend, "He's gotta do what he thinks is right for himself, Hector."

"But even after what you told us about the deferments? You know the cock suckers at the record company ain't gonna let this happen without takin it out on us!" Hector was scared and angry but he tried to keep is voice down. "I can't be in no fucking Vietnam Johnny."

"Just be cool man, we'll talk about it later and figure something out."

When the bus made a meal stop, Johnny carried on the ruse, telling Al that Bobby was still sick. By then Hector had told Kenny about Bobby's escape. As the three of them sat at a table in a coffee shop Johnny had a mutiny on his hands.

"Listen, when this bus gets to Buffalo, I'm grabbing my suitcase and I'm beating feet across the border into Canada even if I gotta swim Niagara Falls to do it," Hector said.

"Don't panic, Hector," Johnny warned.

"When should we panic? Soon as we get off the bus they're gonna know Bobby took off and they're gonna know we covered for him."

"Hectors right Johnny, I don't want to end up like Tommy Gentile," Kenny offered.

"Nothing like that is gonna happen to us."

"Maybe we should all take off…together?" Hector suggested.

"Me and Kenny can't do that. I got a wife and two kids and Kenny's wife is pregnant."

Hector would have none of it, "I'm gonna write my moms a

letter explaining things. Will you see she gets it?"

There was no way Johnny could refuse his friend's request.

By the time the group checked in their hotel, Al knew they were short two people. A head count identified the missing. "So, I suppose no one knows where the fuck these two assholes are?" he questioned Johnny.

"I got no idea, man. Maybe they went sightseeing or something?"

"Bullshit! They skipped out and you know it! You fucking guys put my ass in the ringer and I'm gonna see that you pay for it!"

Johnny knew they had little to fear from this flunky. But the prospect of facing Richie Conforti and Phil Gambetta frightened him.

The Du-Kanes finished out the tour as a duo. No one seemed to mind or notice, especially the audience.

♫♫♫♫♫

Back in New York City they faced the wrath of Alexis Records. Phil Gambetta let them have it with both barrels at a meeting in their downtown business offices. His foul-mouthed curses and threats promised broken limbs and scarred faces. Johnny and Kenny cringed in fear of every shadow for the next two weeks. The reality of the outcome though thankfully less violent was almost as damaging and final.

They were summarily fired from the company and sued for breach of contract. Payments due them from the recent tour were withheld as damages. A punitive sum from a court decision, ruled that any future royalties garnered by their record sales would be withheld.

Both young men received draft notices within weeks of their dismissal. Johnny was granted a deferment because he was the sole support of his wife and two children. Kenny did not fare as well.

Classified 1-A, he was drafted into the Army, part of the induction of some 42,000 men, an increase from 5,400 drafted in January of that same year. Defense Department estimates determined that the war was costing the US Government one billion dollars a day.

Friends and family threw Kenny a going away party at the Castle Harbor German Catering Hall, on Haviland Avenue, in the Bronx. Johnny sent an invitation to Joe Rabin but their old boss didn't show up. The meteoric musical career of one of the finest vocal groups in the country was over.

Chapter Thirty-Eight:

"To the Moon and Beyond"

The moon, the earth's only natural satellite occupies its space in the universe distant by some 238,857 miles from earth. It makes a complete orbit once every 27.3 days and since it is in complete synchronization with the earth, it keeps its face turned to our planet at all times. Nothing in the sky directly behind the moon can be seen from earth. The most significant effect the moon has on the earth is that it's gravitational pull accounts for the changing of the ocean's tides. But as any poet, author or songwriter will tell you the moon also personifies serenity, love, and all things romantic.

By the mid-sixties the moon had become something else, it became a target. In the years between 1959 and 1966 the United States and Soviet Union crash-landed no less than nine unmanned spacecraft on the lunar surface to allow for photographic exploration. Based on these photographs, surface areas became identified as mare, Latin for sea. This included, the Sea of Clouds, the Serpent Sea, and the Sea of Tranquility. The U.S. space program entered its third stage, Project Apollo, charged to accomplish the goal of interplanetary space travel. The moon was designated as the first destination.

As Joseph Rabinowitz lived out his self-imposed exile from the music business, he found little going on to make him miss it. The British still had control, but showed signs of slipping.

In July 1966, the teen magazine, Datebook, printed a quote by John Lennon in which he stated that the Beatles were more popular than Jesus Christ. The remark was taken completely out of context but the ensuing backlash had far reaching effects. Many Christian groups staged “Beatle burnings,” with teenagers throwing Beatles records, photographs and other paraphernalia onto bonfires.

American artists now resorted to gimmicks to help boost record sales. Costumes were one such gimmick and ran the gamut from Egyptian Pharaoh garb to Revolutionary War and Civil War uniforms all the way up to knickers and Lord Fauntleroy suits. Despite the silliness of it all, many of the artists implementing these outfits were quite talented. Their songs garnered many hit records.

But perhaps the ultimate example of silliness occurred when NBC television premiered a thirty-minute, filmed situation comedy series called “The Monkees.” The show, inspired by the two Beatles movies, “A Hard Days Night” and “Help” featured four young, mop topped actors as members of a rock and roll band who week after week found themselves in zany, Marx Brothers type situations cavorting with bikini clad California girls while combating unscrupulous villains often depicted as record company executives or managers.

All the actors playing the Monkees had some real life music experience, but they were still just a manufactured group, drilled and rehearsed until they passed for a real band. They too had hit records and became big stars in the music business. Joseph was astounded by it all.

♫♫♫♫♫

Amid the racial tensions, mistrust of the government, and the overall downward spiral of its culture, Americans sought answers and release in many different ways, including the use of psychedelic drugs. The word psychedelic was a combination of two Greek words meaning mind and manifest. The psychedelic drug experience expanded the mind beyond its normal state of consciousness and perception. The most popular drug Lysergic Acid Diethylamide, also known as LSD, was first synthesized in a laboratory in 1938.

The mind-altering effects were discovered in 1943 when it was used by psychiatrists in the treatment of schizophrenia and other mental disorders.

In the late 1950's, the CIA experimented with the drug in a project called *M K ULTRA,* which used LSD as a mind control and interrogation device. Soon, several mental health professionals, most notably Dr. Timothy Leary of Harvard University received grants to research LSD's potential in a wide range of neuroses. Before long however Leary advocated a more recreational use for the drug. That action brought about his dismissal from Harvard in 1963. He founded a religious sect he called, the League of Spiritual Discovery where LSD became his sacrament. His dogma urged people to turn on to the experiences of LSD, tune in to the messages of their expanded consciousness and drop out of mainstream society.

When Joseph arrived at the huge loft on the top floor of a brownstone on East Thirty-Second Street, he looked around hoping not to be recognized by anyone he knew.

Several area rugs of different shapes and no common pattern covered an old wood planked floor. A variety of couches, chairs and mattresses faced in different directions so that the loft had no central seating area to speak of. The air smelled sweet from the scents of incense and peppermints.

The gathering grew in number to about fifty. Everyone was there to take part in an acid test, an event where both a curious newcomer and seasoned veteran could experience the effects of LSD. Most of them were young, under thirty, others were older, white haired professor types and businessmen dressed in suits. Women wore blouses, work skirts, dresses, and heels. The more casual among them sported jeans, tee shirts, and hippie gear.

Joseph's gaze fell upon a stunningly attractive, dark haired woman in her early forties standing nearby. She wore a clinging white dress. Her make-up and hair-do looked fresh and expensive. They made eye contact and she gave Joseph a broad smile, which he returned rather sheepishly. The movement of several other individuals broke their line of sight and he lost track of her. He began making his way in her general direction, when a soft voice from his immediate right caught him off guard.

"So which is it for you?" the voice asked. Joseph turned to find the woman positioned at his elbow. She was prettier up close with deep, penetrating dark eyes.

"Pardon me?"

"Are you here to turn on, tune in or drop out?"

"A little of each I suppose."

"First timer?" the woman inquired, certain she was right.

"Yes, and you?"

"No, I've been tripping for some time now, out west, Los Angeles mostly. It's a pretty groovin scene out there. My name is Sheila."

"Joe Rabinowitz," he introduced himself as he gently shook her hand. When he let go he noticed a long, slicing scar on the inside of her wrist.

Joseph began to feel at ease with this woman whose smile captivated him. She looked like a socialite, elegant and eloquent, a bit out of place in this gathering.

"So what is it you do, Joe Rabinowitz?" she asked.

"I'm a collector of sorts."

"Well, in that case, why don't you and I collect a couple of comfy chairs before this shindig gets off the ground?"

They found a love seat big enough for just the two of them where they could sit and have a good vantage point to observe what happened around them. Joseph wanted to study the reactions of the others. At the appointed hour, a short, bespectacled man of about thirty in a sports jacket and tie stood behind the wooden counter and called for everyone's attention.

"I'd like to thank you all for attending tonight. My name is Frank Olson and I'll be your spiritual guru for the evening." He didn't look like a guru, more a chemistry teacher. "As most of you already know, tonight's "trip," as we call it, will transport you into a new realm of consciousness. Along the way you'll encounter many altered states of mind. You're encouraged to embrace each one that comes along. Your experience may take several hours but rest assured someone will be here to welcome you back when you return to your earthly vessel."

Joseph was certain the observers were also there to aid any of the participants who might end up having a psychotic reaction to the drug.

A pretty young woman, of about twenty, approached them and offered a silver tray filled with sugar cubes. A liquid dose of LSD, barely visible to the eye topped each cube. They both took one.

"Happy landings," Sheila offered before placing the sugar cube on her tongue, allowing it to melt in her mouth. Joseph followed suit. After the cube completely dissolved he asked her. "About how long before…?"

"People say it's like getting hypnotized, you shouldn't fight it. Try to relax."

The first effects of the drug washed over him slowly, a numbed feeling until it seemed everything around him moved in slow motion. He let his eyes scan the crowd.

One young blonde girl leaned against the upholstered arm of an easy chair fascinated by the movements of her own hands. She held them in front of her face to study them with great intensity. His attention then fell upon the actions of another woman, barely out of her teens. She was perched on the back of a couch, stretching out like a snake on a tree limb. She wore a loose fitting skirt that had risen high up on both thighs. She hovered over the shoulder of an older, chubby woman, a stuck-up type in a business suit, her hair done up in a Beatle style hairdo.

The blonde was reaching down, playing with the ends of the older woman's hair. The brunette responded by throwing her head backward shaking it from side to side as though trying to shoo away an annoying fly. This made the girl behind her giggle as she repeated the action with a similar result. On the third try, the blonde began running the fingers of both hands through the other woman's locks. Now, the chubby one simply let her head fall back onto the bare thigh of the blonde. She reveled in the scalp massage, as did the woman administering it. He also made note of a man in his twenties dressed in a tee shirt and black slacks. He laid on the floor in a fetal position, his head buried in his arms. Joseph thought he heard him sobbing.

The room grew dark. The last thing he remembered was Sheila's face. She now had her head back on the loveseat turned toward him. She still smiled.

As he slipped away, the light and music show that accompanied many such acid tests began. Strobe lights flashed and colored bulbs blinked on the ceiling creating trails of light from one corner of the loft to the other. Joseph closed his eyes just as the music began.

It was a new style, created to accommodate the drug culture, known as 'acid rock.' Lyrics told of dreams, visions or hallucinations sung to loud, driving rhythms featuring lengthy guitar or drum solos and distorted instrumental effects.

Once again in his life, music eased him out of reality. Songs by the signature band of the culture, the Grateful Dead reverberated from the rafters. Even the Beatles made a foray into the psychedelic world when they released their "Sergeant Pepper's Lonely Hearts Club Band" album. The thunderous, electronic final keyboard note of that album's title track greeted Joseph as he returned to the reality of the loft.

He found Sheila looking back at him, her head leaning against his chest. Her hair was no longer perfect but her smile remained intact.

"Welcome home," she said moving away from his midsection.

He peered over her shoulders to a bank of windows displaying daylight.

"You sat with me all this time?" he asked her.

"My flight got in just a few minutes before yours, sweetie."

Joseph stood and stretched. There were about a dozen people left in the loft. Some still in the deep hold of the acid, others slept or stirred. The young blonde and the chubby stuck up woman were gone from the couch. The fetus guy was in their place snoring loudly.

Joseph felt invigorated, more rested than he'd been in months and he had a new found interest in this mysterious woman in white.

"Can I buy you breakfast?" He asked, realizing it was the friendliest thing he'd said to her since they met.

"I need to pee first," Her immodest reply surprised him. Joseph watched as she fumbled into the black high heels she'd kicked off before her voyage, then scurry off to the bathroom.

♫♫♫♫♫

On their way across town they talked about their acid trip. Joseph babbled on incessantly while Sheila called on her own experiences to explain the things he didn't understand.

They ate at a small diner on First Avenue. In that more public setting they abandoned the subject of drug use to become better acquainted. Joseph remained aloof about sharing many details of his past. Sheila proved overly forthcoming talking about herself.

She was forty-four years old currently in the midst of a sabbatical from her job as a Professor at the University of Southern California. She was divorced, a nasty one.

"That's what drove me to this," She showed him the scars on both her wrists, admitting to a suicide attempt, "I thought it would make my husband come back to me, it didn't."

She went on to tell him she had a twenty-two year old son serving time in a California federal prison for attempting to bomb an Army Recruiting Office. Reminiscent of Janet's brother Danny all those years ago, the young man was offered the choice of a jail term or serving in the military. Unlike Danny, Sheila's son, Ryan, chose prison.

"He's been beaten, raped. His father has disowned him and blames me, my *liberal upbringing,* he calls it." At this point she confessed to yet another attempt to end her own life, less than a year ago, this time with pills and booze, "It would have worked too if it wasn't for some nosey neighbor who saw me passed out on our pool deck. She called the cops. Serves me right for trying to get a tan while I killed myself. Just like a woman, huh?"

Her attempt at humor bothered Joseph. He then learned that her resulting sabbatical was more of a suspension levied on her by the University.

"Maybe you need to see a psychiatrist?" Joseph suggested with sincerity.

Sheila laughed loudly, "I *am* a psychiatrist, Joe, Professor of Psychology, assistant to the Department Head. I'm great at giving others advice. I just suck at solving my own problems. I have a steady stream of piss ass students parading through my office begging me to write them letters so they can get a deferment from the draft because of mental problems. Yet, my own son sits in a prison cell brutalized just about every night. That's why these days my mother's little helper comes in the form of a sugar cube with a drop of magic elixir on it."

"What happens if it ever gets to the point where you still can't cope?

"Well, I guess like they say, third time's the charm. But last night and today have been kinda special and that's encouraging," She punctuated her compliment with a flirty glint in her eye and another of her smiles.

They exchanged telephone numbers before Joseph put her in a taxicab promising to call. He did so the very next day. She accepted his invitation to dinner, with the added caveat, "I want you to know, I don't put out on the first date."

But she did put out on that date and every other time they saw one another over the next several weeks. The sex proved most gratifying. Joseph eventually felt secure enough to tell her some things about his work in the music business. She seemed mildly impressed, but never probed for details. She was happy with the now of their budding romance.

♫♫♫♫♫

At 1 pm on January 27th, 1967 at the re-named Kennedy Space

Center in Florida, three astronauts, Virgil Grissom, Ed White, and Roger Chaffee boarded an Apollo space capsule on launching Pad 34. Their mission, to test and evaluate the performance of the Saturn 1B rocket, designed to propel future Apollo flights in America's quest to land a man on the moon. Grissom noticed a sour smell within his space suit. It took three hours to rectify the problem and the air replaced with pure oxygen. At 6:31 pm, Chaffee's voice came over the communications link.

"We have a fire in the cockpit!" Seconds later the link was lost.

A spark from an electrical wire ignited a fire, which went out of control trapping the three men. It took over five minutes for ground crews to open the hatch and reach them. By that time, all three astronauts were dead. As the whole world mourned the loss of three fallen heroes, many began to realize just how costly a journey to the moon might be.

Chapter Thirty-Nine:

"Flower Power"

California became the happening place to be. A huge counter-culture event billed as a human be-in took place in San Francisco at Golden Gate Park, near the intersection of Haight and Ashbury streets. Some 30,000 people turned out. They came dressed in monk's robes, Indian Saris, Paisley blouses and tie-dyed shirts. Many of the women went braless. Both men and women wore their hair in long, flowing lengths topped by cowboy hats or headbands. They smoked pot, dropped acid, drank wine and listened to music ranging from Hindu blessings to plaintive acoustic folk ballads and protest songs. There was also loud "head banging" music by the likes of Big Brother and the Holding Company featuring the dynamic tobacco parched, booze soaked voice of female lead singer, Janis Joplin. Members of the notorious Hell's Angels motorcycle club owned the task of finding lost children.

The print, television, and radio coverage the event received caused a nation-wide interest in the area. Haight-Ashbury came to be seen as a through-the-looking-glass wonderland, a Mecca for free spirited thinkers, anti-war, and anti-establishment supporters alike. Thousands re-located there, scooping up many of the multi-storied wood framed houses that offered a low rent haven for the hippies as they were known.

An entire sub-culture grew in the neighborhood. Stores, called head shops, sold items directly associated with drug use. A free clinic was set up. Doctors, nurses and therapists volunteered their time to treat the ills of the freewheeling inhabitants. Vegetarian cafes, coffee houses and herb shops sprang up in the business district. The hippy culture's pre-occupation with flowers led to the introduction of new terms into the vocabulary, flower child and flower power. Slogans like "make love not war" and "free love" gave evidence to the widespread practice of a new sexual freedom. The phenomenon, its ideals, fashion, and musical influences spread throughout the country.

"They're calling it the summer of love out there," Sheila told Joseph as she put the finishing touches on dinner at her apartment.

Joseph knew the term. He half-heartedly watched a news report on television, certain he was in for another uncomfortable evening of Sheila harping on him to move to the west coast.

Her sabbatical would soon be over and she'd be due back at work. She walked into the living room carrying a glass of sherry wine in each hand. She handed Joseph his glass and sat next to him with one leg folded under the other.

"I spoke to the Dean at the University. He assures me I can be re-assigned to Berkley. Do you realize what that means? We'll be right there in the middle of everything we love. You might even get back into the music business somehow."

He found himself totally at odds with her logic.

"Sheila, I don't mind listening to that music when we're tripping or getting high. But to write lyrics about taking drugs or produce records encouraging kids to get high that would make me feel like some shit heel drug dealer."

It was as forthright as he could be. Sheila became upset.

"Are you saying the Beatles are shit heel drug dealers?" She referred to one of the songs from the Sergeant Pepper LP called "Lucy in the Sky with Diamonds," which made such blatant drug references that the BBC banned it.

"I'm not really the guy you should be talking to about the Beatles," he advised her.

Joseph had no intention of moving to California. Over time, their relationship had been stretched to the limits. She had a lot going for her, she was attractive, smart and sexy, but the state of her mental health made her fragile to say the least. Her favorite catch phrase, "third time's the charm," bore a self-destructive tone Joseph couldn't tolerate any longer. He was delaying the inevitable, fearful breaking up might set her off on a crying jag or worse.

"I'm a New York guy, Sheila. I'd be like a square peg in a round hole out there."

Sheila stood, placed her closed fisted hands on her hips and looked down at him like some scolding schoolteacher.

"That's a rather simplistic answer, don't you think? The whole world is going to hell all around us. The Chinese and the Russians are supporting our enemies in Vietnam. Now the Jews and the Arabs are at each other's throats in the Middle East. Whites and blacks are killing each other in the streets in broad daylight for God's sake."

She spouted her manifesto, a litany of negativity touching on everything from the starving thousands around the world to the race and draft riots taking place in every major city in America. Joseph listened to it all over again. She raised her voice and animated her arm motions.

"We're in such a rush to put a man on the moon. Then what, missile bases on the Sea of Tranquility? Joseph, if the world is in such a hurry to blow itself up can't we, at least, be someplace where people are advocating peace and love until it happens?"

"I'm sorry, Sheila. My mind is made up."

She was stunned, "What about us, Joseph? What about all we have?"

He had no answer.

Sheila felt betrayed. She broke down in tears and would not allow him to console her. She demanded he get out.

In his heart Joseph truly wanted things to end more amicably but his leaving felt like a parole from prison.

He thought that if he walked home it might clear his head but he soon decided he needed a drink. Joseph wandered into a tavern, sat at the bar and tossed a ten-dollar bill onto the hardwood. He didn't look up, even when he felt the bartender's presence across from him.

"Give me a rusty nail," he ordered the scotch based cocktail.

"Mr. Rabin?" a voice asked him.

Joseph looked up. He vaguely recognized the short, somewhat portly older gent wearing a vest and bowtie on the other side of the bar.

"It's me, Mr. Rabin, Michael, I used to tend bar at Patsy's near the Brill Building?"

"Oh yeah, Michael, how are you?" He reached across and shook the bartender's hand.

"I've been fine, Mr. Rabin. Thanks for asking." The bartender moved off and returned a short time later. He placed the old fashioned glass filled to the rim with alcohol and ice in front of him.

"It's been a while since I mixed one of those. You might want to test it."

Joseph took a healthy sip of the cocktail. The drink went down smoothly. His memory of the bartender became more vivid.

"You haven't lost your touch, Mike."

"Man, I sure miss those days at Patsy's when you and all the rest of them music people would come in and play all them great songs in the jukebox."

"Those were the days, alright. But nobody wants to hear that kind of music anymore."

The bartender seemed offended. "Oh, that's where you're wrong, Mr. Rabin. I love all them songs. My wife and I still got all our old records. I know a lot of other people that love 'em too, not this hippie shit they play now."

Joseph finished his drink and slid the empty glass in Michael's direction. "Think you can do that again?"

"You bet."

Joseph nursed the second drink for a good while. Occasionally Michael took a free moment from his duties serving other customers to stop by and continue their chat.

"I used to really like that one group you had, the Du-Kanes.

Whatever happened to those kids, Mr. Rabin?"

"They broke up some time ago."

"Ain't that a shame?" Michael answered. After noticing that Joseph's glass was nearly empty he offered, "Another?"

"Yeah, sure. Third time's the charm, right?"

Some weeks later Joseph heard from a mutual friend that Sheila had indeed gone back to the west coast. The friend didn't have a forwarding address, Joseph determined it was better that way. Whatever it was they had, it was over. So was the summer of love.

♫♫♫♫♫

A heavy police presence invaded the hippie utopia of Haight Ashbury seeking out runaways and making frequent drug busts. Tourists on Gray Line Buses gawked and took pictures of the residents like they were animals in a zoo. A mass exodus took place. People moved to rural communes or hitchhiked across the country to take part in many highly publicized anti-war protests.

Time Magazine printed a cover picture of a pretty, blonde hippie girl placing long stemmed daisies into the rifle barrels of riot police at the Lincoln Memorial in Washington.

Chapter Forty

"In Country"

In the Tay Ninh Province of South Vietnam, combined forces of the U.S. and South Vietnamese Armies conducted search and destroy missions through dense jungle terrain.

Private Kenny Liebermann had become a good soldier. He followed orders, kept out of trouble, and was determined to finish his tour of duty in one piece and return to civilian life.

His squad moved in single-file, slowly and quietly along a narrow piece of ground bordered on the left by deep undergrowth and on the right by a shallow gully some two or three feet deep. Suddenly, but quite discernibly, several loud man-made "boinks" could be heard somewhere close on the left flank. The line of GI's froze in their tracks awaiting the explosions they knew would be only seconds in coming. Mortar shells burst all around him, illuminating the immediate area. Bits and pieces of shrapnel flew everywhere. In the burning undergrowth he caught glimpses of wounded or dying comrades, victims of the attack.

Small arms fire broke out from the bushes on the left. Kenny instinctively sought cover. He jumped into the gully to his right.

The second he landed he felt a sharp pain in his foot. He'd jumped onto a pungi stick, a sharpened bamboo spike placed upright in the earth intended to do exactly what it did to him. Booby traps of this sort were coated with poison. He had to act fast. The stick had penetrated his combat boot just above his right ankle, breaking the skin. There was a lot of blood and it hurt like hell.

Kenny removed the bandana he wore around his neck and

fashioned a tourniquet with a piece of wood he found nearby. He wrapped it around his leg as tight as he could to stem the spread of poison through his bloodstream. The gunfire stopped, indicating the ambush had simply been a quick guerilla strike. Their Viet Cong attackers had already slinked back into the jungle. His buddies would now come looking for wounded comrades.

"Liebermann, you down there, man?" called the familiar voice of his squad leader, Sergeant Saunders.

"Yeah, Sarge. I stepped on a booby trap!"

"Shit! Okay, kid, we're coming to get you. Hold your fire."

After reaching him, the members of his squad rigged a stretcher. They picked him up and were soon humping their way back to base camp. A medic dressed his wound and gave him a shot of strong pain medication. He soon found himself on a med-evac chopper headed for the field hospital.

"Is it bad doc?" Kenny asked the medic tending him and the other wounded men.

"It's badly infected but you'll be okay," the medic answered. "It's a million dollar wound though, I can tell you that. You'll be headed home soon."

"Ahhh, fuck! That means I'm gonna lose my foot."

"Just try to rest, kid."

The helicopter blades started to sound like rim shots on a snare drum. As the pain medication kicked in, Kenny's mind wandered.

"It wasn't me you know?" he said, his voice slurring.

"What's that, trooper?" asked the confused medic.

"It wasn't me that hit that sour note. It was Bobby. He's always fucking up lately."

♫♫♫♫♫

The welcome home party for Kenny at his parent's house on a Sunday afternoon was considerably smaller than the send off he'd had over a year before. Mostly family celebrated his return, his wife, Jeannie, and their two-year-old, and Kenny's sisters, Susan and Carol along with several others. Susan was married to a man named Carl. The couple looked and dressed like full-fledged hippies. Kenny's mother ordered cold cut platters and salads from Dominick's Pork Store, Kenny's favorite.

Johnny and Barbara Seracino arrived late.

After a buffet–style meal, Johnny sat on the large, sectional sofa in the living room. Barbara helped with the food in the kitchen. Kenny appeared at the open doorway between the two rooms. He smiled at his old friend and hobbled across on his crutches. The wound he sustained in Vietnam did indeed cost him his right foot, amputated above the ankle. Johnny scooted to one side so his buddy could sit with him. The top button of his white uniform shirt was open and his necktie loosened considerably. His green uniform jacket adorned with medals and his Purple Heart, lay folded over the back of a chair in the dining room.

"Sorry we didn't get a chance to catch up sooner." he told Johnny.

"That's okay. It's been a big day for you."

Johnny brought his friend up to date on what had gone on in his life since Kenny went overseas.

The owner of the Morris Park Lumber Yard was a fan of their group and offered him a job as assistant manager. Johnny took to his new duties well and before long he was pretty much running the place. It was good money and his celebrity status made him popular with the customers.

Afterward, Kenny said, "I almost didn't recognize you what with that new hairdo and all."

The former lead singer had let his grow long, almost to his shoulders. He also sported long sideburns and a modest Fu-Manchu moustache.

"Yeah, I know, I've changed some. Being stylish my wife calls it."

"Stylish, eh? Maybe I should let my own hair grow, that way I can fit in again too."

"What's that supposed to mean, man? You're home now. Of

course you fit in."

Kenny leaned closer to his friend and lowered his voice.

"I ain't so sure, Johnny. I've had this weird feeling ever since I got back. I can't seem to shake it. Like, this morning when I went to Mass at St. Benedict's with my mom and my sisters. They wanted me to wear my dress uniform because they were proud of me, you know? But when we got to the church, I felt like everyone was staring at me. At first I figured maybe it was because of my foot and the crutches, but after a while I didn't think so anymore. I mean, it was like people looked at me like I done something wrong or something."

Johnny knew he wouldn't be able to provide the explanation his friend needed, many people let their opinions about the war affect the way they looked upon returning veterans.

"Forget all that Kenny," Johnny assured him, "You did your duty. You served your country and you made a great sacrifice. But you're home now, that's all that counts."

Kenny changed the subject. "Hey, man, the V.A. called me yesterday. They want me to come down so I can be fitted for a new foot."

"That's terrific."

"Once I get around okay, my dad says he knows somebody at Con Edison that can maybe get me an office job." He reflected for a moment. "I sure hope they get me one of the newest models. I don't want to have to walk around like the Frankenstein monster with a big clubbed foot," he said with a laugh.

Johnny was surprised that his disabled friend was able to find some humor in his current situation.

♫♫♫♫♫

Late in January 1968, the North Vietnamese launched a massive, surprise counterattack on over one hundred cities during the Tet New Year. Walter Cronkite went to view the aftermath. On his return he announced that the situation in Vietnam was, "…Mired in stalemate…the only rational way out would be to negotiate, not as victors, but as an honorable people who lived up to their pledge to defend democracy and did the best they could."

President Johnson, believing he'd lost the support of the average citizen, stunned the nation by announcing that he'd neither seek nor accept the Democratic Presidential nomination for re-election. The longest war in American history had claimed its biggest casualty.

♫♫♫♫♫

On April 3rd, Dr. Martin Luther King Jr. visited Memphis, Tennessee, to address a rally in support of black sanitation workers who'd been on strike for some three weeks.

Later that night, Dr. King was shot and killed by a sniper's bullet as he stood on a balcony of his Memphis motel. Over 500,000 people attended the funeral service, including President Johnson and all of the major candidates running for President that year. Republican Richard Nixon and Democratic hopefuls Hubert Humphrey, Eugene McCarthy and Robert Kennedy, the brother of the slain President who'd thrown his hat into the ring after Johnson chose not to run.

Violence became a sign of the times. Riots broke out in over 120 American cities resulting in deaths, injuries and more than 20,000 arrests. In Chicago, arson ran rampant. In order to stop looting, Mayor Richard Daley issued orders to his police to shoot to kill.

Chapter Forty-One:

"Florida"

Solomon Rabinowitz suffered a massive heart attack at his home in Florida. Joseph flew down immediately. In a few days, pneumonia set in dealing his father a serious setback. Solomon was not expected to live. Joseph and Myra watched, as he lay helpless in his bed hooked to oxygen tubes and intravenous needles. A monitor displaying his vital signs beeped, keeping time like a metronome at a piano lesson.

Solomon faded in and out of consciousness, recognizing the loved ones at his bedside though barely able to communicate with them. He smiled occasionally holding Myra's hand with what little strength he had left. The next night, Joseph sat vigil alone. He'd been dozing in the visitor's chair, shards of moonlight, slicing in between the slats of Venetian blinds on the window. As Joseph tried to change position he noticed that his father was awake, eyes wide open, what now passed for a smile across his mouth. Convinced that he wasn't dreaming, Joseph sat up and moved his chair closer to the bed. He took his father's hand in his own.

"Your mother went home?" Solomon asked feebly.

"She didn't want to, but yes, she did."

"Good. I've put her through so much lately."

"She doesn't mind."

"She wouldn't say so even if she did."

"You're right."

"Joseph, have I ever told you how proud I am of you?" the question took Joseph by surprise.

"I'm sure you have."

"Well, I'm not so sure. And a father should tell his son that, especially when he is considered a genius."

"Papa, no one has considered me much of a genius for quite some time now."

"The great things you achieve in life can never be taken away from you. And your book of life is far from over, remember that."

Solomon's movements became quite agitated and the beeping monitor reflected that. His father gripped his hand tightly and Joseph sensed there wasn't very much time. He moved closer to his father's face so he'd be sure to hear him.

"Papa, if I'm any kind of genius, it's because it runs in the family. I love you."

Solomon squeezed his son's hand in acknowledgement, and then slipped away.

The two nurses arriving in response to the alarm set off by the heart monitor shooed Joseph away from the bedside. A young doctor rushed in and tried to resuscitate the patient but his gallant efforts failed.

Like most Jews, Solomon did not believe in heaven or any sort of after-life, but Joseph, recalling his own near death experience so many years before in Kentucky, dared to hope that in those last seconds and perhaps even beyond, his father heard the music he loved.

Joseph remained at the hospital until almost daybreak. He timed his arrival at his mother's home hopeful that she'd had gotten a full night's rest. She was still in bed when he got there. He put on a pot of coffee and it was ready by the time she awoke. She knew from her son's demeanor that the news was not good. She sat at the kitchen table and cried when Joseph related the last moments of the man she loved so dearly. They mourned together for the rest of the morning and then set about making Solomon's funeral arrangements.

In the tradition of their religion, the family buried Solomon the next day at the local Jewish cemetery. Joseph and his mother then sat Shiva, a weeklong period of mourning when visitors came to the

Rabinowitz home to pay their respects. The number of friends his parents made since they moved to Florida heartened Joseph. He'd worried about what would happen to his mother now that she was alone. He offered to move to Florida or bring Myra back north, but his mother refused to discuss either of those options.

♫♫♫♫♫

Leo Klein now lived in the affluent south Florida city of Coral Gables. He was saddened when Joseph telephoned with the news of his father's passing but looked forward to seeing his former partner once again when Joseph asked if he could visit. They sat for several hours next to the swimming pool in the backyard of Leo's sprawling Mediterranean style home sipping iced tea. Leo's wife Gloria was off shopping someplace as usual. Never enough diamonds and pearls, Joseph thought to himself.

"And Marlene?" Joseph asked about Leo's daughter now in her late twenties.

"She lives not far from here, has her own law practice" Leo told him proudly. "She's married to a doctor, an obstetrician. All this free love stuff has lots of people having babies."

Leo hadn't changed a bit, in fact he seemed rejuvenated in his retirement.

"This is quite a place you have here," Joseph commented.

"All that money from the record company keeps me going my friend."

"Which reminds me," Joseph produced a folded envelope from his pocket and handed it to Leo who examined the contents.

Joseph didn't receive his royalty checks directly from any of the major music publishing companies. Instead they were forwarded to him by an accountant, Leo's cousin Joshua, who'd handled their financial matters since selling the business. The amounts of the checks were never the same for every period but lately he'd noticed a considerable increase.

"I'm not looking a gift horse in the mouth you understand but do you know anything about this?"

"You no longer keep up on music industry news?"

"These days I'm more interested in the Aqueduct Racing Charts than the Billboard Charts. When did *you* start following the trades?"

"I occasionally enjoy indulging my old habits. You never know, maybe someday someone will write a book about all we've done and I'll be a real celebrity."

"Trust me, Leo, no one is ever going to write a book about any of this."

Leo explained, "There's an English group, they call themselves The Have Knots. They did a cover version of that song of yours, "When He's Around." It went to number one on the British charts. Now it's making a lot of noise here in America. You knew nothing of this?"

Joseph shook his head. He certainly recalled the mammoth first hit record by the Du-Kanes but knew nothing of the English group or the cover version of the song.

"I suppose they updated the thing with screeching guitars and drum riffs that are so loud that it gives you a headache?"

"No, actually they do it as a ballad, a lot like the original, at least as close to what passes for a ballad these days."

Joseph waited for Gloria to return from her shopping spree. She seemed happy to see him and invited him for dinner, but he declined. Joseph and Leo embraced outside the house before driving off in his rental car, leaving Leo to ponder their visit. The question about the royalty checks had thrown him a bit. He felt no sense of regret for not explaining all he knew about the English band the Have Knots. To tell him more may only hurt him. Leo decided that his friend had heard enough sad news already.

♫♫♫♫♫

Lyndon Johnson's decision not to run for re-election turned the Democratic Presidential campaign into a three-way race. Hubert

Humphrey, the current vice-president, would be considered the incumbent. Senator Eugene McCarthy from Minnesota steadfastly opposed the war in Vietnam. He believed his strong showing in the New Hampshire Primary in March made him a force to be reckoned with.

The dynamic personality of Senator Robert Kennedy and the "Kennedy Mystique" put him out in front as summer approached. Many Americans believed Bobby would bring about a return to Camelot and were confident that the younger Kennedy would follow in his brother's footsteps all the way to the White House.

On June 5th, Kennedy gave a victory speech in the Ambassador Hotel in Los Angeles, California. He'd just defeated Eugene McCarthy in the California Primary. As supporters ushered Kennedy through a kitchen passageway, eight gunshots rang out. Kennedy was hit three times. Six other people were wounded. The Palestinian dissident, Sirhan Sirhan, who fired the shots, was apprehended on the spot.

Robert Kennedy died from his wounds. He did follow in the footsteps of his brother John, not to the White House but to a grave in Arlington National Cemetery.

The political conventions for both parties were in stark contrast of each other. Without much fanfare, the Republican's gathered in Miami, Florida in early August nominating former Vice- President Richard M. Nixon to run for President. He set forth a platform rich in rhetoric and veiled promises. He supposedly had a "secret plan" to end the war in Vietnam. In his acceptance speech, he made reference to the fact that he had a good teacher, hoping the public would embrace a return to less violent times similar to the Eisenhower Administration. He even went so far as to rally the delegates with the statement, "let's win this one for Ike."

He could also take great comfort that this time he wouldn't be running against a Kennedy.

Things were much different for the Democrats in Chicago. The convention was targeted by anti-war and civil rights groups intent on using the event as a platform for massive protests certain to gain huge television coverage. Mayor Richard Daley assured party leaders that his police could handle any situation, by force if necessary. Riots ensued with brutal police retaliation all playing for TV cameras and broadcasts around the world. Vice-President Humphrey received the nomination on the first ballot.

During the campaign that followed, there were no scheduled televised debates between the candidates. Nixon obviously learned his lesson from the 1960 race. He did however realize the importance of television when he appeared briefly at the end of a weekly NBC sketch comedy series, "Rowan and Martin's Laugh-In," where he uttered one of that show's more irreverent catch phrases, "sock it to me" putting the line in the form of a question. Hubert Humphrey turned down a similar opportunity.

On Election Day the results went as predicted. The popular vote was ever so close, less than a 1% difference between the two candidates. Nixon received an enormous amount of electoral votes: 301 for him and 191 for the Democrats making him the 37th President of the United States.

Chapter Forty-Two:

"007"

In the waning days of 1968 the landscape of the American music business was a virtual mixed bag of styles and artists. Black oriented music, called soul music, with record labels like Motown, Atlantic, and Stax took a strong hold on the charts with groups like the Supremes, the Temptations, Aretha Franklin, Otis Redding, and Evie Rhodes, who was now a major solo performer. American groups were back in vogue like the Brooklyn Bridge, and Creedence Clearwater Revival. They now posed a serious threat to those English groups that were still holding on in popularity like the Beatles and the Rolling Stones. Newer acts from across the pond that were now achieving success were the Bee Gees and the Have Knots.

It was the Have Knots that interested Joseph most. His royalty checks continued to reflect the success of that group just as Leo told him. He decided he wanted to know more about the group supplementing his income.

He walked into the Colony Record Store on Seventh Avenue, looking for the group's million selling debut LP. He picked it up and after reviewing the song listing on the back cover, he learned that the group had indeed cut cover versions of two of the songs he and Janet wrote. "When He's Around" and an up-tempo tune entitled, "Rye Beach Rock." But he discovered the most surprising detail of all within the body of the album's liner notes. "*...Both of these tunes were penned by the popular American songwriting team of Rabinowitz/Cavelli. Janet Cavelli is often linked romantically to*

Have Knots lead singer, Ian Markham."

That was something Leo neglected to tell him on his visit to Florida. Perhaps he didn't know, but Joseph doubted that. He put the album back in the rack and left the store.

On the evening of December 3rd, NBC television offered a one-hour special called, "Elvis." The show taped and edited from four one-hour sessions represented Elvis Presley's first performances before a live audience in seven years. He appeared tanned and toned in a tight black leather outfit with a bright red electric guitar slung around his neck. Millions tuned in, Joseph among them. The special became the highest rated event of the year.

Joseph also knew that some local AM and FM radio stations were presenting shows dedicated to playing those oldies but goodies over the airwaves. Younger deejays like Gus Gossert in New York started calling it doo wop music.

Joseph remembered what Michael the bartender once told him. If so many people were yearning for a return to the music of the fifties, maybe other careers could be revived.

♫♫♫♫♫

Johnny Seracino settled into his recliner to watch some television on a cold winter evening. His long hair and Fu-Manchu moustache were gone and he now wore his hair parted to one side. As he flipped through the channels with his remote control device he caught sight of his son, Steven, trying to slip out the front door carrying a baseball bat.

"Yo!" he called out stopping the boy in his tracks, "What's with the bat? It's too early for spring training."

"Marie says there's some creepy guy hanging around across the street," Steven's remark caught the attention of his mother finishing the dinner dishes in the kitchen. Johnny rose from his chair and moved behind his wife as she peeked through the café curtains of their kitchen window.

“Omigod! There is somebody out there,” Barbara became unnerved.

“I’ll go outside and have a look.”

“Oh, Johnny, be careful.”

“Here, gimme that,” Johnny said snatching the bat from his son’s hands.

“Lemme go with you?” Steven pleaded.

“You stay put, you hear me?”

As Johnny left the house he raised the collar of his woolen work shirt to brace himself against the wind. He bounced down the short stoop in front of his home positioning the bat so that the man across the street would be sure to see it. Johnny hoped the stranger who wore a heavy topcoat, the brim of a fedora turned down to cover his face would take off in the opposite direction. Instead, the man in the hat started straight toward him.

Johnny raised the bat to a clubbing position when he suddenly recognized the man. It was Joe Rabin.

“Easy there slugger!” Joseph said nervously.

“Jesus, Joe, I coulda killed you, man. My kids thought you was a pervert or something.”

“I’m sorry about that, Johnny. I wasn’t sure I had the right house.”

“Well, let’s not stand out here freezing to death. C’mon inside.”

They turned and walked back to the house. Johnny’s family waited inside the front door, puzzled by what they were seeing.

“Marie was right. It is a pervert,” Johnny told them.

“Then why the hell are you bringing him in here?” Barbara asked until she too recognized the man in the overcoat.

“Hello, Barbara,” Joseph greeted her.

“Joe.”

His unannounced presence made her suspicious.

“I’m sorry if I scared you kids,” Joseph said as Johnny took Joseph’s topcoat and hung it on a hook behind the front door.

“You didn’t scare me,” Steven said exhorting his manhood, “You scared her” he pointed to his younger sister standing next to him.

Once inside the house, the ever-gracious Italian housewife offered her hospitality. "We just finished dinner, but I can fix you a plate?"

"No thank you, Barbara. Maybe just a hot cup of coffee?"

"I can put up a pot of demitasse?"

"That sounds just great sweetheart," Johnny said, "Maybe a shot of Anisette too to fight the cold? We can go down to the basement and talk."

He guided Joseph to the door that would take them downstairs.

"Are you still in the music business, Joe?" Barbara asked before the two men disappeared through the doorway.

"No, Barbara, not for some time now."

"Good."

♫♫♫♫♫

Joseph soon found himself in the comfortable setting of a well decorated furnished basement. Ash wood paneling covered the walls. There was a drop ceiling of white tile and thick pile wall-to-wall carpeting. Something of a homemade bar stood off to one end of the room with three bar stools in front of it. Joseph took a seat on one end of a couch situated in the center of the room. Johnny sat in an easy chair positioned directly opposite a console television, standing caddy corner between two walls.

"You do all this yourself?" Joseph asked.

"Me and a couple of buddies from the lumber yard, yeah, after my folks moved upstate to live with one of my married sisters a few years back."

Joseph scanned to room noticing several of the Du-Kanes gold records hanging on the walls amid some eight by ten glossy promo photos of the group. There were also several of just Johnny and Bobby on a beach somewhere.

"I see you kept some trophies?"

"Yeah, my souvenirs. For old-times sake I guess. Those two of us on the beach were taken by some surfer when we were on tour in California."

"I got a few of them around myself someplace. Your kids ever hear you sing?"

Johnny laughed out loud, "They've heard the records. My kids aren't into those songs. Stevie likes the Doors and Marie digs some girl group. They both got stereos in their rooms, drives me friggin' nuts sometimes."

"What do you tell them about that?"

"I tell 'em to turn that crap down, whaddaya think I tell them?"

The two men enjoyed the humor of it all. Then Joseph decided to test the waters.

"Do you ever hear from any of the other guys in the group?"

"Kenny is still in the neighborhood. He lost a foot in Vietnam. He's pretty much okay now, walks better every time I see him. I don't know where Hector ended up."

"Hector was killed in Vietnam, Johnny," Joseph reported.

"Fuck no!" Johnny sat forward in disbelief, "Last I knew he ran off to avoid the draft."

"That's right. But he tried to sneak back into the country. His family had moved to Pennsylvania. That's where the MP's caught up with him. They inducted him and he was killed in the Tet offensive."

"Poor bastard," the news saddened him. Clearly, Joseph had a lot of information, "And Bobby? I never heard a fucking word about him. He's probably dead somewhere too."

"No, he's alive. He's a blackjack dealer at the Stardust Casino in Las Vegas."

"That son of a bitch. Figures he'd end up someplace where there's plenty of action. You seem to have kept pretty good tabs on all of us. Why is that Joe?"

The time had come for Joseph to get to the point of his visit.

"I want to put the group back together Johnny."

The very thought of it stunned Johnny.

"What the hell for?"

"To do a show, headline a show actually."

"You're dreamin."

"That may well be but I still think it could work."

"Work, how could it work? We've been out of the music business for what, five years? Five years is like fifty."

"I'm not talking about making records or going out on tour or anything like that. I'm talking one night, one big concert with a whole lineup of people from the old days with the Du-Kanes right there at the top."

In the silence that followed, Barbara made her way down the narrow staircase carrying two small demitasse cups. She served her husband and their guest.

"Sip it slow, there's a healthy shot of anisette in each of those," she told the men. Joseph and Johnny figured it might be a good idea to change the topic of conversation with Barbara present, at least for the time being anyway.

"Joe just told me some sad news, honey, Hector Torres was killed in Vietnam."

"Jesus. That's awful. All those young men…for what?"

"And, Bobby Vitale is a card dealer out in Vegas."

"That doesn't surprise me. He was always a wheeler-dealer that one. Did you run into him out there, Joe?" she asked as she sat on the arm of the easy chair next to Johnny.

"No. I haven't been out there."

Barbara, with years of experience as a wise mom recognized the cloud of secrecy in the room. "What's going on here, fellas?"

Johnny happily allowed Joseph explain the details of his plan. There were several points where she might have interrupted his narrative, but to do so would embarrass Johnny and she'd never do that. She remained quiet, but noticed that her husband hung on every word.

"That's quite a dream, huh?" Johnny asked her after Joseph finished.

"As long as you realize that's what it is, just a dream. I mean you might be able to talk Kenny into doing it, poor soul that he is," She directed her next comments at Joseph, "And you know how things ended between you and Bobby. He'd sooner kill you than work for you again. You'd never convince him to go along with it."

Joseph looked at Johnny. He knew his wife was right. Apparently, Joseph had a solution for that.

"I was hoping I wouldn't have to be the one to convince him."

Johnny and Barbara looked at one another, unsure of Joseph's meaning.

"You want *me* to go out to Vegas and pitch this idea to him?" Johnny asked.

"Yes, I do. Actually, I want you both to go. Make it a vacation. A four day junket, all expenses paid."

"Well, what do you think of that?" Johnny asked Barbara.

"I think your old boss is just as cagey as ever."

"I prefer to think of it as just a kind of friendly persuasion." Joseph said with a slightly sinister grin. "You don't have to give me an answer right now, but promise me you'll both think about it anyway?"

"We'll sleep on it," Johnny replied.

With that, the two men followed Barbara upstairs and in another moment, Joseph had his hat and coat on, ready to brace the elements.

"I really enjoyed our little visit," Joseph told his host and hostess.

"Good-bye Joe," Barbara said. He felt quite sure her chilled farewell matched the bitter weather outside.

"I'll call you," Johnny assured him as the two men embraced. Joseph left the house.

The Seracino family closed up the house and the four of them turned in for the night.

When Johnny awoke the next morning he found himself alone in the queen-sized bed. His loins ached from the long, torrid session of lovemaking he and Barbara enjoyed. The musky aroma of sex lingered in the folds of their comforter and bed sheets.

It was an aroma of a different kind that made him stir to full consciousness, that of bacon frying in the kitchen downstairs. He couldn't remember the last time his wife cooked a big breakfast on a weekday morning. He smiled to himself and rolled off the side of the bed to a sitting position. When he looked up he saw Steven standing in the doorway in his underwear, wiping sleep out of his eyes.

"Mom's cooking breakfast?" his son asked.

"Seems like it," Johnny answered. He reached down to the foot of his bed to find his robe. He put it on as he stood and stepped into his slippers.

"Go wash your face," he told Steven.

"Marie is in there."

"Already?" It was another early morning surprise.

Johnny ran his big hand through Steven's tussled hair as he walked passed him. Then he headed down the hall just as the bathroom door opened and his daughter stepped out. She wore a full-length bathrobe, busy putting her long hair up in red berets. Her reaction to the smells emanating from the kitchen was also one of confusion.

"Is it somebody's birthday?"

"No. I don't think so sweetie."

"Then what's with the bacon?"

"Dunno. Maybe it's not for us?"

"Daaad. You're a real joker, you know that?"

Johnny went downstairs and made his way to the dining room. The table was set for four so apparently no company was expected. He continued on and leaned against the wooden archway that opened up into the kitchen.

Barbara stood at the stove and didn't notice him at first. She seemed downright cheery as she worked a spatula through a frying pan filled with bacon. She tipped the pan to keep the grease circulating so the strips wouldn't stick together. After placing the pan back onto the stove she saw Johnny looking at her. They shared a smile between them.

"The kids are worried. What's the occasion?" he asked.

"I woke up in a good mood."

"Same here." He walked up behind his wife and wrapped his

arms around her waist. She leaned back into him. Johnny bent his head forward, nuzzling his way through her thick brown hair to kiss the nape of her neck.

"You're gonna make me burn this," Johnny released her from his grip and stepped back. "Who do you think you are today, James Bond?"

"You complaining Barb?"

"Not me. We haven't spent that much time pleasing one another in quite awhile. I liked it, always did. You want eggs or French toast with this?"

"French toast would be great. I was thinking of calling in sick today."

"To help me around the house?"

"I thought I'd take a ride downtown, go see Joe Rabin maybe." Johnny realized his comment might do him out of his French toast breakfast but Barbara didn't say anything. "That spoil your mood?"

"I guess it would depend on what you went to see him about?"

"Just to talk is all. I'd be lying if I said that some of the things we talked about last night didn't make me curious, get me all stirred up."

"Well, I can attest to the stirred up part that's for sure," a sultry smile accompanied her response. "So you just want to talk to him – you don't plan on signing anything though, right?"

"No. No way…I swear. But, wouldn't it be nice if any of what Joseph told us last night could really, truly happen? I'd like to know you'll stand by me on this, honey."

Her mind took her back to the days before Johnny and the Du-Kanes had success and the fears that she might somehow lose him if he became popular. Instead his stardom brought years of love and security. Even in the declining days and recent times when he was out of the business, he remained a loyal and loving husband. She felt bad for the doubts and jealousy she'd felt. Now Joe Rabin was offering him a chance to shine in the spotlight once again.

"That's exactly where I've been all these years, Johnny. As long as you don't do anything that puts this family on a road headed backwards, I figure that's where I'll stay. Besides, a wild weekend in Las Vegas, without the kids, sounds better and better the more I think about it."

"What time do the kids get home from school today?"

"Not till five or so. They both have glee club."

"Maybe I'll see to it that I get back long before then?" Johnny hoped Barbara recognized his meager attempt at seduction.

"Whatever you say, 007," she replied with a smile.

Chapter Forty-Three:

"Stardust"

The terms Johnny set forth to Joseph, as non-negotiable conditions for a Du-Kanes reunion were simple and specific. He would agree to perform only if the other two surviving members of the group also agreed to appear with him.

It was a risk Joseph was prepared to take. It was also a condition Barbara found agreeable as well, perhaps because she remained confident Joseph would never be able to pull it off.

Kenny came onboard without much hesitation. The young veteran had adapted well to his disability. His prosthetic foot and long hours of painful physical therapy brought him to the point where he walked with a noticeable though not severe limp.

But, his psyche had yet to recover. He still felt the sense of resentment others had for him because of his involvement in the war. He longed to do something to restore his self-respect and dignity. Maybe a return to performing would do just that. Now, all Johnny needed to do was to meet with Bobby. That meant he and Barbara would have their Vegas vacation.

♫♫♫♫♫

The Stardust Hotel/Casino stood at the north end of the Las Vegas Strip. It opened in 1955 and featured a science fiction theme, owing perhaps to the fact that the Nevada Test Site, 65 miles northeast of the city, tested over 20 atomic weapons in the desert. The Stardust's landmark roadside sign stood 188 feet high and incorporated neon and incandescent bulbs in an animation sequence that at night appeared to shower light from the stars above down onto the property.

Their flight from New York had been a long one that included a stopover in Chicago. Johnny and Barbara took a taxi to the hotel where they checked into a room on the ninth floor. They had a commanding view of the stark desert landscape with bare brown mountains in the distance.

After freshening up they ventured down to the casino floor, already crowded with tourists and locals taking full advantage of the many gaming opportunities all around them.

Row after row of slot machines, nicknamed one-arm bandits, made a huge amount of noise. Coins being inserted, the spinning of the reels, and the occasional sound of winning jackpots falling loudly into cheap metal bins located beneath each machine gave players the illusion that lady luck had smiled on them.

There were roulette wheels, crap tables and lines of blackjack tables forming a perimeter around the pit, an area where well dressed employees watched every move customers and dealers made trying to spot any form of cheating.

Johnny approached one such pit boss and asked about Bobby Vitale. He learned he was scheduled to be at work at eight. When he turned to tell Barbara she'd disappeared from his side. He found her a few feet away dropping coins into a slot machine. She said she'd meet him back in their room in time to change for dinner. An hour later, Barbara sadly reported that she'd lost forty dollars.

The couple finished dinner and were back on the casino floor just after eight. Johnny scanned the faces of the dealers stationed behind each blackjack table. He felt certain he'd recognize his old friend, but now wondered what Bobby's reaction would be to seeing him after all this time. In the next blink of an eye he saw Bobby at the last table in the row.

His friend still had his good looks and the gleam in his eye that once captivated females in the audiences he sang to, now had a similar effect on women who gambled at his table.

No longer hesitant, Johnny moved ahead of Barbara at a quickened pace, but he held back for a few minutes until there were no customers playing at the table. He watched as Bobby arranged stacks of colored chips into the metal tray on his side of the table. Johnny's approach went unnoticed.

"Hey, man, you look like a famous singer I used to know," Johnny said casually.

Bobby looked up and recognized his friend immediately.

"Holy shit! I don't believe it!" he said loudly shaking his head in disbelief. He turned and spoke to his pit boss. "Ernie I'm going out on the floor for a minute."

He didn't wait for permission. He walked out from between the line of tables. The two old friends embraced and exchanged greetings.

"Hello stranger," Barbara said coming up behind them. Bobby turned to give her a big kiss and a hug.

"Barbara, so good to see you. You look great!"

"So do you. The desert must agree with you?"

"Yeah, I suppose it does," Bobby answered. He noticed the pit boss Ernie staring his way. "You guys staying here at the hotel?"

"Yeah, till Thursday," Johnny answered.

"I can get an early dinner break at ten. Can we meet then and chat?"

"Sure thing," Johnny said.

"Cool, man. I'll see you then. Have fun okay?" Bobby smiled as he went back to work. Johnny put his arm around Barbara's shoulders as they walked away.

"Geez. That was great wasn't it?" Johnny asked.

"It's real nice seeing him again, yes."

"So what do we do for the next two hours?"

"Well, I don't know about you, but I'm going to invest a few dollars in the machines. You and Bobby have a lot of catching up to do, you guys will want to be alone. I have my room key. I'll see you up there later on okay?"

"Okay, but take it easy on these things will you?" her husband cautioned her.

"I will. I promise," she said kissing him on the cheek before hurrying off to try her luck.

Johnny found a cocktail lounge where a small combo played behind a pretty black female singer. He sat down and ordered a drink but he couldn't focus his attention on the entertainment. He had too much on his mind practicing the spiel he would use on Bobby.

Ten o'clock found the childhood buddies on the roof of the hotel. They sat side by side on the scaffolding that supported the neon sign that spelled out the word Stardust in lettering twenty feet high. Beyond the thousands of neon lights that made up the strip and the rest of the city, the distance in all directions was clothed in deep darkness and invisible horizons. Bobby lit a cigarette.

"A lot different than looking out over Sampson Avenue, eh?" Bobby asked.

"I'll say."

They took turns giving one another a cliff notes version of the events that had transpired since last they'd seen one another. Johnny spoke of the group's breakup, Kenny's war experience and what he knew about Hectors death.

Bobby had sad news to report as well, "While I was stationed in the Pacific, I got word that my mother passed away. The booze finally killed her. My sister Diane still lives with my aunt in New England."

"What have you been up to?" Johnny asked.

"I mustered out of the Navy in San Diego, decided to stay in California. I beach bummed for a while and did some surfing, got to be pretty good at it too. I drove here to Vegas one weekend with a buddy and I never went back."

"What's the attraction?"

"Ha ha. The chicks. The action. Sin city, man, that's what they call it, what better place for a sinner like me?"

"Sounds like it would be a good place for a dreamer too. Like the dreams we had when we were kids."

"We played out that dream a long time ago, Johnny. It ended badly, remember?"

"That's not so say it couldn't happen again."

Bobby laughed, stood and moved to the railing at the edge of the building, "Do you know what you see when you look down there, Johnny?"

Johnny walked to his side and nervously peeked over. "A whole lot of people."

"Not just people, Johnny, those are the dreamers you're talking about. All up and down the strip, dreamers, singers, show girls, and gamblers. They all come here looking to catch lightning in a bottle. But, it's only make believe. Just like this whole town."

"We had a dream once and we made it come true. Maybe we can do it again?"

Bobby could hardly believe his ears. The look in his eyes formed a question Johnny went on to answer. He told Bobby everything – Joe Rabin's visit, the plan to re-unite the group for a concert, all of it. The story stunned Bobby further.

"You're out of your fucking mind. Are you actually gonna let a pimp like Joe Rabin come back into your life after all these years and sell you a bill of goods – give him the chance to fuck you up the ass all over again?"

"Not unless you're right there with me," Johnny explained.

"What?"

"That's the deal I made with Joe. I told him it was all of us or none of us."

"And that's why you came out here to Vegas to talk me into this insanity?"

"Yep."

"And Kenny said yes?" Johnny nodded,"Jesus Christ…you're both nuts." He walked back over to the edge of the building and pointed off in an easterly direction. "You can't see it at night but just over in that direction they're building a brand new hotel…the International. It's gonna be Vegas' biggest and best with all the bells and whistles. You know who they're trying to get to play there?"

Johnny had no clue but felt certain his friend would tell him.

"Elvis Presley, the king of rock and roll. And all the insiders say he's scared…scared of making a comeback."

"Is that it, Bobby are *you* scared?"

"Aren't you?"

"Hell yeah, I'm scared shitless."

"But, you're still willing to try it?"

"Like I said only if you do. Besides, you're forgetting one important detail."

"What's that?"

"You ain't Elvis Presley and neither am I."

The two men rocked with laughter. Bobby needed to get back to work. "I get off at four. Wanna take a ride with me?"

"At four am?"

"Yeah, this is Vegas, man, nobody sleeps in this town. Go back to your room and catch a nap. I'll call your room when I finish my shift."

"Okay, we're in room 907."

The two of them slipped through the roof door and made their way downstairs. Barbara was nowhere around when Johnny got back to their room. He wrote her a note explaining that he planned to meet with Bobby early in the morning and placed it on her pillow. He lay down over the bed covers still fully dressed. He had so much on his mind he had trouble dozing off.

When the phone rang at four he caught it on the third ring. Barbara snored in a deep sleep next to him.

"Hello?" he whispered into the receiver.

"You ready?" the voice on the other end asked.

"Yeah, man, yeah."

"I'm at the front desk.

"Okay, I'll be right down."

Johnny tried to be as quiet as he could in the bathroom. Barbara had left him a note of her own written in lipstick on the medicine cabinet mirror:

Hey you: I won $100.00 bucks in a slot machine!

♫♫♫♫♫

He found Bobby waiting in the lobby. They walked though an exit door leading to the employee's parking lot. Bobby owned a Pontiac, a blue GTO. Once Johnny climbed in to the front bucket seat next to him, Bobby asked, "So, you wanna do some singing?"

"Now?"

"Yeah, I know just the place."

He peeled out of the parking lot, tires screeching onto the first main road behind the strip. At Charleston Boulevard he made a left turn and drove toward the darkness leaving the neon rainbow of the strip behind them. The car ate up the open road until theirs was the only headlights visible in either direction. There were no road signs, no indications of any kind to guide the vehicle, but like some desert creature with uncanny night vision Bobby slowed their progress and navigated the Pontiac off the asphalt. The car bumped and bounced along an unpaved road kicking up a cloud of desert dust.

"This road leads nowhere man," Johnny remarked.

"We're almost there," Bobby said.

They'd come a place called Red Rock Canyon. Even in the pre-dawn light you could make out the steep walls of colored limestone rising majestically on all sides. The shapes and formations of the rocks and cliffs gave the locale a cathedral-like aura.

Bobby pulled the GTO to the edge of a scenic overlook that was invisible moments earlier. Bobby turned off the engine casting them into an unworldly quiet that overwhelmed Johnny.

They got out of the car. Bobby paused to remove a paper bag from the back seat. When they slammed the doors behind them, the resulting sound brought forth a thunderous echo that came back at them tenfold. If they were looking for an echo, they'd come to the right place.

"This place is awesome man," Johnny whispered as though they were indeed in a church.

"I figured you'd like it," Bobby replied. He produced a pint bottle of tequila from the paper bag, he offered a toast before taking a long swig of the contents. "Cheers."

He handed the bottle to his friend.

"To old times," Johnny said. He too took a hearty belt from the bottle.

Bobby began to snap his fingers, establish a beat, set a tempo. It reminded them both of that first day long ago with the record player in Bobby's apartment in the project. He cleared his throat then intoned those nonsense syllables that provided the lead-in to so many great old tunes. Johnny joined in on cue.

Their timing was off, their pipes rusty from time, cigarettes, and booze. They started over and still a third time before making it through entire verses, a chorus and into a bridge.

The natural echo of the canyon walls carried lyrics deep into the last traces of night and back again. They celebrated with long sips of tequila. After the third song they gave themselves an impromptu round of applause. The sound reverberated around them like hundreds of people clapping. It felt good to them. They sang well-passed sunrise.

♫♫♫♫♫

Johnny called Joe Rabin when they got back home to relay the good news. Bobby had agreed to do the show. The Du-Kanes reunion was a go. After hanging up, Joseph picked up the receiver and made another call.

"Hello, Leo? This is Joseph, listen I found a new fad."

Chapter Forty-Four:

"Surprise"

After Leo agreed to provide additional financing, Joseph moved forward with his plans. He enlisted the aid of his old disc-jockey buddy, Jacob Munrow.

Munrow had mellowed with age and dropped the "Big City" moniker from in front of his name. He now worked in FM radio and his three-hour weekly prime time show on Friday and Saturday nights, was extremely popular in the tri-state area. The freedom of the FM format allowed him to include many older tunes in his play list.

They sat on bar stools at a corner section of the tavern where Joseph's bartender friend Michael worked. Joseph came to think of the place as his good luck charm. He impressed Munrow with the details of what he'd done so far.

"I think you might be on to something." Munrow was supportive, yet cautious. "There's a million details goes along with something like this. You need to find a venue, then there's marketing, advertising all that stuff. Frankly, Joseph, I don't think you've got that kind of clout in this town anymore. Out of sight out of mind, you know how that goes."

"But, *you* do, Jacob. If *you* attach your name to it, sign on as Master of Ceremonies *that* will put us over the top. I know it."

"I took a chance on you with Teddy Boyette some years back, and that paid off pretty well for both of us. I suppose I can do it again. All right, count me in."

♫♫♫♫♫

Papers and notes were strewn across the coffee table in Joseph's living room when the doorbell rang, an uncommon occurrence unless he'd ordered pizza or Chinese take-out. It was far too early in the day for that. He stood and opened the door.

It was Janet.

"Hello Joseph." She stood there like some mirage suddenly appearing in the desert. Her hair looked longer, straighter than he remembered. Her eyes were as wide and her smile as bright as ever. She'd fulfilled the prediction he'd made that first day back in Cleveland that she'd become as beautiful as her mother.

She wasn't alone. There, at her side, clutching her hand was a smaller version of herself. Joseph guessed the child to be four years old. She too was blonde and blue-eyed. This wasn't a detail found on any record album liner notes.

"I'm sorry, I know I should have phoned ahead but I wasn't sure I'd be able to stop by," Janet said.

"Please, come in." After entering the apartment, Janet looked around. The little girl was shy. Joseph bent down to her eye level, offered his hand and smiled.

"And what's this pretty little one's name?"

"Danielle Cavelli," she answered softly.

"Well, Danielle, I'm pleased to meet you," she shook his hand and managed a grin. Joseph straightened and looked at Janet. "Cavelli?"

"Danielle's father and I aren't married, Joseph. Dani, this is Mr. Rabinowitz. He's an old friend of mine," there was a slight British inflection in some of the words she spoke, other than that she sounded the same.

"That's a hard name to say mummy," the child replied with a decidedly British accent.

"Shush, Dani, don't be so fresh," Janet scolded her mildly.

"That's okay, sweetheart, you can call me Joe, okay?"

"Hello, Joe," her grin expanded to a full smile.

"What would Danielle say to a nice peanut butter and jelly sandwich and a big glass of milk?" he asked the child.

"Oh, no, Joseph, please don't make a fuss," Janet protested.

"No fuss at all… and a cup of coffee for mom?"

"Only if you let me make it?"

Joseph took their jackets and hung them up. After getting Danielle her snack, they sat her on the floor in front of the television where she quickly became absorbed in an afternoon cartoon show. Joseph and Janet drank their coffee seated at the dining room table. There were a million things he wanted to ask but he had no idea where to start.

"The not being married part, is that your idea or his…Ian isn't it?"

"Yes, Ian Markham. It seems I'm this year's version of Cynthia Lennon." She referred to the wife of Beatle John Lennon, often kept in the background during the group's early tours. "I didn't mind really, for a while. But when some of the press started calling Dani our love child, I decided to keep the two of us out of the spotlight as much as possible. So, you knew about the band then…the songs… Ian?"

"Yeah, sure, they put some extra bread in my royalty checks. Are they here in town?"

"Yes, they're starting a nation-wide tour. They were on the Ed Sullivan show last Sunday, did you see them?"

"No. I've been kind of busy."

"Yes, I see all this paperwork. Do you have a new project?"

"I'm putting together a live concert, a lot of the acts from the old days. I'm even getting the Du-Kanes back together."

"Oh, I think that's so wonderful and very exciting for you." She seemed pleased to hear that he was involved with music again. "Joseph, there was another reason why I stopped by to see you. The band next goes to Florida. There'll be a show in Miami. I wondered if it would be all right if I visited your parents, brought Danielle along to meet them?"

His mood turned somber. "My father passed away last year,

Janet. I was with him when he died."

Her reaction was immediate. Tears came to her eyes.

"I'm so sorry, Joseph, I had no idea."

They both regretted the fact that they'd lost touch so long ago. Janet had written as she'd promised. He even answered her letters for a time. But then, things became so muddled in his life and he lost everything, He decided he had nothing good to tell her so he stopped responding. Not long after, Janet stopped writing.

Joseph wanted to change the subject.

"I think it's a good idea, about Florida I mean. My mother would love to see you…and meet Danielle. I'll call her and arrange it if you'd like?"

"That would be wonderful. Thank you."

"When will you be there?"

"Next weekend."

They chatted for another hour or so, easing into discussions of old memories, laughing at some, and being melancholy over others. Janet didn't ask about any recent relationships and Joseph saw no need to say anything about Sheila. Danielle napped through most of it. When she woke it was time for them to go.

"Thank you for visiting with me, Danielle. I hope I get the chance to see you again sometime?"

"For more cartoons, can we mummy?" the youngster asked.

"We'll see, sweetheart. Thank you for everything Joseph. I'll ring you up in a day or so about Florida?"

"Absolutely, I'll call my mother."

At the door, Janet stood on tiptoes to kiss him on the cheek much the same way she did at Kennedy airport five years ago.

"I'm glad you kept this place. It's still as warm and cozy as ever."

Once she'd gone Joseph thought about what she said. He hadn't felt the apartment as being warm and cozy for a long time. But it seemed that way now as the scent of her lingered all around. Maybe that would last for a while.

They spoke again over the phone two days later. He told her Myra was thrilled that she planned on visiting and he gave Janet the necessary contact information. A week later he received a full report from his mother. He then read in a trade paper that the Have Knots were on their way to the West Coast. Once again, Janet was gone.

In the days that followed Joseph went back to work sifting through the mountain of details associated with putting his show together. He convinced both Mickey Christie and Curtis Tinnsley to come back and help with the event. Mickey would be the sound engineer, Curtis the stage manager, taking charge of the small army of artists and musicians required to make the show run as smoothly and trouble free as possible.

Jacob Munrow also came through. He called in a favor from two theater owners, the Richards Brothers who owned the Majestic Theater on East Forty-fifth Street. The theater sat almost five thousand. It would be a tough nut to crack. Despite that, contracts were signed and the concert scheduled to take place on Saturday, October 18th.

♫♫♫♫♫

At 10:56 pm EDT on July 20th, 1969, American Astronaut Neil Armstrong became the first man to set foot on surface of the moon. Four days earlier, Armstrong and fellow astronauts Edwin "Buzz" Aldrin and Michael Collins took off from the Kennedy Space Center in Florida aboard the Apollo 11 spacecraft. Over one million people had gathered on nearby beaches in the middle of a heat wave to watch the launch. Mission Control Operations at the Manned Spacecraft Center in Houston, Texas helped guide the spacecraft until it achieved Lunar orbit on July 19th.

The next day, Armstrong and Aldrin flew the spidery shaped landing module designated "Eagle" down for a soft landing on the Sea of Tranquility. Armstrong cracked the hatch and descended a nine-rung ladder pausing long enough to pull a handle that activated an RCA black and white television camera. Nearly six hundred million viewers worldwide then viewed the historic event.

The space travelers spent the next two and a quarter hours conducting experiments and gathering almost fifty pounds of rocks and dust samples for testing upon their return to earth. Although they placed an American flag held erect by an aluminum rod because of the Moon's zero gravity, the United States made no claim of colonization or ownership rights. Thy also planted and left a plaque on the surface, which read: *"Here, men from planet Earth set foot on the Moon, July 1969 A.D. We came in peace for all mankind."*

♫♫♫♫♫

The telephone awakened Joseph early the following morning. Janet's voice on the other end of the line stunned him. She was crying.

"Oh, Joseph, isn't it the most amazing thing?" He knew she referred to the moon landing.

"Yes, it's really something."

"President Kennedy promised we'd put a man on the moon by the end of the sixties and we did it," she paused, "I know I sound like some foolish little girl but, can you meet me for dinner tonight?"

"Are you here in New York?" He shook his head in disbelief at the stupidity of his question. "Of course, how about Ecclisse at eight o'clock?"

"Oh, that would be perfect. I'll see you then."

Ecclisse Italian restaurant in Little Italy had been a particular favorite of theirs in the glory days of Chanticleer Records. Joseph was pleased when Janet arrived at the restaurant alone. She'd left Danielle in the care of their traveling nanny. During dinner Janet went all bubbly over the events in the news. Joseph listened with great delight. They drank cappuccino and shared tiramisu as she gave him more details about her visit to his mother. She then got around to the reason why she came back to New York. Apparently she found the Have Knots success more frantic than she'd imagined.

"Fans mobbed the lads wherever we went, always a great crush of screaming girls trying to sneak into our rooms, grab pieces of clothing. It was a nightmare. Being out on the road is no place for a little girl. I made Ian understand that and we agreed I would wait here until the band finished their tour."

Joseph sensed there might be more to it than that, but he didn't press the point.

Janet changed the subject. "How are things going with your project?"

"Quite well. There are still lots of details to work out. You know, I'd love it if you were able to be there?"

"When is it?"

"The middle of October…the 18th."

"I'm sorry Joseph but I'm afraid it's impossible. We're taking an extended holiday in the Bahamas after the tour is over. Then it's back to England to work on a new album."

"I understand, Janet, it would have been nice," he tried to hide his disappointment. "So, what shall we do to work off the effects of this wonderful meal?"

She beamed at him. "Can we make one more stop?"

"Anywhere you like."

They hailed a cab outside the restaurant. Janet told the driver to take them to Battery Park.

Joseph thought it was an odd place for her to want to go so late at night. Most of the tourists were gone and the night people had yet gathered to sleep on the park benches or huddle against the walls that encompassed the centuries old military emplacements. They moved forward to the railing of the promenade looking out on the convergence of the Hudson and East Rivers. The night was clear and the moon was yellow, a bright shiny orb in the sky.

"It looks so much closer now, doesn't it?" Janet asked as she gazed upward.

"Yes, I suppose it does."

"And see how Lady Liberty stands there, her arm straight up in the air pointing almost to the exact spot where the astronauts stood."

A summer wind kicked up off the water blowing her hair all around. She stood transfixed, eyes closed, saying nothing. He would have watched her all night if she didn't eventually turn to him. "I think we need to go now."

He put his arm around her shoulder. They walked back along the promenade. She nestled close into him finding that spot where she'd always fit so perfectly. A taxicab pulled up much too soon to his liking. Joseph opened the back door.

"I can ride with you if you like?" he asked.

"No. You don't need to."

Before entering the cab, Janet paused, looked into his eyes and kissed him on the lips. Joseph closed the door and watched the taxi drive away. Her kiss surprised him, pleasantly...no...more than just pleasantly.

♫♫♫♫♫

Elvis Presley performed fifty-eight consecutive sold out shows at the International Hotel in July, breaking all past Vegas attendance records. Critics and fans alike hailed the shows.

For four days in August an event billed as the Woodstock Music and Art Festival took place on a dairy farm in Sullivan County, New York. The expected crowd of 200,000 swelled to 500,000 causing massive traffic jams on all major highways leading to the site. Heavy rainstorms created deep puddles of mud and there was a shortage of food and bathroom facilities. A wide variety of contemporary rock and roll artists appeared. Early on the last day of the concert, a group named Sha Na Na performed. Consisting of students from Columbia University in New York City, they took their name from the refrain of a number one fifties hit, "Get a Job," by the Silhouettes. They dressed in gold lame suits wore their hair in pompadours, much in the style of

James Dean era greasers. The exhausted throng loved them.

♫♫♫♫♫

Bobby flew to New York a week before the show. He stayed with the Seracino's and on one of his first nights there, Johnny and Barbara invited Kenny and his family over for a reunion dinner of lasagna and her famous meatballs. They toasted Hectors memory with a bottle of Chianti wine.

Johnny had been working on an idea he had for the show. He wanted it to be to be a surprise for both the audience and Joe Rabin, and it would require a good bit of planning and luck to pull it off. He took both Kenny and Bobby into his confidence about the details. Kenny liked the idea. Bobby seemed disinterested.

They had their first meeting with Joseph when rehearsals began the next day. The mood was tense. No one knew what to expect from Bobby. The two men greeted one another with a firm handshake and not much else.

"It's good to see you again," Joseph told him, "I want to thank you for doing this."

"I'm only doing it because Johnny asked me to." His response was cold and Joseph knew he had no right to expect more. Whatever his motive, Bobby came prepared to work. Rehearsals began. Everyone's mood brightened as more and more of the artists scheduled to appear arrived. Those who'd toured together in the old days shared stories and renewed friendships.

Johnny got the chance to speak to Curtis privately and told him about the surprise he'd cooked up. The musical director liked the idea and told Johnny he'd set aside some time to work with the group for what they'd need musically.

"It's gonna work out fine, Johnny. Don't you worry," Curtis assured him.

Chapter Forty-Five:

"Reunion"

The number one song on Billboard's Hot 100 List on October 17, 1969 was "Sugar, Sugar" by the Archies. The song and the group grew out of "The Archie Show," a Saturday morning cartoon show that premiered on CBS-TV in September. It was based on a popular 1941 comic strip. In the show, the teenage characters, Archie, Reggie and Jughead with two girls, Betty and Veronica, form a garage band and sing a song on each show. Two Los Angeles based singers dubbed all the voices heard on the air.

By the next morning, every ticket for Joseph's concert was sold.

"That's quite an accomplishment," Leo boasted sitting in the manager's office of the theater along with Joseph and the Richards brothers. He'd flown up earlier in the week from Florida. Like everyone connected with the show, he was excited that the big day had finally arrived. The promoters discussed some last minute details.

"The Fire Department will allow you to sell about three hundred standing room tickets at the door," Sandy Richards, the older of the two brothers said.

"Better still," Leo remarked after doing a bit of arithmetic in his head.

"We'll open the doors at six-thirty. The whole shebang needs to be over by eleven pm sharp," Sandy's brother Ira offered.

Both theater owners were happy that the concert would be a great success but now they had concerns over security. Despite the fact that the expected crowd would be somewhat older, it was still a rock and roll show. In the past many of those had been the cause of riots.

Joseph understood those concerns. “We’re prepared for any situation which may arise, I can assure you.” That’s the way it would be for the rest of the afternoon – finding solutions to one last minute problem after the other. Control was slowly slipping away from him and into the hands of the highly capable experts he’d gathered around him.

Mickey was there to wire it all. He placed microphones around the stage for optimum effect. He’d sit behind a console of switches, dials and meters to control the levels of sound, making sure instruments didn’t drown out voices and vice versa. No gimmicky multi-tracking possible here. Sound engineering by the seat of your pants, just like the old days.

Curtis put together an orchestra of fifteen of the best musicians money could buy. Gary Tracy was still with him since his high school days, through the Chanticleer years and on out to California where he’d become one of the finest session drummers in the country. The guitarists and keyboard men were mostly from New York, also veterans of many Chanticleer Records studio gigs. He brought his own horn section with him from Los Angeles. They’d worked together on numerous sessions and shows. What they couldn’t read from a music chart they could improvise in an instant.

There were also backup singers, three men and two women. Together or in any mixed combination they would provide harmonies, add depth or act as a crutch for any featured singer unable to hit or hold the notes from their original recordings. One of the men, a singer named Frankie Mesa, would also perform with the Du-Kanes as a replacement for Hector Torres.

An experienced group of stagehands memorized changes involving instruments, microphones or other equipment that needed to be reset, added or removed before each act performed. Even Master of Ceremonies, Jacob Munrow, prepared some anecdotes in case he needed to stall because of some technical malfunction or delay.

The crowd began filtering in at six-forty.

From his vantage point in the wings, Joseph surveyed his audience. Many were in their mid to upper thirties, a portion, younger though not by much. Women outnumbered men and there were a great many couples as well. They dressed in clothes ranging from New York Theater dressy to fall casual. Some even arrived in costume, flowing poodle skirts, tight sweaters and saddle shoes for the women. Some men wore black slacks, tee shirts with cigarette packs rolled up in one-sleeve or leather motorcycle jackets and slicked back hair. The sight amused fellow audience members who pointed and giggled at the sight of these over-thirty teenagers.

A sense of anticipation hovered over the packed house. A smattering of applause and whistles arose as the advertised start time came and went.

Assured that all the bases were covered and there was nothing more for him to do, Joe Rabin, Impresario, fell back to a spot in the wings, to become just another spectator. The houselights dimmed.

"Tonight…" a booming voice came over the public address system, "the Majestic Theater proudly presents, 'An Evening of Solid Gold…a rock and roll musical reunion!'"

A drum roll sounded from behind a thick, blue velvet curtain that separated in the middle to reveal Curtis and his musicians, standing at the ready or seated behind music stands. A huge mock-up of a forty-five RPM record hung from the ceiling in front of red backdrop curtains.

The announcer's voice boomed out once more. "Return with us now to an era of hot rod cars, malt shops, pony tails, and the music of the fabulous fifties!"

A snare drum took up a wild riff joined by guitars, horns and a barrelhouse piano tempo launching into a rocking instrumental version of "Blue Suede Shoes," intended to get the audience going. It did. After the song the crowd broke out in a hearty round of applause. The unseen narrator spoke to them yet again.

"Let's give a warm welcome to a pioneer in the world of R&B blues guitar. He recorded for Chanticleer Records way back in 1956. Here's Charles Bannister!"

Now well past sixty, Bannister moved slowly onto the stage to a smattering of polite applause. Obviously many in the crowd didn't recognize him by name. But when he got to his microphone and counted off into "Bare Legged Woman," the audience cheered loudly. The remainder of Bannister's set was well received. He got a rousing send off when he ambled from the stage.

It was time for Jacob Munrow. The Master of Ceremonies leapt onstage with no introduction. He'd been promoting the concert on his radio show for weeks prior resulting in a great many ticket sales. His loyal and adoring fans recognized him instantly. Some fans jumped out of their seats to cheer him. He stood at the microphone waving and smiling. Long years in show business taught him how to work a crowd. He raised his hands and many of those standing eased back into their seats.

"Good evening everybody and welcome to the show. Let me ask you something, are you ready to rock and roll?" he called out loudly.

"Yeah!" A vast number of voices answered from the opposite side of the footlights. It wasn't enough for the MC.

"Aw, you can do better than that. I said are you ready to rock and roll?"

This time the response came back louder and with much more enthusiasm.

"All right lets bring out four guys from Bedford Styvestant, in Brooklyn. They recorded for the Alexis Records label. Please welcome, the Four Choices!"

This black vocal group represented the only Alexis Records artists on the bill. It was a concession Joseph made to his former competitors, hoping it would placate Richie Conforti and ensure there wouldn't be any trouble with his rivals who were, by this time, having serious financial issues of their own.

Next was Peggy Sue Sylvester, a charming, auburn haired southern belle popular all over the country in 1959 for two big hit records. She was curvaceous and most pleasing to the eye dressed in her signature flowing skirt. The audience reacted well to her set.

The act slated to close out the first half of the show, went way back. The Hollins Twins, veterans of Teddy Boyette's earliest tours. Brother and sister energized the fans with great skill both vocally and musically. Their lush harmony and dueling rockabilly guitar style still worked effectively and brought them a standing ovation that lasted long after the curtains closed signifying the end of the first half.

While the audience members took the opportunity to stretch, smoke or visit the nearest restroom, those behind the scenes were abuzz with activity. The positive reception for the first half of the show started the adrenalin pumping in everyone. Those who'd already performed received congratulations and accolades while high anxiety filled those yet to go on. Leo wiped beads of sweat from his brow with a handkerchief. Joseph found himself breathing a little easier.

As the curtain opened for the second half of the show the orchestra went into a musical interlude as four, female go-go dancers, bounced onto the stage, two from stage left and two from stage right. They were scantily dressed in sleeveless miniskirt dresses and white, thigh high leather boots. Many men in the audience howled and whistled their approval.

After converging center stage the dancers performed a routine demonstrating some of the classic dance crazes. They moved through carefully choreographed steps doing the Loco-Motion, the Jerk, the Mashed Potatoes and of course, Leo's favorite, the Caterpillar. They closed out the segment with the Twist. The audience roared. Jacob Munrow skipped on stage to join them much to the delight of the dancers and the fans. He brought the four girls back to the stage for a bow.

"So, how do like things so far?" he called out. His voice projected into the rafters of the highest balcony. The audience responded with wild applause.

The moment had arrived to bring on the Pixies.

"Ladies and gentleman, you are now in for a real treat," Munrow began his introduction. "It is my distinct pleasure to bring to the stage one of the finest girl groups of the last decade." The audience buzzed with excitement. "Their hits are too numerous to list and I'm sure you'd rather hear them sing than listen to me stand here and talk. So, without further ado, I give you the fabulous Pixies!"

The fans rose as though on command sending a barrage of applause toward the stage. Althea Rhodes and Roberta Johnson moved slowly, their glittering, sequined gowns extended to their ankles. Their vocals were supplemented by two female back up singers seated on stools in a dimly lit corner of the stage. There would be nothing to divert attention from the two principal singers.

They opened their set with one of their biggest hits, "He Belongs To Somebody Else." Althea sang lead with confidence and great strength. No one realized that the voice now singing was not the same one that sang on their classic recordings.

These fans did not come to criticize. They wanted to enjoy the great music they remembered. For the next twenty minutes the group treated them to hit after hit, mixing in cover versions of songs made famous by other girl groups. The reprise of their first number one hit, "The Caterpillar," thrilled everyone. They left the stage only to be brought back for two encores Curtis had prepared for them.

They blew kisses and waved to the audience when they walked off for the final time. Joseph greeted them in the wings, embracing each of them warmly. The Du-Kanes stood nearby.

"They're all ready for you Johnny," Althea told him.

"I don't know how we're gonna follow that, sweetie."

"It's gonna be alright. Sing the songs. That's all they want."

After the girls headed back to their dressing room, Joseph stood with his headliners.

"It's now or never, fellas…are you ready?"

"We won't let you down, boss, don't worry," Bobby replied, surprising everyone.

They heard their intro music, which meant they'd missed Munrow's introduction. It didn't matter.

As agreed they filed onstage slowly, in single file, to make Kenny's limp less noticeable. The crowd went wild. Johnny and Bobby each had their own microphones. Kenny and Frankie Mesa shared a third.

The applause intensified as the group opened with one of their later up tempo hits, "Lucky To Have You." They went for the jugular right out of the box. Another rocking number followed. Bobby took his microphone off the stand. He paraded along the footlights waving to people he couldn't actually see.

Johnny sang lead on the next two songs, album cuts from their first LP. The second tune, a ballad called "I'll never Forget the Night We Met," was the first real test of their harmony. Frankie Mesa proved a superb stand-in. His voice fit the difficult vocal pattern like a glove.

At that point, Johnny engaged in a monologue with the audience.

"We'd like to take a moment to remember a former member of the Du-Kanes. One of our original members from our street corner days, Hector Torres was killed in Vietnam last year." A solemn hush followed a loud groan. The news stunned many in the crowd. "He was a great guy and a wonderful friend. We wish he could have been here with us tonight to join in this celebration. So, we'd like to do a song in Hectors memory."

Single white spotlights fell upon the four singers as they performed the ballad "I Believe," a haunting number, written in the early fifties in an effort to offer solace to those troubled by the Korean War. The song had also been a hit for a street corner group called the

Earls who also lost one of its members in the military. After the last harmonious note, the Du-Kanes lingered in their positions, heads bowed in an added moment of tribute.

The group was in full command. At a pre-arranged signal, Kenny fell back to help Curtis conduct the orchestra in a rousing musical introduction. The group performed a segment of three of their up tempo tunes, highlighted by Bobby doing a wild dance routine flanked by Frankie and Johnny.

The next portion of the show was more intimate as the boys re-visited their days at the Throggs Neck Community Center. They sang two Acappella songs with no musical accompaniment.

Then, it was time for Johnny's surprise. He looked over at Curtis and nodded. Curtis signaled the orchestra. The musicians hastened to get the appropriate music charts onto their stands. Joseph noticed this unexpected change. He became concerned, rose from his seat and looked at Leo, who merely shrugged.

Back onstage, Johnny explained, "Right now, we have a little surprise, not just for you but also for the man responsible for putting this whole show together." He looked to the wings. He had Joseph's full and undivided attention. "Many of us performing tonight were once members of the same close knit family. Charles Bannister, the Hollins Twins, the Pixies and the Du-Kanes all recorded for Chanticleer Records. A man named Joe Rabin started that record label and turned it into an empire. He discovered us, many while we were just kids, and made us all big stars. But there was one artist, the original star of the Chanticleer label who made it possible for all of us who followed…the late, great Teddy Boyette."

The audience rose en masse recognizing the name and the talent of the singer gone too soon. "So, as a tribute to Teddy and as a way of showing our appreciation to Joe Rabin, we've put together a medley of Teddy's tunes and we'd like to do it for you now."

For the next several minutes, the vocal group delivered short snippets of Teddy's songs ranging from "Move it on Over" to the spiritual, "The Old Wooden Cross."

It made for another show stopping moment
Bobby moved forward to set up the next song.

"A few months ago, three courageous men took a very long trip to the outer regions of space. Two of them became the first humans to set foot on the surface of the moon. Some years back the Du-Kanes had a number one hit with a song that spoke of that very same place. It was called Bouncing a Kiss off the Moon. We'd like to dedicate it to the heroes of Apollo 11."

Their stirring rendition thrilled the audience. Every note, every gesture was perfect. They took a synchronized bow at the end of the song. When the ovation began to subside, Curtis cued his musicians into the instantly recognizable, haunting opening strains of "When He's Around."

The response almost drowned out the music. Johnny had to cup his ear with an open hand to make sure his falsetto remained on key.

Joseph had reworked the arrangement. The tempo was a bit slower than the original and a new, longer instrumental bridge extended the song to an even longer length. The audience didn't mind they would have listened to it all night long.

As the final notes reverberated through the theater, a tidal wave of adulation began in the upper balconies, cascaded down through the mezzanine sections, on into the orchestra seats before crashing against the stage.

The four young men bowed in unison and waved to the now standing throng. They filed off in much the same way they entered almost a full hour before.

The crowd would have none of it. Chants for more rose from the audience. The Du-Kanes barely had time to wipe the perspiration from their faces and accept congratulatory hugs from Joseph, Leo, and Jacob before whisked back for their encores. They'd chosen the popular Jackie Wilson tune, "Lonely Teardrops," that featured a long guitar solo. Johnny and Bobby were out front extolling the audience to clap and jump around.

Their second encore was a tune by another Bronx group, Dion and the Belmonts, "Teenager in Love." Whenever Bobby reached the point in the song where he sang the lyrics…"Each time I ask the stars up above…" the entire audience came back with the next line… "Why must I be a teenager in love?" The reaction was sustained and deafening. The show dangerously approached the mandatory cut off time as Jacob approached the microphone.

"Let's bring everybody back one more time. C'mon everybody, come on out here!"

All the performers filtered out and huddled at the center of the stage.

"Joe, Joe Rabin," Jacob called out, "Get out here, man. We owe all this to you."

Joseph stepped from the wings to anchor this impromptu chorus line at its center. The band stuck up the chords for what would be the show's grand finale, a most appropriate sign off tune recorded by the Spaniels in 1954. "Goodnite Sweetheart, Goodnite." Soon, everyone in the building, performer and fan alike swayed to the music and sang together.

After each verse, several of the singers peeled away to leave the stage. When Curtis brought the song to a rousing finish, Joseph stood alone. The houselights came up.

Joseph's thoughts went out to those watching from some other exalted place. His father, proud at his son's rekindled success, his friend Danny Cavelli, who surely would have come to enjoy this great music and Chanticleer, his mentor, who taught him what it meant to understand not just the music but also the mysteries of life. And, of course, Teddy, the young man whose talent started it all.

A sudden feeling of melancholy waved over him. Here he was, rejuvenated, re-born, his past successes vindicated. He was alone, without the only woman he ever really loved, a woman he lost because he became selfish. He let his love of music take precedence over what he felt for her. And, he was *still* selfish. Why couldn't he have both his wife and his renewed success? Conflicting emotions of exhilaration and emptiness filled his being.

♫♫♫♫♫

In lower mezzanine section 124, row b, seat number seven, Janet stood with the others. Fans around her made their way to the exits still buzzing about the show, she watched tearfully as Joseph walked from the stage, the heavy curtain closed behind him.

In recent days, she'd made some important decisions in her life. She decided she would not return to England. A maelstrom of scandal was about to rain down on Ian Markham involving his drug abuse. She could never allow Danielle to be exposed to all that attention and publicity. Instead, they would remain in America to make a new start.

One more decision remained. She thought about going back to her hotel and try to get some sleep, but she was probably too wound up for that. If she made her way backstage she might be able to get a message to Joseph. Maybe he'd be happy to see her, perhaps even invite her to share this triumphant moment with him and the others.

She decided to go backstage.

THE END

CPSIA information can be obtained at www.ICGtesting.com
Printed in the USA
BVOW070305241011
274307BV00001B/1/P